Together for
Christmas

DEBBIE MACOMBER

BRENDA NOVAK

SHEILA ROBERTS

RAEANNE THAYNE

mira

Recycling programs
for this product may
not exist in your area.

ISBN-13: 978-0-7783-0990-1

Together for Christmas
First published in 2014. This edition published in 2020.
Copyright © 2014 by Harlequin Books S.A.

5-B Poppy Lane
First published in 2006. This edition published in 2020.
Copyright © 2006 by Debbie Macomber

When We Touch
First published in 2012. This edition published in 2020.
Copyright © 2012 by Brenda Novak, Inc.

Welcome to Icicle Falls
First published in 2012. This edition published in 2020.
Copyright © 2012 by Sheila Rabe

Starstruck
First published in 2006. This edition published in 2020.
Copyright © 2006 by Harlequin Books S.A.

This edition published by arrangement with Harlequin Books S.A.

For questions and comments about the quality of this book, please contact us at
CustomerService@Harlequin.com.

Mira
22 Adelaide St. West, 40th Floor
Toronto, Ontario M5H 4E3, Canada
BookClubbish.com

Printed in U.S.A.

Contents

5-B Poppy Lane   7
DEBBIE MACOMBER

When We Touch   113
BRENDA NOVAK

Welcome to Icicle Falls   255
SHEILA ROBERTS

Starstruck   309
RAEANNE THAYNE

5-B Poppy Lane

DEBBIE MACOMBER

Prologue

IT WAS EARLY AFTERNOON, CHRISTMAS EVE. SNOW was falling lightly, adding to the festive atmosphere inside and out. Helen Shelton fussed with the decorations in her small Cedar Cove duplex, making sure everything was in place. The tree, a real one, featured the ornaments she'd started acquiring when she'd married Sam in 1946. He'd bought her many of these, and as she hung them carefully on the branches she'd relived their history, hers and Sam's. He'd died almost thirty years ago but she remembered every Christmas they'd spent together.

The Nativity pieces were arranged on her coffee table with the Infant Jesus nestled in the manger, surrounded by the other familiar figurines. A large evergreen wreath hung on her front door. The house was redolent with the scents of spruce and spice—ready for Christmas.

Helen wanted everything perfect when her only grand-daughter and her husband arrived. In preparation she'd mulled cider and baked Ruth's favorite Christmas cookies from an old gingerbread recipe; they'd first made it together when Ruth was a child. Even now, after all these years, Helen remembered the thrill she'd felt when her granddaughter was born. Oh, she loved her grandsons, but for a grandmother there was something special about a girl.

The doorbell chimed and Helen peeked outside to see her dear friend Charlotte Rhodes standing on the porch. Delighted, she opened the door and quickly ushered Charlotte inside. They were both getting on in years, and Helen suspected neither of them had many Christmases left. She didn't have a fatalistic view of life by any means, but she was a practical woman. Helen knew what it was to face death. She had no fear of dying.

"Merry Christmas," Charlotte said, unwrapping a hand-knit lace scarf from around her neck. Her friend was the most exquisite knitter. Many a time she'd assisted Helen with her knitting projects. She gave her the confidence to try new things. Why, with Charlotte's help a few years back, Helen had completed a complicated Fair Isle sweater. She still felt a bit of pride whenever she wore that sweater. She was a competent knitter in her own right; she didn't mean to discount her skills. But Charlotte had such an encouraging way about her, and not just when it came to knitting. Helen had confided in Charlotte about what had happened to her during the war, and Charlotte had urged her to share it with her family. Eventually, she had....

"Merry Christmas," Helen said, taking Charlotte's coat and scarf and hanging them up. She led her friend into the kitchen. "This is such a pleasant surprise."

"I knew your granddaughter and her husband were stop-

ping by, so I brought some of my green tomato mincemeat."
She removed two beribboned jars from her ever-present knitting bag.

"Oh, Charlotte, *thank* you." Helen accepted the jars and put them on the counter to admire. Charlotte was well aware that Helen had a weakness for her homemade green tomato mincemeat.

"Consider this a small Christmas gift," Charlotte said, looking pleased at Helen's reaction.

"Didn't you say it was too much work this year?" Helen could swear Charlotte had claimed she was finished with canning. And who would blame her?

"I did say that, and then I took a look at all those green tomatoes and I couldn't help myself. Besides, Ben swears mincemeat is his favorite pie."

"I thought your peach pie was his favorite."

Charlotte actually blushed. Those two had been married for several years now but they still behaved like newlyweds. It always made Helen smile.

"Ben says that about all my pies."

"Well, I'm very happy to get these. I'll make a pie for tonight's dessert." Helen automatically set the teakettle on the burner, dropping tea bags into her best china pot.

"What time is your granddaughter getting here?"

Helen glanced at the kitchen clock. "Not for several hours. Around five."

Charlotte pulled out a chair and sat down, reaching into her voluminous bag for her knitting. Socks again. Charlotte was never without her knitting, and these days it was usually socks. Helen had recently made socks, too, but not ones you'd wear. She'd knit both Ruth and Paul Christmas stockings to hang by the fireplace. Because of the intricate pattern, it had taken her the better part of three months. She planned to give them their made-with-love Christmas stockings when they exchanged gifts that evening.

It wasn't long before the tea was ready and the two of them sat across the table from each other, a plate of the gingerbread cookies between them.

"I've met your granddaughter, haven't I?" Charlotte asked, picking up her teacup and frowning slightly.

"Yes, don't you recall? Ruth certainly remembers you."

"She does?"

"It was a few years ago. She was in quite a state when she came by to visit. She was absolutely beside herself because she wasn't sure what to do about Paul."

Charlotte looked confused.

"That was shortly after they met," Helen explained, surprised her friend had apparently forgotten the episode, since Charlotte had answered Ruth's knock at the door. "They'd been corresponding for a while. Paul was in the marines. Well, he still is, but that's not the point."

Charlotte chose a cookie. "It's coming back to me now," she said. "They had a lovely romance, didn't they?"

"Oh, yes."

She took a bite. "Mmm. Delicious. Now, remind me again how they met."

Helen settled back in her chair and picked up her own cup of tea. This was such a wonderful story. Her own love story was part of it, too. All those years ago during the Second World War. There were fewer and fewer people who knew what that war had *really* been like.

For more than fifty years she'd refused to talk about that time, refused to even think about her adventures and ordeals. She'd lost so much—and yet, she'd gained, too. At the urging of the few friends she'd confided in, including Charlotte, she'd finally told Ruth what had happened. Ruth and her Paul.

Afterward, her granddaughter had said that her experiences were more than family history; they were *history.*

"Helen," Charlotte murmured, shaking her out of her reverie. "You were going to tell me about Ruth and Paul."

"Oh, yes. The story of how they fell in love..." She settled back, listening to the comforting click of Charlotte's needles, and began.

One

RUTH SHELTON HURRIED OUT OF HER CLASS-room-management lecture at the University of Washington, where she was completing her master's of education degree. Clutching her books, she dashed across campus, in a rush to get home. By now the mail would have been delivered to her small rental house three blocks from the school.

"Ruth," Tina Dupont called, stopping her in midflight. "There's another antiwar rally this afternoon at—"

"Sorry, I've got to run," Ruth said, jogging past her friend and feeling more than a little guilty. Other students cleared a path for her; wherever she was headed must have seemed urgent—and it was, but only to her. Since Christmas, four months ago, she'd been corresponding with Sergeant Paul Gordon, USMC, who was stationed in Afghanistan. There'd been recent reports of fighting, and she hadn't received a letter or an email from Paul in three days. Three interminable days. Not since they'd initially begun their correspondence had there been such a lapse. Paul usually wrote every day and she did, too. They emailed as often as possible. Ruth had strong feelings about the war in Iraq, although her opinions didn't match those of her parents.

Earlier in the school year, Ruth had been part of a protest rally on campus. But no matter what her political views on the subject, she felt it was important to support American troops wherever they might be serving. In an effort to do that, Ruth had voluntarily mailed a Christmas card and letter to a nameless soldier.

Paul Gordon was the young man who'd received that Christmas card, and to Ruth's surprise he'd written her back and enclosed his photograph. Paul was from Seattle and he'd chosen her card because of the Seattle postmark. He'd asked her lots of questions—about her history, her family, her interests—and closed with a postscript that said he hoped to hear from her again.

When she first got his letter, Ruth had hesitated. She felt she'd done her duty, supported the armed services in a way she was comfortable doing. This man she'd never met was asking her to continue corresponding with him. She wasn't sure she wanted to become that involved. Feeling uncertain, she'd waited a few days before deciding.

During that time, Ruth had read and reread his letter and studied the head shot of the clean-cut handsome marine sergeant in dress uniform. His dark brown eyes had seemed to stare straight through her—and directly into her heart. After two days, she answered his letter with a short one of her own and added her email address at the bottom of the page. Ruth had a few concerns she wanted him to address before she could commit herself to beginning this correspondence. Being as straightforward and honest as possible, she explained her objections to the war in Iraq. She felt there was a more legitimate reason for troops to be in Afghanistan and wanted to know his stand. A few days later he emailed her. Paul didn't mince words. He told her he believed the United States had done the right thing in entering Iraq and gave his reasons. He left it up to her to decide if she wanted to continue their correspondence. Ruth emailed him back and once again listed her objections to the American presence in the Middle East. His response came a day later, suggesting they "agree to disagree." He ended the email with the same question he'd asked her earlier. Would she write him?

At first, Ruth wasn't going to. They were diametrically opposed in their political views. But in the end, even recognizing the conflict between their opinions, she did write. Their correspondence started slowly. She enjoyed his wry wit and his unflinching determination to make a difference in the world. His father had fought in Vietnam, he said, and in some ways the war in Afghanistan seemed similar—the hostile terrain, the unpredictability of the enemy, the difficult conditions. For her part, she mentioned that at twenty-five she'd returned to school to obtain her master's of education degree. Then, gradually, without being fully aware of how it had happened, Ruth found herself spending part of every day writing or emailing Paul. Despite the instant nature of email, and its convenience, they both enjoyed interspersing their on-line messages with more formal letters. There was something so…permanent about a real letter. As well, depending on his duty assignment, Paul didn't always have computer access.

After they'd been corresponding regularly for a couple of months, Paul asked for her picture. Eventually she'd mailed him her photograph, but only after she'd had her hair and makeup done at one of those "glamour" studios. Although she wasn't fashion-model beautiful, she considered herself fairly attractive and wanted to look her absolute best for Paul, although she didn't entirely understand why it mattered so much. For years, she'd been resigned to the fact that she wasn't much good at relationships. In high school she'd been shy, and while she was an undergraduate, she'd dated a little but tended to be reserved and studious. Her quiet manner didn't seem to appeal to the guys she met. It was only when she stepped in front of a classroom that she truly became herself. She loved teaching, every single aspect of it. In the process, Ruth lost her hesitation and her restraint, and to her astonishment discovered that this enthusiasm had begun to spill over into the rest of her life. Suddenly men started to notice her. She enjoyed the attention—who wouldn't?—and had dated more in the past few months than in the preceding four years.

For the picture, her short brown hair had been styled in loose curls. Her blue eyes were smiling and friendly, which was exactly the impression she hoped to convey. She was a little shocked by the importance of Paul's reaction—by her need that he find her attractive.

She waited impatiently for his response. A week later she received an email. Paul seemed to like what he saw in her photograph and soon they were writing and emailing back and forth at a feverish pace. A day without some form of communication from Paul felt empty now.

Ruth had never had a long-distance relationship before, and the growing intensity of her feelings for this man she'd never met took her by surprise. She wasn't a teenager with a schoolgirl crush. Ruth was a mature, responsible adult. Or at least she had been until she slipped a simple Christmas card into the mailbox—and got a reply from a handsome marine sergeant named Paul Gordon.

Ruth walked quickly to the rental house she shared with

Lynn Blumenthal, then ran up the front steps to the porch. Lynn was eighteen and away from home and family for the first time. The arrangement suited both of them, and despite the disparity in their ages and interests, they'd gotten along fairly well. With her heart pounding hard, Ruth forced herself to draw in a deep breath as she started toward the mailbox.

The screen door flew open and Lynn came out. "What are you doing home?" she asked, then shook her head. "Never mind, I already know. You're looking for a letter from soldier boy."

Ruth wasn't going to deny the obvious. "I haven't heard from him in three days."

Lynn rolled her eyes. "I don't understand you."

"I know." Ruth didn't want to get into another discussion with her roommate. Lynn had made her feelings about this relationship known from the outset, although as Ruth had gently tried to tell her, it was none of her business. That didn't prevent the younger woman from expressing her views. Lynn said that Ruth was only setting herself up for heartache. A part of Ruth actually agreed, but by the time she realized what was happening, she was emotionally involved with Paul.

"You hardly ever see Clay anymore," Lynn chastised, hands on her hips. "He called and asked about you the other night."

Ruth stared at the small black mailbox. "Clay and I are just friends."

"Not according to him."

It was true that they'd been seeing each other quite a bit following a Halloween party last October. Like her, Clay Matthews was obtaining his master's of education, and they seemed to have a lot in common. But her interest in him had started to wane even before she'd mailed that Christmas card to Paul. The problem was, Clay hadn't noticed.

"I'm sorry he's disappointed."

"Clay is decent and hardworking, and the way you've treated him the last few months is…is terrible." Lynn, who at five foot ten stood a good seven inches taller than Ruth, could be intimidating, especially with her mouth twisted in that grimace of disapproval.

Ruth had tried to let Clay down easily, but it hadn't worked. They'd gone to the library together last Thursday. Unfortunately, that had been a mistake. She'd known it almost right away when Clay pressured her to have coffee with him afterward. It would've been better just to end the relationship and forget about staying friends. He was younger, for one thing, and while that hadn't seemed important earlier, it did now. Perhaps it was wrong to compare him to Paul, but Ruth couldn't help it. Measured against Paul, Clay seemed immature, demanding and insecure.

"You said he phoned?" Frowning, she glanced at Lynn.

Lynn nodded. "He wants to know what's going on."

Oh, brother! Ruth couldn't have made it plainer had she handed him divorce papers. Unwilling to be cruel, she'd tried to bolster his ego by referring to all the positive aspects of his personality—but apparently, that had only led him to think the opposite of what she was trying to tell him. He'd refused to take her very obvious hints, and in her frustration, she'd bluntly announced that she wasn't interested in seeing him anymore. That seemed pretty explicit to her; how he could be confused about it left Ruth shaking her head.

The fact that he'd phoned and cried on her roommate's shoulder was a good example of what she found adolescent about his behavior. She was absolutely certain Paul would never do that. If he had a problem, he'd take it directly to the source.

"I think you're being foolish," Lynn said, and added, "Not that you asked my opinion."

"No, I didn't," Ruth reminded her, eyeing the mailbox again. There was an ornamental latticework design along the bottom, and looking through it, she could tell that the day's mail had been delivered. The envelope inside was white, and her spirits sank. There *had* to be something from Paul. If not a real letter, then an email.

"He wanted me to talk to you," Lynn was saying.

"Who did?" Ruth asked distractedly. She was dying to open the mailbox, but she wanted to do it in privacy.

"Clay," Lynn cried, sounding completely exasperated. "Who else are we talking about?"

Suddenly Ruth understood. She looked away from the mailbox and focused her attention on Lynn. "You're attracted to him, aren't you?"

Lynn gasped indignantly. "Don't be ridiculous."

"Sit down," Ruth said, gesturing toward the front steps, where they'd often sat before. It was a lovely spring afternoon, the first week of April, and she needed to clear the air with her roommate before this got further out of hand.

"What?" Lynn said with a defensive edge. "You've got the wrong idea here. I was just trying to help a friend."

"Sit," Ruth ordered.

"I have class in twenty minutes and I—" Lynn paused, scowling at her watch.

"Sit down."

The eighteen-year-old capitulated with ill grace. "All right, but I know what you're going to say." She folded her arms and stared straight ahead.

"I'm fine with it," Ruth said softly. "Go out with him if you want. Like I said earlier, I'm not interested in Clay."

"You would be if it wasn't for soldier boy."

Ruth considered that and in all honesty felt she could say, "Not so."

"I don't understand you," Lynn lamented a second time. "You marched in the rally against the war in Iraq. Afghanistan isn't all that different, and now you're involved with Paul what's-his-face and it's like I don't even know you anymore."

"Paul doesn't have anything to do with this."

"Yes, he does," Lynn insisted.

"I'm not going to have this conversation with you. We agree on some points and disagree on others. That's fine. We live in a free society and we don't have to have the same opinion on these issues or anything else."

Lynn sighed and said nothing.

"I have the feeling none of this is really about Paul," Ruth said with deliberate patience. She hadn't known Lynn very long; they lived separate lives and so far they'd never had a problem. As roommates went, Ruth felt she was fortunate to have found someone as amicable as Lynn. She didn't want this difference of opinion about Clay—and Paul—to ruin that.

The other girl once again looked pointedly at her watch, as if to suggest Ruth say what she intended to say and be done with it.

"I don't want to see Clay," she said emphatically.

"You might have told him that."

"I tried."

Lynn glared at her. "You should've tried harder."

Ruth laughed, but not because she was amused. For whatever reason, Clay had set his sights on her and wasn't about to be dissuaded. Complicating matters, Lynn was obviously interested in him and feeling guilty and unsure of how to deal with her attraction.

"Listen," Ruth said. "I didn't mean to hurt Clay. He's a great guy and—"

"You shouldn't have lied to him."

Ruth raised her eyebrows. "When did I lie to him?"

"Last week you said you were going to visit your grandmother in Cedar Cove and that was why you couldn't go out with him this weekend. I overheard you," she murmured.

Oh, that. "It was a white lie," Ruth confessed. She definitely planned to visit her grandmother, though. Helen Shelton lived across Puget Sound in a small community on the Kitsap Peninsula. Ruth had spent Thanksgiving with her grandmother and visited for a weekend before Christmas and then again close to Valentine's Day. Her last visit had been early in March. She always enjoyed her time with Helen, but somehow the weeks had slipped away and here it was April already.

"A lie is a lie," Lynn said adamantly.

"Okay, you're right," Ruth agreed. "I should've been honest with Clay." Delaying had been a mistake, as she was now learning.

That seemed to satisfy her roommate, who started to get to her feet. Ruth placed her hand on Lynn's forearm, stopping her. "I want to know why you're so upset about this situation with Clay."

"I told you…. I just don't think this is how people should treat each other."

"I don't like the way Clay's put you in the middle. This is between him and me. He had no right to drag you into it."

"Yes, but—"

"You're defending him?"

Lynn shrugged. "I guess."

"Don't. Clay's a big boy. If he has something to say, then he can come to me all on his own. When and if he does, I'm going to tell him *again* that I'm no longer interested in dating him. I'm—"

"Stuck on some gun-wielding—"

A look from Ruth cut her off.

"Okay, whatever," Lynn muttered.

"What I want you to do is comfort him," Ruth said, patting Lynn's arm.

"I could, I suppose."

"Good," Ruth said, hoping to encourage her. "He might need someone to talk to, and since you're sensitive to his feelings, you'd be the perfect choice."

"You think so?"

Ruth nodded. Lynn stood up and went inside to get her books; she left with a cheerful goodbye as if they'd never had an argument. With her roommate gone, Ruth leaped off the step and across the porch to the mailbox. Lifting the top, she reached inside, holding her breath as she pulled out the electric bill in its white envelope, a sales flyer—and a hand-addressed airmail letter from Sergeant Paul Gordon.

Two

April 2

My Dear Ruth,

We've been out on a recon mission for the last four days
and there wasn't any way I could let you know. They
seemed like the longest four days of this tour, and not
for the reasons you might think. Those days meant I
couldn't write you or receive your letters. I've been in
the marines for eight years now and I've never felt like
this about mail before. Never felt this strongly about a
woman I've yet to meet, either. Once we were back in
camp, I sat down with your letters and read through
each one. As I explained before, there are times we can't
get online and this happened to be one of those times.
I realize you've probably been wondering why I wasn't

in touch. I hope you weren't too concerned. I would've written if I could.

I have good news. I'm coming home on leave....

RUTH READ PAUL'S LETTER TWICE. YES, HE'D definitely said he was headed home, to Seattle, for two weeks before flying to Camp Pendleton in California for additional training. He hoped to spend most of his leave with her. His one request was that Ruth make as much time for him as her studies would allow and, if possible, keep her weekends free.

If Ruth thought her heart had been beating hard a few minutes earlier, it didn't compare to the way it pounded now. She could barely breathe. Never had she looked forward to meeting anyone more.

Sitting on the edge of her bed, Ruth picked up the small framed photograph she kept on her nightstand. Paul's image was the first thing she saw when she woke and the last before she turned off her light. In four months, he'd become an important part of her life. Now, with his return to Seattle, their feelings for each other would stand the real test. Writing letters and email messages was very different from carrying on a face-to-face conversation....

At the end of his letter, Paul suggested they meet at 6:00 p.m. on Saturday, April 16, at Ivar's restaurant on the Seattle waterfront. She didn't care what else was on her schedule; any conflicting arrangement would immediately be canceled.

Rather than begin her homework, Ruth sat down and wrote Paul back, her fingers flying over the computer keys as she composed her response. Yes, she would see him there. Nothing could keep her away. While she was nervous at the prospect of meeting Paul, she was excited, too.

Her letter was coming out of the printer when the phone

rang. Absently Ruth grabbed the receiver, holding it against her shoulder as she opened the desk drawer and searched for an envelope.

"Hello?"

"Ruth, it's your grandmother."

"Grandma," Ruth said, genuinely pleased to hear from Helen. "I've been meaning to call you and I haven't. I'm sorry."

Her grandmother chuckled. "I didn't call to make you feel guilty. I'm inviting you to lunch."

"When?"

"In a couple of weeks—on Sunday the seventeenth if that works for you. I figured I'd give you plenty of time to fit me into your schedule. I thought we'd sit out on the patio, weather permitting, and enjoy the view of the cove."

Her grandmother's duplex was on a hill overlooking the water with the lighthouse in the distance. Her grandparents had lived in Cedar Cove for as long as Ruth could remember, and Helen had stayed there after her husband's death. Because Ruth had been born and raised in Oregon, she'd visited the small Washington town often through the years. "I've wanted to get over to see you."

"I know, I know, but unless we both plan ahead, it won't happen. In no time you'll have your master's degree and then you'll move on and we'll both regret the missed opportunities. I don't want that."

"I don't, either." Her grandma Shelton was Ruth's favorite relative. She was highly educated, which wasn't particularly common for a woman her age, and spoke French and German fluently. She'd worked as a translator from the 1950s through the '80s, specializing in French novels, which she translated into English. Her father hadn't said much about his mother's life prior to her marriage, and one of the reasons Ruth had chosen to attend the University of Washington was so she could get to know her grandmother better.

"I can put you down for lunch, then?"

"Yes, that would be lovely." Her gaze fell on Paul's letter and Ruth realized that the date her grandmother had suggested was the first weekend Paul would be in town. He'd specifically asked her to keep as much of that two-week period free as she could. She wanted to spend time with him and yet she couldn't refuse her grandmother. "Grandma, I'm looking at my calendar and—"

"Is there a conflict?"

"Not…exactly. I've sort of got a date," she said, assuming she and Paul would be seeing each other. It would be ideal if he could join her. "It isn't anything official, so I—"

"Then you do have another commitment."

"No…" This was getting complicated. "Well, not exactly," she said again.

"I wasn't aware that you were dating anyone special. Who is he?"

The question hung there for a moment before Ruth answered. "His name is Paul Gordon and we aren't really dating." She would've continued, except that her grandmother broke in.

"Your parents didn't say anything about this." The words were spoken as if there must be something untoward about Paul that Ruth didn't want to divulge.

"No, Mom and Dad wouldn't," Ruth said, not adding that she hadn't actually mentioned Paul to her parents. She'd decided it wasn't necessary to enlighten them about this correspondence yet. Explaining her feelings about Paul to her family would be difficult when everyone knew her political views. More important, she wasn't sure how she felt about him and wouldn't be until they'd met.

So far, they were only pen pals, but this was the man she dreamed about every night, the man who dominated her thoughts each and every day.

"Grandma, I haven't said anything to Mom and Dad because I haven't officially met Paul yet."

"Is this…" Her grandmother hesitated. "Is this one of those…those *internet* relationships?" She spit out the word as though meeting a man via the internet was either illegal or unseemly—most likely both.

"No, Grandma, it's nothing like that."

"Then why don't your parents know about him?"

"Well, because…because he's a soldier in Afghanistan." There—it was out.

Her announcement was greeted by silence. "There's something wrong with that?" she eventually asked.

"No…."

"You say it like you're ashamed."

"I'm *not* ashamed," Ruth insisted. "I like Paul a great deal and I'm proud of his service to our country." She downplayed her political beliefs as she expanded on her feelings. "I enjoy his letters and like him more than I probably should, but I don't like the fact that he's a soldier."

"You sound confused."

Ruth sighed. That was certainly an accurate description of how she felt.

"So this Paul will be in Seattle on leave?"

"Yes. For two weeks."

"He's coming here to meet you?"

"His family also lives in the area."

"Invite him along for lunch," her grandmother said. "I want to meet him, too."

"You do?" Ruth's enthusiasm swelled. "That's great. I

thought of it, but I wasn't sure how you'd feel about having him join us."

"I meant what I said. I want to meet him."

"We've only been writing for a few months. I don't know him well, and…" She let the rest fade.

"It'll be fine, Ruth," her grandmother assured her. Helen always seemed to understand what Ruth was feeling. She'd found ways to encourage the special bond between them.

"Grandpa was a soldier when you first met him, wasn't he?" Ruth remembered her father telling her this years ago, although he'd also said his mother didn't like to talk about those years. Ruth assumed that was because of Grandpa Sam's bad memories of the war, the awful things he'd seen and experienced in Europe. She knew her grandparents had met during the Second World War, fallen in love and married soon afterward. Ruth's father had been born in the baby boom years that followed, and her uncle Jake had arrived two years later. Ruth was Helen's only granddaughter, but she had three grandsons.

"Oh, yes." She sighed wistfully. "My Sam was so handsome, especially in his uniform." Her voice softened perceptibly.

"How long did you know him before you were married?"

Her grandmother laughed. "Less than a year. In wartime everything's very intense. People married quickly because you never knew if you'd still be alive tomorrow. It was as if those of us who were young had to cram as much life into as short a time as possible."

"The war was terrible, wasn't it?"

Helen sighed before whispering, "All war is terrible."

"I agree," Ruth said promptly.

"So you and this soldier you've never met are discussing marriage?" her grandmother asked after a moment.

"No!" Ruth nearly choked getting out her denial. "Paul and me? No, of course not. I promise you the subject has never even come up." They hadn't written about kissing or touching or exchanged the conventional romantic endearments. That didn't mean she hadn't *dreamed* about what it would be like to be held by Paul Gordon. To kiss him and be caressed by him. She'd let her imagination roam free....

"So you say," her grandmother said with amusement in her voice. "By all means, bring your friend. I'll look forward to meeting him."

That was no doubt true, Ruth thought, but no one looked forward to meeting Paul Gordon more than she did.

Three

"HOW DO I LOOK?" RUTH ASKED HER ROOM-
mate. She hated to sound so insecure, but this was
perhaps the most important meeting of her life and Ruth was
determined to make a perfect impression.

"Fabulous," Lynn said, her face hidden behind the latest
issue of *People* magazine.

"I might believe you if you actually looked at me." Ruth
held on to her patience with limited success. The relationship
with her roommate had gone steadily downhill since the confrontation on the porch steps two weeks earlier. Apparently
Clay wasn't interested in dating Lynn. What Ruth did know
was that Clay hadn't contacted either of them since, and her
roommate had been increasingly cold and standoffish. Ruth
had tried to talk to her but that hadn't done any good. She
suspected that Lynn *wanted* to be upset, so Ruth had decided

to go about her own business and ignore her roommate's disgruntled mood. This might not be the best strategy, but it was the only way she could deal with Lynn's attitude.

Her roommate heaved a sigh; apparently lifting her head a couple of inches required immense effort. Her eyes were devoid of emotion as she gave Ruth a token appraisal. "You look all right, I guess."

These days, that was high praise coming from Lynn. Ruth had spent an hour doing her hair, with the help of a curling iron and two brushes. And now it was raining like crazy. This wasn't the drizzle traditionally associated with the Pacific Northwest, either. This was *rain*. Real rain. Which spelled disaster for her hair, since her umbrella wouldn't afford much protection.

If her hair had taken a long time, choosing what to wear had demanded equal consideration. She had a pretty teal-and-white summer dress from last year that made her eyes look soft and dreamy, but the rain had altered *that* plan. Now she was wearing black pants and a white cashmere sweater with a beige overcoat.

"You're meeting at Ivar's, right?"

"Right." Ruth didn't remember telling her roommate. They were barely on speaking terms.

"Too bad."

"Too bad what?"

Lynn sighed once more and set aside the magazine. "If you must know, soldier boy phoned and said you should meet him outside the restaurant." She grinned nastily. "And in case you haven't noticed, it's pouring out."

"I'm supposed to meet him outside?"

"That's what he said."

Ruth made an effort not to snap at her. "You didn't think to mention this before?"

Lynn shrugged. "It slipped my mind."

Ruth just bet it did. Rather than start an argument, she collected her raincoat, umbrella and purse. Surely she would receive a heavenly reward for controlling her temper. Lynn would love an argument but Ruth wasn't going to give her one; she wasn't going to play childish games with her roommate. The difference in their ages had never seemed more pronounced than it had in the past two weeks.

Because of the rain, Ruth couldn't find convenient street parking and was forced to pay an outrageous amount at a lot near the restaurant. She rushed toward Ivar's, making sure she arrived in plenty of time. Lynn's sour disposition might have upset Ruth if not for the fact that she was finally going to meet the soldier who'd come to mean so much to her.

Focusing on her hair, dress and makeup meant she'd paid almost no attention to something that was far more important—what she'd actually say when she saw Paul for the first time. Ideas skittered through her mind as she crossed the street.

Ruth hoped to sound witty, articulate and well-informed. She so badly wanted to impress Paul and was afraid she'd stumble over her words or find herself speechless. Her other fear was that she'd take one look at him and burst into tears. It could happen; she felt very emotional about meeting this man she'd known only through letters and emails.

Thankfully, by the time she reached Ivar's, the rain had slowed to a drizzle. But it was still wet out and miserably gray. Her curls, which had been perfectly styled, had turned into tight wads of frizz in the humid air. She was sure she resembled a cartoon character more than the fashion model she'd strived for earlier that afternoon.

After the longest ten-minute wait of her life, Ruth checked her watch and saw that it was now one minute past six. Paul was late. She pulled her cell phone from her bag; unfortunately Paul didn't answer *his* cell, so she punched out her home number. Perhaps he'd been delayed in traffic and had called the house, hoping to connect with her.

No answer. Either Lynn had left or purposely chosen not to pick up the receiver. Great, just great.

To her dismay, as she went to toss her cell phone back inside her purse, she realized the battery was low. Why hadn't she charged it? Oh, no, that would've been *much* too smart.

All at once Ruth figured it out. Paul wasn't late at all. Somehow she'd missed him, which wouldn't be that difficult with all the tourist traffic on the waterfront. Even in the rain, people milled around the area as if they were on the sunny beaches of Hawaii. Someone needed to explain to these tourists that the water dripping down from the sky was cold rain. Just because they'd dressed for sunshine didn't mean the weather would cooperate.

Despite her umbrella, her hair now hung in tight ringlets all around her head. Either of two things had happened, she speculated. Perhaps her appearance was so drastically changed from the glamour photo she'd sent him that Paul hadn't recognized her and assumed she'd stood him up. The other possibility was even less appealing. Paul had gotten a glimpse of her and decided to escape without saying a word.

For a moment Ruth felt like crying. Rather than waste the last of her cell phone battery phoning her roommate again, she stepped inside the restaurant to see if Paul had left a message for her.

She opened the door and lowered her umbrella. As she did, she saw a tall, lean and very handsome Paul Gordon get up from a chair in the restaurant foyer.

"Ruth?"

"Paul?" Without a thought, she dropped the umbrella and moved directly into his embrace.

Then they were in each other's arms, hugging fiercely.

When it became obvious that everyone in the crowded foyer was staring at them, Paul finally released her.

"I was outside—didn't you tell Lynn that's where we were meeting?"

"No." He brushed the wet curls from her forehead and smiled down at her. "I said inside because I heard on the weather forecast that it was going to rain. And—" he rolled his eyes "—I forgot my cell phone. I'm not used to carrying one around."

"Of *course* you said inside." Ruth wanted to kick herself for being so dense. She should've guessed what Lynn was up to; instead, she'd fallen right into her roommate's petty hands. "I'm so sorry to keep you waiting."

A number of people were still watching them but Ruth didn't care. She couldn't stop looking at Paul. He seemed unable to break eye contact with her, too.

The hostess came forward. "Since your party's arrived," she said with a smile, "I can seat you now."

"Yes, please." Paul helped Ruth off with her coat and set the umbrella beside several others so it could dry. Then, as if they'd known and loved each other all their lives, he reached for her hand and linked her fingers with his as they walked through the restaurant.

The hostess seated them by the window, which overlooked the dark, murky waters of Puget Sound. Rain ran in rivulets down the tempered glass, but as far as Ruth was concerned it could have been the brightest, sunniest day in Seattle's history.

Paul continued to hold her hand on top of the table.

"I was worried about what I'd say once we met," she said. "Then when we did, I just felt so glad, the words didn't seem important."

"I'd almost convinced myself you'd stood me up." He

yawned, covering his mouth with the other hand, and she realized he was probably functioning on next to no sleep.

"Stood you up? I would've found a way to get here no matter what." She let the truth of that show in her eyes. She had the strongest feeling of *certainty,* and an involuntary sense that he was everything she'd dreamed.

He briefly looked away. "I would've found a way to get to you, too." His fingers tightened around hers.

"When did you last sleep?" she asked.

His mouth curved upward in a half smile. "I forget. A long time ago. Maybe I should've suggested we meet tomorrow instead, but I didn't want to wait a minute longer than I had to."

"Me, neither," she confessed.

He smiled again, that wonderful, intoxicating smile.

"When did you land?" she asked, because if she didn't stop staring at him she was going to embarrass herself.

"Late this morning," he told her. "My family—well, you know what families are like. Mom's been cooking for days and there was a big family get-together this afternoon. I wanted to invite you but—"

"No, I understand. You couldn't because—well, how could you?" That didn't come out right, but Paul seemed to know what she was trying to say.

"You're exactly like I pictured you," he said, leaning forward to touch her cheek.

"You imagined me drenched?"

He chuckled. "I imagined you beautiful, and you are."

His words made her blush. "I'm having a hard time believing you're actually here," she said.

"I am, too."

The waitress came for their drink order. Ruth hadn't even looked at her menu or thought about what she'd like to drink.

Because she was wet and chilled, she ordered hot tea and Paul asked for a bottle of champagne.

"We have reason to celebrate," he announced. Then, as if it had suddenly occurred to him, he said, "You do drink alcohol, don't you?"

She nodded quickly. "Normally I would've asked for wine, but I wanted the tea so I could warm up. I haven't decided what to order yet." She picked up the menu and scanned the entrées.

The waitress brought the champagne and standing ice bucket to the table. "Is there something special you're celebrating?" she asked in a friendly voice.

Paul nodded and his eyes met Ruth's. "We're celebrating the fact that we found each other," he said.

"Excellent." She removed the foil top and wire around the cork and opened the bottle with a slight popping sound. After filling the two champagne flutes, she left.

Ruth took her glass. "Once again, I'm so sorry about what happened. Let me pay for the champagne, please. You wouldn't have had a problem finding me if I'd—"

"I wasn't talking about this evening," he broke in. "I was talking about your Christmas card."

"Oh."

Paul raised his glass; she raised hers, too, and they clicked the rims gently together. "Do you believe in fate?" he asked.

Ruth smiled. "I didn't, but I've had a change of heart since Christmas."

His smile widened. "Me, too."

Dinner was marvelous. Ruth didn't remember what she'd ordered or anything else about the actual meal. For all she knew, she could've been dining on raw seaweed. It hardly mattered.

They talked and talked, and she felt as if she'd known Paul

her entire life. He asked detailed questions about her family, her studies, her plans after graduation, and seemed genuinely interested in everything she said. He talked about the marines and Afghanistan with a sense of pride at the positive differences he'd seen in the country. After dinner and dessert, they lingered over coffee and at nine-thirty Paul paid the tab and suggested they walk along the waterfront. She eagerly agreed. Her umbrella was now merely an encumbrance because the rain had stopped, so they brought it back to her car before they set off.

The clouds had drifted away and the moon was glowing, its light splashing against the pier as they strolled hand in hand. Although she knew Paul had to be exhausted from his long flight and the family gathering, she couldn't deny herself these last few minutes.

"You asked me to keep the weekends free," Ruth murmured, resting her head against his shoulder.

"Did you?"

She sighed. "Not tomorrow."

"Do you have a date with some other guy?"

She leaned back in order to study his face, trying to discern whether he was serious. "You're joking, right?" she said hesitantly.

He shrugged. "Yes and no. You have no obligation to me and vice versa."

"Are *you* seeing someone else?"

"No." His response was immediate.

"I'm not, either," she told him. She wanted to ask how he could even *think* that she would be. "I promised my grandmother I'd visit tomorrow."

"Your grandmother?" he repeated.

"She invited you, too."

He arched his brows.

"In fact, she insisted I bring you."

"So you've mentioned me to your family."

She'd told him in her letters that she hadn't. "Just her. We've become really close. I'm sure you'll enjoy meeting her."

"I'm sure I will, too."

"You'll come, won't you?"

Paul turned Ruth into his arms and gazed down at her. "I don't think I could stay away."

And then he kissed her. Ruth had fantasized about this moment for months. She'd wondered what it would be like when Paul kissed her, but nothing she'd conjured up equaled this reality. Never in all her twenty-five years had she experienced anything like the sensation she felt when Paul's mouth descended on hers. Stars fell from the sky. She saw it happen even with her eyes tightly closed. She heard triumphant music nearby; it seemed to surround her. But once she opened her eyes, all the stars seemed to be exactly where they'd been before. And the music came from somebody's car radio.

Paul wore a stunned look.

"That was…very nice," Ruth managed.

Paul nodded in agreement, then cleared his throat. "Very."

"Should I admit I was afraid of what would happen when we met?" she asked.

"Afraid why? Of what?"

"I didn't know what to expect."

"I didn't, either." He slid his hand down her spine and moved a step away. "I'd built this up in my mind."

"I did, too," she whispered.

"I was so afraid you could never live up to my image of you," Paul told her. "I figured we'd meet and I'd get you out of my system. I'd buy you dinner, thank you for your letters and emails—and that would be the end of it. No woman could possibly be everything I'd envisioned you to be. But you are, Ruth, you are."

Although the wind was chilly, his words were enough to warm her from head to foot.

"I didn't think you could be what I'd imagined, either, and I was right," Ruth said.

"You were?" He seemed crestfallen.

She nodded. "Paul, you're even more wonderful than I'd realized." At his relieved expression, she said, "I underestimated how strong my feelings for you are. Look at me, I'm shaking." She held out her hand as evidence of how badly she was trembling after his kiss.

He shook his head. "I feel the same way—nervous and jittery inside."

"That's lack of sleep."

"No," he said, and took her by the shoulders. "That's what your kiss did to me." His eyes glittered as he stared down at her.

"What should we do?" she asked uncertainly.

"You're the one with reservations about falling for a guy in the service."

Her early letters had often referred to her feelings about exactly that. Ruth lowered her gaze. "The fundamental problem hasn't changed," she said. "But you'll eventually get out, won't you?"

He hesitated, and his dark eyes—which had been so warm seconds before—seemed to be closing her out. "Eventually I'll leave the marines, but you should know it won't be anytime in the near future. I'm in for the long haul, and if you want to continue this relationship, the sooner you accept that, the better."

Ruth didn't want their evening to end on a negative note. When she'd answered his letter that first time, she'd known he was a military man and it hadn't stopped her. She'd gone into this with her eyes wide open. "I don't have to decide right away, do I?"

"No," he admitted. "But—"

"Good," she said, cutting him off. She couldn't allow their differences to come between them so quickly. She sensed that Paul, too, wanted to push all that aside. When she slipped her arms around his waist and hugged him, he hugged her back. "You're exhausted. Let's meet in the morning. I'll take you over to visit my grandmother and we can talk some more then."

Ruth rested her head against his shoulder again and Paul kissed her hair. "You're making this difficult," he said.

"I know. I'm sorry."

"Me, too," he whispered.

Ruth knew they'd need to confront the issue soon. She could also see that settling it wasn't going to be as easy as she'd hoped.

Four

PAUL MET RUTH AT THE SEATTLE TERMINAL AT ten the next morning and they walked up the ramp to board the Bremerton ferry. The hard rain of the night before had yielded to glorious sunshine.

Unlike the previous evening, when Paul and Ruth had talked nonstop through a three-hour dinner, it seemed that now they had little to say. The one big obstacle in their relationship hung between them. They sat side by side on the wooden bench and sipped hot coffee as the ferry eased away from the Seattle dock.

"You're still thinking about last night, aren't you?" Ruth said, carefully broaching the subject after a lengthy silence. "About you being in the military, I mean, and my objections to the war in Iraq?"

He nodded. "Yeah, there's the political aspect and also the

fact that you don't seem comfortable with the concept of military life," he said.

"I'm not, really, but we'll work it out," she told him, and reached for his free hand, entwining their fingers. "We'll find a way."

Paul didn't look as if he believed her. But after a couple of minutes, he seemed to come to some sort of decision. He brought her hand to his lips. "Let's enjoy the time we have today, all right?"

Ruth smiled in agreement.

"Tell me about your grandmother."

Ruth was more than willing to change the subject. "This is my paternal grandmother, and she's lived in Cedar Cove for the past thirty years. She and my grandfather moved there from Seattle after he retired because they wanted a slower pace of life. I barely remember my grandfather Sam. He died when I was two, before I had any real memories of him."

"He died young," Paul commented sympathetically.

"Yes.... My grandmother's been alone for a long time."

"She probably has good friends in a town like Cedar Cove."

"Yes," Ruth said. "And she's still got friends she's had since the war. It's something I admire about my grandmother," she continued. "She's my inspiration, and not only because she speaks three languages fluently and is one of the most intelligent women I know. Ever since I can remember, she's been helping others. Although she's in her eighties, Grandma's involved with all kinds of charities and social groups. When I enrolled at the University of Washington, I intended for the two of us to get together often, but I swear her schedule's even busier than mine."

Paul grinned at her. "I know what you mean. It's the same in my family."

By the time they stepped off the Bremerton ferry and took

the foot ferry across to Cedar Cove, it was after eleven. They stopped at a deli, where Paul bought a loaf of fresh bread and a bottle of Washington State gewürztraminer to take with them. At quarter to twelve, they trudged up the hill toward her grandmother's duplex on Poppy Lane.

When they arrived, Helen greeted them at the front door and ushered Paul and Ruth into the house. Ruth hugged her grandmother, whose white hair was cut stylishly short. Helen was thinner than the last time Ruth had visited and seemed more fragile somehow. Her grandmother paused to give Paul an embarrassingly frank look. Ruth felt her face heat as Helen spoke.

"So, you're the young man who's captured my granddaughter's heart."

"Grandma, this is Paul Gordon," Ruth said hurriedly, gesturing toward Paul.

"This is the soldier you've been writing to, who's fighting in Afghanistan?"

"I am." Paul's response sounded a bit defensive, Ruth thought. He obviously preferred not to discuss it.

In an effort to ward off any misunderstanding, Ruth added, "My grandfather was a soldier when Grandma met him."

Helen nodded, and a faraway look stole over her. It took her a moment to refocus. "Come, both of you," she said, stepping between them. She tucked her arm around Ruth's waist. "I set the table outside. It's such a beautiful afternoon, I thought we'd eat on the patio."

"We brought some bread and a bottle of wine," Ruth said. "Paul got them."

"Lovely. Thank you, Paul."

While Ruth sliced the fresh-baked bread, he opened the wine, then helped her grandmother carry the salad plates out-

side. An apple pie cooled on the kitchen counter and the scent
of cinnamon permeated the sunlit kitchen.

They chatted throughout the meal; the conversation was
light and friendly as they lingered over their wine. Every now
and then Ruth caught her grandmother staring at Paul with
the strangest expression on her face. Ruth didn't know what
to make of this. It almost seemed as if her grandmother was
trying to place him, to recall where she'd seen him before.

Helen had apparently read Ruth's mind. "Am I embarrassing your beau, sweetheart?" she asked with a half smile.

Ruth resisted informing her grandmother that Paul wasn't
her anything, especially not her beau. They'd had one lovely
dinner together, but now their political differences seemed to
have overtaken them.

"I apologize, Paul." Helen briefly touched his hand, which
rested on the table. "When I first saw you—" She stopped
abruptly. "You resemble someone I knew many years ago."

"Where, Grandma?" Ruth asked.

"In France, during the war."

"You were in France during World War II?" Ruth couldn't
quite hide her shock.

Helen turned to her. "I haven't spoken much about those
days, but now, toward the end of my life, I think about them
more and more." She pushed back her chair and stood.

Ruth stood, too, thinking her grandmother was about to
carry in their empty plates and serve the pie.

Helen motioned her to sit. "Stay here. There's something
I want you to see. I think perhaps it's time."

When her grandmother had left them, Ruth looked at Paul
and shrugged. "I have no idea what's going on."

Paul had been wonderful with her grandmother, thought-
ful and attentive. He'd asked a number of questions during
the meal—about Cedar Cove, about her life with Sam—and

listened intently when she responded. Ruth knew his interest was genuine. Together they cleared the table and returned the dishes to the kitchen, then waited for Helen at the patio table.

It was at least five minutes before she came back. She held a rolled-up paper that appeared to be some kind of poster, old enough to have yellowed with age. Carefully she opened it and laid it flat on the cleared table. Ruth saw that the writing was French. In the center of the poster, which measured about eighteen inches by twenty-four, was a pencil sketch of two faces: a man and a woman, whose names she didn't recognize. Jean and Marie Brulotte.

"Who's that?" Ruth asked, pointing to the female.

Her grandmother smiled calmly. "I am that woman."

Ruth frowned. Helen had obviously used a false name, and although she'd seen photographs of her grandmother as a young woman, this sketch barely resembled the woman she knew. The man in the drawing, however, seemed familiar. Gazing at the sketch for a minute, she realized the face was vaguely like Paul's. Not so much in any similarity of features as in a quality of…character, she supposed.

"And the man?"

"That was Jean-Claude," Helen whispered, her voice full of pain.

Paul turned to Ruth, but she was at a complete loss and didn't know what to tell him. Her grandfather's name was Sam and she'd never heard of this Jean or Jean-Claude. Certainly her father had never mentioned another man in his mother's life.

"This is a wanted poster," Paul remarked. "I speak some French—studied it in school."

"Yes. The Germans offered a reward of one million francs to anyone who turned us in."

"You were in France during the war and you were *wanted?*"

This was more than Ruth could assimilate. She sat back down; so did her grandmother. Paul remained standing for a moment longer as he studied the poster.

"But…it said Marie. Marie Brulotte."

"I went by my middle name in those days. Marie. You may not be aware that it was part of my name because I haven't used it since."

"But…"

"You and Jean-Claude were part of the French Resistance?" Paul asked. It was more statement than question.

"We were." Her grandmother seemed to have difficulty speaking. "Jean-Claude was my husband. We married during the war, and I took his name with pride. He was my everything, strong and handsome and brave. His laughter filled a room. Sometimes, still, I think I can hear him." Her eyes grew teary and she dabbed at them with her linen handkerchief. "That was many years ago now and, as I said, I think perhaps it's time I spoke of it."

Ruth was grateful. She couldn't let her grandmother leave the story untold. She suspected her father hadn't heard any of this, and she wanted to learn whatever she could about this unknown episode in their family history before it was forever lost.

"What were you doing in France?" Ruth asked. She couldn't comprehend that the woman she'd always known as a warm and loving grandmother, who baked cookies and knit socks for Christmas, had been a freedom fighter in a foreign country.

"I was attending the Sorbonne when the Germans invaded. You may recall that my mother was born in France, but her own parents were long dead. I was studying French literature. My parents were frantic for me to book my passage home, but like so many others in France, I didn't believe the country would fall. I assured my mother I'd leave when I felt it was no longer safe. Being young and foolish, I thought she was overreacting. Besides, I was in love. Jean-Claude had asked me to marry him, and what woman in love wishes to leave her lover over rumors of war?" She laughed lightly, shaking her head. "France seemed invincible. We were convinced the Germans wouldn't invade, convinced they'd suffer a humiliating defeat if they tried."

"So when it happened you were trapped," Paul said.

Her grandmother drew in a deep breath. "There was the Blitzkrieg.... People were demoralized and defeated when France surrendered after only a few days of fighting. We were aghast that such a thing could happen. Jean-Claude and a few of his friends decided to resist the occupation. I decided I would, too, so we were married right away. My parents knew nothing of this."

"How did you join the Resistance?" Paul asked as Ruth looked at her grandmother with fresh eyes.

"Join," she repeated scornfully. "There was no place to *join,* no place to sign up and be handed a weapon and an instruction manual. A group of us students, naive and foolish, offered resistance to the German occupation. Later we learned there were other groups, eventually united under the leadership of General de Gaulle. We soon found one another. Jean-Claude and I—we were young and too stupid to understand the price we'd pay, but by then we'd already lost some of our dearest friends. Jean-Claude and I refused to let them die in vain."

"What did you do?" Ruth breathed. She leaned closer to her grandmother.

"Whatever we could, which in the beginning was pitifully little. The Germans suffered more casualties in traffic accidents. At first our resistance was mostly symbolic." A slow smile spread across her weathered face. "But we learned, oh yes, we learned."

Ruth was still having difficulty taking it all in. She pressed her hand to her forehead. She found it hard enough to believe that the sketch of the female in this worn poster was her own grandmother. Then to discover that the fragile, petite woman at her side had been part of the French Resistance...

"Does my dad know any of this?" Ruth asked.

Helen sighed heavily. "I'm not sure, but I doubt it. Sam might have mentioned it to him. I've only told a few of my friends. No one else." She shook her head. "I didn't feel I could talk to my sons about it. There was too much that's disturbing. Too many painful memories."

"Did you...did you ever have to kill anyone?" Ruth had trouble even getting the question out.

"Many times," Helen answered bluntly. "Does that surprise you?"

It shocked Ruth to the point that she couldn't ask anything else.

"The first time was the hardest," her grandmother said. "I was held by a French policeman." She added something derogatory in French, and although Ruth couldn't understand the language, some things didn't need translation. "Under Vichy, some of the police worked hard to prove to the Germans what good little boys they were," she muttered, this time in English. "I'd been stopped and questioned, detained by this pig of a man. He said he was taking me to the police station. I had a small gun with me that I'd hidden, a seven millimeter."

Ruth's heart raced as she listened to Helen recount this adventure.

"The pig didn't drive me to the police station. Instead he headed for open country and I knew that once he was outside town and away from the eyes of any witnesses, he would rape and murder me."

Ruth pressed her hand to her mouth, holding back a gasp of horror.

"You'd trained in self-defense?" Paul asked.

Her grandmother laughed. "No. How could we? There was no time for such lessons. But I realized that I didn't need technique. What I needed was nerve. This beast of a man pulled his gun on me but I was quicker. I shot him in the head." She paused at the memory of that terrifying moment. "I buried him myself in a field and, as far as I know, he was never found." She wore a small satisfied look. "His mistake," she murmured, "was that he tightened his jaw when he reached for his gun—and I saw. I'd been watching him closely. He was thinking of what might happen, of what could go wrong. He was a professional, and I was only nineteen, and yet I knew that if I didn't act then, it would've been too late."

"Didn't *you* worry about what could happen?" Ruth asked, unable to grasp how her grandmother could ever shoot another human being.

"No," Helen answered flatly. "I *knew* what would happen. We all did. We didn't have a chance of surviving, none of us. My parents would never have discovered my fate—I would simply have disappeared. They didn't even know I'd married Jean-Claude or changed my name." She stared out at the water. "I don't understand why I lived. It makes no sense that God would spare me when all my friends, all those I loved, were killed."

"Jean-Claude, too?"

Her eyes filled and she slowly nodded.

"Where was he when you were taken by the policeman?" Paul asked.

Her grandmother's mouth trembled. "By then, Jean-Claude had been captured."

"The French police?"

"No," she said in the thinnest of whispers. "Jean-Claude was being held by the Gestapo. That was the first time they got him—but not the last."

Ruth had heard about the notorious German soldiers and their cruelty.

Helen straightened, and her back went rigid. "I could only imagine how those monsters were torturing my husband." Contempt hardened her voice.

"What did you do?" Ruth glanced at Paul, whose gaze remained riveted on her grandmother.

At first Helen didn't answer. "What else could I do? I had to rescue him."

"You?" Paul asked this with the same shock Ruth felt.

"Yes, me and…" Helen's smile was fleeting. "I was very clever about it, too." The sadness returned with such intensity that it brought tears to Ruth's eyes.

"They eventually killed him, didn't they?" she asked, hardly able to listen to her grandmother's response.

"No," Helen said as she turned to face Ruth. "I did."

Five

"YOU KILLED JEAN-CLAUDE?" RUTH REPEATED incredulously.

Tears rolling down her cheeks, Helen nodded. "God forgive me, but I had no choice. I couldn't allow him to be tortured any longer. He begged me to do it, begged me to end his suffering. That was the second time he was captured, and they were more determined than ever to break him. He knew far too much."

"You'd better start at the beginning. You went into Gestapo headquarters?" Paul moved closer as if he didn't want to risk missing even one word. "Was that the first time or the second?"

"Both. The first time, in April 1943, I rescued him. I pretended I was pregnant and brought a priest to the house the Gestapo had taken over. I insisted with great bravado that they force Jean-Claude to marry me and give my baby a name. I didn't care if they killed him, I said, but before he died I wanted him to give my baby his name." She paused. "I was very convincing."

"So you weren't really pregnant?" Ruth asked.

"No, of course not," her grandmother replied. "It was a ploy to get into the house."

"Was the priest a real priest?"

"Yes. He didn't know I was using him, but I had no alternative. I was desperate to get Jean-Claude out alive."

"The priest knew nothing," Ruth said, meeting Paul's eyes, astounded by her grandmother's nerve and cunning.

"The Father knew nothing," the older woman concurred, smiling grimly. "But I needed him, so I used him. Thankfully the Gestapo believed me, and because they wanted to keep relations with the Church as smooth as possible, they brought Jean-Claude into the room."

Ruth could picture the scene, but she didn't know if she'd ever possess that kind of bravery.

"Jean-Claude was in terrible pain, but he nearly laughed out loud when the priest asked him if he was the father of my child. Fortunately he didn't have to answer because our friends had arranged a distraction outside the house. A fire-bomb was tossed into a parked vehicle, which exploded. All but two Gestapo left the room. I shot them both right in front of the priest, and then Jean-Claude and I escaped through a back window."

"Where did you find the courage?" Ruth asked breathlessly.

"Courage?" her grandmother echoed. "That wasn't courage. That was fear. I would do anything to save my husband's life—and I did. Then, only a few weeks later, I was the one who killed him. What took courage was finding the will to live after Jean-Claude died. *That* was courage, and I would never have managed if it hadn't been for the American soldier who saved my life. If it hadn't been for Sam."

"He was my grandfather," Ruth explained to Paul.

"I want to know more about Jean-Claude," Paul said, placing his arm around Ruth's shoulders. It felt good to be held by him and she leaned into his strength, his solid warmth.

Her grandmother's eyes grew weary and she shook her head. "Perhaps another day. I'm tired now, too tired to speak anymore."

"We should go," Paul whispered.

"I'll do the dishes," Ruth insisted.

"Nonsense. You should leave now," Helen said. "You have better things to do than talk to an old lady."

"But we *want* to talk to you," Ruth told her.

"You will." Helen looked even more drawn. "Soon, but not right now."

"You'll finish the story?"

"Yes," the old woman said hoarsely. "I promise I'll tell you everything."

While her grandmother went to her room to rest, Ruth and Paul cleaned up the kitchen. At first they worked in silence, as if they weren't quite sure what to say to each other. Ruth put the food away while Paul rinsed the dishes and set them inside the dishwasher.

"You didn't know any of this before today?" he asked, propping himself against the counter.

"Not a single detail."

"Your father never mentioned it?"

"Never." Ruth wondered again how much her father actually knew about his mother's wartime adventures. "I'm sure you were the one who prompted her."

"Me?" Paul asked. "How?"

"More than anything, I think you reminded her of Jean-

Claude." Ruth tilted her head to one side. "It's as if this woman I've known all my life has suddenly become a stranger." Ruth finished wiping down the counters. She knew they'd need to leave soon if they were going to catch the ferry.

"Maybe you'd better check on her before we go," Paul said.

She agreed and hurried out of the kitchen. Her grandmother's eyes opened briefly when Ruth entered the cool, silent room. Reaching for an afghan at the foot of the bed, Ruth covered her with it and kissed the papery skin of her cheek. She'd always loved Helen, but she had an entirely new respect for her now.

"I'll be back soon," Ruth promised.

"Bring your young man."

"I will."

Helen's response was low, and at first Ruth didn't understand her and strained to hear. Gradually her voice drifted off. Ruth waited until Helen was asleep before she slipped out of the room.

"She's sleeping?" Paul asked, setting aside the magazine he was reading when Ruth returned to the kitchen.

Ruth nodded. "She started talking to me in French. I so badly wish I knew what she said."

They left a few minutes later. Absorbed in her own thoughts, Ruth walked down the hill beside Paul, neither of them speaking as they approached the foot ferry that would take them from Cedar Cove to Bremerton.

Once they were aboard, Paul went to get them coffee from the concession stand. While he was gone, Ruth decided she had to find out how much her family knew about her grandmother's war exploits. She opened her purse and rummaged for her cell phone.

Paul brought the coffee and set her plastic cup on the table.

Ruth glanced up long enough to thank him with a smile. "I'm calling my parents."

Paul nodded, tentatively sipping hot coffee. Then, in an obvious effort to give her some privacy, he moved to stand by the rail, gazing out at the water.

Her father answered on the third ring. "Dad, it's Ruth," she said in a rush.

"Ruthie! It's nice to hear from you."

Her father had never enjoyed telephone conversations and generally handed the phone off to Ruth's mother.

"Wait—I need to talk to you," Ruth said.

"What's up?"

That was her dad, too. He didn't like chitchat and wanted to get to the point as quickly as possible.

"I went over to see Grandma this afternoon."

"How is she? We've been meaning to get up there and see her *and* you. I don't know where the time goes. Thanksgiving was our last visit."

How is she? Ruth wasn't sure what to say. Her grandmother seemed fragile and old, and Ruth had never thought of her as either. "I don't know, Dad. She's the same, except—well, except she might have lost a few pounds." Ruth looked over at Paul and bit her lip. "I...brought a friend along with me."

"Your roommate? What's her name again?"

"Lynn Blumenthal. No, this is a male friend."

That caught her father's attention. "Someone from school?"

"No, we met sort of...by accident. His name is Paul Gordon and he's a sergeant in the marines. We've been corresponding for the past four months. But Paul isn't the reason I'm phoning."

"All right, then. What is?"

Ruth dragged in a deep breath. "Like I said before, I was visiting Grandma."

"With this marine you're seeing," he reiterated.

"Yes." Ruth didn't dare look at Paul a second time. Nervously, she tucked a strand of hair behind her ear and leaned forward, lowering her voice. "Grandma was in France during World War II. Did you know that?"

Her father paused. "Yes, I did."

"Were you aware that she was a member of the French Resistance?"

Again he paused. "My father said something shortly before he died, but I never got any more information."

"Didn't you ask your mother?"

"I tried, but she refused to talk about it. She said some things were better left buried and deflected all my questions. Do you mean to say she told you about this?"

"Yes, and, Dad, the stories were incredible! Did you know Grandma was married before she met Grandpa Sam?"

"What?"

"Her husband's name was Jean-Claude."

"A Frenchman?"

"Yes." She tried to recall his surname from the poster. "Jean-Claude… Brulotte. That's it. He was part of the movement, too, and Grandma, your *mother,* went into a Gestapo headquarters and managed to get him out."

"My mother?" The question was loud enough for Paul to hear from several feet away, because his eyebrows shot up as their eyes met.

"Yes, Dad, *your* mother. I was desperate to learn more, but she got tired all of a sudden, and neither Paul nor I wanted to overtax her. She's taking a nap now, and Paul and I are on the ferry back to Seattle."

Ruth heard her father take a long, ragged breath.

"All these years and she's never said a word to me. My dad did, as I told you, but he didn't give me any details, and I never believed Mom's involvement amounted to much—more along the lines of moral support, I always figured. My dad was over there and we knew that's where he met Mom."

"Did they ever go back to France?" Ruth asked.

"No. They did some traveling, but mostly in North America—Florida, Mexico, Quebec…"

"I guess she really was keeping the past buried," Ruth said.

"She must realize she's getting near the end of her life," her father went on, apparently thinking out loud. "And she wants us to know. I'm grateful she was willing to share this with you. Still, it's pretty hard to take in. My mother…part of the French Resistance. She told me she was in school over there."

"She was." Ruth didn't want her father to think Helen had lied to him.

"Then how in heaven's name did she get involved in that?"

"It's a long story."

"What made her start talking about it now?" her father asked.

"I think it's because she knows she's getting old, as you suggested," Ruth said. "And because of Paul."

"Ah, yes, this young man you're with."

"Yeah."

Her father hesitated. "I know you can't discuss this with Paul there, so give us a call later, will you? Your mother's going to want to hear about this young man."

"Yes, Daddy," she said, thinking with some amusement that she sounded like an obedient child.

"I'll call Mom this evening," her father said. "We need to set up a visit ourselves, possibly for the Memorial Day weekend."

After a quick farewell, she clicked off the phone and put it back in her purse.

Paul, still sipping his coffee, approached her again. She picked up her own cup as he sat down beside her.

"I haven't enjoyed an afternoon more in years," Paul said. "Not in years," he added emphatically.

Ruth grinned, then drank some of her cooling coffee. "I'd like to believe it was my company that was so engaging, but I know you're enthralled with my grandmother."

"And her granddaughter," Paul murmured, but he said it as if he felt wary of the fact that he found her appealing.

Ruth took his hand. "We haven't settled anything," he reminded her, tightening his hold on her fingers.

"Do we have to right this minute?"

He didn't answer.

"I want to see you again," she told him, moving closer.

"That's the problem. I want to see you again, too."

"I'm glad." Ruth didn't hide her relief.

Paul's responding smile was brief. "Fine. We'll do this your way—one day at a time. But remember, I only have two weeks' leave."

She could sense already that these would be the shortest two weeks of her life.

"By the time I ship out, we should know how we feel. Agreed?"

"Agreed."

He nodded solemnly. "Do you own a pair of in-line skates?" he asked unexpectedly.

"Sure, but I don't have them in Seattle. I can easily rent a pair, though."

"Want to go skating?"

"When?"

"Now?"

Ruth laughed. "I'd love to, with one stipulation."

"What's that?"

Ruth hated to admit how clumsy she was on skates. "If I fall down, promise you'll help me up."

"I can do that."

"If I get hurt…"

"If you get hurt," Paul said, "I promise to kiss you and make it better."

Ruth had the distinct feeling that she wasn't going to mind falling, not one little bit.

Six

Helen Shelton
5-B Poppy Lane
Cedar Cove, Washington

April 23

Dearest Charlotte,
Forgive me for writing rather than calling. It must seem
odd, since we're neighbors as well as friends. It's just that
sometimes writing things out makes it easier to think
them through....

I have some news, by the way. You haven't met my
granddaughter, Ruth, but you've heard me speak of
her. Well, she was over last week with a soldier she's
been writing to, who's on leave from Afghanistan. He's

a delightful young man and it was easy to see that her feelings for him are quite intense. His name is Paul Gordon. When Ruth first introduced us, I'm afraid I embarrassed us both by staring at him. Paul could've been Jean-Claude's grandson, the resemblance is that striking.

For the past few weeks, I've been remembering and dreaming about my war experiences. You've encouraged me for years to write them down. I've tried, but couldn't make myself do it. However... I don't know if this was wise but I told Ruth and her young man some of what happened to me in France. I know I shocked them both.

My son phoned later the same day, and John was quite upset with me, especially since I'd told Ruth and not him. I tried to explain that these were memories I've spent most of my life trying to forget. I do hope he understands. But Pandora's box is open now, and my family wants to learn everything they can. I've agreed to allow Ruth to tape our conversations, which satisfies everyone. I'm afraid you're right, my dear friend—I should've told my children long ago.

Do take care of yourself and Ben. I hope to see you soon.

Bless you, dear Charlotte,
Your friend always,
Helen

"I WANT YOU TO MEET MY FAMILY," PAUL SAID A little more than a week after their first date. They'd spent every available moment together; they'd been to the Seattle Center and the Space Needle, rowing on Lake Washington, out to dinner and had seen a couple of movies. Sitting on the campus lawn, he'd been waiting for Ruth after her last class of the day. He stood when she reached him, and Ruth saw that he wasn't smiling as he issued the invitation.

"When?"

"Mom and Dad are at the house."

"You mean you want me to meet them *now?*" Ruth asked as they strolled across the lush green grass toward the visitors' parking lot. If she'd known she was meeting Paul's parents she would've been better prepared. She would've done something about her hair and worn a different outfit and...

"Yeah," Paul muttered.

Ruth stopped and he walked forward two or three steps before he noticed. Frowning, he glanced back.

"What's going on here?" she asked, clutching her books to her chest.

Paul looked everywhere but at her. "My parents feel they should meet you, since I'm spending most of my time in your company. The way they figure it, you must be someone important in my life."

Ruth's heart did a happy little jig. "Am I?" she asked flirtatiously.

A rigid expression came over him, betraying none of his feelings. "I don't know the answer to that yet."

"Really?" she teased.

"Listen, Ruth, I'm not handing you my heart so you can break it. You don't want to be involved with a soldier. Well, I'm a soldier, and either you accept that or at the end of these two weeks, it's over."

He sounded so...so military. As if he thought a relationship could be that simple, that straightforward. Life didn't divide evenly into black-and-white. There were plenty of gray areas, too. All right, so Paul had a point. In the back of her mind, Ruth hoped that, given time, Paul would decide to get out of the war business. She wasn't the kind of woman who'd be content to sit at home while the man she loved was off in some faraway country risking his life. Experiencing dreadful things. Suffering. Maybe dying.

"You'd rather I didn't meet your family?" she asked.

"Right."

That hurt. "I see."

Some of her pain must have been evident in her voice, because Paul came toward her and tucked his finger beneath her chin. Their eyes met for the longest moment. "If my family meets you, they'll know how much I care about you," he said quietly.

Ruth managed to smile. "I'm glad you care, because I care about you, too," she admitted. "A *lot*."

"That doesn't solve anything."

"No, it doesn't," she said, leaning forward so their lips could meet. She half expected Paul to pull away, but he didn't.

Instead, he groaned and forcefully brought his mouth to hers. Their kiss was passionate, deep—honest. She felt the sharp edges of her textbooks digging painfully into her breasts, and still Ruth melted in his arms.

"You're making things impossible," he mumbled when he lifted his head from hers.

"I've been known to do that."

Paul reached for her hand and led her into the parking lot. "I mentioned your grandmother to my parents," he said casually as he unlocked the car doors.

"Ah," Ruth said, slipping into the passenger seat. "That explains it."

"Explains what?"

"Why your family wants to meet me. I've brought you to *my* family. They feel cheated."

Paul shook his head solemnly. "I really don't think that's it. But...speaking of your grandmother, when can we see her again?"

"Tomorrow afternoon, if you like. I talked to her this morning before my classes and she asked when we could make a return visit."

"You're curious about what happened, aren't you?" Paul asked as he inserted the key into the ignition.

"Very much," Ruth said. Since their visit to Cedar Cove, she'd thought about her grandmother's adventures again and again. She'd done some research, too, using the internet and a number of library books on the war. In fact, Ruth was so fascinated by the history of the Resistance movement, she'd found it difficult to concentrate on the psychology essay she was trying to write.

She'd had several days to become accustomed to the idea of Helen's exploits during the Second World War. And yet she still had trouble imagining the woman she knew as a fighter for the French Resistance.

"She loved Jean-Claude," Paul commented.

Ruth nodded. Her grandmother had loved her husband enough to kill him—a shocking reality that would not have made sense at any other time in Helen's life. And then, at some point after that, Helen had met her Sam. How? Ruth wondered. Helen said he'd rescued her, but what were the circumstances? When did they fall in love? Family history told her that Sam Shelton had fought in the European campaign during the Second World War. He'd been in France toward the end of the war, she recalled. How much had he known about Helen's past?

Ruth could only hope her grandmother would provide some answers tomorrow.

The meeting with Paul's family was going well. Ruth was charmed by his parents, who immediately welcomed her. Barbara, his mother, had an easy laugh and a big heart. She brought Ruth into the kitchen and settled her on a stool at the counter while she fussed with the dinner salad.

Paul and his father, Greg, were on the patio, firing up the grill and chatting. Every now and then, Ruth caught Paul stealing a glance in her direction.

"I want to help," Ruth told his mother.

"Nonsense," Barbara Gordon said as she tore lettuce leaves into a large wooden bowl. "I'm just so pleased to finally meet you. It was as if Paul had some secret he was keeping from us."

Ruth smiled and sipped her glass of iced tea.

"My father was career military—in the marines," Barbara said, chopping tomatoes for the salad. "I don't know if that was what induced Paul to join the military or not, but I suspect it had an influence."

"How do you feel about him being stationed so far from home?" Ruth asked, curious to hear his mother's perspective. She couldn't imagine any mother wanting to see her son or daughter at that kind of risk.

Barbara sighed. "I don't like it, if that's what you're asking. Every sane person hates war. My father didn't want to fight in World War II, and I cried my eyes out the day Greg left for Vietnam. Now here's my oldest son in Afghanistan."

"It seems most generations are called upon to serve their country, doesn't it?" Ruth said.

Barbara agreed with a short nod. "Freedom isn't free—for us or for the countries we support. Granted, in hindsight some of the conflicts we've been involved in seem misguided, but unfortunately war appears to be part of the human condition."

"Why?" Ruth asked, although she didn't really expect a response.

"I think every generation has asked that same question," Barbara said thoughtfully, putting the salad aside. She began to prepare a dressing, pouring olive oil and balsamic vinegar into a small bowl. "Paul told me you have a problem with his unwillingness to leave the marines at the end of his commitment. Is that right?"

A little embarrassed by the question, Ruth nodded. "I do."

"The truth is, as his mother, I want Paul out of the marines, too, but that isn't a decision you or I can make for him. My son has always been his own person. That's how his father and I raised him."

Ruth's gaze followed Paul as he stood with his father by the barbecue. He looked up and saw her, frowning as if he knew exactly what she and his mother were talking about. Ruth gave him a reassuring wave.

"You're in love with him, aren't you?" his mother asked, watching her closely.

The question took Ruth by surprise. "I'm afraid I am." Ruth didn't *want* to be—something she hadn't acknowledged openly until this moment. He'd described his reluctance to hand her his heart to break. She felt the same way and feared he'd end up breaking hers.

There seemed to be a tacit agreement not to broach these difficult subjects during dinner.

The four of them sat on the patio around a big table, shaded by a large umbrella. His mother had made corn bread as well as the salad, and the steaks were grilled to perfection. After dinner, Ruth helped with the cleanup and then Paul made their excuses.

"We're going to a movie?" she whispered on their way out the door, figuring he'd used that as a convenient pretext for leaving.

"I had to get you out of there before my mother started showing you my baby pictures."

"I'll bet you were a real cutie."

"You should see my brother and sister, especially the nude photos."

Ruth giggled.

Instead of the theater, they headed for Lake Washington and walked through the park, licking ice-cream cones, talking and laughing. Ruth couldn't remember laughing with anyone as much as she did with Paul.

He dropped her off after ten, walked her up to the front porch and kissed her good-night.

"I'll pick you up at noon," he said. "After your morning class."

"Noon," she repeated, her arms linked around his neck. That seemed too long. Despite her fears, despite the looming doubts, she *was* in love with him.

"You're sure your grandmother's up to having company so soon?" he asked.

"Yes." Ruth pressed her forehead against his shoulder. "I think the real question's whether we're ready for the next installment. I don't know if I can bear to hear exactly what happened to Jean-Claude."

"Perhaps not, but she needs to tell us."

"Yes," Ruth said. "She couldn't talk about it before."

"I know." Paul kissed her again.

Ruth felt at peace in his arms. Only when she stopped to think about the future, *their* future, did she become uncertain and confused.

Seven

RUTH AND PAUL SAT WITH HELEN AT THE kitchen table in her Cedar Cove house as rain dripped rhythmically against the windowpane. The day was overcast and dreary, as it frequently was during spring in the Pacific Northwest.

Helen reached for the teapot in the middle of the table and filled each of their cups, then offered them freshly baked peanut-butter cookies arranged on a small dessert plate. Ruth recognized the plate from her childhood. She and her grandmother had often had tea together when she was a youngster. Her visits to Cedar Cove were special; her grandmother had listened while Ruth chattered endlessly, sharing girlish confidences. It was during those private little tea parties that they'd bonded, grandmother and granddaughter.

Today the slow ritual of pouring tea and passing around

cookies demanded patience. Ruth badly wanted to throw questions at Helen, but she could see that her grandmother would resume her story only when she was ready. Helen seemed to be bracing herself for this next installment.

"I've been thinking about the things I mentioned on your last visit," Helen finally said, sipping her tea. Steam rose from the delicate bone-china cup. "It was a lot for you to absorb at one time."

"I didn't know *anything* about your adventures, Grandma." And they truly were adventures, of a kind few people experienced these days. *Real* adventures, with real and usually involuntary risks.

Helen grimaced. "My children didn't, either. But as I said before, it's time." Helen set the fragile cup back in its saucer. "Your father phoned and asked me about all of this." She paused, a look of distress on her face. "I hope he'll forgive me for keeping it from him all these years."

"I'm sure he will," Ruth told her.

Helen obviously wanted to believe that. "He asked me to tell him more, but I couldn't," she said sadly.

"I'm sure Dad understood."

"I couldn't relive those memories again so soon."

Ruth laid a comforting hand on her grandmother's arm. This information of Helen's was an important part of her family history. Today, with Helen's agreement, she'd come prepared with a small tape recorder. Now nothing would be lost.

"Jean-Claude had a wonderful gift," her grandmother said, breaking into the story without preamble. "He was a big man who made friends easily—a natural leader. Our small group trusted him with our lives."

Paul smiled encouragingly.

"Within a few minutes of meeting someone, he could figure out if he should trust that person," Helen continued. "More and more people wanted to join us. We started with a few students like ourselves, who were determined to resist the Nazis. Soon, others found us and we connected with groups across France. We all worked together as we lit fires of hope."

"Tell me about the wanted poster with your picture and Jean-Claude's," Ruth said.

Her grandmother smiled ruefully, as if that small piece of notoriety embarrassed her. "I'm afraid Jean-Claude and I acquired a somewhat exaggerated reputation. Soon almost everything that happened in Paris as part of the Resistance movement was attributed to us, whether we were involved or not."

"Such as?"

"There was a fire in a supply depot. Jean-Claude and I wished we'd been responsible, but we weren't. Yet that was what prompted the Germans to post our pictures." A smile brightened her eyes. "It was a rather unflattering sketch of Jean-Claude, he told me, although I disagreed."

"Can you tell me some of the anti-Nazi activities you were able to undertake?" Ruth asked, knowing her father would want to hear as much of this as his mother could recall.

Helen considered the question. "Perhaps the most daring adventure was one of Jean-Claude's. There was an SS officer, a horrible man, a pig." This word was spit out, as if even the memory of him disgusted her. "Jean-Claude discovered that this officer had obtained information through torturing a fellow Resistance member, information that put us all at risk. Jean-Claude decided the man had to die and that he would be the one to do it."

Paul glanced at Ruth, and he seemed to tell her that killing an SS officer would be no easy task.

Helen sipped her tea once more. "I feared for Jean-Claude."

"Is this when he…died?" Ruth asked.

"No." For emphasis, her grandmother shook her head. "That came later."

"Go on," Paul urged.

"One night Jean-Claude left me and another woman in a garden in the suburbs, at the home of a sympathetic school-teacher who'd made contact with our group. He and his wife went out for the evening. Jean-Claude instructed us to dig a grave and fill it with quicklime. We were to wait there for his return. He left with two other men and I was convinced I'd never see him again."

"But you did," Ruth said.

The old woman nodded. "According to Jean-Claude, it was either kill the SS officer or he would take us all down. He simply knew too much."

"What did Jean-Claude do?"

"That is a story unto itself." Helen sat even straighter in her chair. "This happened close to the final time he was captured. He knew, I believe, that he would die soon, and it made him fearless. He took more and more risks. And he valued his own life less and less." Her eyes shone with tears as she gazed out the rain-blurred window, lost in a world long since past.

"The SS officer had taken a room in a luxury hotel on the outskirts of Paris," Helen went on a minute later. "He was in the habit of sipping a cognac before retiring for the evening. When he called for his drink, it was Jean-Claude who brought it to him wearing a waiter's jacket. I don't know how he killed the SS man, but he did it without alerting anyone. He made sure there was no blood. The problem was getting the body out of the hotel without anyone seeing."

"Why? Couldn't he just leave it there?"

"Why?" Helen repeated, shaking her head. "If the man's body had been discovered, the entire staff would have been

tortured as punishment. Eventually someone would have broken. In any event, Jean-Claude smuggled the body out."

"How did he do it?"

"Jean-Claude was clever. His friends hauled him and the
body of the SS officer up the chimney. First the dead man and
then the live one. That was necessary, you see, because there
was a guard at the end of the hallway."

"But once they got to the rooftop, how did he manage?"

"It was an effort," Helen said. "Jean-Claude told me they
tossed the body from that rooftop to the roof of another building and then another—an office building. They lowered him
down in the elevator. When the men arrived with the body,
we all worked together and buried him quickly."

"The SS officer's disappearance must have caused trouble
for the Resistance," Paul said.

Helen nodded ardently. "Oh, yes."

"When was Jean-Claude captured the second time?" Ruth
asked. She was intensely curious and yet she dreaded hearing
about the death of this brave man her grandmother had loved.

Helen's eyes glistened and she lifted her teacup with an un-
steady hand. "It isn't what you think," she prefaced, and the
cup made a slight clinking sound as it rattled against the saucer. Helen placed both hands in her lap and took a moment to
compose herself. "We were headed for the Metro—the subway. By then I'd bleached my hair and we'd both changed our
appearances as much as possible. I don't think my own mother
would have recognized me. Jean-Claude's, either," she added
softly, her voice a mere whisper.

Paul reached for Ruth's hand, as if sensing that she needed
his support.

When her grandmother began to speak again, it was in
French. She switched languages naturally, apparently with-

out realizing she'd done so. All at once, she covered her face and broke into sobs.

Although Ruth hadn't understood a word, she started crying, too, and gently wrapped her arms around her grandmother's thin shoulders. Hugging her was the only thing she could do to ease this remembered pain.

"It's all right, it's all right," Ruth cooed over and over. "You don't need to tell us any more."

Paul agreed. "This is too hard on her—and you," he said.

They stayed for another hour, but it was clear that reliving the past had exhausted her grandmother. She seemed so frail now, even more than during the previous visit.

While her grandmother rested in her room, Ruth cleared the table. As she took care of the few dishes, her eyes brimmed with tears again. It was agonizing to think about the horrors her grandmother had endured.

"When she was speaking French, she must've been reliving the day Jean-Claude died," Ruth said, turning so her back was pressed against the kitchen counter.

Paul nodded. "She was," he answered somberly.

Ruth studied him as she returned to the kitchen table, where he sat. "You said you speak French. Could you understand what she was saying?"

He nodded again. "At the Metro that day, Jean-Claude was picked up in a routine identity check by the French police. Through pure luck, Helen was able to get on the train without being stopped. She had to stand helplessly inside the subway car and watch as the police hauled him to Gestapo headquarters." Paul paused long enough to give her an odd smile. "The next part was a tirade against the police, whom she hated. Remember last week when she explained that some of the French police were trying to prove their worth to the

Germans? Well, apparently Jean-Claude was one of their most wanted criminals."

"They tortured him, didn't they?" she asked, although she already knew the answer.

"Yes." Paul met her eyes. "Unmercifully."

Ruth swallowed hard.

"Helen tried to save him. Disregarding her own safety, she went in after him, only this time she went alone. No sympathetic priest." Paul's face hardened. "They dragged her into the basement, where Jean-Claude was being tortured. They had him strung up by his arms. He was bloody and his face was unrecognizable."

"No!" Ruth hid her eyes with both hands.

"They taunted him. Said they had his accomplice and now he would see her die."

Ruth could barely talk. "They...were going to...kill Helen—in front of Jean-Claude?"

"From what she said, it wouldn't have been an easy death. The point was for Jean-Claude to watch her suffer—to watch her die a slow, agonizing death."

"Dear God in heaven."

"She didn't actually say it," Paul continued. "She didn't have to spell it out, but Jean-Claude obviously hadn't been broken. Seeing her suffer would have done it, though, and your grandmother knew that. She also knew that if he talked, it would mean the torture and death of others in the Resistance." Paul looked away for a moment. "Apparently he and his friends had helped a number of British pilots escape German detection. At risk was the entire underground effort. Jean-Claude knew more than anyone suspected."

"Helen couldn't let that happen," Ruth said.

"No, and Jean-Claude understood that, too."

"Remember when she said she was the one who killed him? She didn't mean that literally, did she?"

"She did."

This was beginning not to make sense. "But...how?"

Paul braced his elbows on the table. "Her voice started to break at that point and I didn't catch everything. She talked about a cyanide tablet. I'm not sure how she got hold of it. But I know she kissed him.... A final kiss goodbye. By this stage she was too emotional to understand clearly."

The pieces started to fall together for Ruth. "She gave him the pill—you mean instead of taking it herself?"

"That's what it sounded like to me," he said hoarsely.

"Was this when he asked her to kill him? And then she kissed him and transferred the pill?"

"I think so." Paul cleared his throat, but his voice was still rough. "She said Jean-Claude had begged her to kill him. He spoke to her in English, which the Germans couldn't understand."

Ruth pictured the terrible scene. Helen and Jean-Claude arguing. If Helen swallowed the pill, she'd be dead and the Gestapo would lose their bargaining chip. Even knowing that, Jean-Claude couldn't bear to see his wife die. It truly would have broken him.

"Speaking in another language added enough confusion that she had the opportunity to do what he asked," Ruth speculated.

"Last time she told us about being driven by fear instead of courage," Paul reminded her. "I'm sure she didn't stop to think about what she was doing—she couldn't. Nor could she refuse Jean-Claude."

Ruth wanted to bury her face in her hands and weep.

"Jean-Claude thanked her," Paul said.

"She would have refused." Ruth could see it all in her mind, the argument between them.

"I'm convinced she did refuse at first. She loved Jean-Claude—he was her husband."

Ruth couldn't imagine a worse scenario.

Paul's voice dropped slightly. "She said Jean-Claude had never begged for mercy, never pleaded for anything, but he told her he couldn't bear any more pain. Above all, he couldn't bear it if they killed her. He begged her to let him die."

"He loved her that much," Ruth said in a hushed whisper.

"And she loved him that much, enough to spare him any more torture, even at the risk of her own death."

"They didn't kill her, though," Ruth said, stating the obvious. "Even though they must have figured out that she was responsible for his death?"

Paul's eyes widened as if he couldn't explain that any more than she could. "She didn't say what happened next."

Ruth stood, anxious now to see her grandmother before they left. "I'm going to check on her."

Ruth went to her grandmother's room to find her resting fitfully. Helen's eyes fluttered open when Ruth stepped quietly past the threshold.

"Have I shocked you?" Helen asked, holding out her hand to Ruth.

"No," Ruth told her grandmother, who had to be the bravest woman she'd ever know. She sat on the edge of the bed and whispered, "Thank you, Grandma—for everything you did. And for doing Paul and me the honor of sharing it with us."

Helen smiled and touched her cheek. "You've been crying."

Taking her grandmother's hand between her own, she kissed the old woman's knuckles. A lump filled her throat and she couldn't find the words to express her love.

"When did you meet Grandpa?" she finally asked.

Helen smiled again and her eyes drifted shut. "Two years later. He was one of the American soldiers who came with Patton's army to free us from the concentration camp."

This was a completely different aspect of the story.

"When it was learned that I was an American citizen, I was immediately questioned and when my citizenship was verified, I was put on a ship and sent home."

"Two years," Ruth said in a choked voice. "You were in a camp for *two years?*" Just when she thought there was nothing more to horrify her, Helen revealed something else.

"Buchenwald.... I don't want to talk about it," Helen muttered.

No wonder her grandmother had never spoken of those years. The memories were far worse than the worst Ruth had been able to imagine.

Her grandmother brushed the hair from Ruth's forehead. "I want you to know I like your young man."

"He reminded you of Jean-Claude, didn't he?"

Her smile was weak, which told Ruth how drained this afternoon's conversation had left Helen. "Not at first, but then he smiled and I saw Jean-Claude in Paul's eyes." She swallowed a couple of times and added, "I wanted to die after Jean-Claude did. I would've done anything if only the Germans had put me out of my living hell. They knew that and decided it was better to let me live and remember, each and every day, that I'd killed my own husband." A tear slid down her face. "I can't speak of it anymore."

Ruth understood. "I'll leave you to rest. Try to sleep."

Her grandmother's answering sigh told Ruth how badly she needed that just then.

"Come back and see me soon," she called as Ruth stood.

"I will, I promise." She bent down to kiss the soft cheek.

Paul was waiting for her in the living room, flipping

through the *Cedar Cove Chronicle,* but he got up when she returned. "Is she all right?"

Ruth shrugged. "She's tired." Her eyes were watering again, despite her best efforts not to cry. She couldn't stop thinking about the pain her grandmother had endured and kept hidden all these years.

Paul held open his arms and she walked into his embrace as naturally as she slipped on a favorite coat. Once there, she began to cry—harsh, broken sobs she thought would never end.

Eight

AS BEFORE, RUTH AND PAUL SPOKE LITTLE ON the ferry ride back to Seattle.

Ruth's entire perspective on her grandmother had changed. Until now, she'd always viewed the petite, gentle woman as... well, her grandmother. All of a sudden Ruth was forced to realize that Helen had been young once, and deeply involved in events that had changed or destroyed many lives. She'd been an ordinary young woman from a fairly privileged background. She'd been a student, fallen in love, enjoyed a carefree existence. Then this ordinary young woman had been caught up in extraordinary circumstances—and risen to their demands.

Ruth was curious about the connection between her grandmother's life during the war and her life afterward. Clearly the link was her grandfather, whom she'd never had a chance to know.

Paul stood with Ruth at the railing as the ferry glided through the relatively smooth waters of Puget Sound. The rain had stopped, and although the sky remained cloudy and gray, the air was fresh with only the slightest hint of brine.

"Every story I hear leaves me amazed that this incredible woman is my grandmother," Ruth said fervently, grateful that Paul was beside her.

"I know. I'm overwhelmed, and I just met her."

They exchanged tentative smiles, and then they both sighed—in appreciation, Ruth thought, of everything Helen Shelton had been and done.

"I wish I'd known my grandfather," she said. "He seems to have been the one who gave my grandmother a reason to live. He loved her and she loved him." Ruth knew that from every word her grandmother and her dad had said about Sam Shelton.

"How old were you when he died?" Paul asked.

"Two or so." She turned so she could look directly at Paul. "When I saw my grandmother in her bedroom, she said he was with a group of soldiers who freed the prisoners in the concentration camp."

"She was in a concentration camp?"

Ruth nodded. "She was there at least a couple of years."

Paul frowned, obviously upset.

"I can't *bear* to think what her life was like in one of those obscene places," Ruth said.

"It would've been grim. You're right—they were obscene. Places of death."

Ruth didn't welcome the reminder. "I'm so glad you've been with me on these visits," she told him. Paul's presence helped her assimilate the details her grandmother had shared. He'd given her a feeling of comfort and companionship as they'd listened to these painful wartime experiences. Ruth believed there was something about Paul that had led Helen to divulge her secrets.

After the ferry docked, they walked along the Seattle waterfront, where they ate clam chowder, followed by fish-and-chips, for dinner. Their mood was somber, and yet, strangely, Ruth felt a sense of peace.

The next day, after her classes, she hurried back to her rental house and ran into Lynn. As much as possible, Ruth had avoided her roommate. Her relationship with Lynn had been awkward ever since the argument over Clay. Lynn's lie, which she'd told in an effort to keep Ruth from meeting Paul, hadn't helped.

Lynn was coming out just as Ruth leaped up the porch steps. Her roommate hesitated.

Ruth did, too. She'd never said anything to Lynn about her intentional mix-up that first night she was meeting Paul. Her classes would be over in June, and she was more than ready to move out.

"Hi," Lynn offered uncertainly.

Ruth's pace slowed as she waited, half expecting Lynn to make some derogatory remark about Paul. Because Ruth had been with him so often lately, she'd had very little contact with her roommate.

"Are you seeing Paul again?" The question lacked the scornful tone she'd used when referring to him previously. She seemed more prompted by curiosity than anything else.

"We're meeting some friends of his later. Why?" Ruth couldn't help being suspicious. If he'd phoned with a change of plan, she needed to know about it. She knew from experience that Lynn couldn't be trusted to relay the message.

Lynn shrugged. "No reason."

"Is there something you aren't telling me?" Ruth's voice was calm.

Her roommate had the grace to blush. "He didn't call, if that's what you're asking."

"Like I could believe you."

"You can—okay, maybe what I did that night was stupid."

"Maybe?" Ruth echoed.

"All right, it was. I was upset because of Clay." She didn't meet Ruth's eyes. "I thought Clay was really hot and you dumped him for soldier boy, and I thought that was just wrong."

"I don't need you to decide who I'm allowed to date." Ruth couldn't keep the anger out of her voice. What Lynn had tried to do still rankled. If her cell phone battery hadn't been low, she and Paul might have missed each other completely. That sent chills down her spine.

Lynn released a long sigh. "I'll admit it—you were right about Clay."

"How so?"

"He's...he's stuck on himself."

Ruth suspected that meant he wasn't interested in Lynn.

"I... I like Paul," her roommate confessed.

Ruth wasn't even aware that Lynn had met him and said so.

"He stopped by one afternoon when he thought you were back from class, only you weren't, and I was here. We talked for a bit. Then he left to look for you at the library."

Funny that neither had mentioned the incident earlier. "I had the impression you were dead set against him."

"Not him," Lynn said. "I'm against the war in Iraq.... I thought you were, too."

"I don't like war of any kind. This war or any war, including Afghanistan. Still, the United States is involved in the Middle East, and no matter what, it's our young men and women who are fighting there. Politics aside, I want to support our troops."

"I know." Lynn suddenly seemed to find something absolutely mesmerizing about her shoes.

Ruth moved past her on the porch. "I'd better go in and change."

"Ruth," Lynn said sharply. Ruth turned to face her. "I'm sorry about the other night. That really was an awful thing to do. I was upset and I took it out on you."

Ruth had pretty much figured that out on her own. "Paul and I connected, so no harm done."

"I know, and I'm glad you did because I think Paul is great. I know he's a soldier and all, but he's a nice guy. I only met him once, but I could see he's ten times the man Clay will ever be. He's the kind of guy I hope to meet."

Paul had obviously impressed her during their brief exchange. She wondered what they'd talked about.

"All's well that ends well," Ruth said.

"Shakespeare, right?" Lynn asked. "In other words, all is forgiven?"

Ruth laughed and nodded, then started into the house.

Paul picked her up at five-thirty and they drove to a Mexican restaurant in downtown Kent. Paul had arranged for her to meet his best friend.

Brian Hart and his wife, Carley, were high school sweethearts and Brian had known Paul for most of his life.

"We go way back," Brian said when they were introduced. He slid out of the booth and they exchanged handshakes, with Paul standing just behind Ruth, his hand on her shoulder.

"I'm pleased to meet you both." They were a handsome couple. Carley was a delicate blonde with soulful blue eyes, and her husband was tall and muscular, as if he routinely worked out.

"We're pleased to meet you, too," Carley said when Ruth slipped into the booth across from her.

Paul got in beside Ruth.

"I insisted Paul introduce us," Carley said as she reached for a chip and dipped it in the salsa. "Every time we tried to get together during his leave, he already had plans with you."

Ruth hadn't thought of it that way, but realized she'd monopolized his time. "I guess I should apologize for that."

"We only have the two weeks," Paul explained.

"You'll be back in Seattle after the training, won't you?" Brian asked.

"Maybe, but…" Paul hesitated and glanced at Ruth.

"We only just met and…" Ruth let the rest fade. He would be back and they'd see each other again, but only if she could accept his career in the military.

This fourteen-day period was a testing time for them both, and at the end they had a decision to make.

"I'm giving Ruth two weeks to fall head over heels in love with me." Paul said it as if it were a joke.

"If she doesn't, there's definitely something wrong with her," Carley joked back.

Ruth smiled, but she felt her heart sinking. She hadn't made her decision yet; the truth was, she'd been putting it off until the last possible minute.

Time was dwindling and soon, in a matter of days, Paul would be leaving. She wasn't ready—wasn't ready to decide and wasn't ready for him to go.

Brian and Carley had to be home before eight because of their babysitter, so they left the restaurant first.

Ruth had enjoyed the spicy enchiladas, the margarita and especially the teasing between Paul and Brian. Carley had told story after story of the two boys and their high school exploits, and they'd all laughed and joked together.

Paul and Ruth lingered in the booth over cups of dark coffee, gazing into each other's eyes. He'd switched places so he could sit across from her. If she'd met him under any other circumstance, there'd be no question about her feelings. None! It was so easy to fall in love with this man. In fact, it was already too late; even Paul's mother had seen that. Ruth *knew* him. After all the letters and emails, all the conversations, she felt as if he'd become part of her life.

"I know what you're thinking," Paul said unexpectedly.

"What am I thinking?" she asked with amusement.

"You're wondering why I find life in the military so attractive."

She shrugged. "Close."

"Do you want to know my answer?"

Ruth was aware of his reasons, but wanted to hear him out, anyway. "Sure, go ahead."

"I like the structure, the discipline, the knowledge that I'm doing something positive to bring about freedom and democracy in the world."

This was where it got troubling for Ruth.

Before she could state her own feelings, Paul stopped her. "I know you don't agree with me, and I accept that, but I am who I am."

"I didn't challenge that—I wouldn't."

He stiffened, then reached for his coffee and held it at arm's length, cupping his hands around the mug. "True enough, but the minute I started talking, you looked like you wanted to challenge my answer."

She hadn't known her feelings were that transparent.

"I guess now is as good a time as any to ask where I stand with you."

"What do you mean?" An uneasy feeling began to creep up her spine. They had only a couple of days before he was scheduled to leave, and she was going to need every minute of that time to concentrate on this relationship.

"You know what I'm asking, Ruth."

She did. She met his eyes. "I'm in love with you, Paul."

"I'm in love with you, too." He stretched his hand across the table and intertwined their fingers.

Her heart nearly sprang out of her chest with happiness and yet tears filled her eyes.

To her astonishment, Paul laughed. "This is supposed to be a happy moment," he told her.

"I *am* happy, but I'm afraid, too."

"Of what?"

"Of you leaving again. Of your involvement in the military. Of you fighting in a war, any war."

"It's what I do."

"I know." Still, she had difficulty reconciling her emotions and beliefs with the way Paul chose to make his living.

"But you don't like it," he said, his voice hard.

"No."

He sighed harshly. "Then tell me where we go from here."

Ruth wished she knew. "I can't answer that."

His eyes pleaded with her. "I can't answer it for you, Ruth. You're going to have to make up your mind about us."

She'd known it would come down to this. "I'm not sure I can. Not yet."

He considered her words. "When do you think you'll be able to decide?"

"Let's wait until you've finished your training and we see each other again.... We'll both have a better idea then, don't you think?"

"No. I might not be coming back to Seattle. I have to know soon. Now. Tonight." He paused. "I realize I sound unfair and pushy, and I apologize."

"Apologize for what?" she asked. Her hand tightened

around his fingers. She could feel him pulling away from her, if not physically, then emotionally.

"I've been trained to be decisive. Putting things off only leads to confusion. We've been writing for months."

"Yes, I know, but—"

"We've spent every possible minute of my leave together."

"Yes...."

"I love you, Ruth, but I won't lie to you. I'm not leaving the marines. I've chosen the military as my career and that means I could be involved in conflicts all over the world. I have to know if you can accept that."

"I..."

"If you can't, we need to walk away from each other right now. I don't want to drag this out. You decide."

Ruth didn't want a part-time husband. "I want a man who'll be a husband to me and a father to my children. A man of peace, not war." She didn't mean to sound so adamant.

Paul didn't respond for a long moment. "I think we have our answer." He slid out of the booth and waited for her. They'd paid earlier, so there was nothing to do but go out to the parking lot.

Ruth wasn't finished with the conversation, even if Paul was. "I need time," she told him.

"The decision's made."

"You're pressuring me," she protested. "I've still got two days, remember?"

"It doesn't work that way," he said.

"But this isn't fair!"

"I already admitted it wasn't." He opened the passenger door, and a moment later, he joined her in the car. "I wish now I'd waited and we still had those two days," he said bleakly. "But we don't."

He started the car and Ruth noticed that his fingers had tensed on the steering wheel.

Ruth bit her lip. "Sure we do. Let's just pretend we didn't have this conversation and enjoy the time we have left. You can do that, can't you?" Her voice took on a pleading quality.

"I wish I could, but… I can't." He inhaled deeply. "The decision is made," he said again.

They didn't have much to say during the rest of the ride to the university district. When Paul pulled up in front of the rental house, Ruth noticed the lights were on, which meant Lynn was home.

They sat side by side in the car without speaking until Paul roused himself to open his door. He walked around to escort her from the passenger side, then accompanied her to the porch.

Ruth half expected him to kiss her. He didn't.

"Will I see you again?" she asked as he began to leave.

He turned back and stood there, stiff and formal. "Probably not."

"You mean this is it? This is goodbye…as if I meant nothing…as if we were strangers?" She felt outraged that he could abandon her like this, without a word. It was unkind and unfair…and life wasn't that simple.

"Is there anything left to say?" he asked.

"Of course there is," she cried. She didn't know what, but surely there was *something*. Hurting and angry, Ruth gestured wildly with her arms. "You can't be serious! Are you really going to walk away? Just like that?"

"Yes." The word was devoid of emotion.

"You aren't going to write me again?"

"No."

This was unbelievable.

"Call me?"

"No."

She glared at him. "In other words, you're going to act as if you'd never even met me, as if I'd never mailed that Christmas card."

A hint of a smile flickered over his tightly controlled features. "I'm certainly going to give it my best shot."

"Fine, then," she muttered. If he thought so little of her, then he could do as he wished. She didn't want to be with a man who didn't care about her feelings, just his own.

Nine

TRUE TO HIS WORD, PAUL DIDN'T GET IN TOUCH with her after their Tuesday-night dinner. The first day, her anger carried her. Then she convinced herself that he'd contact her before he left for Camp Pendleton. Not so. Paul Gordon—correction, *Sergeant* Paul Gordon, USMC—was out of her life and that was perfectly fine with her. Only it wasn't.

A week later, as she sat in her "Theories of Learning" class, taking notes, her determination faltered. She wanted to push all thoughts of Paul out of her mind forever; instead, he was constantly there.

What upset her most was the cold-blooded way he'd dismissed her from his life. It seemed so easy for him, so…simple. She was gone for him, as if she meant nothing. That hurt, and it didn't stop hurting.

Ruth blinked, forcing herself to listen to the lecture. If she flunked this course, Paul Gordon would be to blame.

After class she walked across campus, her steps slow and deliberate. She felt no urge to hurry. But when her cell phone rang, she nearly dropped her purse in her eagerness. Could it be Paul? Had he changed his mind? Had he found it impossible to forget her, the same way she couldn't forget him? A dozen more questions flew through her mind before she managed to answer.

"Hello?" She sounded excited and breathless at the same time.

"Ruth." The familiar voice of a longtime friend, Tina Dupont, greeted her. They talked for a few minutes, and arranged to meet at the library at the end of the week. Four minutes after she'd answered her cell, it was back in her purse.

She was too restless to sit at home and study, which was how she'd spent every night since her last date with Paul, so she decided to go out. That was what she needed, she told herself with forced enthusiasm. Find people, friends, a party. Something to do, somewhere to be.

Although it was midafternoon, she took the bus down to the waterfront, where she'd met Paul the first night. That wasn't a smart idea. She wasn't up to dealing with memories. Before she could talk herself out of it, Ruth hopped on the Bremerton ferry. A visit with her grandmother would lift her spirits in a way nothing else could. Besides, if Helen felt strong enough, she wanted to hear the rest of the story, especially the role her grandfather had played.

As she stepped off the foot ferry from Bremerton to Cedar Cove, it occurred to Ruth that she should've phoned first. But it was unlikely her grandmother would be out. And if she was, Ruth figured she could wander around Cedar Cove for a while. That would help fill the void threatening to swallow her whole.

The trudge up the hill to her grandmother's house seemed twice as steep and three times as long. Funny, when she'd been with Paul, the climb hadn't even winded her. That was because she'd been laughing and joking with him, she remembered—and wished she hadn't. Alone, hands shoved in her pockets, she felt drained of energy.

Reaching 5-B Poppy Lane, she saw that the front door to her grandmother's duplex stood open, although the old-fashioned wooden screen was shut. The last remaining tulips bloomed in primary colors as vivid as the rainbow. Walking up the steps, Ruth rang the doorbell. "Grandma! Are you home?"

No one answered. "Grandma?"

Alarm jolted through her. Had something happened to her grandmother? She pounded on the door and was even more alarmed when a white-haired woman close to her grandmother's age came toward her.

"Hello," the older lady said pleasantly. "Can I help you?"

"I'm looking for my grandmother."

The woman unlatched the screen door and swung it open. "You must be Ruth. I don't think Helen was expecting you. I'm Charlotte Rhodes."

"Charlotte," Ruth repeated. "Helen's spoken of you so often. It's wonderful to meet you."

"You, too," Charlotte said, taking Ruth's hand. "I'm happy to make your acquaintance."

Ruth nodded, but she couldn't stop herself from blurting out, "Is anything wrong with my grandmother?"

"Oh, no, not at all. We're sitting on the patio, talking and knitting. Helen's counting stitches and asked me to get the door. She assumed it was a salesman and my job was to get rid of him...or her." Charlotte laughed. "Not that *I'm* much good at that. Just the other day, a Girl Scout came to my door selling cookies. When I bought four boxes, she announced that every kid comes to my house first, because I'll buy anything. Especially for charity."

Ruth grinned. "I think my grandmother must be like that, too."

"Why do you suppose she sent *me* to the door?" Charlotte joked. "Your grandmother's knitting a Fair Isle sweater. It's her first one and she asked me over to get her started."

"Perhaps I should come back at a more convenient time?" Ruth didn't want to interrupt the two women.

"Nonsense! She'd never forgive me if you left. Besides, I was just gathering my things to head on home. My husband will be wondering what's kept me so long." Charlotte led the way through the house.

As soon as Ruth stepped onto the brick patio, her grandmother's eyes lit up with pleasure. "Ruth! What a welcome surprise."

Ruth bent forward and kissed Helen's cheek.

Charlotte Rhodes collected her knitting, saying she'd talk to Helen at the Senior Center on Monday, and left.

"Sit down, sit down," Helen urged, motioning at the chair next to her. "Help yourself to iced tea if you'd like." Strands of yarn were wrapped around both index fingers as she held the needles. One was red, the other white. "You can find a glass, can't you?"

"Yes, of course, but I'm fine," Ruth assured her, enjoying the sunshine and the sights and sounds of Cedar Cove. The earth in her grandmother's garden smelled warm and clean— the way it smelled only in spring. Inhaling deeply, Ruth sat down, staring at the cove with its sparkling blue water.

"Where's Paul?" her grandmother asked, as if noticing for the first time that he wasn't with her.

Ruth's serenity was instantly destroyed and she struggled to disguise her misery. "He went to the marines' camp in California."

"Oh." Her grandmother seemed disappointed. "I imagine you miss him."

Ruth decided to let the comment slide.

"I liked him a great deal," her grandmother said, rubbing salt into Ruth's already wounded heart. Helen's focus was on her knitting, but when Ruth didn't immediately respond, she looked up.

Ruth met her eyes and exhaled forcefully. "Would you mind if we didn't discuss Paul?"

Her request was met with a puzzled glance. "Why?"

Ruth decided she might as well tell her. "We won't be see-ing each other again."

"Really?" Her grandmother's expression was downcast. "I thought highly of that young man. Any particular reason?"

"Actually," Ruth said, "there are several. He's in the mili-tary, which you already know."

Her grandmother carefully set her knitting aside and reached for her glass of iced tea, giving Ruth her full atten-tion. "You knew that when you first met, I believe."

"Yes, I did, but I assumed that in time he'd be released from his commitment and return to civilian life. He told me that won't be the case, that the military's his career." *In for the long haul,* as he'd put it. Granted, she'd known about his dedication to the marines from the beginning, but he'd known about her feelings, too. Did her preferences matter less than his?

"I see." Her grandmother studied her.

Ruth wondered if she truly did. "What really upsets me is the heartless way he left. I told him I wasn't sure I could live with the fact that he'd chosen the military." The memory an-gered her, and she raised her voice. "Then Paul had the au-

dacity to say I wouldn't be hearing from him again and he…
he just walked away." Ruth hadn't planned to spill out the
whole story minutes after she arrived, but she couldn't hold
it inside a second longer.

Her grandmother's response shocked her into silence. Helen
smiled.

"Forgive me," her grandmother said gently, leaning forward to give Ruth's hand a small squeeze. "Sam did something similar, you see."

The irritation died instantly. "I wanted to ask you about
my grandfather."

A peaceful look came over Helen. "He was a wonderful
man. And he saved me."

"From the Germans, you mean?"

Helen shook her head. "Technically, it was General Patton
and the Third Army who saved us. Patton knew what Buchenwald was. He knew that a three-hour wait meant twenty-
thousand lives because the Germans had been given orders
to kill all prisoners before surrendering. Against every rule of
caution, Patton mounted an attack, cutting off the SS troops
from the camp. Because of his decisive move, the Germans
were forced to flee or surrender. By that time, the German
soldiers knew they were defeated. They threw down their
guns and surrendered. Sam was with Patton on the march, so,
yes, he contributed to my rescue and that of countless others.
But when I say your grandfather saved me, I mean he saved
me from myself."

"I want to hear about him, if you're willing to tell me."
Ruth straightened, perching on the edge of her seat.

Her grandmother closed her eyes. "I cannot speak about
the years in Buchenwald, not even to you."

Ruth reached for Helen's hand, stroking the soft skin over
the gnarled and prominent knuckles. "That's fine, Grandma."

"I wanted to die, wished it with all my heart. Without Jean-Claude, it was harder to live than to die. Living was the cruelest form of punishment." Tears pooled in her eyes and she blinked them away.

"When the Americans came," Helen continued, "the gates were opened and we were free. It was a delicious feeling—freedom always is—but one never appreciates it until it's taken away. The soldiers spoke English, and I went to them and explained that I was an American. I had no identification or anything to prove my claim, so I kept repeating the address where my parents lived in New York. I was desperate to get word to them that I was alive. They hadn't heard from me in almost five years.

"One of the soldiers brought me to their headquarters. I was completely emaciated, and I'm sure my stench was enough to nauseate anyone standing within twenty feet. The young man then took me to his lieutenant, whose name was Sam Shelton. From that moment forward, Sam took care of me. He saw that I had food and water, clothes and access to showers and anything else I needed."

Ruth shuddered at the thought of her grandmother's physical and mental condition following her release.

Her grandmother paused to take a deep breath, and when she spoke again, it was in another language, what Ruth assumed was German. Pressing her hand on Helen's, she stopped her. "Grandma, English, please."

Her grandmother frowned. "Sorry."

"Was that German?"

She shrugged, eyes wild and confused. "I don't know."

After all those years inside a German camp, it made sense that she'd revert to the language. In her mind she'd gone back to that time, was reliving each incident.

"Go on. Please," Ruth urged.

Helen sighed. "I don't remember much about those first days of freedom."

Ruth could easily understand that.

"Still, every memory I have is of the lieutenant at my side, watching over me. I was hospitalized, and I think I slept almost around the clock for three days straight, waking only long enough to eat and drink. Yet every time I opened my eyes, Sam was there. I'm sure that's not possible, but that's how I remember it."

She picked up her tea with a trembling hand and sipped the cool liquid. "After a week—maybe more, I don't know, time meant nothing to me—I was transported out of Germany and placed on a ship going to America. Sam wrote out his name and home address in Washington State and gave it to me. I didn't know why he'd do that."

"Did you keep it?" Ruth asked.

"I did," Helen confessed, "although I didn't think I'd ever need it. By the time I got back to New York, I was still skin and bones. My own parents didn't even recognize me. My mother looked at me and burst into tears. I was twenty-four years old, and I felt sixty."

Ruth was in her twenties and couldn't imagine living through any of what her grandmother had described.

"Five months after I got home, Sam Shelton knocked on the door of my parents' brownstone. I'd gained weight and my hair had grown back, and when I saw him I barely remembered who he was. He visited for two days and we talked. He'd come to see how I was adjusting to life in America."

Ruth had wondered about that, too. It couldn't have been easy.

"I hadn't done very well. My parents owned a small bakery and I worked at the counter, but I had no life in me, no joy. Now that I was free, I felt I had nothing to live for. My husband was dead, and I was the one who'd killed him. I told this American soldier, whom I hardly knew, all of this. I told him I preferred to die. I told him everything—not one thing did I hold back. He listened and didn't interrupt me with questions, and when I was finished he took my hand and kissed it." The tears came again, spilling down her cheeks. "He said I was the bravest woman he'd ever known."

"I think you are, too," Ruth said, her voice shaky.

"Sam told me he was part of D-day," Helen said. "His company was one of the first to land on Omaha Beach. He spoke of the fighting there and the bravery of his men. He'd seen death the same way I had. Later, in the midst of the fighting, he'd stumbled across the body of his own brother. He had no time to mourn him. He didn't understand why God had seen fit to spare him and not his brother.

"This lieutenant asked the very questions I'd been asking myself. I didn't know why I should live when I'd rather have died with Jean-Claude—or instead of him." She paused again, as if to regain her composure.

"After that, Sam said he'd needed to do a lot of thinking, and praying, and it came to him that his brother, his men, had sacrificed their lives so that others could live in freedom. God had spared him, and me, too, and it wasn't up to either of us to question why. As for Jean-Claude and Tim, Sam's brother, they had died in this terrible but necessary *war*. For either of us to throw away our lives now would be to dishonor them— my husband and Sam's brother."

"He was right, you know."

Her grandmother nodded. "Sam left after that one visit. He wished me well and said he hoped I'd keep in touch. I waited a week before I wrote the first letter. Sam hadn't given me many details of his war experiences, but deep down I knew they'd been as horrific as my own. In that, we had a bond."

"So you and Grandpa Sam wrote letters to each other."

Helen nodded again. "For six months we wrote, and every day I found more questions for him to answer. His letters were messages of encouragement and hope for us both. Oh, Ruth, how I wish you'd had the opportunity to know your grandfather. He was wise and kind and loving. He gave me a reason to live, a reason to go on. He taught me I could love again—and then he asked me to marry him." Helen drew in a deep breath. "Sam wrote and asked me to be his wife, and I said no."

"You refused?" Ruth asked, incredulous.

"I couldn't leave my parents a second time…. Oh, I had a dozen excuses, all of them valid."

"How did he convince you?"

Her smile was back. "He didn't. In those days, one didn't hop on a plane or even use the phone unless it was a dire emergency. For two weeks he was silent. No letters and no contact. Nothing. When I didn't hear from him, I knew I never would again."

This was the reason her grandmother had smiled when Ruth told her she hadn't heard from Paul.

"I couldn't stand it," Helen admitted. "This soldier had become vitally important to me. For the first time since Jean-Claude died, I could *feel*. I could laugh and cry. I knew Sam was the one who'd taken this heavy burden of pain from my shoulders. Not only that, he loved me. Loved me," she repeated, "and I'd turned him down when he asked me to share his life."

"What did you do next?"

Helen smiled at the memory. "I sent a telegram that said three words. *Yes. Yes. Yes.* Then I boarded a train and five days later, I arrived in Washington State. When I stepped off the platform, my suitcase in hand, Sam was there with his entire family. We were married two weeks later. I knew no one, so he introduced me to his best friends and the women they loved. Those four became my dearest friends. They were the people who helped me adjust to normal life. They helped me find my new identity." She shook her head slowly. "Not once in all the years your grandfather and I were together did I have a single regret."

Ruth's eyes were teary. "That's a beautiful love story."

"Now you're living one of your own."

Ruth didn't see it like that. "I don't want to be a military wife," she said. "I can't do it."

"You love Paul."

Ruth noted that her grandmother hadn't made it a question. Helen knew that Ruth's heart was linked with Paul's. He was an honorable man, and he loved her. They didn't need to have the same political beliefs as long as they respected each other's views.

"Yes, Grandma, I love him."

"And you miss him the same way I missed Sam."

"I do." It was freeing to Ruth to admit it. The depression that had hung over her for the past week lifted.

All at once Ruth knew exactly what she was going to do. Her decision was made.

Ten

BARBARA GORDON ANSWERED THE DOORBELL, and the moment she saw Ruth, her eyes lit with delight. "Ruth, I'm so glad to see you!"

Ruth was instantly ushered into the house. She hadn't been sure what kind of reception she'd get. After all, she'd disappointed and possibly hurt the Gordons' son.

"I was so hoping you'd stop by," Barbara continued as she led her into the kitchen.

Obediently Ruth followed. "I came because I don't have a current address for Paul."

"You plan on writing him?" Barbara seemed about to leap up and down and clap her hands.

"Actually, no."

The happiness drained from the other woman's eyes.

"I know it's a bit old-fashioned, but I thought I'd send him a telegram."

The delight was back in place. "Greg," she shouted over her shoulder. "Ruth is here."

Almost immediately Paul's father joined them in the kitchen. His grin was as wide as his wife's had been. "Good to see you, good to see you," he said expansively.

"What did I tell you?" Barbara insisted.

The two of them stood there staring at her.

"About Paul's address?" Ruth prodded.

"Oh, yes." As if she'd woken from a trance, Barbara Gordon hurried into the other room, leaving Ruth alone with Paul's father.

It was awkward at first, and Ruth felt the least she could do was explain the reason for her visit. "I miss Paul so much," she told him. "I need his address."

Greg Gordon nodded. "He's missing you, too. Big-time."

Ruth's heart filled with hope. "He said that?"

"Not in those exact words," Greg stated matter-of-factly. "But rest assured, my son is pretty miserable."

"That's *wonderful*." Now it was Ruth who wanted to leap up and down and clap her hands.

"My son is miserable and you're happy?" Greg asked, but a teasing light glinted in his eyes.

"Yes… No… Yes," she quickly amended. "I just hope he's been as miserable as I have."

Greg's smile faded. "No question there."

The phone rang once; Barbara must have answered it right away. Within a few minutes she returned to the kitchen, carrying a portable phone. "It's for you."

Greg started toward her.

"Not you, honey," she said, gesturing at Ruth. "The call is for Ruth."

"Me?" She was startled. No one knew she'd come here. Anyone wanting to reach her would automatically call her cell. Her frown disappeared as she realized who it must be.

"Is it Paul?" she asked, her voice low and hopeful.

"It is. He thinks Greg's about to get on the line." She clasped her husband's elbow. "Come on, honey, let's give Ruth and Paul some privacy." She was halfway out of the room when she turned back, caught Ruth's eye and winked.

That was just the encouragement Ruth needed. Still, she felt decidedly nervous as she picked up the phone resting on the kitchen counter. After the way they'd parted, she didn't know what to expect or how to react.

"Hello, Paul," she said, hoping to sound calm and confident, neither of which she was.

Her greeting was followed by a slight hesitation. "Ruth?"

"Yes, it's me." Her voice was downright cheerful—and more than a little forced.

"What are you doing at my parents' place?" he asked gruffly.

"Visiting."

Again he paused, as if he wasn't sure what to make of this. "I'd like to speak to my father."

"I'm sorry, he and your mother left the room so you and I could talk."

"About what?" He hadn't warmed to her yet.

"Your calling ruins everything," she told him. "I was going to send you a telegram. My grandmother sent one to my grandfather sixty years ago."

"A telegram?"

"I know it's outdated. It's also rather romantic, I thought."

"What did you intend to say in this telegram?"

"I hadn't decided. My first idea was to say the same thing Helen said to my grandfather. It was a short message—just three little words."

"I love you?" He was warming up now.

"No."

"No?" He seemed skeptical. "What else could it be? Helen loved him, didn't she?"

"Oh, yes, but that was understood. Oh, Paul, I heard the rest of the story and it's so beautiful, so compelling, you'll see why she loved him as much as she did. Sam helped her look to the future and step out of the past."

"You're avoiding the question," he said.

That confused her for a moment. "What's the question?"

"Do you love me enough to accept me as a marine?"

"I wasn't sending *that* answer by way of Western Union." The answer that was going to change her life....

"You can tell me now," he said casually.

"Before I do, you have to promise, on your word of honor as a United States marine, that you'll never walk away from me like that again."

"You think it was easy?" he demanded.

"I don't care if it was easy or not, you can't ever do it again." His abandonment had hurt too much.

"All right," he muttered. "I promise I'll never walk away from you again."

"Word of honor?"

"Word of honor."

He'd earned it now. "I'm crazy about you, Paul Gordon. *Crazy.* Crazy in love with you. If having the marines as your career means that much to you, then I'll adjust. I'll find a way to make it work. But you need to compromise, too, when it comes to my career. I can't just leave a teaching job in order to follow you somewhere."

The last thing Ruth expected after her admission was a long stretch of silence.

Then, "Are you serious? You'll accept my being in the military?"

"Yes. Do you think I'd do this otherwise?"

"No," he told her. "But what you don't know is that I've been thinking about giving up the marines."

"Because of me?"

"Yes."

"You were?" Never once had it occurred to Ruth that he'd consider such a thing.

"My dad and I have had a couple of long talks about it," he went on to say.

"Tell me more."

"You already know this part—I'm crazy about you, too. I wasn't convinced I could find a way to live the rest of my life without you. One option I've looked into is training. I've talked to my commander about it, and he thinks it's a good possibility. I'd be able to stay in the marines, but I'd be stationed in one place for a while."

Ruth slumped onto a kitchen stool, feeling deliciously weak, too weak to stay upright. "Oh, Paul, that's wonderful!"

"I felt like a fool," he said. "I made my big stand, and I honestly felt I was right, but I didn't have to force you to decide that very minute. My pride wouldn't allow me to back off, though."

"Pride carried me the first week," she said. "Then I went to see my grandmother, and she told me how she met my grandfather at the end of the war. Their romance was as much of an adventure as everything else she told us."

"She's a very special woman," Paul said. "Just like her granddaughter."

"I'll tell you everything later."

"I can't wait to hear it. I'm just wondering if history might repeat itself."

"How?"

"I'm wondering if you'll be my wife."

"That's the perfect question," Ruth said, and it *was* perfect for what she had in mind.

She closed her eyes and sighed deeply. "I do believe I'll send you that telegram after all."

Yes. Yes. Yes.

Epilogue

PAUL REACHED FOR RUTH'S HAND BENEATH THE dining-room table. Ruth smiled and gave his hand a squeeze.

"Dinner was fabulous, Grandma," Ruth said. She'd never expected her grandmother to go to all this effort. "I wish you hadn't worked so hard, though. Paul and I would've taken you out to eat."

"Nonsense. It's Christmas Eve. Besides, I rarely get the opportunity to cook for anyone these days. I enjoyed it. And it's such a treat to have the two of you all to myself."

"Thank you so much for everything—especially the stockings. You know we'll treasure them."

"And thank *you,* my darling, for the beautiful memoir you've created."

Ruth had made a new version of Helen's story, including

a number of photographs she'd found through her research. She'd scanned the poster declaring Helen and her first husband, Jean-Claude, criminals. She'd also inserted some details Helen had remembered more recently. Finally, she'd had it professionally bound and it was, even if she said so herself, a beautiful piece of work. The memoir was for her grandmother, true, but it was also for everyone in the Shelton family, now and in the future.

Ruth stood and carried the empty dinner plates to the sink. "Paul and I will do the dishes."

"No need."

"We insist," Paul said.

"I don't want to waste a minute of our time together with dishes," Helen told him. "I hardly ever see you as it is."

"Well, that should be changing soon," Ruth said with a smile.

"I've requested Seattle as my next duty station," Paul explained. "My parents are here, too, and we both love the Pacific Northwest."

"California is fine, but this is where we want to make our home," Ruth added.

"Let me get coffee—and the pie," Helen said, walking into the kitchen behind them.

"You mean, there's pie, as well as those yummy cookies?" Paul's eyes lit up.

"Green tomato mincemeat. The tomatoes are from Charlotte Rhodes's garden. It's the best you'll ever taste."

"I love mincemeat," Ruth said, resisting the urge to poke her husband, who was making a face.

Helen smiled. "Give it a try and if you don't like it, I also have fruitcake."

"I believe I'll pass on both."

Ruth's grandmother ignored his comment and quietly

dished up three small slices of pie with vanilla ice cream. Ruth helped her bring the plates into the dining room. Paul followed, carrying two cups and saucers, steaming with freshly brewed coffee. Ruth had declined, saying the pie was enough for her.

"One taste," she said, waving her fork at him.

Paul grinned. "I doubt anyone could refuse you, Ruth. Especially me."

"You keep thinking that, okay?"

Ruth watched as her husband sliced off a sliver of the pie. She laughed when she saw his expression change.

"Hey, this is *good*."

Helen looked equally pleased. "I'll tell Charlotte she made a convert out of you." She paused to sip her coffee. "What are your plans for Christmas Day?"

Paul reached for Ruth's hand once more. "First, we're making you breakfast tomorrow morning. It's the least we can do." Helen had invited them to stay the night, and they'd accepted. "Then we're driving to Seattle to spend the day with my parents."

"And we're going to visit Mom and Dad for New Year's," Ruth said.

"Our Christmas vacation worked out perfectly, since I was able to get a week's leave at the same time Ruth finished teaching for the semester."

"There's nothing like being with family over the holidays." Helen nodded.

"I couldn't agree more." Ruth turned to her husband, who sent her a smile. "Besides, we have news to share…the kind of news we wanted to tell you in person."

Helen stared at them expectantly.

"We're going to make you a great-grandma," Ruth announced, and awaited her grandmother's reaction. To her surprise, Helen said nothing.

"Grandma Shelton, did you hear?" Paul prodded.

Helen's face broke into a huge smile. "Congratulations. When are you due?"

"Not until June."

"June? What a perfect month for a birthday."

"Oh, Grandma, you'd say that about any month."

"Probably," Helen agreed. "I apologize for not responding right away. I was trying to calculate if I had enough time to knit you a special baby blanket and an extra Christmas stocking before then. I suspect I do."

"Oh, Grandma," Ruth said, struggling not to laugh.

"This is a blessed Christmas," Helen said simply, happiness radiating from her face. "There was a time I didn't believe I'd ever know joy again and yet I feel it every single day."

"Merry Christmas, Grandma."

"Merry Christmas to both of you. No—" she raised her coffee cup in a toast "—to all *three* of you."

★ ★ ★ ★ ★

When We Touch

....

BRENDA NOVAK

Prologue

Present Day

IT WAS KYLE HOUSEMAN.

Olivia Lucero hesitated when she saw her ex–boyfriend through the peephole, even though she'd already yelled, "Coming," at the sound of his knock. It had been three years since he'd broken her heart by marrying her sister, Noelle. He and Noelle were now divorced, but it was still awkward to confront him, especially on her own.

"What's wrong?" Lorianna Beck, a friend who'd come to town for Victorian Days, a celebration Whiskey Creek hosted every Christmas, held her coffee cup in one hand and rubbed her eyes with the other.

Olivia forced a smile and shrugged. "Nothing," she said, and finished turning the knob so she could open the door.

A hint of relief eased the anxiety on Kyle's forehead. His hands were shoved deep in the pockets of his jeans and, when she'd spotted him through the peephole, he'd been wearing a scowl. "Thank God you're home," he said.

That wasn't the greeting she'd expected. She'd assumed he'd come to see Brandon. Whenever Kyle showed up these days, he asked for her husband. They were finally establishing a relationship, but it was still tentative.

"Brandon's at the shop," she said, maintaining a polite smile. After her husband had retired from professional skiing, he'd opened a ski-and-snowboard shop in the center of town. He was usually out of the house early, particularly during the cold season—not that there'd been much snow this year.

"I'm not looking for Brandon." Kyle's breath misted in the morning air. "I was hoping I could have a few minutes to speak with you alone."

Olivia glanced over her shoulder at Lorianna, who was sitting at her kitchen table. Although she and Lorianna, the wife of one of Brandon's old ski buddies, had bonded quickly, Lorianna was a relatively new friend. She had her own problems, and that—rather than Victorian Days—was the real reason for her visit. But Olivia wasn't sure she wanted to share anything too personal with her. Besides, with the issues Lorianna was facing, the poor woman was going through enough.

When Olivia turned back, she could tell that Kyle hadn't realized that she had company. Lorianna had arrived late last night, so she hadn't been seen around town. And she didn't have a car with her, parked out front or otherwise. She'd flown in from Denver, and Olivia and Brandon had picked her up at the Oakland Airport. "It looks like this might be a bad time," he said. "So maybe…maybe you can call me later?"

"Wait! Don't go on my account." Lorianna dried what was left of her tears and jumped to her feet. "I'm no reason to post-

pone anything. I was just about to get in the shower, anyway."
She scurried out of the kitchen before Olivia could argue, so
Olivia stepped back and waved Kyle inside. She wasn't dressed
for company. She'd yanked on some sweats when she rolled
out of bed, brushed her teeth and pulled her blond hair into a
ponytail, but she was curious enough to hear what Kyle had
to say that she wasn't concerned about her appearance.

"Who was that?" he asked, once Lorianna's footsteps could
be heard on the landing overhead.

She and Kyle had grown up in the same small Gold Country
town and knew almost all the same people. Olivia could understand why he'd be slightly surprised to find a stranger in her
house. "Have you ever heard Brandon talk about Jeff Felix?"

"The skier? The guy he hated when he first started his career?"

"That's the one. According to Brandon, Jeff was sort of…
arrogant when they first met. But they're good friends now
that they no longer compete."

Kyle cocked an eyebrow at her. "If that was Jeff, he's had
an especially good sex change."

She chuckled. "That's his wife, Lorianna."

"She seemed upset. Is she okay?"

"She'll be fine."

"Where's he?"

"Home in Denver. He was too busy with the restaurant
they recently opened to join her, and she wanted to see Victorian Days."

"She doesn't seem too impressed so far."

"She hasn't been yet. That'll be tonight. And she's working through a few…issues."

"So she's staying with you?"

"For a short time." Until she could make a few decisions
about her life—or Christmas arrived next week. Whichever

came first. Olivia had agreed to provide a temporary safe haven where Lorianna could rest, relax and do some soul-searching under the guise of hanging out with a new friend.

Kyle scratched his head. "I didn't mean to chase her off."

"It's okay. I'm sure she doesn't mind." She motioned at a chair. "Have a seat while I get you a cup of coffee."

He didn't say anything, but he seemed ill at ease as he waited, looking around at the Christmas tree in the other room, the garland running up her staircase railing and the other decorations and furniture. She guessed that he was wondering if this was how their house would have looked if they'd ended up together.

"Thanks," he said when she brought him his cup. Then his gaze lowered to her belly and she guessed he was thinking about the baby. She and Brandon had made the announcement last week, so word was getting around. Obviously, he'd heard.

She slid the cream and sugar closer. She knew him so well—or used to—that she could've fixed his coffee for him, exactly the way he liked it. "So...what's going on?"

His chest lifted as he took a deep breath. "Your mother came to see me last night."

A jolt of concern went through her as she perched on the edge of her own seat. "She did? *Why?*"

He grimaced. "She asked me to help heal her family."

Olivia clenched her jaw. "Let me guess—she's worried about Noelle."

"Yes."

"That's why you're here? To patch things up between my sister and me?"

"If I can."

"That's all in the past," she said in a tone indicating they should leave it there.

"I realize that, but it hasn't been forgotten, not if you and Noelle can't be in the same room—not even at Christmas."

Olivia stood and went to the counter to get her herbal tea. Why hadn't her mother come to *her* about this? Nancy never faced what was bothering her head-on. Instead, she tried to ignore it or slip around it somehow, which irritated Olivia. "What happened wasn't all your fault, Kyle," she said.

"Still, I'm sorry for my part in it."

"I know. You've apologized and…and I've forgiven you."

"Have you?"

She shifted beneath his intense regard. "Yes."

"Then maybe that's the problem. She doesn't understand how you can forgive me but not your own sister."

Olivia couldn't stifle a bitter laugh. "Because I know my sister! Does my mother think I don't understand what Noelle did? How badly she wanted to steal you from me? How calculated she was in her approach? I mean…was there even a baby, Kyle?"

He sighed and rubbed his chin without answering.

"You can't say for sure, can you? You don't even know whether she was lying about that."

"I saw the pregnancy test results. There was a baby. I'm just not sure if she miscarried, like she claims, or…"

"It says a lot that you're still not sure, don't you think?"

"Look, I understand your anger. Trust me, I can get angry over Noelle, too. But we can't escape the past and hang on to it at the same time. Noelle is my ex. Of course I'm going to have complaints about her. We wouldn't be divorced if we could get along. What upsets me is that your relationship with her—with your whole family—is compromised, even three years later, because of me. It makes me wonder if I'll ever be able to atone for what I did."

"It's not you who needs to atone! That's the thing."

"What we did takes two. I'm fully aware of that—and if I wasn't, there've been plenty of people telling me," he added drily.

She'd been one of them. "So what do you want me to do?"

"Give Noelle another chance. Let this Christmas be a fresh start."

"I'd be a fool to trust her again! She would love nothing more than to do the same thing with Brandon."

"He'd never make the same mistake I did."

Fortunately, she could count on that. "I can't believe you came to help my mother."

"She wants to put her family back together. And I want the same thing, for you more than her. What good does it do to hold a grudge?"

"Who wouldn't hold a grudge after what Noelle did?"

"That may be true, but it ended well." He lowered his voice. "Look at what you've got. Look how happy you and Brandon are."

He had a point. Without Noelle, she probably would've married Kyle herself, and then she would never have known what she was missing. Kyle was wonderful, but Brandon was more than she could have dreamed. At odd moments, she did feel gratitude for finding that kind of love.

"It would be easier to forgive her if she was even the slightest bit contrite," she said. "Or if I had some hope that she wouldn't stab me in the back again at the first opportunity."

"She's jealous of you. She wants what you have. Somehow, no matter what happens, no matter how hard she tries, you always end up better off."

"And I've felt bad for her before. But I don't anymore. She's her own worst enemy."

"I know it's not easy to forgive someone who doesn't deserve it."

It was almost impossible. Especially in this situation. Olivia wasn't sure she was capable of such a magnanimous gesture, but Kyle seemed to be suggesting that he thought she was.

What if she could let go of her resentment? What if she could put her family back together again, allow them to look forward to holiday gatherings as they used to? For her parents' sakes if not Noelle's?

As enraging as it had been that her mother had supported Noelle through the whole painful debacle of her marriage to Kyle, in her heart Olivia understood why she'd behaved as she did. Nancy had known that her "good" daughter would be okay in the end. It was Noelle who worried her. Noelle screwed up so much she needed someone to be on her side when the rest of the world walked out.

"Damn it," she grumbled.

"What?"

"You know what. But I'll think about it."

He nodded. "Thanks. I hate the fact that…that there are any residual negative effects of what I did, especially when it comes to you."

He still loved her. Olivia could feel it. If she could wave some magic wand that would heal his heart and free him from regret, she would. So why couldn't she feel the same way about her sister?

There were a lot of reasons. But she needed to overcome them. She had so much, Noelle so little.

"You'll find someone else someday," she whispered as she gave him a brief hug and walked him to the door.

"What was that all about?"

Olivia had just said goodbye to Kyle when Lorianna appeared, dressed in a robe and wearing a towel wrapped around her head.

"Nothing important. Aren't you going to get dressed?

There's a Christmas shop down the street that might cheer you up."

"I was going to ask if I could borrow a blow-dryer. I forgot mine."

"Of course. There's one under the sink in the master."

"I'll get it, but you really won't tell me who that man was? Here I've been blubbering on and on about my problems—ever since I got up this morning—and you're going to keep yours all to yourself?"

Olivia considered her new friend. Maybe it would help Lorianna to know that she wasn't the only one trying to forgive someone for something painful. Maybe that was even the reason fate had brought them together. "You've been wondering if you can get over the fact that your husband's been with someone else."

"I don't think I can," she said, sounding adamant. "My heart is broken. My trust is destroyed."

"Well, I'm trying to move beyond a hurtful situation, too. I've just got a little more perspective on it—thanks to the passage of time."

Lorianna studied her more closely. "What kind of situation?"

Olivia smiled. "Are you sure you don't want to finish getting ready first? Because it's a long story."

Lorianna pulled off the towel and fluffed her hair with her hands. "I'll let it air-dry," she said. "I'd rather hear this."

One

RETURNING FOR HER SISTER'S WEDDING would've been difficult had it merely meant pretending to be a happy and supportive bridesmaid. But being in charge of the whole event? That added insult to the most heart-wrenching emotional injury Olivia Arnold had ever sustained.

As she drove back to Whiskey Creek for the first time since learning that Noelle would be marrying Kyle Houseman—the man she'd been dating herself until three months ago—she wished she'd had the nerve to refuse her parents. Noelle tried to beat Olivia at anything and everything she did. It had been that way since they were children.

But Olivia planned weddings for a living. She was also the family peacemaker, so it came naturally to try to forgive, to move on. And, as her mother had pointed out, she was the one who'd asked Kyle if they could take a "break" while she moved to Sacramento to build her business. She'd wanted one year to see if she could develop it into something spectacular in a bigger city before marrying Kyle and settling down in Whiskey Creek.

Given all that, how *could* she refuse to help? Especially when she could save her father so much money?

Despite her determination to soldier on through everything that was happening, an odd sense of panic welled up as she reached the edge of town. Pulling over just beyond the sign that said Welcome to Whiskey Creek, The Heart of Gold Country, she tried to get hold of herself but almost turned her Acura around. Within an hour, she could be home in Sacramento. She could hide away until this wedding was a distant memory and, if she was lucky, avoid her sister and new brother-in-law for a decade or two. Maybe by then she'd be able to face them without wanting to cry.

And why shouldn't she turn back? If she stayed, the humiliation of the next few days would be as painful as the heartbreak. Whiskey Creek was a town of only two thousand people. Thanks to the fact that she and Kyle had been a couple for three years, and had separated so recently, she couldn't possibly escape the whispers, the pitying looks or the condolences of the friends and neighbors who'd known her most of her life.

"Shit. Shit, shit, shit!" Bumping her forehead against the steering wheel, she pictured Kyle kissing "the bride" and groaned at the disappointment and betrayal. Noelle had waited for just the right moment. When Olivia was in Sacramento, trying to experience something new before starting her life with Kyle. When he was alone and not coping well with the separation. Then she'd made her move. Olivia wasn't sure she'd ever be able to forgive her sister, especially since it was Olivia's own tears and confidences that had armed Noelle. They'd never been particularly close, but they came from the same family and had lived under the same roof until Olivia relocated to Sacramento last February. That gave Noelle certain insights she wouldn't otherwise have had.

But if she left, if she ran, her sister would know she was just as hurt today as she had been that terrible evening the horrible truth—that Kyle and Noelle had been seeing each other—came out. Why give Noelle the pleasure? Why confirm that her sister, younger by two years—which only made it worse—had finally landed the coup de grâce of their sibling rivalry?

"Ahhhhh!" She pounded the steering wheel with her fists this time, before hitting everything else in sight. Somehow, seeing her hometown looming ahead had destroyed her restraint. Rage seemed to be a monster growing in strength and power until it was bursting out of her chest—

A knock on the window interrupted her in midsob. She'd been so focused on her distress, on screaming and beating her dashboard, she hadn't heard anyone approach.

Mortified to realize she had a witness to her behavior, she turned to see a tall, blond man dressed in a white T-shirt, khaki shorts and flip-flops. His mouth, tense with some emotion, made a slash in his face beneath a pair of mirrorlike sunglasses.

Oh, God… Despite those glasses, it wasn't a cop, as she'd expected. Worse—it was Kyle's stepbrother, Brandon Lucero. He was younger than Kyle by a year, which made him almost a year older than her, and he appeared to be…concerned. No doubt he thought she'd lost her mind.

He might as well have caught her with her pants down. It would've been less embarrassing. Her only consolation was that Brandon wasn't likely to tell Kyle what he'd seen, even if he connected it to the upcoming wedding. There was no love lost between the two men. They'd lived together while in high school, after Kyle's older sister had married and moved away and his father married Brandon's mother. But that hadn't made them friends.

Brandon waited to speak until she rolled down the window. "You okay?" he asked, his teeth a stark contrast to his golden tan.

After getting abusive with the interior of her innocent car, her right hand hurt so badly she was afraid she'd fractured it. She cradled it in her lap, hoping he wouldn't notice the swelling, and wiped her other hand over her wet cheeks. This kind of behavior wasn't like her.

"Don't I look okay?" she countered as if she hadn't just lost control.

"Babe." He shook his head. "Tell me this has nothing to do with Kyle."

She dabbed at her eyes, inadvertently smearing her mascara, which she wiped onto her white shorts. Cut low at the hips and high on the leg, they'd been purchased with one goal in mind—turning male heads. In her current situation, she needed the ego boost. But her pride in the body she'd worked so hard to slenderize and tone had gone out the window, along with her composure. What did it matter if she looked better than she ever had? Noelle was marrying the man Olivia thought would be *her* husband. "Would you believe I broke a nail?"

His biceps bulged, stretching the sleeves of his T-shirt as he folded his arms. "Not a chance. Want to try something else?"

"No. Who cares if you think I'm an idiot?" she grumbled as she pushed her long hair out of her face. "You've never liked me much to begin with."

This seemed to surprise him. "What gave you that impression?"

"I don't know." She managed a facetious smirk. "Maybe the way you scowl every time you see me? Or, if you can't avoid me, which is always your first choice, you just grunt so you don't have to say hello?"

He scowled when she'd expected him to laugh. "Would you believe I was saving you from myself?"

"No."

"I can be chivalrous when I want to be."

"That's definitely not an adjective I'd use to describe *you*. I'm sure all the women with broken hearts you've left behind would agree with me."

His scowl darkened. "What women with broken hearts?"

She could've named a few. Some of them were acquaintances. He was a tempting challenge—few could refuse him. But he didn't give her the chance to be more specific. He was still talking.

"I'm going to assume you're angry or you wouldn't have said that. You're obviously having a bad day."

Ah, the understatement of the year. And since she had to face Kyle and Noelle as well as her parents in the next few minutes, her day was going to get worse.

"We had a class together, remember?" he added. "I took you to my junior prom. I've always liked you just fine."

She couldn't see his eyes, but she sensed that they were moving over her, taking inventory of what her clothes revealed. Instinctively she wanted to cover up. The only thing stopping her was the sure knowledge that doing so would draw more attention to her atypical attire. "And—" he grinned "—from what I can see so far, I'm going to like the new you even more."

What had she been *thinking* when she'd put on this outfit? If Kyle didn't regret what he'd done by now, a pair of short shorts and a low-cut blouse wouldn't do the trick. It was too late to save what they'd had, anyway. It wasn't as if she could take him back.

"I dressed in a weak moment," she explained, her face burning. "I needed to feel attractive."

"Mission accomplished." He whistled. "You could stop traffic. You stopped me, didn't you?"

She considered the amusement on his face. "I'm pretty sure you thought I was having engine trouble."

"To be honest, I thought a bee had gotten into your car and you were under attack."

"Thanks for the visual. That helps with the embarrassment. But it wasn't that bad."

His eyebrows rose above his sunglasses. "It was alarming. But back to your changed wardrobe. I don't think showing that much skin is the best way to recover." He scratched his smooth-shaven chin. "I mean... I'd hate to see you wind up with the wrong kind of guy. *Again.*"

"Kyle was the wrong kind of guy?" She was anxious to hear his justification for that statement. The general belief was that *Brandon* was the less reliable of the two. Kyle had attended UC Berkeley on an academic scholarship while getting a degree in electrical engineering. He'd started his own company manufacturing solar panels after that, which was currently making him rich. He was strong, kind, talented.

Maybe he wasn't *quite* as handsome as his stepbrother, but his attention wasn't nearly as fleeting, either.

"For you he was *completely wrong,*" Brandon maintained as if he'd been able to see it all along.

The uncertainty she'd always felt in his presence returned. She'd caught him watching her since that prom. Most of the time he turned away the second she noticed, but occasionally their eyes met and held, and she remembered how badly she'd once wished he'd call. "Who would be better?" she challenged.

Mouth quirking up on one side, he said, "Why don't you

follow me to my place and put yourself back together before you walk into the lion's den? We can talk about it."

It was a kind suggestion. One she never would've expected—not from him. But she could guess why he was suddenly so helpful. He'd love nothing more than to shove a connection with her in Kyle's face.

And therein lay the appeal of his offer....

"Do you think your stepbrother will hear about it if I do?" she asked.

He chuckled softly. "We can make sure of it."

That kind of petty revenge was beneath her. But the idea of turning the tables on Kyle, and by extension Noelle, was tempting. "He'd hate it," she mused. "Whether he's marrying my sister or not." She knew because of that last call, the apology, the crack in his voice when he'd said he'd always love her. The memory of it brought fresh tears to her eyes....

A truck was coming up from behind. To get out of its way, Brandon stepped close enough that she could pick up his scent in the air that blasted into her car as the truck whooshed by. He smelled as good as he looked. But that was no surprise. She recalled dancing with him as a sophomore, pressing her nose into his warm neck in an effort to remember his scent. She'd instinctively known that was the only part of Brandon a girl could safely capture.

"He wouldn't want you to be with anyone else, but me least of all," he agreed.

Obviously he liked the idea of upsetting Kyle as much as she did. Problem was...associating with Brandon came with a certain amount of risk. For one, the way she was dressed could be misleading. He might assume she'd changed, become promiscuous, like the girls he usually preferred. And what if she fell into her own trap? Brandon was like a meteor. He burned hot and bright as he crashed through a woman's orbit, but he left a lot of damage in his wake and nothing, no one, slowed him down. Although some girls welcomed the thrill of try-ing—he never lacked for female companionship—Olivia was already nursing a broken heart. She had no business being alone with this man, especially while she was on the rebound.

On the other hand, she was tired of trying to turn the other cheek. She was also tired of being so darn careful with her love life. Kyle was supposed to have been a wise choice, a man who wanted to settle down and have a family. And look how well that had turned out. He was having a family, all right. *With her sister.* Noelle was pregnant, hence the rush on the wedding. Her mother wanted Noelle married off before she started to show.

"Are you coming?" Brandon asked when she didn't answer.

Were they going to be allies? She found that a bit ironic, considering that, after prom, they'd never even been friends. She'd been one of the few who'd understood that wanting Brandon would only end in misery. "If I go to your house, it doesn't mean I'll be sleeping with you," she said, taking a stab at his motivation for inviting her.

He jammed his fists into the pockets of his baggy shorts. "Kyle won't know that."

Her injured hand was beginning to throb. She should head to her parents' house, change into something more sensible and make an ice pack. She was supposed to arrive in time for dinner. But if she showed up there in the next few minutes, they'd question her about her red eyes even if she concocted a good excuse for her hand. She couldn't stand the thought of that, especially if they cornered her in front of Noelle, who would know exactly what was wrong and take great satisfac-tion in being the cause of it.

"Do you have an ice pack?" she asked, finally letting him see her injury.

He slid his sunglasses down to take a look, and she felt the full effect of those eyes, which were several shades lighter than hazel. "Do *I* have an ice pack?"

"You have a lot of them." Of course he did. As a professional skier, he probably needed one often.

"Come with me and you'll feel better in a few minutes. I guarantee it."

She squinted up at him. *I think that's what I'm afraid of,* she thought but all she said was, "Thanks."

Two

OLIVIA HAD NEVER BEEN INSIDE BRANDON'S
house. Kyle had driven her past it once, when they'd
been coming back from a picnic near the old mine. Brandon
had been abroad at the time, or they never would've taken
the chance of running into him. Kyle preferred to have as little contact as possible. Since then, she'd noticed the turnoff
that led to his solitary cabin whenever she drove up this way
to hike or bike. Brandon had always been a bit of a mystery
to her. Or maybe it was just that ever since she'd sat in front
of him in Chemistry she'd felt his magnetism as much as any
girl. There'd even been a few times over the years when she'd
been tempted to swing by his house.

She could understand why he'd like living here, with the
peace and quiet and the spectacular view afforded by one
wall made entirely of glass. His home reminded her of the

Swiss Family Robinson Treehouse, probably because it was two stories high and dug out of the mountain—very much a part of nature. As if that wasn't unusual enough, a telescope held pride of place in the middle of the living room, beneath a giant skylight.

Most people wouldn't put a telescope in the living room because it would obstruct their view of the television. But Brandon's TV was in the loft area above. Down here, various geodes and old weapons, artifacts and sculptures lined bookshelves that also contained a surprising array of books, mostly nonfiction. She spotted one on astronomy, another on Buddhism and a third on the history of China.

"China?" she murmured while he was in the kitchen, getting her some ice. She'd never taken him for a scholar. Since he made his living as an extreme skier, he was often videotaped plunging down the steepest slopes in the world. She thought he was foolish to risk his life doing a thing like that *once,* let alone again and again, but there appeared to be some fringe benefits to his job besides the high pay and adrenaline rush. Obviously it had taken him to many different countries.

"Are you an art collector?" she called, studying several paintings.

He came into the room carrying the most technically advanced ice pack she'd ever seen. "Not really. I pick up what appeals to me. Most of it's from unusual places. I love to travel."

"I can tell." He was consumed by wanderlust. No wonder he'd never, to her knowledge, become serious about one particular woman. It was tough to maintain a relationship under such circumstances.

"What about you?" he asked.

She pulled her gaze from a photograph of an African woman holding the hand of a child in some faraway jungle she'd probably never see. "I don't get the opportunity very often."

Although she'd been planning weddings and other events since she'd graduated from Sac State with a degree in business administration, moving to Sacramento had required she take on some expenses that she'd never had before. Not only was she living on her own for the first time since renting a small house with three other girls in college, she'd leased an office and was paying for advertising in the hope of attracting new clients. The money she'd saved while living with her parents once she'd returned to Whiskey Creek needed to be held in reserve, just in case.

"Would you like to see more of the world if you could?" he asked.

She fingered an elephant carved out of wood. "Absolutely," she replied, but she wasn't really considering the possibility. She was too preoccupied wondering how the Brandon suggested by this house could be so different from what she'd taken him to be, which was much more the typical jock.

"I'm planning a backpacking trip across Nicaragua in a few weeks." He bent to look into her face. "You could come with me."

The idea of escaping held massive appeal. But she wasn't sure it was a legitimate offer. Most people didn't extend invitations like that off the cuff. "You're going across the entire country?"

"Nicaragua's not that big."

"I have a feeling it might seem big if you're *walking.*"

He smiled. "That's the best way to see it."

She didn't know much about South America. She'd always been more concerned with the geography she navigated right here in California—especially finding the right place to live after leaving Whiskey Creek. "I wish I could," she said in a throwaway statement that took for granted he hadn't been serious.

He didn't press the issue. He motioned to a soft leather couch. "Have a seat. Let's get this on your hand."

She was tempted to choose one of the hammock-style chairs that hung from the ceiling instead. They had, no doubt, come from Mexico or some other country and looked comfortable. But, in deference to her injured hand, she decided against getting into something she might have difficulty getting out of.

Once she was settled in, he examined her hand before putting the ice pack on it. "You should get this x-rayed."

"I couldn't have broken any bones throwing a tantrum," she said, but she knew that was denial talking. She just didn't want to face that she might've caused herself some stiff medical bills and the inconvenience of going home in a cast.

"I'm not so sure," he responded. "If the pain doesn't go away in the next day or so, definitely have it checked."

He should know about broken bones. Not long ago, he'd tumbled off a cliff in Switzerland and broken his right leg in three places. They'd replayed the footage of it on the local news over and over. Almost everyone had seen it. As a result of that spill, he'd been on crutches, convalescing for much of the last year she and Kyle were dating. In the past twelve months she'd seen him around town more often than she had in the ten or so years since prom.

He arranged the ice pack on her hand and headed back to the kitchen.

"Do you ever get lonely out here?" she asked, looking toward the giant window directly across from her. From where she sat, she couldn't see the water, but she knew the river cut through the ravine below.

"Not really."

That was a stupid question, she told herself. Why would he get lonely? He could have a woman visit anytime he wanted.

"Do you ever get lonely in Sacramento?" he called back.

After living at home with her family since college, and dating Kyle for three of those years—seeing him every day—Sacramento had been a big change. She'd been *more* than lonely;
she'd been positively bereft. But no one wanted to hear someone sniveling on and on about a past relationship. Other than
that lapse of sanity in her car, she thought she'd managed to
absorb the pain without showing how bad she really felt. "I
try to keep myself so busy I don't even have time to think
about stuff like that."

"No wonder you lost your cool."

His response surprised her. "Excuse me?"

"You haven't dealt with the blow."

"I refuse to feel bad about a man who could do what Kyle
did. That's all."

He reappeared with some painkillers and a glass of water.
"Here, take these."

She swallowed the pills, then eyed him dubiously when
he said, "To be honest, I don't understand why you're here."

"You invited me," she pointed out, purposely misunderstanding.

"You know what I mean."

With a wince, she adjusted the ice pack. "Everyone's wondering whether I'll show up. I felt it was best to come back
with my head held high. Not coming would only have confirmed to Kyle and Noelle that I'm still hurt."

"I admire your courage, but..."

He thought she'd bitten off more than she could chew.
That episode in the car proved it. "I won't break down again."

"There's no shame in loving someone, Olivia."

As if he knew anything about it. She almost said that, but
stopped herself. Why be unkind? *He* wasn't the person who'd
wronged her. She knew better than to give him the chance.
"There is if that someone is marrying your sister," she grum-

bled. "Everyone's watching me, waiting for the tears to flow." And he'd actually witnessed them....

His expression softened. "Kyle screwed up."

"I appreciate the sentiment, even if you are sort of obligated to say that to someone who's going through what I am."

He didn't try to convince her he'd meant it more honestly. "Just because you're in town doesn't mean you have to stay," he said. "I'm the only one who's seen you."

"You're suggesting I leave? Miss the wedding? She's my sister."

"That goes both ways. Most people would say she had no business hooking up with your boyfriend."

The fact that Kyle had been her boyfriend made him that much more desirable for Noelle. It was a strange but undeniable dynamic. Noelle had always coveted what she had. "What good would it do to nurse my resentment? To tear my family apart?" she asked. "Besides, I *have* to attend the wedding. I'm planning it."

His thick eyebrows jerked together. Because he'd removed his sunglasses the moment they walked into the house, she could see his eyes. She wasn't sure that was a *good* thing. They were so beautiful they could render a woman helpless with a single, smoldering glance—especially a woman who needed to feel desired again.

"You're *planning* it?" he said. "Why the hell would you do that?"

The anger in his voice made her stiffen. "That's what I do for a living. That's what I've been doing since college."

"Doesn't mean you had to do *this* wedding. Why didn't you say no?"

"To my *parents*?"

"They had no right asking *you*."

"They couldn't afford anyone else. I have all the contacts.

I could do it much more easily than they could themselves. Besides, they *want* me to forgive her. They want to maintain peace and harmony in the family."

"That's bullshit. They should've protected you, told her to elope."

Olivia had never dreamed she'd be commiserating with Brandon Lucero. Apparently their mutual dislike of Kyle had pulled them onto the same team. "Why haven't you ever gotten along with your stepbrother?" she asked.

"Kyle's not bad," he replied. "Not anymore." He returned to the kitchen a third time and came back with two glasses of wine, one of which he handed to her.

"That didn't really answer my question."

"I was fifteen when he came into my life."

"And?"

He seemed reluctant to continue, acting as if it was in the past and didn't matter anymore. But she could tell it did.

"Oh, come on," she said. "He was sleeping with my sister within a week of our break. We weren't even supposed to be seeing other people. I'm not going to stick up for him."

"There's no need for anyone to stick up for *him*. Everyone knows *I'm* the black sheep."

"You're saying he's had it easier than you?"

He took a sip of his wine. "By the time he came into my life, it'd been ten years since my dad died."

"I heard he was in a plane crash. Is that true?"

"It was his own plane. He loved to fly. But there was a malfunction...."

"I'm sorry."

"I was only five when it happened." He sat across from her. "But by the time my mother remarried, I was comfortable, no longer craving a father or a brother. My mother and I were doing just fine."

"Until she met Bob Houseman and everything changed."

He nodded. "Suddenly I lost the company of my friends and found myself in a new town, a new school. Not only that but I had this father figure who was bossing me around and laying down strict rules. I had a brother, too, who meant the absolute world to him, which meant I could never compete. That made having a dad more of an illusion than a reality." He studied the wine in his glass. "The worst part was how it affected my mother. She was so eager to please them both that I was quickly relegated to the backseat, expected to understand and adapt." He fell silent before finishing with, "There were just a lot of changes."

So he felt that Kyle and Kyle's father had stolen his previous life and his mother from him. When she looked at it from his point of view, she could see why. It sounded as if Kyle had been in a better position to enjoy the new family dynamic. It would be hard to start over in high school, hard to have your position usurped.

Was that why he'd used his good looks and charisma like a weapon?

"How do you feel about Kyle now?" she asked.

"None of what bothered me then seems to matter anymore. I've come to terms with it."

She got the feeling that wasn't completely true. Maybe the animosity had died down, but… "Do you think you'll ever be close?"

"Probably not. Imagine taking two boys with strong personalities, competitive personalities, both oldest sons, and trying to force one to become 'the little brother' after years and years of living a different life. Although I was younger, I refused to let Kyle best me at anything, and he resented the constant challenge."

"I'm sure it didn't help that you went your own ways so soon after your parents were married."

"I don't follow you...."

"You never really got a chance to adjust." Kyle had headed off to college just two years after the wedding, right after she and Brandon went to Brandon's junior prom, which was something that had always bugged Kyle—even though he and Olivia weren't dating back then. By the time he returned, Brandon was gone. Then they started their careers and, with Brandon out of town so much, it'd been easy for Kyle to forget he even had a stepbrother. Most of the time, he hadn't wanted to talk about Brandon, just his older sister, with whom he was close.

"Actually I think we were both relieved by the separation," he said with a wry grin.

"If he finds out I'm here, you could be looking at another challenge to your relationship."

He winked at her. "I'm willing to take that risk."

She glanced around the room. "You're willing to take *any* risk."

His eyes never left her face. She could feel his close regard, even though she avoided eye contact. "Only if I want something badly enough."

Olivia's phone rang, saving her from a response. She was glad. Whether or not he'd meant what he'd said as a pickup line, she'd felt a tingle down to her toes. She prayed her reaction was because her self-esteem had hit an all-time low. She needed to heal before she involved herself in another relationship, especially with someone so likely to use her without a second thought.

She checked caller ID. It was her mother. Nancy had been expecting her and must be getting worried. They were supposed to make the favors for the reception after dinner to-night. Olivia had the supplies in her trunk.

Sending Brandon a look asking his forbearance, she over-came her reluctance to take this call and answered, infusing as much lift into her voice as possible. "Hello?"

"Where are you? I was sure you'd be here by now."

Olivia allowed herself a grimace. "I, uh, had a little acci-dent."

"With your car?"

"No. I tripped while loading up and hurt my hand. So I'm running late."

Brandon was watching her, but she continued to avoid his gaze.

"How bad is it? You didn't break any bones..."

"I doubt it," she said, removing the ice pack to take a look.

"Do you need Dr. Harris to x-ray it?"

"We'll see. I'll be there shortly."

"Dinner's at six."

She heard the subtle threat in that statement. They'd eat without her if she wasn't there. "I'll make it."

"Good. Kyle and Noelle are here waiting."

"I bet they are."

Her mother had to have heard the sour note in her voice, but, wisely, she didn't react to it. Since the news of Noelle's pregnancy, Nancy had done her best to minimize Olivia's previous relationship with Kyle. The way she told the story, Noelle was marrying an "old friend" of her other daughter's. Never mind that she and Kyle had slept together. Never mind that they'd talked about marriage themselves.

"Hurry. We have a lot to do."

"See you soon." After she hung up, she returned her at-tention to Brandon. "It was very gallant of you to rescue me from my imaginary bee attack, but I've got to go."

"You sure you're ready for what lies ahead?"

"No, but I never will be. It's like going in for a root canal. Better to get the pain over with." She rolled her eyes. "No-elle and Kyle are anxiously awaiting my arrival."

"Lucky you," he said drily.

"Exactly."

"Where are you staying?"

"My parents'."

He made a face. "Isn't your sister living there?"

She drank the rest of her wine, put her glass on the coffee table and got up. "Until Saturday night, when her new husband whisks her off to wedded bliss."

"You're more forgiving than I am."

"I could pay for a hotel, but I'd be a hundred bucks poorer. How would that bother them?"

"Good point." He stood, too. "Just don't let loose on any inanimate objects again. You might break your other hand."

"I've learned my lesson," she responded, but just hearing her mother's voice had put a lump in her throat. She couldn't help feeling betrayed by her parents, too, because they were so eager to throw their support behind this wedding. She knew they had a grandchild at stake, but still...

After using his bathroom to fix her makeup, she found Brandon standing at the window, looking outside. "What do you think? Can you tell I've been crying?"

"I never would've guessed."

She suspected he might be placating her, but she didn't push. "Maybe I should change into something more conservative."

"Are you kidding?" He whistled. "Let Kyle eat his heart out."

That almost made her smile, until she imagined the reality of the next few hours. "*I'll* probably be the miserable one."

Although he continued to study her, she could tell he'd

shifted gears. "If it gets too bad, you could always come back here."

She raised her eyebrows. "So we could…"

His grin turned her knees to water. "Sleep. Of course. And I won't charge you for the room."

"Maybe you'd let me check out your big telescope," she said, widening her eyes in feigned innocence.

"If you want to see the stars, I could give you a night to remember," he said, playing along.

She laughed. "The ultimate revenge?"

"No," he said, growing serious. "What I've wanted since prom."

"That's why you dropped me off at the end of the night and have avoided me ever since?"

"I knew I wasn't what you needed. You're too sensitive."

He was right. That had been true then, and it was true now. If someone as trustworthy and admired as Kyle could hurt her so terribly, how would she ever survive the kind of emotional damage someone like Brandon could wreak?

"But I'll go easy on you," he added with a grin. "My number's in your phone, in case you need it."

"Thanks." She was surprised he'd taken the liberty. She was a little flattered, too. But she had no intention of returning. She hadn't been with a man in three months. That wouldn't have seemed like a long time before her relationship with Kyle, but it felt like an eternity now that she knew what she was missing. She *couldn't* come back. She'd only get herself into trouble if she did, because it wasn't Brandon's telescope she wanted him to share.

Three

KYLE'S WORK TRUCK, A FORD F-150, SAT IN HER parents' driveway. Olivia had expected to see it, but her heart sank all the same.

Taking a breath, trying to bolster herself, she got out of her Acura and started toward the front door, rolling her suitcase behind her with a sense of determination and purpose that belied the pain.

You can do this. Just keep your chin up and try to forget that this is Kyle and Noelle. Pretend they're no different from any of the other couples you've worked with.

It was a wedding, a job, she told herself. But she hadn't been home since she'd moved away. Her only contact had been through her mother, who shared various details over the phone, like Kyle buying a new car because Noelle "hated" trucks.

Olivia felt strange marching up to her parents' front door

knowing that nothing was as it used to be, that Kyle wasn't waiting for her in quite the same way as he'd waited for her in the past.

"I've entered *The Twilight Zone*," she muttered.

She spotted a flurry of movement at the window. Then the door flew open and her mother descended on her. "There you are! I've been worried. Let me see what you've done to your poor hand."

Grateful for the distraction, she displayed her injury.

"Oh, dear." Her mother's eyebrows knitted. "Look at that. Of all times for something like this to happen. Well, come on in. We'll get some ice. Maybe we'll be able to put you on the left side when we take the wedding pictures so the swelling doesn't show."

"I don't need to be in the pictures at all," she said before she could stop the words.

Nancy's smile faded. The expression on her face suggested she was about to respond, but whether she was going to warn her not to ruin the wedding, or say she was sorry about what Olivia must be feeling, Olivia never heard because Kyle strode out to greet her.

Olivia thanked God that Noelle wasn't with him. Seeing him was bad enough. He seemed reluctant yet eager to approach, which added more confusion to the emotions currently assaulting her.

"I'm glad you're safe," he said.

Their eyes met briefly before she jerked hers away, but he kept his smile stubbornly in place as he hurried to assist with her suitcase.

Obviously he'd been anticipating this moment and was prepared for it. Olivia had tried to prepare, too. Little good it had done her. Nausea threatened to ruin her calculated indifference.

"I've got it." She made an effort to keep the resentment from her voice, but it was impossible. No doubt he picked up on her tone. They were too familiar with each other for him to miss the slightest nuance. She knew the strength of his arms and how wonderful it felt to have them close around her, the rough texture of his jaw, the fullness of his lips and how soft yet demanding they could be when he kissed....

Why had this person she'd trusted so deeply betrayed her? There were moments, moments like now, when she couldn't believe that their lives had taken such a dramatic turn.

He attempted to grab her case in spite of her refusal, but she hung on and kept walking, leaving him no choice but to fall back and follow.

"Where's Dad?" she asked her mother as they reached the front patio, an attractive covelike entrance to her parents' rambler.

"Out back, grilling some steaks."

Olivia didn't ask where Noelle was. She didn't want to see her sister.

The smell of a home-cooked meal enveloped her as soon as she entered the house—evoking the only pleasant sensation Olivia had experienced since she'd left Brandon's. Everything else cut like broken glass.

A buzzer went off in the kitchen, and her mother hurried to remove whatever she had on the stove. "We didn't want to eat without you," she said, raising her voice to be heard, "but it was getting late. I'm glad you arrived in time."

Olivia didn't comment. She'd promised herself she wouldn't complain, wouldn't wallow in self-pity, wouldn't start a fight. But how she wished she could miss this meal. No aroma could be tempting enough to make her want to stay.

Sensing Kyle's presence at her elbow, she left her suitcase and pivoted to go back outside, already eager for a reprieve from the tension twisting her stomach. "I've got the stuff for the wedding favors in my trunk. I'll grab it."

"Not with your hand hurt," Kyle said. "Let me."

"No, thanks. I can manage." She had no intention of allowing him to do anything. But, to her chagrin, he joined her, anyway. So she tried to ignore him. She didn't want to see him any more than she wanted to see her sister, didn't want to hear him, either, or confront the reality of what they used to be and what they were now.

Once they were out of earshot of her mother, he caught her elbow to get her to face him and lowered his voice. "I'm so sorry, Olivia. I know… I know how hard this must be. It's killing me that I'm causing you pain."

He seemed sincere, but maybe he was just being arrogant. She'd begun to doubt everything she'd ever known about him, except the physical sensations that had been such a major part of their relationship. Looking at him made her crave the familiarity they'd enjoyed. Since Carly, her best friend, had moved to Phoenix to accept a job offer with Southwest Airlines, Kyle had become both friend and boyfriend. Losing his friendship hurt as much as all the rest.

Battling the threat of tears, she manufactured another smile. "You're not causing me pain," she said. "As a matter of fact, I'm already seeing someone else."

Dropping his hand, he blinked in surprise. "Your mother said… I mean, she didn't mention that."

"I haven't told her about him. There's enough going on around here. This is *your* week, *your* wedding. I'll save my announcements for later."

Did he go pale? Or was that her imagination?

"Is it someone in Sac?" he asked.

She could've said yes and left it at that. She wasn't entirely sure why she didn't. Maybe it was because a mere name wouldn't have the same effect. "No, actually. He's from Whiskey Creek. Someone you know quite well."

A muscle flexed in his cheek. "Who?"

She'd already gone too far. But the same desperate compulsion that had overtaken her in the car when she injured her hand seemed to goad her now, until the name that would hurt him most passed her lips. "Brandon."

The color returned to his face, staining his cheeks a bright red. "My *stepbrother?*"

"You're not really related," she reminded him. "That happens to be important to me, even though it wasn't to you."

He seemed to struggle with words. "His mother is married to my father."

"You lived together for two years. Sadly I've had to put up with Noelle my whole life."

He shook his head as if she'd just coldcocked him. "Brandon?" he said again. "You've got to be joking."

She lifted her chin. "Why?"

"Because he'd be terrible for you!"

"In what way?" she challenged.

"He…he doesn't know what it means to really love anyone. The second he gets bored, or a skiing opportunity presents itself, he'll be gone and you may never hear from him again."

She sneered. "Funny *you* should say that."

"I know I let you down." He lowered his voice. "But…that doesn't mean I don't care about you."

"Did you think I'd mope around indefinitely?"

"No, of course not. That isn't what I want. I want you to be happy."

She smiled broadly. "Brandon makes me happy."

A scowl replaced his stunned expression. "Don't cut off your nose to spite your face, Olivia. He hasn't been able to maintain one serious relationship. He'll only hurt you in the end."

She popped the trunk. "I doubt it. Thanks to you, I'm older and wiser than I was."

"You're no match for him. He'll take advantage of how innocent and trusting you are and how deeply you love—"

"I'm not planning to marry him." She rolled her eyes. "I'll leave making the Big Commitment to you and my dear sister. Brandon's good in bed. Right now, that's all I need."

When he sagged a little, her heart twisted so painfully she almost admitted the truth. She couldn't hurt Kyle regardless of what he'd done to her. But Noelle's voice, filled with suspicion, rang out from the patio. "What's taking so long?"

Olivia raised the trunk lid, revealing the many boxes of wedding paraphernalia she'd borrowed from River City Resort Club & Spa. She'd been planning to tote it all in herself, regardless of her throbbing hand. She wanted to stay busy, focused. But if Kyle was going to dog her footsteps, she figured he could handle the job.

"Looks like there's more here than I remembered. If you could bring it into the living room, we'll get started on the wedding favors right after we eat. I have to leave soon. Brandon's expecting me," she said and walked past her sister without saying hello.

Four

WHEN HIS MOTHER SHOWED UP ON HIS DOOR-
step, Brandon was relieved Olivia was gone. He didn't
feel he owed it to his stepbrother to stay away from her or
anything like that. After what Kyle had done, Brandon considered Olivia fair game for any guy, even him. But he knew
his mother would get involved if she saw Olivia at his place—
and if there was any way to keep his mother from getting involved, it was always best to go that route. Otherwise, she'd
give him no peace.

"Hi, what are you doing here?" he asked as he swung the
door wide. She rarely came over. But he'd let her past few
calls go to voice mail. He'd heard enough about the wedding,
hadn't wanted to hear any more.

That had been a mistake. Instead of leaving him alone, she'd
come to harangue him in person.

"I was on my way home and thought I'd stop by," she said.

Sure, that made sense. Except his place wasn't on the way to or from anywhere. Only teenagers and hikers bothered to visit the old mine or the trails he loved so much.

"Can I come in?" she asked, sounding slightly miffed that he hadn't already offered.

Belatedly he realized he was still blocking the entrance. "Of course." He stepped aside so she could move past him. Then he placed his arms around her in the obligatory hug.

"Have you picked up your tux for the wedding?" she asked as soon as he released her.

"Not yet."

"Brandon!" Cocking her head, she gave him that searching look that said he was about to get a stern lecture. "You're not going to do anything to ruin this wedding, are you? Because I'm counting on you. Just once I'd like you to go along with what we have planned and behave yourself. Can you do that? For me?"

"No problem." He tried to play it straight, but it was difficult not to grimace. He hated the way she catered to Kyle and Kyle's father. Maybe if she'd give them hell every once in a while, he wouldn't have to establish their boundaries on his own.

"Good. I'm glad to hear it. I'll grab your tux when I hit town. If you wait too long, they'll be closed."

"There's always tomorrow, Mom."

"The wedding rehearsal is tomorrow. There'll be a lot to do as it is."

"I can get my own tux!"

Obviously put out by his refusal to let her take control, she sniffed. "And you'll make the rehearsal?"

"Of course."

"On time and sober?"

"When have I ever shown up anywhere drunk?" he asked. As an athlete, he worked against the clock as it was. Age would slow him down fast enough; he wasn't about to destroy his body with alcohol.

"I'm just covering all the bases," she told him.

For Kyle…. "Maybe I'm not the one you should be worried about," he said.

"What do you mean?

"Maybe you should pay Kyle a visit instead, see if you can get him to call off the coming travesty."

She looked as though he'd just stuck her with a pin. "Why would I do that?"

He made a face that suggested she was crazy for even asking. "Because he's about to ruin his life?"

For a moment, she seemed torn, but ultimately took the party line. "We don't know that."

"Maybe *you* don't, but I do."

"Granted, Noelle isn't the woman Olivia is," she said, relenting, "but…it's his choice. We have to respect his wishes."

Brandon leaned one shoulder against the wall. "Were you aware that Olivia's been planning the wedding?"

She slid her purse farther up her arm. He wasn't sure how, at five-two and a hundred and twenty pounds, she managed to haul that thing around. It had to weigh thirty pounds. But she didn't go anywhere without it. "Nancy mentioned she was helping, yes."

"I can't believe they'd expect her to do that."

"They told me they thought it would be cathartic for her."

"To plan the wedding of the man she loves—to her *sister*? Come on! I think it was just cheaper."

"It wasn't my place to make that decision, either," she said, but at least her tone of voice acknowledged that she agreed with him.

"*Someone* should've told them to plan it themselves," he grumbled.

"I'm sure it's fine. Olivia's a very forgiving, wonderful woman. And someday she'll find an equally wonderful man."

Brandon pictured Olivia sitting on the side of the road, tears streaming down her face as she gazed up at him. Even completely disheveled, she was the prettiest woman he'd ever seen. "How wonderful would he need to be?" he asked.

His mother frowned at him. "Excuse me?"

"Never mind." He'd known all along, ever since he'd held Olivia in his arms at prom, that he couldn't have her. If he was going to get involved with a woman, she had to be like him, able to enjoy a quick, passionate affair and then move on.

Because, as soon as ski season arrived, he'd be gone again.

Noelle was angry during dinner. Olivia could feel her sister's animosity. She wasn't sure why Noelle felt *she* had the right to be upset. She wasn't the injured party. But every few seconds she'd glance over at Kyle, who was keeping his eyes on his plate, before sending Olivia an accusing glare.

What did she think happened before she came upon them outside?

Olivia didn't care. Not really. Most of the slights Noelle perceived were imagined. It'd always been that way. Olivia just wanted to get the wedding favors assembled so she could leave. She couldn't stay here, as planned. The unspoken hurt and anger were too agonizing.

But she wouldn't go to Brandon's. Sacramento wasn't that far. Although it would waste time and gas, she'd drive home and come back in the morning. She did, however, have to tell Brandon what she'd said to Kyle. She wasn't looking forward to that conversation. She'd already embarrassed herself once where he was concerned.

After dinner, Kyle went in to watch a true crime show with her father, Noelle disappeared into her bedroom to do whatever she felt she needed to do to prepare for her wedding and Olivia helped her mother wash dishes. Olivia had just started to relax, thanks to the comfort of routine, when Noelle called to her from the bedroom.

"Can you come and tell me how to wear my hair?" she asked, but Olivia wasn't fooled. Noelle had played nice long enough. She'd obviously decided on a bit of honesty to pierce the thin veneer of civility that had carried them this far. Olivia wasn't opposed to that herself.

"I'll be right back," she told her mother.

Nancy's forehead creased in worry, as if she, too, suspected that Noelle wasn't interested in opinions on her hair, but she nodded, and Olivia silently promised to do all she could to keep her temper in check. Fighting wouldn't improve the situation. Noelle and Kyle were going to have a baby. She needed to keep that in mind, especially if she wanted to be part of her niece's or nephew's life. The child was innocent and deserved the support of his or her entire family. Olivia just hoped that someday she'd be able to look at her sister's offspring, at *Kyle's* offspring, without cringing.

Maybe it'd be easy. Maybe Noelle would have a little girl who was a much better person than her mother....

"Are you thinking of an updo?" she asked as she walked down the hall.

Noelle was waiting by the door. She closed it as soon as Olivia walked in. "What are you doing?" she whispered harshly.

Olivia studied her flushed face. She was pretty; there was no denying that. They both had wide blue eyes, long blond hair and even features, but Noelle, shorter by two inches, had a curvier figure, which probably made her more attractive. Despite that, Olivia had never been jealous. Due to Noelle's demanding nature, self-absorption and terrible mood swings, she'd never been particularly popular with the opposite sex. Olivia figured men could sense that her looks wouldn't be worth the cost of involvement. She'd always thought Kyle understood that, too. "I don't know what you mean," she said.

"You know *exactly* what I'm talking about!"

Did Noelle believe Olivia had said something inappropriate to Kyle? That she was trying to stir up trouble?

Olivia started to explain that she was at a complete loss when Noelle made the reason for her anger clear. "You're seeing *Brandon? Really?* Kyle's *stepbrother?*"

At first, because of Noelle's emphasis on the family connection, Olivia assumed she was worried about how that might make Kyle feel. Neither one of them had any right to complain, of course, but the threat of looking like a hypocrite had never stopped Noelle. She believed the entire world should bow at her feet—which made Olivia suddenly realize that Noelle wasn't angry on Kyle's behalf. She expected Kyle to fight his own battles and cope with his own difficulties. She expected that of everyone, except herself. The only way Noelle could be *this* upset was if Olivia's actions affected her *personally.*

And then Olivia remembered. For most of one summer, Noelle had had the worst crush imaginable on Brandon. She'd done everything possible to gain his attention, including driving past his house numerous times a day, calling him incessantly, showing up wherever she guessed he might be. Olivia had forgotten that, largely because it'd been so long ago—eight years or more. And he hadn't given her so much as a second look. When August rolled around, he told her flat-out that he wasn't remotely interested and she'd better quit stalking him or he was going to the police.

The police threat came—understandable enough—after

she'd spied on him with another woman, but his unequivo-
cal rejection had done significant damage to Noelle's ego.

"Why are you smiling?" Noelle snapped.

Olivia sobered. "I guess I still don't understand why you're
upset."

Noelle grabbed her arm. "I'm upset because you're doing
this on purpose! You're trying to ruin my wedding!"

"What?" Olivia jerked loose. "I've been planning your wedding—*for free!* Not only have I donated hours and hours of
my time, I've called in favors from all the vendors I've ever
worked with."

"For Mom and Dad. Not for me."

Olivia couldn't argue with that.

"This is your revenge," she continued. "This is how you
think you'll get the last laugh."

"What are you talking about?" Noelle had liked a lot of
boys over the years. She couldn't claim proprietary interest in
all of them. Besides, after that summer she'd never had a nice
thing to say about Kyle's stepbrother.

"I'm talking about you sleeping with Brandon!"

So Kyle had shared that information. "I don't see why my
being with Brandon would bother you. You're in love with
Kyle, right? You're having his baby. And because of that baby,
he's marrying you."

"Not because of the baby!" she cried, stamping her foot.
"Because he loves me! I knew you'd try to cheapen it, try to
convince yourself that he's still in love with you. But he's not.
He hates that the two of you were ever together!"

When they talked on the phone for the last time, Kyle had
said the years they'd spent together were the best of his life,
but Olivia didn't give him away. His feelings had probably
already changed.

"Fine. He hates that we were together. He hates me. I don't

care. He's all yours now. You got exactly what you wanted. So enjoy him and leave me alone."

"I didn't get pregnant on purpose. I know you think I did."

"At this point, it doesn't matter what I think." She turned to go but Noelle wasn't finished yet.

"Does Brandon know?"

Olivia hesitated with her hand on the doorknob. "Know what?"

"That I'm pregnant?"

Why would he care? "Of course he does. Everyone in town knows."

"Your relationship with him won't last," she said suddenly, changing tactics. "He isn't the marrying kind."

"Fortunately, after what I've been through in the past few months, I'm only looking for some fun." Unable to resist, she lowered her voice. "And, God, can he provide it!"

Kyle had the hardest time keeping his eyes from gravitating to Olivia. She looked better than ever—tall, tan, hair streaked from the sun. But, despite her shapely legs—which happened to be his favorite part of the female anatomy—her appearance had nothing to do with how he felt. She'd always been beautiful to him, the only woman he'd ever loved. Just seeing her made his determination falter.

How had he gotten into such a terrible mess? These days, he constantly asked himself that. But he had no answer—except the obvious. He'd been an idiot, foolish enough to make the kind of mistake that would change his life forever.

He wished he could stop time, demand everyone back up and let him start over. But he'd seen the results of the pregnancy test. With a baby coming, there were no second chances.

"*Honey,* you have to put *three hugs* and *three kisses* in each box," Noelle said.

He blinked at the foil-wrapped chocolate candies. Wasn't that what he'd been doing? He opened the last wedding favor he'd assembled. She was right. He'd put in five kisses and only one hug. He'd thought, as long as they each included six pieces, it wouldn't matter. They had more than enough of both kinds. But every little detail mattered to Noelle.

"Got it." He smiled as congenially as possible to keep Olivia and her parents from knowing how badly Noelle's voice grated on him.

Three kisses, he silently mimicked. *And three hugs.* Along with a scrap of paper that read, *What's the earth with all its art, verse, music worth—compared with love, found, gained, and kept? —Robert Browning*

"Kyle, is something wrong?"

He glanced up to see his future mother-in-law watching him. He hadn't realized he'd slipped into inactivity. He was sitting there, staring at that damn line of Robert Browning's.

"No." His cheek muscles ached with the effort of yet another smile. "I was just wondering if I'd remembered to invite my aunt Georgia."

"You invited her," Noelle said without looking up. "You had so many on your list I had to cut twenty from mine, remember?"

He didn't know if he was supposed to apologize. He'd tried to keep his list small. His was certainly smaller than hers, by a significant margin. He hadn't wanted a big wedding. Given the situation, he much preferred they forgo the embarrassment of being married in Whiskey Creek and fly to Vegas. It seemed crazy to celebrate the hardest thing he'd ever done.

But thanks to Noelle's insistence on creating the fanfare she'd always craved for her wedding, they were looking at a long, painful weekend. One that included Olivia, making it impossible to avoid the fact that, if not for one foolish night, this could've been *their* wedding.

Actually, he'd been with Noelle more than one night. It had been a whirlwind couple of weeks, during which she'd flirted and teased and cajoled and pleased. Caught in the aftermath of Olivia's proposing a break and moving to Sacramento because she didn't want to settle down without experiencing a little more of life, he'd been feeling rejected, unsure she'd ever really come back and angry enough to tell himself he didn't have to suffer while she was gone. Their break hadn't been *his* idea. The fact that they weren't together but weren't really apart left him feeling irritable and foolish.

And this was where it had gotten him....

Suppressing a groan, he started filling boxes again.

"Did you find the right tie and cummerbund for your tux?" Olivia asked. It was the first time she'd initiated any conversation between them. He would've been grateful for her attention, would've seen it as a hopeful sign that she might eventually be able to forgive him, except he knew she was only asking as the wedding planner.

"I have."

"And your groomsmen have the right ones, as well?"

"Probably. I've told them where to go."

"You need to check."

"I will."

"Do they know the rehearsal dinner tomorrow has been moved to seven instead of six-thirty?"

He kept forming little boxes and filling them with the appropriate chocolate candy before adding them to the stack in the middle of the table. The women took over from there, tying on a delicate pink ribbon imprinted with Kyle's and Noelle's names and the date of their wedding.

Two days. The worst will be over in two days.... "I've notified them of that, too."

"Even Brandon?"

He'd invited Brandon to be in the wedding party for the sake of his parents. He felt it would be too obvious a slight to leave him out. But other than receiving a brief email confirming his participation, Kyle hadn't heard from his stepbrother. "Even Brandon."

"I'll double-check with him tonight."

The idea of Olivia spending time with Brandon for any reason made Kyle flinch. She hadn't meant much to him when the two of them went to a prom together years ago. But she meant a lot to him now. "I can email him again."

"Why don't you just call him?"

He met her gaze. "Maybe I will."

Ham, as Olivia's father was called, paused in his work to raise his eyebrows at this exchange. But, as usual, he didn't say anything. Sometimes Kyle wished he would. He wished *someone* would admit that this wedding was a huge mistake. Because he couldn't. If Noelle wanted to marry him, he had no choice. He had to stand up and do the right thing or he wouldn't be able to live with himself later.

Five

RELIEVED TO BE AWAY FROM HER PARENTS' house, Olivia dialed Brandon's number as she sat in her car, letting the engine idle in the empty parking lot of Just Like Mom's. The diner was closed, along with almost everything else in town, including the touristy shops dedicated to Whiskey Creek's gold rush heritage. It was late enough that she was hesitant to start the long drive home. She was tired. And she wasn't optimistic that facing her empty apartment would be that much better than crashing in her old bedroom. She seemed to be miserable no matter what.

"I'm not sure how to break this to you," she said as soon as Brandon answered.

"Break what to me?" he responded, his voice husky, which made her wonder if she'd awakened him. "You *couldn't* have found someone with a bigger telescope."

She knew he was teasing but, feeling herself flush, decided to ignore the innuendo. "I, uh, told a little white lie about you."

"Did it make me look good or bad?" He didn't sound too excited by the prospect either way.

"Maybe a little opportunistic?"

"Okay. Let me have it."

She drew a deep breath. "Kyle and Noelle think we're seeing each other."

"That's it?"

"Not quite."

"I'm waiting...."

"They also think we're sleeping together."

"Really."

"I don't know what got into me," she said. "Kyle pulled me aside and said it was killing him to know he was causing me pain, and I... I couldn't stand being so transparent and vulnerable. So I told him I'm not hurting at all, that I'm already seeing someone else."

"Me."

"Right. I could've named someone from Sacramento. That's what I *should've* done, obviously. He couldn't have proven that one way or the other. But..."

"It wouldn't have been half as much fun."

"No, it wouldn't have had the same impact." She'd found Noelle's reaction even more satisfying than Kyle's, but she didn't mention that. She was fairly sure her sister would be a sore subject with Brandon, even after the number of years that had passed since she'd invaded his privacy. "I hope you're not too sorry you stopped to help me."

"Not at all. I just wish I could've seen Kyle's face."

She smiled as she remembered. "He went white as a sheet."

"Good. Maybe it gave him the jolt he needs."

"In what way?"

"I haven't given up hope that he'll come to his senses and call the whole thing off."

Olivia pictured Kyle and Noelle as they'd been at dinner. They hadn't seemed particularly close, but they were dealing with a lot of stress, even more than normally accompanied a wedding. She wasn't convinced she could get an accurate reading from what she'd seen. "Maybe he loves her."

"You and I both know who he loves."

She hadn't expected Brandon to be so candid. "There *is* the baby—"

"Jumping into a marriage destined to end in divorce won't help the baby." He lowered his voice in a way that demanded an honest answer. "Would you take him back?"

"No!"

"You're done with him no matter what he does, no matter how much he begs?"

"He won't beg. You know Kyle. Once he's made up his mind, that's it. He'd never embarrass Noelle, my parents or your family by backing out. Whatever else he might be, he's a man of his word. But I'm done with him."

"And now you're all mine."

The zap she'd experienced earlier, the one that left her feeling slightly giddy, struck again, like a lightning bolt out of the clear blue sky. Which made no sense. She was still in love with Kyle—although their relationship was completely and totally *over*.

Assuming it was basic chemistry, the kind that could come out of nowhere even with a complete stranger, she shrugged off her reaction. He was merely referring to what she'd said earlier. "Or so they think. I'm sorry I went that far. I had no right to drag you into something that could have long-term repercussions inside your own family. But…it won't turn out to be a big deal. I let both him and Noelle know it's not serious. We don't have to go around holding hands or anything. Maybe a smile or two at the wedding—that's all."

"You're saying you implied we're not making love, just having sex."

"Exactly. But I made sure they knew it was mind-blowing." She tried to joke a little herself but the images that flashed through her head—images of Brandon's mouth on hers—made her words anything but funny.

"There's only one problem," he said.

"What's that?"

"If you told them it was casual, they already know you were lying."

For some reason, she was having difficulty catching her breath. "What makes you say that?"

"Honey, you're not capable of casual."

She'd certainly been more circumspect than he had. But that didn't mean she couldn't play the same game of Catch Me If You Can. "How do you know? I'm just as capable of being free and easy as anyone else."

"You're speaking from experience? You've had other 'free and easy' relationships?"

She thought of the two men she'd slept with. Both had been long-term, steady boyfriends. "Not yet," she admitted. "But after what I've been through, I'm not looking for a commitment. I think everyone understands that. Emotional entanglements are too…sticky and…and confining." The memory of Kyle coming forward to tell her he'd been with Noelle made her want to bang her head on the steering wheel again. "Not to mention painful," she added. "And when they don't work out you have to deal with regret for getting involved in the first place."

"I couldn't have said it better myself."

"Why shouldn't I have my fun just like everyone else?" she asked, warming to her defiance. "I'm an adult. I can do whatever I want."

"Now you're getting me excited."

She heard the humor in his voice but chose to ignore it. "Maybe I've been playing it too safe. Maybe I wouldn't be the one nursing a broken heart if I was willing to take a walk on the wild side once in a while."

"I'll buy that."

Again, she ignored the subtle smile in his voice because she loved feeling empowered. Just the idea of breaking the rules and getting away with it seemed to revive her flagging spirits. She could fight back if she wanted to!

But her enthusiasm dimmed as fast as it had dawned when he said, "Great. Come on over. Venus is out tonight. I'll show you."

Shit. She'd gone too far. She'd merely wanted him to respect her as someone equally competent to make that choice. Instead he'd called her bluff.

Suddenly feeling the need to backpedal, she searched for a good excuse. "I would, but…you're not the right kind of guy for my first hookup."

"Are you kidding?" he said. "I'm the *perfect* guy. And I'm volunteering."

"That's kind of you, but…it wouldn't be…*smart*."

"Define smart."

"We wouldn't gel. We're not…compatible."

"Because…"

She swallowed hard. He knew he appealed to women, knew she was no exception. What would he accept that would allow her to save face? "I'd be a boring partner for a thrill-seeker like you."

"That's like saying you have to wash your hair," he said

flatly. "If you're stepping up your game, you're really going to have to do better."

"It's not as lame as you're making it sound."

"It's worse. Face it. You're all talk."

"No, I'm not," she said. "Think of the women you've been with. The variety. The experience. I'd be…meat and potatoes when you're used to caviar."

"Olivia?"

It wasn't hot outside. As a matter of fact, it was a bit chilly. Yet she was sweating. "Yes?"

"Why don't you let me decide what turns me on?"

Because she'd long ago eliminated Brandon as a romantic possibility. She knew she couldn't remain as aloof as he did. He seemed to sense the same thing, seemed to understand that she wasn't good at dealing with someone like him. "You've never even acted interested."

"Do you remember prom?" he asked.

Of course she did. That night was tucked away in a special file in her brain, one she accessed every now and then so she could relive his good-night kiss. No one else had ever kissed her in quite the same way.

But she didn't want to think about that now. She was too scared. And not just because of her recent experience with Kyle. She'd been scared of Brandon from the beginning. "That was years ago."

"I know. But I've wanted you ever since. I'll be here if you change your mind," he said and hung up.

Olivia pressed her good hand over her face. She wasn't sure what had just happened, how she and Brandon had rounded the corner from "acquaintances who'd once had a class to-gether and went to a school dance" to "I've wanted you ever since" in such a short time. She figured it was her fault. She'd sent the wrong signals, especially when she'd had to let Brandon know she'd been telling others they were having sex. She supposed it was natural for him to take advantage if he sensed an opportunity. But she couldn't accept what he'd offered, no matter how reckless and angry and fatalistic she might be feeling. One night with him would be enough to set her recovery back by months.

Somehow, her life just kept getting more complicated....

She told herself to head back to her parents' house and turn in. She had so much to do in the morning. She had an early appointment with the events coordinator at the Pullman Mansion, where they were having the wedding and the reception. She also had to track a shipment of candy jars she'd ordered on the internet to find out why they hadn't yet arrived. And if those jars weren't going to make it in time, she needed to come up with an alternative. After that, she was scheduled to meet with the florist to see about adding lights to the centerpieces, and then the DJ so she could provide him with a playlist. All before the rehearsal dinner.

This wedding had to go without a hitch, had to run more smoothly than any event she'd ever planned, or she'd get the blame for anything that went wrong. After all her efforts, she certainly didn't want to be accused of sabotage. If she wanted to let her parents down, she could've done that by refusing to handle it in the first place.

Too bad she didn't have internet, or she could work on her computer right here, she thought with a frown. Her parents had service, but she was still dragging her feet about returning there. She preferred to wait until Kyle had gone and Noelle was in bed, and she didn't think she'd let enough time pass for that to have happened.

Briefly she considered renting a room at one of the two bed-and-breakfasts in town. They'd have internet. But she didn't dare spend the money. Her savings was off-limits. Besides, one of Kyle's best friends owned The Gold Nugget. That crossed it off her list right there.

Sexy Sadie's, a local bar fashioned after an old-time saloon, caught her eye. It was down the street. The place wasn't usually crowded on weeknights but Thursdays were busier than Monday through Wednesday. She watched several people come and go, was contemplating stopping there for a drink, when her cell phone rang.

It was Kyle. She almost didn't answer. They had nothing to say to each other. But if he was at her house, her mother, father or sister had likely asked him to pass on a message. She had to stop thinking of him as her ex and start thinking of him as her brother-in-law.

"Ick," she muttered but, with a sigh, hit the talk button. "What can I do for you?"

"You can answer one question," he replied.

This didn't sound as though he was planning to pass on a message. "Does Noelle know you're calling me?"

He didn't answer. "Are you already with Brandon?"

"No."

"Are you really seeing him?"

She curled her fingernails into her palms. Making up a relationship that didn't exist was pathetic. She should never have done it. Look what had happened with Brandon as a result! Just the thought of him lying in his bed, waiting for her, made her yearn for more than the memory of that one kiss all those years ago.

"No!" she said, as much to herself as him.

He seemed surprised by the energy of her answer, but he was probably too relieved to comment on the intensity behind it. "Thank God."

"Not that it should matter to you," she added, feeling more sane.

"I know, it's just... I believed you."

After the doubt Brandon had shown that anyone would be convinced they were seeing each other, she knew she should feel vindicated. But he obviously understood who she was better than Kyle did. Which was odd. "Even though I've been living in Sacramento for the past few months?" she said.

"He'd be willing to make the drive. He has a thing for you. I could sense his interest the whole time you and I were together."

Strange though it seemed, given their limited contact over the years, she'd always had a thing for him, too. She'd just never allowed herself to entertain the possibility of letting it go anywhere. "Jealousy's making you blind."

"I'm not blind to anything! He likes tall blondes."

"Doesn't mean he likes *all* tall blondes."

"I'm telling you we almost got into a fight at Thanksgiving because of the way he kept looking at you."

Olivia hadn't noticed anything amiss, nothing beyond the usual push-pull she felt whenever Brandon was around. He'd shown up for dinner, but he'd stayed only long enough to eat. As far as she was concerned he'd done nothing wrong.

"He didn't even speak to me," she said.

"He might try now."

"So you're...what? Giving me fair warning?"

"I'm letting you know that getting involved with him wouldn't be a smart move. You remember how he treated your sister—"

"I like that better than how *you've* treated my sister!"

"Ouch," he said but she ignored him.

"Besides, that was years ago, when he was home from college for the summer. And she was *stalking* him, Kyle. She

spied on him with another woman. That would make anyone angry."

"That's not the way she tells the story. She says he was pursuing her, leading several women on at the same time."

Because she didn't want to admit the truth. He'd discover
that was a common occurrence. "I believe Brandon."

"Over your own sister?"

"Yes. Absolutely. Look, I appreciate all the brotherly love,
but—"

"*Brotherly* love?" he broke in. "Would you just...stop?
Please? Do you think this is any easier for me?"

The desperation in his voice surprised her.

"I screwed up," he went on. "And now I'm paying the price.
But I don't want you to suffer any more than you already have
because of my stupidity."

Somehow his words made her even angrier than if he'd said
he adored her sister and always had. "If you're having second
thoughts, I'm not the one to talk to."

There was a long silence. Then he said, "I realize that."

"What is it you hold against Brandon, anyway?" she asked.
"It can't have anything to do with him mistreating Noelle,
because you didn't like him *before* he threatened her with a
restraining order."

"You know how he is. He's stubborn and egotistical and...
and difficult to get along with."

She wrapped her arms around herself and stared out at the
town she loved so much. Kyle had cost her even this. She'd
planned to come back but now...she felt as if she'd been cast
adrift, as if Whiskey Creek was no longer her anchor. "How
does that affect me?"

"He can't commit, and as much as you're trying to pretend
you're not looking for love, I know you too well. He's not the
kind of man you need."

As if Kyle was any better! He'd set himself up with that statement. But this time she let it go. "Have you talked to him recently?"

"I don't need to."

"Maybe you're going by dated information. Maybe he's matured and you're missing out on having a great brother."

"I'm not missing out on anything."

"You could cut him a little slack, you know. He's in your wedding party."

"For the sake of my parents."

She understood how familial obligation played a role this weekend. She doubted she'd even be attending the wedding were it not for Nancy and Ham. "Now you know why I'm here."

"I knew that before."

Again, the door opening and closing at Sexy Sadie's caught her eye. "I have to go."

"Wait—"

"For what, Kyle? Get some sleep. You'll need to be in top form this weekend."

He'd dared to call her, so she knew he wasn't with Noelle. Her sister was probably in bed, getting her beauty rest. That meant she could return to her parents'.

But Olivia couldn't go back there quite yet. Telling herself she'd have just one drink, she drove down the street and parked in front of the bar.

Six

BRANDON'S PHONE WOKE HIM. "HELLO?" HE muttered, squinting to see the time displayed on his digital alarm.

He was pretty sure it read 1:10 a.m.

"Brandon?"

Olivia. He recognized her voice immediately—although he could tell there was something wrong. "Yes?"

"I'm sorry, Brandon."

She sounded genuinely distraught. "For what, honey? It's okay that you didn't come over. I wasn't really expecting you."

"I meant for b-bothering you in the middle of the night."

When she sniffed, he gripped the phone harder. She was crying. "That's okay, too. What's wrong?"

"Um…do you think… Would it be too much trouble… I hate to ask this, but…"

"Where are you?" He was awake enough to hear that she was slurring her words. That, together with the loud music in the background, indicated she was at a bar. But, if so, where? In Sac? Or in Whiskey Creek?

"S-s-sexy S-S-Sadie's!" she announced, laughing. "I think I'm drunk. I was only going to have one drink, but... I don't know what happened."

"You had more."

"Yep."

He'd assumed she left town. He'd known she'd never show up at his place. "Do you need me to come get you?"

"Would you?" She seemed infinitely relieved.

"Of course." He rolled out of bed and began to dress. "Where's your car?"

"Out front. But I don't think... I don't think I should drive, Brandon. It wouldn't be safe. I might hurt some...somebody. I wouldn't want to hurt anybody."

"You're not going to get behind the wheel, sweetheart."

"No, but... I shouldn't have called *you*. Today's the first time we ever really talked since prom so...it's rude, right? To do that to a new friend?"

"Is that what we are?"

"Aren't we?"

He smiled at her distress. "Of course we are."

"Okay, good. Anyway, I'd call someone else but...all my other friends belong to Kyle."

"They what?"

"They're *his* friends. Callie and Eve and Riley and Ted and Cheyenne..."

She seemed to lose her train of thought before she could name all the members of the tight clique Kyle had belonged to since grade school. Rattling them off by memory wouldn't be that easy to do sober, since there were at least ten.

"Losing them, along with everything else, must've been hard." Her own friends had gotten married or taken jobs elsewhere, but most of Kyle's had remained here in Whiskey Creek and were as close as ever. A lot of people envied the support and friendship they gave each other. He doubted they liked her any less, but he could see why she could no longer hang out with them.

"Cheyenne's *so* nice," she was saying. "Even with that monster of a mother. Can you believe she grew up living in motels and clunker cars? That she had to *beg* on street corners? What kind of life would that be?"

He found his shoes and headed to the kitchen for his keys. "Cheyenne's nice," he agreed.

"And here I am wallowing in self-pity because my boyfriend got my sister pregnant. I should be more grateful."

"You'll get through this."

"Do you think she did it on purpose?"

"I wouldn't put it past her."

"Me, neither," she responded. "I wish I could talk to Cheyenne about it. But…it's not the same with Kyle's friends now. They have to be…have to be loyal to him. They were *his* friends first. I know they feel bad about what's happened, but… what can they do? No more Fridays at the coffee shop for me." She'd added a singsong quality to her voice, but that quickly fell away. "I wish… I wish it could be different. I wish—"

"Olivia?" He interrupted because he'd heard her voice crack and knew she was about to break down again. "Don't think about Cheyenne or any of Kyle's other friends—"

"Who aren't *my* friends anymore," she broke in, but he didn't let her distract him.

"I'm coming, okay? I've got my keys in my hand. I'll talk to you when I get there."

"I'm sorry, Brandon. You shouldn't have to come out so late."

"I don't mind," he said. "Just stay put. I'm on my way."

"Thank you. I'm so tired. Maybe if I get some sleep tomorrow will be better."

"Of course it will. Don't worry about anything. I'll take care of you." He strode to his front door. "Now let me talk to Fisk."

She didn't need to ask who Fisk was. He'd been bartending at Sexy Sadie's since they were kids. "Sure. Goodbye, Brandon. You're coming for me, right? You're coming now? And you'll show me the stars?"

A smile tugged at his lips. "If that's what you want, honey. Give the phone to Fisk."

"Okay...."

The music got even louder as the phone changed hands. Then Brandon heard the boom of Fisk's deep voice. "'Lo?"

"Fisk, Brandon Lucero."

"Oh, hey, Brandon. What's up?"

"I wanted to ask if you'd keep an eye on Olivia until I get there. Can you do that for me?"

"I would, but—"

"No buts. Don't let her go anywhere."

Fisk lowered his voice. "I doubt she could make it to the door. That's why I called Kyle a few minutes ago. I know he's seeing her sister these days—what a mess that is—but as soon as I said I was going to call Noelle she wouldn't give me her phone, and I didn't have the number for any of her friends or family. So it was Kyle or no one."

Brandon had been jogging to his truck. At this, he stopped. "Don't let him take her."

"I just wanted someone to get her home safe."

"*I'll* see to that."

"I'm not sure I'll be able to stop him, Brandon. You'd better get here quick."

"Shit." Brandon hit the end button as he fired up his truck and roared out of his driveway.

By the time Brandon arrived at Sexy Sadie's, Kyle was already there. But he didn't have to worry about Olivia leaving with his stepbrother. She was clutching the bar for all she was worth, wouldn't even stand, despite Kyle gripping her shoulders and urging her to get up.

"Let go of her," Brandon said, coming up on him from behind.

At the sound of his voice, Kyle whipped around. "What the hell are *you* doing here?"

"I came to take her home."

Fisk had watched him walk in. Now he hurried over to address them. "I don't want any trouble, boys."

Brandon lifted a hand to reassure the bartender that they weren't going to cause a scene but kept his focus on Kyle. "She doesn't need your help, bro. I've got it from here."

Olivia turned a beseeching expression on him. "Don't let him take me, Brandon."

"I won't, honey. Just get your purse off the floor, and we'll go home and look through the telescope."

Her pretty blue eyes filled with tears but she blinked them back. "That's...good." Releasing the bar, she got up, managed to sidestep Kyle even though he reached for her and staggered right into Brandon's arms.

"I'm *so* glad you're here," she said, clinging tightly to him.

He let his arms close around her, once again feeling that inexplicable protectiveness he'd experienced all those years ago when they danced at prom.

The menacing look on Kyle's face made Brandon wonder

if he'd be able to keep the promise he'd just given Fisk. Kyle didn't seem willing to let Olivia go without a fight. "You need to take her to her parents'," he said, his voice threatening, low.

Fisk stepped forward. "Come on now. Let Brandon handle it, Kyle. I shouldn't have called you. You have no say anymore."

"I'll let her leave with someone else but not him," Kyle shot back.

Brandon arched an eyebrow. "She's the one who called me."

"Olivia—" Kyle started but she wouldn't even look at him.

Brandon backed off enough to see into her face. "Do you want to go to your parents' house? Your sister's probably waiting up for you. You know how concerned she is about your welfare. You wouldn't want Noelle to worry, right?"

"You son of a bitch," Kyle ground out.

"I'm just asking the question." Brandon spread his hands, smiling when Olivia insisted she definitely *didn't* want to see her sister.

"That comes as a real surprise, honey," Brandon said and returned his gaze to Kyle. "I think she's made her desires clear."

A growl sounded deep in Kyle's throat and he clenched his fist as if he'd throw a punch.

Prepared to put Olivia behind him in case he had to defend himself, Brandon stiffened. But Fisk grabbed Kyle before he could do anything stupid.

"Calm down, buddy," Fisk said in a low voice. "I'm sure you could cause some serious damage, but I think your brother could, too. You don't want to wind up with a shiner for your wedding."

"Don't hurt him!" Fresh tears caught in Olivia's long lashes when she saw Fisk shoving Kyle back. "Please, don't hurt him."

Her panic over Kyle's well-being showed that she still cared about him, and that took the fight out of him. Dropping his hands to his sides, he watched her with such agony that, for the first time ever, Brandon felt a degree of sympathy for his stepbrother. Maybe the way Kyle's life had intersected with his own wasn't what Brandon would've wished for, but Kyle was obviously in a great deal of pain.

"I'm sorry." Kyle shook his head. "I'm so sorry."

He was speaking to Olivia, but she didn't respond to him. She'd already closed her eyes and turned as if she couldn't bear to look at him another second.

"I won't let anything happen to her." Brandon had to offer his stepbrother that much comfort as he guided her out.

Seven

BRANDON FELT AS IF HE DESERVED A MEDAL. He'd managed to stop Olivia when she'd started peeling off her clothes. There'd been one moment when he'd almost succumbed—when she locked her arms around his neck and tried to pull him into bed with her. She kept insisting she could do casual sex, and, Lord, did he want to believe her. With her body up against his, the silk of her panties coming out the back of her loosened shorts, he'd nearly thrown honor and decency to the wind. Thoughts like, "Just one kiss, one taste, one touch..." went through his head but considering the desire raging through him, he'd known that was all the spark it would take to start a conflagration. Sternly reminding himself that she wasn't in any condition to give consent, he helped her remove the shorts she was so intent on getting off but refused every advance.

And now he was paying the price. Tense and completely unsatisfied, he tossed and turned while the girl he'd dreamed about for over a decade lay in the next room wearing nothing but her T-shirt and a pair of pretty panties. He felt her soft skin in his mind every time he closed his eyes.

The memory alone made him hard.

He could only hope she'd want him as badly in the morning, but he knew her better judgment would take over by then. As much as she *thought* she wanted a wild affair, something to fill the sudden loneliness, it was all too typical of being on the rebound. She wasn't the type to take sex lightly, which was why he'd always been careful to keep a safe distance. He wouldn't be good for someone like her. He was too devoted to his freedom.

Frustrated with his inability to shut down, he rolled over to search for his phone on the nightstand. For the past hour, he'd been debating whether to send Kyle a text. He figured he might as well be gallant all the way around.

She's in the guest room asleep. Safe and sound. Get some rest. Big weekend ahead.

He hoped that would bring Kyle some peace.

A return text quickly confirmed that Kyle was still awake, which wasn't a surprise. If Kyle felt half as torn about his upcoming marriage as Brandon suspected, he might walk the floor all night.

You better not have touched her.

"So much for trying to do you a favor," he grumbled and scrolled through his pictures, looking for one his mother had sent him, months ago, from Thanksgiving. It was a group shot with Kyle and Olivia and the whole family.

As he stared at her image, at her and Kyle smiling for the camera, he remembered how difficult it had been to see them together. He didn't want to sacrifice the life he had, but she'd always been a temptation. He'd hated the idea that his stepbrother, of all people, would end up with her, knew it would make every family event a challenge.

The ding signaling another text drew Brandon from his thoughts.

Have you been calling her since we took our break? Did you wait even that long before making your move?

What does it matter to you? he replied. Aren't you getting married this weekend?

Have you been chasing her?

Brandon didn't bother to deny the attraction. Was waiting to see if you were going to wake up and realize you're ruining your life.

This time when there was no response, Brandon figured it was just as well. They weren't close enough to be so blunt with each other. He leaned over to return his phone to the nightstand—but another message appeared.

I have no choice.

Propping his pillows behind his back, he typed, Yes, you do. Don't let your sense of duty drag you into making a bad situation worse.

What about the baby?

What about it? Did you ever think she might've gotten pregnant on purpose? That she's manipulating you? Brandon wouldn't put it past her.

She's still pregnant. You're telling me you wouldn't even try to create a family?

You can support the baby, be a good father regardless. Maybe it's not optimal to do it single, but you can make it work. That sort of thing happens all the time.

There was a long wait before the next text came in. Brandon had just decided Kyle must've gone to sleep when he heard the reply arrive.

Not to me it doesn't. I want my kid to have my name, my presence. I don't want to be a part-time dad with a stepparent joining the action.

Brandon could sense the resolve in those words. He could easily understand the sentiment behind them, too. But he was afraid that Kyle's background and misguided nobility were pulling him into a nightmare of catastrophic proportions.

So how should he answer? What Kyle did or didn't do wasn't any of his business. He'd spent the past decade telling himself he didn't really care about his stepbrother. But...he couldn't help admiring Kyle's determination to fall on his sword. He was a much better person than Brandon had ever given him credit for. Maybe Bob had a right to be so damn proud. Brandon couldn't have made himself marry Noelle.

But no one—even Olivia—knew her the way he did. Although he was trying to believe she'd grown up and changed, he'd seen her at her worst, when she was obsessed and un-relenting and so narcissistic he couldn't even *like* her. He'd done everything he could to discourage her from pursuing him eight years ago, to let her know he wasn't interested. But it made no impact whatsoever. If anything, she became *more* determined. He'd come home to find her waiting in his driveway, turn to see her staring in his window, "bump" into her so many times a day she could only be following him. He couldn't imagine a woman so out of touch with reality and the wants and desires of other people being successful in a marriage, even to a white knight like Kyle, who was willing to do 90 percent of the work.

I wish you'd listen to me, he wrote. There's something missing in Noelle.

I already know she had a crush on you. She was just being young and stupid and too forward.

Too forward? Her behavior went far beyond that. You're saying the Noelle she is now would never cross the lines she crossed back then?

Of course not, Kyle responded. Anyway, I could never undo the damage I've done. I can't go back to Olivia while Noelle has my baby. I might as well have some integrity and stand up and take responsibility for my actions.

Brandon wanted to reiterate that he'd be sorry if he married Noelle. But what good would it do? Kyle had made up his mind and nothing was going to change it. Then you need to let go of Olivia.

Again, Kyle's answer took a while to arrive. But Brandon waited because he knew it would come.

Won't be easy.

★ ★ ★

Olivia woke up to a splitting headache. It took effort just to open her eyes. Thank God the room was dark. She could see sunlight peeking around the cracks in the blinds, enough that she could make out an overburdened desk, a computer, a ship in a bottle and some tribal masks on the wall—but she didn't recognize any of it. Where was she?

Then it came to her. She'd gotten drunk last night, and Brandon had brought her home. She could remember him fighting to keep her clothes on. She could also remember trying to kiss him. She'd wanted him so badly....

Surprisingly enough, he was the one who'd resisted. "You're not interested?" she'd breathed.

"Not like this, sweetheart," he'd told her and helped her remove only her shorts before tucking her in. She'd gotten the impression he'd been tempted despite those words, was fairly certain he'd almost turned back at the door. But she was embarrassed all the same. Now both of the Arnold girls had thrown themselves at him.

Kyle's actions had knocked her on her butt and she couldn't seem to get her legs under her again. She never would've behaved like that otherwise.

Brandon interrupted her moment of regret with a brisk knock. "Olivia? You awake?"

She cringed at the fact that she was going to have to face him, and so soon. She'd made a complete fool of herself last night, first by getting drunk, then by trying to get him into bed. She still wasn't sure what he'd meant by, "Not like this." Was he saying he didn't want to take advantage of her while she was under the influence of alcohol? Or that he didn't want to become a surrogate for Kyle?

She couldn't imagine he'd refrain because of Kyle. Brandon

probably preferred she be in love with someone else. Then he wouldn't have to worry about her falling in love with him.

"I'm awake, but I'm not very happy about it," she replied.

He poked his head inside. Freshly showered and wearing a black V-neck T-shirt with a pair of well-worn jeans and flip-flops, he looked better than ever—which was saying a lot. She wasn't sure what accounted for that, unless just getting to know him made him more and more attractive. Maybe it was that she finally had some respect for him, since he'd re-jected her advances.

"How are you feeling?" he asked.

She shoved a hand through her messy hair. "Like roadkill."

He chuckled. "I was afraid of that. Would you like some-thing to eat?"

Could her stomach tolerate food? She didn't dare take the risk. "No, but a pain pill would be nice." She knew he had some; he'd provided it yesterday. "What time is it?"

"Nearly nine."

"Oh, no!" She shot out of bed, then staggered and nearly fell.

Somehow, he managed to get inside the room quickly enough to catch her and guide her back to the bed.

"I've missed my first appointment," she explained, rais-ing her good hand to her pounding head. "I was supposed to meet Abby, the event planner at the Pullman Mansion, at eight. I've got to go!"

He frowned at her. "I don't think you're up to it."

She'd been stupid to drink last night. She wasn't used to that much alcohol. "I don't have any choice." Her tongue felt thick and unwieldy. "Have you seen my phone?" She glanced around but couldn't locate it.

"Your purse is out on the counter."

When she started to get up, he pressed her back. "I'll get it."

He returned with a glass of water, two ibuprofen tablets and her purse, which contained her phone. At least she hadn't left it at the bar last night. She figured, at this point, she should be grateful for the little things.

"She's tried to reach me five times," she said as she checked her call record. "My mother and Noelle have both called twice." She lifted her eyes to his. "What am I going to tell them?"

"I say you tell them that you're not feeling well and to get by the best they can without you."

"I can't do that! The wedding's tomorrow night." She rubbed her temples, hoping to mitigate some of the pain. The hand she'd injured was no longer swollen, but it was still sore, which didn't help with her hangover.

He urged her to swallow the painkillers and watched as she obeyed. "Fine. Get in the shower. I'll call and tell them you're on your way." He took the glass. "Then I'll drive you to your car."

It wouldn't go over very well to have Brandon act as her secretary when she'd blown such an important appointment. They'd assume she was purposely causing problems, that it was a vindictive attempt to strike back at Noelle. But it would postpone the confrontation until she felt more equipped to handle it. And letting them believe she was having an affair was better than the pathetic truth that she wasn't handling Kyle and Noelle's union quite as nonchalantly as she'd planned.

Regardless of anything else, she deserved one small rebellion, didn't she?

"Thanks." She handed him her phone. "They're right there on my list of favorites."

"Towels are on the rack to the left of the sink," he said. "You'll see them."

Despite the pressure she was feeling to hurry, she could only move gingerly. She made her way to the door before turning back. "Did Kyle come to the bar last night?"

He met her eyes. "He did."

"I thought maybe I dreamed that part."

"No."

They stared at each other for a few seconds. Olivia didn't understand why, but she couldn't look away.

"You could steal him back if you want," he said at length. "You know that, right?"

He was serious. He was telling her that if Kyle was the man she really wanted to be with, she could fight for him and would probably win.

But it wasn't so simple. There were other people involved. Not to mention the baby.

"I wouldn't want to hurt the people that would hurt," she said.

"Despite what Noelle has done to you?"

She sighed. "Yes."

"Then you must not want him enough."

"I don't," she said. "Not anymore." That didn't mean what she was going through didn't hurt. The disappointment, the disillusionment, the sense of betrayal and the blow to her self-esteem were very real and ever-present, especially when she was in Whiskey Creek. But she couldn't get back with Kyle knowing he had a child with her sister. How would they interact with that child? How would they interact with her family?

At least, for the first time since falling in love with Kyle, she was feeling desire for another man. The excitement that brought told her life after Kyle was possible; she just had to be careful or she'd land herself in an even worse situation.

"I'm glad to hear it," he said.

Suddenly she became very conscious of the fact that she was wearing nothing but her panties and shirt. She was better covered than if she were wearing a bathing suit. But what had almost happened last night, what she'd *wanted* to have happen, made her feel very exposed.

The way his gaze traveled over her body, as intimate as a caress, made her breasts tingle. She struggled to find her voice. "Did I really try to rip off my clothes when you put me to bed?"

He grinned, which was answer enough.

"Thought so." She'd actually brought it up so she could apologize. "I'm sorry. From what you said on the phone, I assumed that...that you might welcome a bed partner."

"You think I was rejecting you?"

She felt her eyebrows slide up. "Weren't you? I slept alone last night."

"Next time ask me when I have the option of saying yes."

Eight

OLIVIA HAD LEFT HER LUGGAGE AT BRANDON'S
house. Since she didn't have a better place to stay, it'd
seemed silly to lug it in so she could get ready, then lug it back
out. He would have done the carrying for her, of course. He
was a gentleman that way. But since her family already knew
she was with him, there was no reason to leave his cabin on
their account. He'd invited her to use his guest room for as
long as she wanted, and she figured she might as well take
him up on it.

That meant she'd be going back....

"Olivia, what do you think?"

She blinked before focusing on her mother, who was wearing a flowery dress and had her hair sectioned off in rollers
with a scarf tied over the lot, making her look very 1960s
housewife. "About what?"

"The bows that go on the chairs!" The impatience in Nancy's voice suggested she'd already asked once. "Noelle doesn't think they match the table runners. Are you sure these are the shade we ordered?"

Removing the sunglasses she'd been using to hide her bloodshot eyes, Olivia tried to focus. She'd expected these meetings to be difficult. But she was so preoccupied with Brandon, she was finding them more of a nuisance than a challenge.

"They're a shade off," she admitted. "I borrowed these from River City to save money, remember? That's what you wanted me to do."

"But will they look bad?" Nancy refastened a roller that was threatening to fall. Olivia had tried to convince her that a round brush and a blow drier would give her the curl she wanted, but she insisted her hair looked best when she "put it up" for a day—and she was going all out for the wedding.

"I think they'll be fine," Olivia assured her. "They won't be right up against each other. See?" She held the two fabrics a few inches apart. "You won't notice they're not exact, especially with all the shades of pink and peach in the flower arrangements."

"I don't know...." Noelle shot her an accusing glower. "I thought they'd match better than *that*."

She said this as if it was Olivia's fault they didn't, although it had been Noelle's choice. She'd wanted to save money on the chair covers so she could get a pair of very expensive heels, which wouldn't even show beneath her dress.

Noelle wanted this to be the wedding of the century, which was so unrealistic. But it wasn't only the color of the chair bows that was bothering her. She'd been hostile all morning. Olivia could *feel* the animosity; she just wasn't sure of the cause. Was it the difficulty of pulling off an event like this? Or was it that Noelle knew Kyle had called her last night? That he'd come to the bar to get her?

Maybe she'd been the cause of a fight....

Or was Noelle upset that she was hanging out with Brandon?

The suspicion that her sister was once again jealous of the man in her life—even though she and Brandon weren't as romantically involved as Noelle thought—made Olivia nervous. After everything Noelle had done to get Kyle, including, possibly, a purposeful pregnancy, she had no business even noticing Brandon.

"Regardless, it's too late to change now," Olivia said. Normally she would've gone to greater pains to reassure the bride, but she meant that statement in more ways than one. Noelle had made her decision. And in the process, she'd hurt and embarrassed Olivia, cost their parents a great deal of money by demanding such an expensive wedding, made a public fool of Kyle and humiliated herself.

Now she was carrying Kyle's baby.

It was time for her to quit being so selfish.

"We could do without the bows," her mother suggested, obviously trying to placate Noelle.

"Is that what you want?" Olivia turned to her sister, making it clear by her tone that she didn't care either way.

Noelle pressed her fingers to her eyes. "Ugh! This is turning into a nightmare! Some wedding planner *you* are. I thought having a wedding was supposed to be fun."

"I think it helps to be in love," Olivia murmured. Fortunately Nancy didn't hear. Abby was showing her where they'd set up the table for all the candy.

"I *am* in love!" Noelle insisted.

"With Kyle or Brandon?" Olivia asked.

Noelle's lips thinned and her eyes grew so cold they gave Olivia chills. "You're trying to ruin my wedding!"

Seriously? Was that all she was concerned about? There was so much more at stake!

"I'm afraid you're going to ruin Kyle's *life*," she responded, realizing, for the first time, that what she'd suffered might turn out to be paltry by comparison.

"How'd it go today?" Brandon asked as he let her in.

Olivia was so tired she could scarcely move. This week had been emotionally draining. Add to that her late night at the bar, and a day spent in her sister's company, and she was ready to crawl into bed. She hadn't even taken the time to have lunch. She'd been running too late, so she'd gone all day without a meal. But they had to be at the rehearsal dinner in an hour. She'd eat then.

"It was weird," she told him.

He went into the kitchen as she dropped onto his couch.

"It's always weird when your sister is marrying the man you love," he said.

Love? Or loved? She couldn't decide anymore.

She thought back on the past seven hours. Her sister had grown more and more hateful throughout the day. Olivia felt sorry for their mother, who'd worked extra hard to stay positive and enthusiastic in the face of their long, sullen silences. "It got even weirder than that," she said.

"In what way?" He brought her a sliced orange, which she accepted gratefully.

"I'm beginning to feel sorry for Kyle, if that makes any sense."

"Makes all the sense in the world to me. I feel sorry for him, too."

She offered him a tired grin. "That's harsh. Just because she stalked you for a few months?"

A chuckle let her know he understood she was teasing. "It

was the creepiest thing I've ever been through, seeing her face staring in at me through the window."

"I suspect she still has a thing for you."

He tried to shrug it off. "Don't say that."

"It's true. Our...relationship is driving her crazy. I'd tell her we haven't slept together, but I don't think she'd believe me."

"She's getting married. It shouldn't matter to her either way."

She savored the sweetness of the orange he'd given her. "Unless she's only in it for the shoes."

"The shoes?"

"The trappings, the party, the celebration, the attention. This wedding shines a bright light on her and announces to everyone in Whiskey Creek that Kyle, a guy highly admired, prefers her to every other woman, including me."

"The sad truth is...he doesn't."

"I don't even care anymore." Pushing her plate away, she leaned back and closed her eyes. "All I want is for this wedding to be over."

"You're exhausted."

She didn't answer. She told herself she could rest for fifteen minutes. Then she had to get ready. She had to get through the rehearsal dinner. But Brandon nudged her before she could drift off. "Come on. Nap on the bed. It'll be more comfortable."

"I can't move," she objected, but that didn't deter him. He simply scooped her up and carried her down the hall.

When he took her to his room instead of hers, she didn't have the energy to protest. At the moment, she was worthless as a sex partner. She just hoped he'd curl up beside her, lend her his strength and his warmth. But the next thing she knew, she was facedown on his pillow, breathing in the scent that lingered there—the same scent that clung to his body—as his fingers massaged the tight muscles in her neck and shoulders.

She groaned. "Why are you being so nice to me?"

He laughed softly. "Don't trust it. Considering what you do to me, I have only evil intentions."

"Would it make you any less of a villain to lie down with me?"

"I suppose that wouldn't hurt my reputation too much," he said wryly and scooted in beside her.

With his shoulder as her pillow and his fingers moving gently through her hair, she felt oddly content as she drifted off.

A screech woke Brandon from a dead sleep. One look at Olivia, blinking awake next to him, told him she hadn't made that sound. She was as startled as he was. So what—

Then the sound came again—*"O-li-via!"*—and he realized what was going on. "Shit! The rehearsal dinner!"

Olivia was already scrambling off the bed, but she didn't have a chance to speak before Noelle started screaming again.

"I know you're in there, damn you!" She banged on the door. "How could you? *How could you do this to me?*"

"What time is it?" Olivia cried.

"Nearly eight."

Her face went pale. "Oh, God! I overslept."

Brandon felt terrible. "I'm sorry. I never intended to fall asleep. I just shut my eyes for a minute."

She rubbed her face as if trying to get her bearings. "We have to go."

Galvanized into action, he hopped out of bed. "You go change. I'll answer the door."

"No, I'll answer. She's so upset there's no telling what she might say."

"Exactly." He gave her a little push. "Better if she says it to me. She can't hurt me, and it might blow off some of the steam. Get ready."

Although reluctant to let him handle her temperamental sister, she seemed to understand the urgency of showing up at the dinner party—where the rest of the wedding party was waiting for them.

"I've got it," he assured her, and she hurried into the bathroom.

"Olivia!" Noelle yelled.

He opened the door before she could knock again.

She immediately stepped back so she could look up at him. "Where's my sister?"

"Getting ready. You can head back. We'll be there as soon as we can."

"You'll be there? Why weren't you there *an hour* ago?"

He stepped out and closed the door so that Olivia wouldn't have to hear this. "We fell asleep, okay? I'm sorry about that—"

"You're not sorry for anything!" She looked a little crazed with her hair falling out of whatever was holding it up. "You're busy banging my sister when it's supposed to be *my* turn!"

Knowing she couldn't have meant that quite the way it sounded, he raised his eyebrows, giving her a chance to clarify.

"To have what I want," she said, her cheeks flashing red. "To have everyone's cooperation. It's *my* wedding. This isn't about you…or her!"

"Then don't make it about us," he said. "Go ahead and enjoy it. We aren't standing in your way."

"Yes, you are! She's my planner! She's supposed to be there taking care of things!"

He lowered his voice, hoping she'd do the same. "The wedding isn't until tomorrow, Noelle. Everything will be fine. Just…calm down, okay? Your sister doesn't need you to flip out right now."

"You're worried about what *she* needs? What about *me?*"

"What about you?" he retorted. "Have you ever stopped to consider how what you've done—what you're doing—might be making *her* feel?"

She narrowed her eyes at his mussed hair and wrinkled clothes. "I *know* what she's been feeling," she said and stomped away.

Olivia was so self-conscious about entering the ballroom more than an hour late, and with Brandon at her side, she could barely stand it. But she couldn't turn back time. And since Noelle had probably announced that she'd found them together, Olivia saw no benefit in appearing separately. Bringing two vehicles to the rehearsal wasn't going to fool anyone. She'd actually been glad that, with her nerves in such a riot, she hadn't needed to drive the steep mountain road from Brandon's house to town.

The instant they stepped through the door, twenty-four sets of eyes turned in their direction. Kyle's family. Her family. Lindsey Manelli, Noelle's maid of honor and best friend. The tight-knit group Kyle had grown up with, including the female members, who were in Noelle's line because she wouldn't have had much of a line without them.

Olivia had expected to attract everyone's attention—the entire party had been waiting for her—yet she still felt her stomach muscles tighten. Brandon, on the other hand, seemed to take it in stride. He smiled as if he was completely relaxed and had no reason to be embarrassed. And he kept his hand at the small of her back, encouraging her to follow his lead.

She tried, but her smile faltered when her father pinned her beneath a disapproving stare. She'd figured her mother would squawk and Noelle would rant and then pout. She'd known their reactions wouldn't be easy to take—she still had that to look forward to—but this was harder. Unlike her mother, who refused to see her sister's shortcomings, her father knew Noelle had problems. Although he obviously loved his younger daughter, Ham often shook his head in disgust when she was being shallow or selfish.

With Olivia, however, it was different. She had always been able to maintain his respect. But with that came high expectations. And she'd just let him down.

Trying not to allow his disappointment, her sister's angry glare or Kyle's stony expression to attack her confidence, she apologized to the wedding party at large, without providing an excuse for her tardiness. Then she ran through a brief rehearsal just to make sure everyone was aware of how the ceremony should proceed. Fortunately Abby, from the Pullman Mansion, had taken over in her absence, so they already knew what she was telling them.

Then they were off to the upscale restaurant in the front of the mansion, where Kyle had booked a private room for everyone to have a steak dinner. The chicken or pasta would've been cheaper. Olivia had pointed that out. But Noelle had insisted that she could never serve less than the best at *her* wedding. And since Kyle was paying for it, Noelle was getting everything she wanted—the most expensive meal on the menu along with some fancy Napa Valley champagne.

"Was being in his bed worth it?" Noelle hissed in Olivia's ear.

Olivia turned to see her sister filing into the room behind her as everyone fanned out, trying to find a seat.

"Worth what?" She edged toward the middle table, where the bride and her family and the groom and his family were to sit. She was hoping to avoid a confrontation by slipping away before Noelle could really engage her, but Noelle managed a parting shot all the same.

"Looking like a slut in front of both our families and all of Kyle's friends!"

Those friends used to be her friends, until Noelle had stolen Kyle and made it too awkward for Olivia to hang out with them. Incensed to think her sister would dare take that tack after what *she'd* done, Olivia almost let her have it. But then she glanced up and caught Brandon watching her. As he walked through the crowded room, he gave her a half smile and a wink that reminded her to take it on the chin—or at least pretend to.

Ignoring Noelle and Gail DeMarco, Noah Rackham, Baxter North, Callie Vanetta, even Cheyenne Christensen, her favorite of Kyle's friends, as well as the rest of them, Olivia began to circle the center table. She was hoping to put several place settings between her and Noelle. But her sister had saved the seat next to her.

"Olivia, why don't you sit here by me?" she said as sweetly as if she hadn't just called Olivia a slut.

Olivia suspected her sister of trying to keep her from sitting beside Brandon, but she had no intention of doing that, anyway—not under the watchful eyes of both sets of parents, neither of whom seemed pleased by their friendship. Maybe they believed Noelle and thought she and Brandon were trying to ruin the wedding.

"Noelle!" Kyle's chastening tone surprised Olivia. Clearly he wasn't happy. He seemed to be cautioning his fiancée against baiting her, but Noelle ignored him.

"Well?" Her sister lifted her eyebrows.

Feeling Kyle's parents' attention on her, Olivia suppressed her anger. She'd be damned if she'd let Noelle make her look any worse than she already did. "Coming."

Once they were all seated, the tension eased enough for

polite conversation. Everyone joined in except Kyle. He remained silent, drinking far more than he ate.

Noelle didn't seem to notice that her groom was upset. Her gaze darted to Brandon every few seconds, even though he didn't pay her the slightest attention. When he did look up, it was to catch Olivia's eye.

Determined to get through the meal as fast as possible, Olivia concentrated on her salad and champagne and tried to block out everything else. But Brandon's mother whispered something to him, and Olivia couldn't help straining to hear what was said.

"Why on earth were you so late? You promised me you'd be on your best behavior!"

"I *am* on my best behavior," he said with a mock scowl that nearly made Olivia laugh. He hadn't answered his mother's question, but when he leaned back and put his arm around her, she seemed so pleased by the loving gesture that she let the rest go.

Smooth, Olivia thought. *Too* smooth. She was going to have to be careful not to fall for him like everyone else.

Nine

KYLE FELT AS IF THE NIGHT WOULD NEVER END. He knew he was drinking too much, but he had to do something. Otherwise, he'd get into a public argument with his soon-to-be wife. Noelle was playing games, taunting Olivia wherever and whenever she could. She didn't realize that it made her look jealous and inferior and foolish.

This was the woman he was marrying. But the sense of doom that acknowledgment brought him wasn't the worst of what he was suffering. Not tonight. The worst was watching Brandon and Olivia together. The way they'd walked into the room, united against everyone else. The intimacy of the looks they exchanged across the table. The smiles. They were captivated with each other. He'd never seen his brother so attentive to a woman. He wanted to believe Brandon was just trying to get under his skin, but he knew better. Brandon had his faults. He was competitive and stubborn and deter-mined to live life on his own terms, but he was honest, and he wasn't petty.

Kyle had expected this wedding to be difficult, but it was proving to be almost impossible.

"So have you decided where you'll live?" his future mother-in-law asked.

This had been a subject of much contention. He wanted to stay in the same house he'd been living in for five years, the one he'd had built near his manufacturing plant. It wasn't big or ostentatious, but it was comfortable and convenient.

Noelle wanted him to buy her a mansion in town. She worked at a dress boutique, making minimum wage, and used the excuse that it was closer to her job.

"We're going to knock down the old Foreman house right there on the turn as you leave town and build our dream home," Noelle gushed.

Kyle gaped at her. Where had *that* come from? She'd been trying to talk him into that plan, but he'd never agreed. "No, we're not," he said. "Noelle will be moving in with me."

"We can't live in that cracker box!" she snapped. "Where will we put the baby?"

"There's room." He finished his champagne and searched for the waiter. "I can move the storage I have over to the plant."

"But there's no need to go to the trouble. If we build in town, we can have everything just the way we want."

The way *she* wanted. That was all that ever mattered.

He could tell he was making his parents uncomfortable by not respecting her wishes, but the alcohol was interfering with his ability to control the negative thoughts and emotions ris-ing to the surface. "I'm not ready to build in town."

"That's not what you said when we talked about it last,"

Noelle pressed, despite the look he gave her, asking her to drop it. "You said you'd think about it."

He shrugged. "I have. The answer's no."

"What I want doesn't count?" Her voice grew shrill. "We're going to stay in that dump just because *you like it?*"

His place was one of the nicest in the area. It wasn't even close to being a "dump." She was just trying to get her own way, like the spoiled child she really was, but before he could say so, someone touched his shoulder.

"Hey, you."

Gail had left her table in the middle of the main dish to rescue him. He knew that as soon as her gaze cut to the waiter filling his glass on the other side.

"What's up?" he said.

"I have a toast I want to do tomorrow," she replied, "but I'd like to check with you to see if what I've got planned is okay. Do you have a minute?"

He glanced around the table at all the faces watching him and managed to conjure up what he hoped was a passable smile. "Of course." He dipped his head toward the rest of them. "Excuse us."

"Don't you want me to come?" Noelle asked. "I should probably know about it, if it's for the wedding."

"Um…" As Gail's eyes shifted to his fiancée, Kyle was willing to bet only he knew how much Gail disliked her.

"It's actually a surprise," Gail said. "For you! So…it would be better if you stayed here, okay?"

Obviously flattered, Noelle preened for Brandon as if this somehow proved her importance. Then Brandon turned to Kyle, and he might as well have said, "You're a fool if you go through with this," because it was written all over his face.

"What about your dinner?" Noelle's mother piped up.

"Can't you talk about the toast after you finish? You've hardly eaten a thing!"

Kyle put his napkin to the side of his plate. "I'm too excited to eat," he said, even though excitement played no role.

Eager to escape, he followed his friend out of the room and then out of the restaurant to a patio that was empty except for a few lingering diners who congregated around a table at one end.

"What's going on?" he murmured.

"That's what I'm wondering," she said, turning to confront him. "I've never seen you drink so much at someone else's rehearsal dinner—and this is your own!"

"I'm fine. I—"

She squeezed his arm. "Kyle, please. If the rest of the gang could've gotten out of that room without making it look too odd, they'd be here with me, trying to talk some sense into you."

He knew where this was going. "She's having my baby, Gail."

She pressed two fingers to each temple. "I know! I understand you feel responsible for that. And I admire how determined you are to do the right thing. But... I can't bear to see you unhappy. We all feel like we're attending your funeral instead of your wedding!"

The others must have shared the details of the past few weeks with her because he hadn't had the chance to say much since she hit town. She lived in L.A., was the only member of their group to have moved away and had been gone since starting her public relations firm over a decade ago.

Normally he loved it when she came home. She had the best stories about the movie stars she represented. At last count, she was working with several box office hits, including Hollywood heavyweight Simon O'Neal. But they hadn't had a chance to catch up on any of that this time around.

"It's just extra hard," he said. "With Olivia here."

"I've let my work take over my life, so I'm no expert on relationships," she said. "But…if you won't cancel this, you should at least put it off until you're more confident in your decision."

He laughed. "Are you kidding me? The wedding's tomorrow, Gail. There's no way I can change anything." If he backed out, he feared Noelle would make it impossible for him to ever see his child. As long as she got her way, she was tractable. But if he embarrassed or upset her, she'd fight him on everything.

"Kyle—"

"There you are."

They both turned to see Eve, who managed The Gold Nugget, the bed-and-breakfast owned by her family.

"Did you tell him what we think?" she asked Gail.

Gail shot Kyle a meaningful glance. "I told him."

Eve gave him a stern look. "So are you going to call it off?"

Once again, he searched for a better way to handle the situation but couldn't find one. "No. I'm going to be a father. Nothing can take precedence over that."

They were almost out of the room, almost free, when Kyle's father caught up with Brandon and pulled him off to one side. "So what are you doing to keep busy now that the cast is off?" he asked.

Olivia gritted her teeth at being detained. She couldn't wait to leave, to put the rehearsal dinner behind them and return to the peace of Brandon's secluded cabin. She needed to regroup, but she couldn't allow her eagerness to show. Everyone was watching her too closely, wondering if she'd been late in some passive-aggressive attempt to make her unhappiness known.

"Just working out every day, trying to get in shape for the season."

Brandon answered Bob's questions politely, but Olivia could tell he was purposely playing up the ski-bum image. He'd already told her that spring and summer were almost as busy as fall and winter. When she'd acted surprised, he'd explained that he had to meet with his sponsors, be available to film commercials and participate in photo shoots, most of which required travel to New York or Los Angeles. He also had to appear at various events, including children's camps and autographings, and increase his presence on social networking sites. Professional skiing was a business as much as a sport, and the stacks of paperwork on his desk—mostly contracts of one kind or another—seemed to prove it. So did the poster samples he'd been sent. One showed him dropping, seemingly without effort, down the face of an alarmingly steep mountain wearing an expensive brand of ski gear. Another captured his smiling face in a pair of Oakley goggles with ice crystals caught in the beard growth along his jaw.

He could've told his stepfather about these things. He could also have mentioned that he was making a tremendous amount of money. Although they hadn't spoken about that aspect, Olivia could tell it was true. But Brandon refused to vie for Bob's approval, and Olivia couldn't help but respect that.

"Can the leg take another season?" This question was spoken with apparent concern, but Olivia heard the subtext. Bob thought Brandon should hang up his skis and get serious about life.

She guessed Brandon interpreted his tone the same way and that made her sad. Brandon was one of the best skiers in the world, yet Bob treated him as if he hadn't accomplished anything. He seemed to think Brandon should be a horse breeder like him, or something else more "legitimate," like Kyle.

"Leg's getting stronger all the time," Brandon assured him. "It'll be fine."

Olivia imagined the pain Brandon must've suffered from that injury. Another daunting descent would require courage, but she had no doubt he'd do it. His daring made her smile.

She was still smiling when she realized that Brandon was watching her with a speculative expression. He had somehow guessed that her smile was related to him. His lips quirked slightly as if he was tempted to grin back at her, even though a grin wasn't appropriate to the conversation he was having with the disapproving Bob.

"Well, you've got several months before you go back to Europe. You want to learn what it's like to put in a hard day's work, come on out to the stables," Bob was saying. "We've got our hands full this year. Might be a great way to make some extra cash."

Brandon thanked him for the opportunity but begged off, saying he was going backpacking in Nicaragua. That didn't win him any points with Bob, but it made Olivia chuckle. Brandon knew just how to tweak his stepfather's nose without appearing to be impolite.

She turned to hide her mirth and came face-to-face with Brandon's mother. Paige had been talking to Nancy and Ham, who'd just left.

"I'm sorry about how things worked out for you with Kyle," Paige said, almost conspiratorially. "We miss seeing you at the house."

"I miss you, too," Olivia responded, feeling an odd tug for what used to be.

"Brandon's far more of a handful," she responded. "But it's *impossible* not to love him."

Another warning—in case Olivia wasn't already a believer. "We're just friends," she said, but Paige had already started a separate conversation with Cheyenne Christensen, whose mother was suffering from cancer. Olivia didn't think Paige had heard the rejoinder.

"What'd she say?" Brandon had finally broken away from his stepfather.

"She said she loves you."

Taking hold of her elbow, he guided her out. "Was she shaking her head as if it was against her will?" he asked with a laugh.

Olivia had been so eager to get to Brandon's house, but even before they walked through the door she knew she wouldn't be able to unwind the way she'd envisioned. They no longer had to cope with the myriad emotions swirling around the wedding party. Her father's disappointment with the way she'd handled the evening. Noelle's jealousy. Kyle's sullenness. The palpable concern of Kyle's friends. All of that suddenly seemed so distant...part of another lifetime. Instead they had to cope with each other, and that was almost more difficult, because every word they'd spoken on the drive back, every accidental touch as he let her in, felt like foreplay to a sexual encounter she knew she'd be foolish to allow.

It wasn't so unusual for a woman in her situation to want to jump into bed with the next handsome guy. Another relationship, one with a quick flame, could assuage the loneliness and ease the sting of rejection. But, oddly enough, this was different. It didn't feel as if Brandon would be a substitute for Kyle. It felt as if *Kyle* had always been a substitute for *Brandon!*

She was fairly certain the rebound experience wasn't supposed to work like that and couldn't figure out why her situation was so different. She and Kyle had only been apart for about four months, and thanks to his betrayal, those four months had been the most miserable of her life. That meant she still loved him, didn't it?

So how could she care more about being with Brandon than she did about being hurt and angry over Kyle's Big Mistake? What he'd done meant they could never be together again.

But that didn't seem to matter so much anymore.

"Would you like some herbal tea?" Brandon asked as she put her purse on the counter.

"What kind do you have?"

"A blend I found in Thailand." He reached into a cupboard to get the box, which he showed her. "You should try it."

She pictured them drinking tea together, talking into the night and eventually ending up in his bed. She wanted that exact scenario so badly she almost chose satisfaction over caution.

Maybe she would have, if not for his mother's words: *It's impossible not to love him.*

She had an inkling that might be true. She'd always been drawn to Brandon, but never more so than in the past two days. She figured it was better to get away while she could. So, after a brief hesitation, she shook her head. "No, thanks. I've got to get up early. I wouldn't want to oversleep the way I did today."

She halfway hoped he'd try to convince her to stay up with him. But he didn't. He told her he understood and added a polite good-night.

Forcing a smile to hide her disappointment, she nodded, but before she turned away, she caught sight of something that held her fast. When he moved, a grimace crossed his face and he shifted to take his weight off the leg he'd broken in his skiing accident.

"Are you okay?" She'd heard him say his doctors had been able to put him back together, that he was healed and already training for the next season.

His expression cleared instantly. He even exerted normal pressure on his leg while putting away the tea. "Of course. Why?"

"I just thought..." She stopped herself. He wouldn't be planning to walk across Nicaragua if his leg was causing him trouble. She must've imagined that he felt pain. Or maybe he'd just twisted it, which could make anyone wince. "Never mind," she said. "See you in the morning."

Ten

SOMETHING WOKE OLIVIA A FEW HOURS LATER. She wasn't sure what—until she listened carefully. Then she realized it was the TV. Although the house was otherwise dark and quiet, she could hear the drone of voices and wondered what Brandon was watching.

It had to be late.

She checked her phone on the nightstand. Sure enough, it was three-thirty.

She tried to go back to sleep. It wasn't any of her business what Brandon was doing. But after lying awake for another twenty minutes, she got up to see if he was okay. Maybe he needed someone to cover him and turn off the TV....

He had a television in his bedroom. She'd seen it when they'd napped in there before. But that wasn't where she found him. Perhaps he'd thought he'd keep her awake if he used that one. Or he liked the loft better, because he was there, asleep in a recliner.

He'd changed into an old T-shirt and a pair of basketball shorts. That he'd wanted to get comfortable didn't come as any surprise, but his leg in a brace and buried beneath half a dozen ice packs did.

"Oh, God." She hadn't imagined the flicker of pain on his face earlier. Although he'd masked it quickly, there was no doubt now. Besides the brace and the ice, she saw a bottle of prescription pain medication on the table beside him. Obviously his leg was still giving him a great deal of trouble.

Her presence and the two words she'd uttered were enough to wake him. He opened his eyes and looked at her. Then he tried to sit up and grab for the remote, but it had fallen out of his hands and onto the floor.

She retrieved it for him, but by then she'd already seen what he probably didn't want her to see. He'd been watching the footage of his own fall. From what she could tell, his support crew was a couple of hours into trying to get him help. She could see the dark speck he made on the mountain, hear the helicopter from which they were filming and the frantic discussion going on between the cameraman and the pilot. She could also feel the tremendous concern, the sheer urgency of the situation. According to the stopwatch on the screen, whoever held the camera had been filming for two hours and forty-four minutes, but rescuers hadn't yet been able to reach Brandon on that steep slope.

How long did he have to lie there, in a crumpled heap, waiting? She'd never thought about that. She'd seen the same clip as everyone else—the part where he lost control and tumbled like a rag doll down the cliff, hitting rocks and trees along the way—but not this extended version. This wasn't for public consumption. She hadn't even considered how hard it would be for emergency help to get to him or how it must've felt for him to lie there suffering. It was a miracle they'd been able to rescue him at all.

"Are you wondering how you survived?" she asked.

He scratched his head as he relaxed into his seat. "I'm wondering how I screwed up so badly, how I put myself in that position in the first place."

"You're good at what you do, Brandon, but...anyone can make a mistake. Especially on a slope like that."

He took the remote and snapped off the TV as if he couldn't bear to see any more, and she frowned as she studied his leg. "I hope you're really going backpacking across Nicaragua in two weeks because, if I remember right, I was invited to join you."

"I'll take you next summer." He shifted so he could remove the ice packs on his leg.

"So that invitation—it was just a fake?" Nudging his hands away, she stripped off the packs.

"Sort of. I have to leave town, but I won't be doing any backpacking."

"Where are you going?"

Obviously uncomfortable revealing this information, he cleared his throat. "There's a doctor in Europe. Thinks he can fix my leg." He motioned to a small refrigerator in the corner near the wet bar. "The packs go in there."

Apparently sitting up with his leg in a brace wasn't an unusual occurrence. "You need another operation?" she asked as she opened the fridge.

"At least one," he answered. "In order to regain full range of motion, it might take more."

"And you're not telling anyone because..."

Velcro rasped as he removed the brace and set it beside his chair. "I can't risk losing my sponsors. If they think I'll no longer be a force in the industry, they'll sign someone else."

"I see." She folded her arms. "And you haven't told anyone here at home because you're afraid we might leak the truth to the press?"

"Figured if I'm going to lie, I might as well be consistent among all my friends."

"What about your family?"

"What family?"

"Your mother loves you, Brandon."

"And she loves Bob and Kyle and will soon have a grand-baby. I'm a big boy. I've made my decision and I'll live with the results. There's no need to worry her."

How many times had his parents warned him not to take the risks he took? "That's gallant of you. I think. Except, if I was your mother, I'm pretty sure I'd want to know."

"I've considered that. But if I tell her, I essentially tell my stepfather, too, and I don't want to hear him say, 'I told you so.' I especially don't want to put up with having him act as if I deserve this."

She could understand his feelings. She'd heard Bob expound on the subject of Brandon and his choice of career before, when she was at the Housemans' with Kyle. At the time, she'd agreed with him. Now she felt...torn. She wanted Brandon to be happy, wanted to see him excel at what he loved. She just didn't want him to lose his life chasing the next adrenaline rush.

"I heard the condescending way he was talking to you tonight." Groggy from sleep and possibly the painkiller, he seemed a little out of it, so she helped him to his feet. "Let's get you to bed."

"My stepfather is a pain in the ass," he grumbled, but he settled an arm over her shoulders so he could take some of the pressure off his bad leg.

She decided it was better not to comment on that, since

she'd once been sympathetic to Bob's frustrations where Brandon was concerned. "Back to Nicaragua."

"Are you sorry the trip's off?"

"I'm wondering why you invited me to go at all."

"Wishful thinking."

An adventure like that had sounded nice. It still did.

"And I knew you'd refuse," he added.

He also knew it made a great cover, a believable cover, for the length of time he'd be gone. She had to hand it to him, he was good at hiding the problem. Until he'd winced earlier, she'd never even suspected. "And if I hadn't?" she asked.

"You could come to Europe with me, travel around while I recuperate—as long as you stop by to see me once in a while."

She could imagine how lonely that would be—to have an operation in a foreign county when all your friends and family thought you were having such a great time they didn't bother to write or call. But, assuming he wasn't any more serious about having her join him in Europe than he'd been about Nicaragua, she let that comment slide. "You made yourself climb these stairs. Maybe if you didn't push yourself so hard, your leg would have a chance to heal on its own."

"Stairs are the least of my worries. I'm going to have to do much more than climb up to my loft if I want to hang on to my career."

He was scared, she realized. Scared that everything he'd been was somehow gone. He had to recreate himself.

She could relate to that. She'd embraced moving to Sacramento, had been eager to have a year to herself to see what she could do to expand her professional aspirations. But then her life had taken the Kyle-Noelle detour and she'd been floundering ever since.

"Would it be so terrible to retire?" Finished navigating the stairs, she guided him into the hall. "Surely you can't expect to ski such dangerous runs forever."

"No, not forever. Just another two or three years. I'm not ready to give it up. When I go out, it'll be on *my* terms."

The conviction in his voice told her that even if his efforts didn't pay off, he'd put up one hell of a fight. "Then I believe you'll make a comeback. If not this season, the next."

He didn't respond. She feared he knew her encouragement was simply that—encouragement.

"For now you need to get some sleep," she said. "Or you won't convince anyone that leg has healed."

They'd reached his room. She hesitated at the entrance, expecting him to continue on himself, but, keeping one arm around her shoulders, he touched her face with the opposite hand.

When she looked up at him, he held her chin so that she couldn't look away as he murmured, "Come to bed with me."

Brandon knew Olivia had every reason in the world to say no. She'd just been through a terrible breakup. She probably wasn't over Kyle. The last thing she needed was to make love with a man who'd soon be leaving, most likely for months. At the moment, he had no clue where his life was going, whether he'd ever ski again, what he'd do if his comeback turned out to be a bust.

But he couldn't help trying to capture and hold on to the special quality that made her so difficult to forget.

"Brandon—"

At the distress in her voice, he released her. He wouldn't pressure her, didn't want her to regret giving in once it was all over. "Never mind, honey. I know it's been a hell of a year for you." Figuring she'd hurry to her own room, he limped to the bed and dropped onto the mattress. His damn leg was aching again. Some days were worse than others. Tonight, the pain had gotten so bad he thought it might drive him insane.

But then she was there with her clothes off, and the pain disappeared beneath a flood of euphoria.

Olivia supposed she'd known this was coming. Brandon had always been different from the other boys and, as an adult, he was different from the other men she knew, too. So even though a lot had changed in recent months, nothing had *really* changed. Meeting him again had shown her that as much as she'd cared about Kyle, she'd already accepted that their romantic relationship was over. She'd gotten further beyond the heartbreak of it than she'd dreamed.

"That's it, honey," Brandon whispered as she slid her hands up under his T-shirt to run her fingers over the ridge of his pectoral muscles, his nipples, the sprinkling of soft hair that covered his chest. She liked that he was encouraging her to cast her inhibitions aside, to touch and taste him as eagerly as he was touching and tasting her. They hadn't even bothered to turn off the lights. Being able to see his expressions and reactions added a whole other dimension.

When her bare skin first came into contact with his, he sucked air between his teeth and held her still as if he needed a moment to recover. "You've got me so excited I can hardly breathe," he whispered hoarsely.

She loved the power that knowledge gave her. He probably realized she would or he wouldn't have made the admission. He was generous that way, and she appreciated it. "There's just one problem…"

He gazed up at her. "What is it?"

"I don't want to hurt your leg."

Even the guttural sound of his laugh made her happy. "I

don't want you to worry about that," he said. "All I can feel is how badly I want you. Kiss me."

When her mouth met his, Olivia groaned. It felt as if she'd been waiting for this day since the last time he'd kissed her, in high school. Closing her eyes, she parted her lips and welcomed his tongue in her mouth, enjoying the fact that she was in control and he didn't seem to mind.

"You kiss even better than you feel," he told her.

"Good. Because I want to kiss you again."

He rolled her beneath him as the kiss grew wetter and more heated. Then, anchoring her hands to the mattress above her head, he lowered his head.

Olivia gasped when his mouth closed over her breast. She was so wound up, so desperate to release the building tension, she wanted to rake her nails down his back. But she could only arch into him because he was still restraining her hands.

"Ah, you like that?" he murmured as his tongue made arousing circles.

She liked *him.* She almost said so—almost blurted out that these sensations would be meaningless to her if he were anyone else. But she knew that would make him uncomfortable. *It's impossible not to love him,* his mother had said. That was true—but it was equally true that he'd never commit.

He spent considerable time on her other breast, the sensitive skin on the inside of her arms and her neck before releasing her wrists. Then she was free to touch him wherever she wanted, and she took full advantage of it—until his mouth returned to hers and his fingers found the part of her that wanted him most.

"Brandon…" Her voice caught on his name.

He was so engrossed it took him a second to respond. "What, sweetheart?"

He sounded dazed. She knew she probably sounded the

same. Or maybe she sounded desperate. She was certainly *feeling* desperate, craved nothing more than the completion he promised.

"Do you have birth control?" she asked. "Because I... I have nothing."

"I bought some condoms this morning." His mouth was at her breast again but his fingers...they were torturing her even more sweetly.

"This morning?" she repeated.

He lifted his head long enough to grin at her. "I was thinking positive."

She cocked an eyebrow at him. "Oh, you were."

"Couldn't help hoping."

Catching handfuls of his hair, she laughed as he settled himself between her legs.

"Do it now," she whispered.

He kissed her tenderly. "I've waited a long time for this."

She liked that they'd left the lights on, that she could see him. He was male beauty and athletic grace. "God, I love—"

He hesitated. "What?" he whispered when she stopped.

She'd been about to say, "Everything about you." Those exact words almost came out despite her efforts to hold them back, but she managed a more acceptable substitution. "The way you make love."

He stared down at her. "Thank you. I love the way you make love, too."

That was nice of him, she thought. He sounded so sincere. Then she locked her legs around his hips, drawing him as deep as possible.

Eleven

BRANDON REACHED FOR OLIVIA BEFORE HE even opened his eyes, but she was no longer in his bed. His hands met with cool, crisp sheets instead. Only a hint of her perfume remained.

He rolled toward the scent, breathing it in, remembering. Then he shoved himself up on his elbows to listen.

Silence. She wasn't showering. She wasn't moving around in the kitchen.

She was gone from more than just his bed.

"Damn," he muttered, disappointed. But at least his leg wasn't painful. The terrible ache that was becoming such a part of his life had disappeared as completely as Olivia had. Of course, given how often they'd made love in the past three or four hours, he had too many biochemicals flowing through his bloodstream to feel anything unpleasant. Still, these days he checked for pain every time he woke up because he never knew when just walking was going to be a battle.

Today was a good day. He was exhausted after being up so much of the night, but it was the kind of exhaustion that comes with complete satisfaction. The only thing better would to be to feel her bare skin under his hands one more time.

He almost drifted back to sleep. But then he began to wonder if she was gone until she ran some errands, until after the wedding, or for good.

Dragging himself out of bed, he tested his leg to see if it would complain when he put pressure on it, breathed a sigh of relief when it didn't and went to check the other bedroom.

"Already?" he grumbled when he saw it.

She'd taken her suitcase with her.

"Are you really with Kyle's brother?" Nancy asked.

Olivia had been so busy this morning pulling together the last-minute details of the wedding that she'd managed to avoid spending any time alone with her mother or her sister. To get everything done, she'd had to stay focused. When Nancy and Noelle stopped for lunch, Olivia grabbed a sandwich and moved gratefully on without them to get the right colored candy for the reception.

Fortunately the jars she'd ordered online had arrived. That meant she didn't have to use the less attractive ones she'd bought yesterday. But now that the chairs, tables and decorations were in place, and the caterers, minister and disc jockey were primed and ready, she only had to make sure everyone was prepared for the photographer at three. So she and her mother were getting a manicure while Noelle was having her hair curled and stacked in an arrangement that could've been featured in *Bride Magazine*.

"No. Brandon and I are just friends," she said, pretending to be preoccupied with her nails so she wouldn't have to look up.

"You're staying with him," her mother pointed out. "You're staying with him instead of us."

The nail tech left to see to a walk-in customer. Olivia wished she'd come back. "He has an extra room, Mom."

"You're saying you slept in it last night?"

Olivia wished she could insist she had. She *should've* stayed in her own bed. She'd been a fool to get up and go find him, a fool to allow herself to get in so far over her head.

Did she want to be mooning over Kyle's stepbrother for the rest of her life?

Definitely not—but she had a feeling it might go that way. She'd never had such a strong reaction to any man. Since they'd been together, she hadn't been able to think of anything besides the tender way he'd held her and the feel of his mouth on hers—not to mention the many intimate places he'd put his hands.

She'd come to Whiskey Creek brokenhearted over Kyle and would be leaving brokenhearted over Brandon. That shouldn't have been possible in such a short time. But it was her own fault. She hadn't given herself a chance to recover from Kyle before taking on an even bigger threat to her peace of mind.

"More or less," she muttered when her mother leaned forward, demanding an answer to where she'd slept.

"More or less?" Nancy echoed. "Oh, no! Noelle was right. She told me the two of you are sleeping together, but I didn't want to believe it. I don't know what's wrong with you girls. First her, and now you! You'll do anything to hurt each other."

"What's happened between Brandon and me has nothing to do with her or Kyle. We aren't trying to hurt anyone."

"Then why are you getting involved with someone so close to both of them?"

"Brandon has never been close to Noelle. He hasn't even been close to Kyle. And I'm not 'getting involved' with him. I admit things got out of hand this weekend. I… I haven't been myself, wasn't prepared to deal with…temptation." *Or not in such a potent form,* she added silently. "It's not every day that your sister gets pregnant by the man you thought you'd marry yourself," she went on. "Don't you think that could throw a girl off track?"

Her mother winced, but Olivia could see the nail tech finishing with the other client and wanted to wrap up the conversation before she returned.

"Anyway, it's over," she continued. "I'm heading home after the wedding and trying to forget this weekend ever happened."

"So it's not an ongoing relationship."

She pasted a pleasant expression on her face because the nail tech was walking toward them. "Of course not. Brandon's going backpacking across Nicaragua in two weeks. Then he's got the ski season. Who knows when he'll be back in Whiskey Creek? And I've already moved my business to Sacramento, just like I planned." A plan that had sounded so ideal in the beginning but had, in the end, cost her so much.

The worry lines on her mother's face softened. "That's a relief."

"Why would it matter to you?" Olivia asked.

"Our lives are complicated enough at the moment. I don't like what Noelle has done, but I can't change it, either. At least I know Kyle will make a good husband. That gives me hope that we can all get past the rough start. I'm not sure I'm convinced of Brandon's integrity."

"Maybe he has more integrity than you think."

Her mother had no chance to reply because Noelle suddenly appeared from the other side of the salon. "Well?"

Even Olivia had to admit she looked beautiful. "Kyle will love it," she said.

★ ★ ★

Pictures seemed to take forever. Noelle had decreed that Kyle was not to see her before the ceremony, so the groom and his men were sequestered in a different area of the mansion than the bride and her ladies. Callie Vanetta, one of Kyle's best friends and part of the group he'd grown up with, owned a photography studio on Sutter Street, near the center of town, and was handling the pictures like the pro she was. First, she photographed Kyle, his best man and other groomsmen while Noelle did her makeup. Then Callie came to the bridal suite, where she snapped shots of Noelle getting ready with her maid of honor and bridesmaids.

Feeling more like a robot than a human being, Olivia smiled and nodded and offered her fair share of compliments. They toasted the wedding with delicate flutes of champagne, and took pictures of the process. They admired Noelle's veil and jewelry and hair, and took pictures of that. They hugged and laughed and watched Noelle gaze into a giant mirror, and took even more pictures.

As soon as possible, Olivia faded into the background. She wanted this part, which required so much pretending, to be over. But she didn't want the next part—the wedding—to begin. Then she'd have to face Brandon. Although she'd been able to avoid him so far, that wouldn't be the case much longer.

"Olivia, I…"

Olivia turned from the window overlooking the patio where the ceremony would take place to see Callie standing at her elbow.

"I just… I wanted to say I'm sorry," she whispered. "For… what's happened."

Olivia managed a brief smile, but then Noelle, who'd gone into the bathroom, returned and asked if they should take a picture of her by the window, looking down at the altar below.

"Good idea." Olivia squeezed Callie's arm as she moved past, to let her know she was okay. But she felt a little guilty accepting Callie's sympathy, or anyone else's. She knew Callie would be surprised to learn she wasn't brooding over Kyle.

Brandon didn't get to escort Olivia. Noah Rackham was her partner and had been from the beginning. But she was right in front of him. He couldn't take his eyes off her. He kept hoping she'd turn and acknowledge him in some way, maybe give him a smile that indicated she'd enjoyed last night as much as he had. But ever since she'd entered the room she'd kept her eyes averted and her attention on what was going on around them—on everything *but* him. He hoped it was because she was under pressure to make sure this wedding was a success.

The music swelled as Kyle, followed by the first of the groomsmen and bridesmaids, walked down the aisle. Riley and Olivia were after Eve and Baxter, two more of Kyle's friends. Brandon watched as they moved into the dazzling sunshine, and waited several beats before stepping "on deck" with Cheyenne Christensen.

"I can't believe he's going through with this," his partner muttered as she slipped a hand through the crook of his arm.

Her words surprised him. Kyle's friends were so loyal to him that they generally ignored Brandon when he was at home.

"What did you say?" he asked.

She turned distressed eyes on him. "I feel like someone should stop the wedding."

"And that someone should be..."

"How about you?" she responded, but she grinned when she said it and he couldn't help chuckling.

"It's too late to save him now," he said.

She ducked her head, presumably so that the guests twisting around in their seats, trying to catch a glimpse of the rest of the wedding party, wouldn't see her disapproval. "I know." Then they stepped into the sunlight, too, and pandered to the crowd and Callie's camera as they approached the minister, where they separated.

Brandon thought he saw Olivia looking at him as he released Cheyenne. He smiled to see if he could get her to smile back, but she glanced away so quickly he wasn't sure she'd really seen him. He caught Kyle glaring at him a second later so he moved on without missing a beat.

Once the line was assembled, the traditional wedding march blasted from the speakers and Noelle appeared on her father's arm. As she glided toward her waiting groom, Brandon thought maybe he *should* speak up. He would have, if he'd believed it might make a difference.

But Kyle wouldn't thank him for it. His stepbrother was determined to go to the guillotine, so Brandon kept his mouth shut as the two repeated their vows, kissed and exchanged rings.

The congratulations came next but, in Brandon's opinion, they were rather subdued. *Does anyone think this marriage has a chance?*

Kyle held his bride's hand, but his gaze strayed almost immediately to Olivia, who seemed determined not to look in his direction, either.

As soon as Callie Vanetta had finished taking pictures now that the men and women were together, Brandon made his way over to Olivia. "Everything's working out perfectly," he said. "You've done a great job."

When she turned to face him, he again tried to get a read on what she was feeling. But she didn't give him the opportunity. "Thanks," she said and moved away.

Olivia knew people were keeping a close eye on her, wondering if it was breaking her heart to see Kyle marry her sister. She could hear them murmuring. "Poor thing... Can you believe he went through with it?" and "She even planned the whole wedding!"

She did her best to bear up under the scrutiny. Their pity humiliated her. But she'd expected as much and couldn't focus on it. Not with Brandon in the room. It was all she could do not to head straight over to him, especially since he seemed so confused by her withdrawal. He'd tried, several times, to approach her.

He was kind to show his support. She appreciated his attempts to make this god-awful night a bit better. But she feared that if she spent even two seconds in his company he'd realize he'd been right all along—she wasn't cut out for casual sex. She couldn't say how it had happened, but she'd somehow lost a piece of her heart in that encounter, which was definitely information she didn't want him to have.

So she avoided him at all costs.

"Are you seeing Brandon?"

Cheyenne stood at the candy table next to her. Olivia had been so busy refilling the jars she hadn't noticed her. "No. Of course not." She cleared her throat. "We're just friends."

"Does *he* know that?"

She swallowed. "Pardon?"

"I've never seen him look at a friend the way he looks at you."

Following Cheyenne's line of sight, she saw Brandon leaning against the wall with a drink in one hand. He had a frown on his face and that didn't change when their eyes met.

She nodded politely, but this time *he* didn't respond. "He's been very...supportive," she said, forcing herself to turn away.

"I've always thought he's not as bad as people make him sound," Cheyenne said. "A lot of that criticism stems from jealousy, don't you agree? People have a hard time accepting someone who soars so high. Someone who dares to break all the rules."

Olivia wondered why Brandon was on his feet and wished he'd sit down and give his leg a rest. "It's great how much he enjoys the things he loves."

"I think he'd like to enjoy you, too." Her lips curved in a conspirator's grin, but before Olivia could say anything, the toasts started and Cheyenne moved back to her table.

The best man, Noah Rackham, spoke first. He talked about the length of his friendship with Kyle and how Kyle's marriage would make their group of friends larger.

Olivia flinched at that. She'd always thought *she'd* be the next official member of their clique. Then Nancy got up—Ham wasn't the type—and told her new son-in-law how excited she was to have him as part of the family. She related a cute story about Kyle coming to her rescue once when her car wouldn't start. Everyone smiled because it was endearing, and they'd expect nothing less from Kyle, but Nancy didn't add that he'd done it when he was *her* boyfriend, not Noelle's.

Kyle's father got up after Nancy and said he'd always been able to depend on Kyle and how proud of him he was.

As the toasts wore on, Olivia began to see a pattern. Everyone had praise for Kyle, but no one had much to say about Noelle.

Determined to be big enough to overlook the circumstances that had brought them to this point, Olivia retrieved her glass from the dessert table, where she'd left it when she restocked the candy, and lifted it high. "I'd also like to offer a toast."

She regretted her impulsiveness when everyone looked at her. A sudden hush swept through the room, attaching more weight to what she was about to say than she wanted. She got the impression that there were people who hoped to see her break down in public, or perhaps berate her sister as Noelle deserved. But Olivia merely wanted everyone to know that she supported the union and was no longer bitter about how this wedding had come to pass.

Stubbornly maintaining a congenial smile, she turned toward the new couple. She wished she could extol her sister's many virtues, but...she couldn't. So she settled for a few simple words to show everyone that she harbored no animosity. "To the bride and groom. I wish you health, happiness, prosperity and...abiding love."

Although everyone else applauded, the despair on Kyle's face made it difficult to drink to her own toast. His expression told her he knew what her words really meant. She'd cut him loose. She'd stopped carrying a torch for him. She thought Noelle would appreciate that, but her sister seemed as crestfallen as Kyle. Maybe, now that Olivia no longer wanted Kyle, Noelle wasn't sure she wanted him, either. Noelle couldn't even console herself with the fact that she'd soon be living in a mansion. From Noelle's grumblings while they were at the salon earlier, Kyle hadn't relented and agreed to build her the house of her dreams.

A few others offered toasts, all of them Kyle's friends, except for Noelle's maid of honor. Then the dancing started.

Breathing a sigh of relief that the night was nearly over, Olivia put down her glass and automatically glanced over to where she'd last seen Brandon. But he wasn't there anymore. After a quick search, she caught sight of him, recognized his blond head at the door.

He was leaving.

Twelve

"BRANDON."

Brandon refused to turn when Olivia called his name. He kept walking through the gardens even when she hurried after him and grabbed his hand.

"Brandon, wait. I—"

"What?" he snapped, stopping so suddenly that she had to back up to avoid running into him. "What could you possibly have to say to me after treating me like I don't exist?"

Taken aback by the depth of his anger, she stared at him. She didn't know what to say, how to explain. Everything that came to her was wrong. Or far beyond what she should feel after so short a time.

"I... I'm sorry," she mumbled and turned before he could see the tears in her eyes. But this time he came after her. He reached her before she could enter the building. And she was pretty sure he cursed when he kissed her.

Brandon had no idea what had happened at the wedding. If Olivia had been confused, or hurt, or embarrassed. But she was in his arms now and that took the sting away, made it easy to forgive her, to chalk her remoteness up to everything she'd been through in the past few months. When her lips gave way beneath his, allowing him to taste the warm wetness of her mouth, he couldn't even remember why he'd been mad.

"There you are," he breathed as her arms circled his neck. "I've missed you."

She smiled against his mouth. "I've missed you, too."

It didn't matter that it had only been a day. He meant what he'd said, and he could tell she did, too. Eager to take anything she was willing to give him, he groaned as she ground her hips against his. He knew what she wanted. He wanted the same thing. But they couldn't risk being seen, couldn't be caught making out like this.

It would've made more sense to take her home, but he was rattled enough by her earlier behavior to fear she'd change her mind again if he waited. So he pulled her into the shelter of some trees, where they had a degree of privacy.

"You're all I've thought about," he admitted, framing her face with his hands.

"Funny you should say that. You're all I've thought about, too," she said, and then they were kissing again and straining to get closer and she started to remove his belt.

Olivia knew what she was doing was crazy. She'd never behaved like this before—but she'd never felt like this before, either, never wanted a man as she wanted Brandon. Instead of stopping him when he slipped a hand inside her dress, she encouraged him, shifting so he could reach what he wanted to touch. Only the fear that what they were doing might cause him to injure his leg gave her pause.

"Don't hurt yourself," she murmured.

"I'm fine," he whispered. "All I need is you."

"But your leg…"

"I'm being careful," he said, but he didn't seem to be keeping that promise when he put on a condom and lifted her up against the building.

It was over almost as fast as it had begun. Sheer excitement crashed into frantic need for an incredible few minutes, obliterating every bit of pent-up longing. She could hear the music, smell the roses, but all she could feel was Brandon moving inside her.

Afterward, his heart pounded hard and fast beneath her ear and his chest rose and fell as he struggled to catch his breath.

"I've never done it at a wedding before," he told her with a chuckle.

She tilted her head back to look up at him. "I've never done it *anywhere* in public."

Lowering her gently to the ground, he kissed her temple. "I'm a bad influence."

"No. It was my fault as much as yours."

He straightened his clothes while she straightened hers. Then he offered her his hand. "Let's get out of here, go home."

She shook her head.

"Do you have to stay for a while? I hope not. I want more of you."

"I'm sorry, but—" she bit her lip "—this is goodbye, Brandon. I'm not going back to your place."

His eyebrows drew together. "What are you talking about?"

He wasn't used to being denied. But she knew it was better to leave him wanting more. To end on a positive memory.…

"I've got my life and you've got yours. I don't even live here."

"So? You're not far. Why not enjoy each other for as long as we can?"

She wanted to walk away while she still had the strength to do it with some dignity. It was important to her self-esteem. He was leaving the country in two weeks, anyway. "Because you were right."

"About..."

"I'm not capable of casual."

He lifted her chin with one finger. "What if—" he started but another voice interrupted.

"Olivia? Olivia!"

Noelle was looking for her.

"Where are you?" her sister cried.

"Damn," she whispered and began to step out of the trees, but he tugged her back. "I'm not ready to let you go."

She wasn't sure if he was referring to this moment or their relationship in general. But it didn't matter either way. "It'll be easier now than later," she said. Then she slipped out.

Hoping to *rejoin* the wedding without bringing attention to herself, Olivia drew a deep breath and smoothed her hair. But Noelle saw her as soon as she entered the room and came straight for her.

"Where have you *been?*" her sister demanded. "Everyone's been asking about you. Grandma and Grandpa are tired. They want to say goodbye."

Olivia struggled to appear serene, but the intensity of what she'd just experienced had left her shaken. "Outside, getting some fresh air."

Her sister's eyes narrowed. Had she noticed Olivia's flushed face and Brandon's recent departure and put the two together? "Doing what?"

"Nothing." At the suspicion in Noelle's voice, she couldn't help turning to see if Brandon was behind her, but he wasn't.

Noelle raised one hand to pluck a leaf from her hair. "At my wedding, Olivia? At my wedding?"

Olivia told herself to cross the room and say goodbye to her grandparents and everyone else. But she couldn't bring herself to stay another second. She'd given this weekend all she had. And still she felt as though she'd failed more than she'd succeeded. "I'm leaving," she said. "I hope you enjoy your honeymoon."

"Wait! Who's going to clean up?" Noelle called, but Olivia ignored her. She walked faster and faster until she was outside, running. Her parents and their friends could clean up. Kyle's friends could help. She'd done all she could.

When she reached her car, she got in, locked the doors and peeled out of the lot.

It wasn't until she was almost at her apartment that she realized she'd received a text nearly half an hour earlier. It was from Brandon: I wish you'd change your mind.

Olivia never came back. And she didn't call him. As one day led to the next the week after the wedding, Brandon held out hope that she might relent and see him. He knew what they'd shared was special. Wondered how she could hold out, given the strength of their attraction.

But he didn't hear from her. He told himself to move on without her. He'd known all along that he wasn't the kind of man she needed. He was too caught up in his career. And right now he had a battle of epic proportions on his hands if he expected to get back on a pair of skis. He didn't need to be involved with a woman who could distract him the way she could.

Everything he told himself was logical and true, but that didn't make her any easier to forget.

By Wednesday, he broke down and called her. She didn't pick up, but he left a message on her voice mail. "Call me. This is nuts. I want you so much I can't think straight."

On Thursday, he texted her twice. Are you really going to do this to me? and I smell you, taste you every time I close my eyes.

He was dying to see her again and he made no effort to hide it. But that didn't seem to matter. Although he tried calling her one last time, he received no reply.

Friday, when his parents invited him to dinner, he accepted immediately and was grateful for the diversion—until Kyle and Noelle showed up. They must've returned early. They were supposed to be on their honeymoon until Sunday night.

"Did you have a wonderful time?" his mother gushed as Bob let them in.

"It was—" Noelle sent Kyle a sulky look "—fine."

"Fine?" Paige blinked in confusion. "You went to Napa Valley. There isn't a more beautiful place on earth."

Noelle lifted her nose in the air. "There was nothing wrong with the scenery. It was Kyle. He insisted on working the whole time we were gone."

"I have a company to run," he explained. "I had to take a few calls. Nothing big."

"Maybe it wasn't big to you." Noelle regarded Brandon with an accusatory air, but he had no idea how she could blame him for anything. "You weren't the one who was always waiting," she snapped at Kyle.

Kyle seemed embarrassed, which was, no doubt, Noelle's intent. "I gave you plenty of attention," he grumbled, and surprised Brandon by appearing relieved to see him. "How's the leg?"

Brandon hadn't heard that question in a while. Only Olivia knew he was still having problems with it. But the pain it caused him had been getting harder and harder to hide. "Fine. It's been fine since I got the cast off."

Fortunately Kyle didn't question that. "Great. When do you go to Nicaragua?"

Paige drew Noelle into the kitchen while Brandon answered. "Next Friday."

Kyle shot a look at his father, who was turning off the TV. "I wish I could go with you," he said in a low voice, intended only for Brandon.

Brandon scowled at him. "Damn it, Kyle."

He didn't say anything. He just pinched the bridge of his nose as if the past week had been one of the hardest he'd ever endured.

"I wish you weren't so damn noble," Brandon muttered.

"It wasn't my nobility that got me into this mess."

Brandon chuckled as Bob came back toward them.

"What?" He looked between them.

Kyle answered. "Nothing," he said, but he didn't seem bothered that his father could overhear when he asked, "How's Olivia?"

An image of her, naked beneath him, popped into Brandon's mind, making the craving he felt for her that much worse. "I wouldn't know."

Kyle studied him for a moment. "If you care about her, don't let her go." He sounded jealous but resigned to the idea. "She's crazy about you. I could tell."

Brandon was so shocked that Kyle would encourage him, he couldn't decide how to respond. Fortunately his mother saved him the trouble by entering the room, carrying a hot casserole. Noelle was right behind her with some rolls.

"Come on over and sit down," she said. "Dinner's served."

Olivia had almost called Brandon a million times. She wanted to respond to his messages, to see him again. But she knew that if he was leaving in a week there was no point.

He'd go on his way and forget about her. She didn't need to grow even more attached to him.

But it had been a long, lonely week since the wedding. It didn't help that Kyle texted her on Sunday: Brandon seemed lost at dinner Friday.

There was no context to let her decipher his meaning or his intent. She planned to ignore it but ultimately wrote back: What does that have to do with me?

Everything, came the reply.

Aren't you supposed to be on your honeymoon? she typed.

Work brought me back early.

A few seconds later, he added a Thank God that almost made her laugh. She knew, in a way no one else probably did, what he was talking about. Noelle was not an easy person to take for long periods of time.

I refuse to feel sorry for you, she texted back.

He followed up with a wink and that brought a smile to her lips. "Poor Kyle." She was just glad she hadn't heard from her sister. She was also glad that it was wedding season and she'd signed three new clients. The added work, along with trying to hang some pictures and decorate her apartment, was keeping her busy, giving her a good excuse not to drive back to Whiskey Creek—even though, when she stopped working for five seconds, that was exactly where her heart wanted to take her.

Thirteen

KYLE, OF ALL PEOPLE, CALLED TO SAY GOODBYE. "Do you have everything? Do you need a ride to the airport?" he asked.

Brandon glanced at the luggage he'd packed. He'd hired a car to take him to Sacramento. He was meeting his agent, Scott Jones, for lunch before heading to the airport. To pay a driver to come all the way out to Whiskey Creek was expensive, but he couldn't let any of his friends or family see that he wasn't taking a backpack.

"I'm covered," he replied. "Thanks, though."

"Your plane leaves at five?"

He grimaced as he shifted. His leg was giving him so much trouble today. It was getting worse all the time. "Five-thirty."

After this small talk, there was a slight pause. "Okay. Have a nice trip."

Brandon stopped Kyle before he could hang up. "You thought you'd offer me a ride because…"

"When she was here for the wedding, Olivia told me something I've decided might be true."

He hadn't realized Olivia and Kyle had had much chance to talk, or were even on speaking terms. That toast at the wedding had been so generous it had blown Brandon away. He couldn't imagine many other women being able to forgive so quickly that they could wish a sister well despite the hurt she'd caused. "What did Olivia say?"

"That I should try talking to you now and then. That I might be missing out on having a great brother."

A fresh pang of longing shot through Brandon. He hadn't talked to Olivia since their encounter in the gardens during the wedding, but his desire to hear her voice hadn't diminished. If anything it had grown stronger. "She did?"

"I told you how much she admires you."

"I remember. I'm still not sure why you bothered to do that."

"I missed out. Doesn't mean you have to," he said and hung up.

Brandon stared at his phone. He wanted to call Olivia one more time, to at least be able to say goodbye. But a honk let him know the car had arrived. He had to get his luggage outside or he'd be late for lunch, which could potentially make him late for the airport.

Today Brandon was leaving for Europe and his surgery. Olivia had received a text from him a few days ago telling her he'd like to stop in to say goodbye. She wanted to say goodbye to him, too, but she knew it would be too difficult to see him again, knowing what lay ahead. She was worried about his leg, about his career, about his being in Europe on his own for weeks, maybe months, while he recuperated. She hated that he hadn't told anyone else what he was doing. That meant even his parents wouldn't be there to support him. As far as they were concerned, he was off on another grand adventure. If anything, they felt mildly annoyed that he didn't seem to be growing up.

She sighed as she clicked on one YouTube clip of him after another. He was truly an impressive skier. She loved watching him plunge down those treacherous mountains. He seemed able to conquer the impossible. There was an inherent thrill in seeing someone who mattered so much to her do something so magical. But she also cringed with each new descent. She knew he was addicted to the adrenaline and all the benefits the sport brought him, and if he continued, he might not survive.

Her phone rang just as she was trying to make herself go to the office. She had work to do, work that was piling up because she couldn't seem to quit thinking about Brandon.

For a split second, she thought maybe it was him on the phone. But it wasn't. He'd stopped calling a few days ago. This was Noelle. Her sister was trying to reach her for the first time since the wedding.

Unable to deal with Noelle on this of all days, she set her phone aside. But a minute later, she heard the buzz of an incoming text.

"What do you want?" she grumbled and checked her messages.

Brandon's off on his Nicaragua trip for God knows how long. He probably won't even remember your name when he gets back, her sister had written.

Noelle couldn't seem to help herself. She just had to be spiteful.

Olivia nearly responded with some sarcastic remark about the difficulty of marriage and good luck getting Kyle to give her that house in town—or earning Kyle's love, for that matter. But her mother had told her Noelle was having a tough time adjusting to married life. Apparently stealing Kyle hadn't brought her the happiness she'd thought it would. So, instead of unleashing all the hurtful things she was dying to say, Olivia wrote, I wish Brandon the best.

Then she went to get showered. Noelle was right on one account. Brandon would forget her soon enough.

Lunch with Scott was tense. His agent was the only one, besides Olivia, who knew that Brandon's leg wasn't healing properly, the one who'd arranged the operation to fix it. He had a vested interest in seeing Brandon succeed, so he clearly wasn't happy when Brandon came toward him, unable to walk without a slight limp.

"It's worse?" he said.

Some days, like today, the pain was so bad Brandon almost couldn't tolerate it. "A lot worse." He hated to hear himself say that, but there it was.

Scott cursed, looked away, then forced a smile. "Dr. Shapiro will take care of you. He's the best leg man in the world. A real miracle-worker."

Brandon nodded and listened as Scott detailed what they'd accomplish next season. Neither one of them admitted that, if the operation didn't work, his career was finished. It wasn't a possibility they could even acknowledge.

By the time the waitress brought the check, Brandon was eager for lunch to be over. He'd thought seeing Scott would be helpful, motivating, encouraging, but he found that their visit had depressed him instead. It was the worry in Scott's eyes.

"When do you have to be at the airport?" Scott asked.

Brandon glanced at his watch. "Half an hour. We'd better go."

They rode in silence. There wasn't much more to say. Brandon had a rough few weeks ahead of him, with uncertainty his only companion.

When they arrived, Scott insisted on parking and taking Brandon's luggage. That in itself told Brandon his agent was deeply concerned. How many times had Scott brought him here and dropped him at the curb?

Too many to count. But Brandon didn't argue. He figured he'd be on his own all too soon.

They were in line at the ticket counter when he received a text from Olivia. He couldn't believe she'd finally responded.

What she'd written came as an even bigger surprise: Before you go, I just want you to know that I've never felt about anyone else the way I feel about you. You own my heart, Brandon. I think you have since prom. So please, be safe. I want to see you on the slopes next fall.

"What is it?" Although Scott had been getting anxious to leave—making calls and answering texts while they waited—he was watching Brandon now, too curious to be distracted by the passing time.

"A friend," he replied, but he realized almost as soon as those words came out of his mouth that she was much more than a friend. He'd never felt about anyone else the way he felt about her, either.

"I can help you here, sir." The gal at the ticket counter smiled, expecting him to approach. But he couldn't move.

"Brandon?" Scott had already dragged his luggage to the scale.

"I can't do this," he said, remaining right where he was.

Scott's eyes nearly popped out of his head. "*What?* Are you crazy?"

The reason behind the fear that had been gripping his stomach for days suddenly became clear. It wasn't only his career he was afraid of losing. "I have to see someone."

"I have no idea what you're talking about," Scott said. "See who?"

Waving the family behind him to the counter in his place, Brandon stepped out of line.

His shocked agent hurried over with his bags. "What are you doing?" he whispered. "If you miss this plane, you'll miss your operation. And I'm not sure when we'll be able to reschedule. This doctor is booked. Do you hear me? He's world-famous."

"I can't leave her," he said simply.

"Can't leave *who,* for crying out loud?" Scott jerked on his tie, trying to loosen it. "You have to get on this plane! Do you want to ski next season or not?"

He wanted to ski. But that was no longer *all* he wanted. "Drive me back to Sacramento or I'll take a cab," he said and wrenched his suitcase from Scott's hand.

Olivia felt much better after texting Brandon. She knew she'd probably never see him again—unless it was to bump into him occasionally while visiting Whiskey Creek. But at least she'd finally had the guts to be honest with him about her feelings. Somehow that seemed important, whether he wanted to hear what she had to say or not. It wasn't as if she expected anything in return. She'd spoken the truth so he would know how hard she'd be praying for his health and well-being while he was gone. That was all. He needed someone to know, someone to care.

Now she'd given him that.

"Are you okay?"

She had a prospective bride in her office, looking at samples of table linens. "Of course. Why?"

The girl cocked her head. "You've got tears in your eyes."

Olivia dabbed at the corners. "I was just thinking of a friend."

"Must be a close friend."

She nodded. As brief as her time with Brandon had been, she felt closer to him than anyone else.

She'd finished the appointment and was packing her briefcase with swatches and magazines—she had to meet another bride at River City Resort Club & Spa tomorrow morning—when she heard the buzzer that indicated someone had walked into the small anteroom outside her office. She didn't have any employees, couldn't afford payroll, so she called out, "Welcome to Weddings by Olivia. I'll be right there."

"Could you hurry?" came the response. "I've got a plane to catch."

Brandon! Olivia's heart jumped into her throat as she scrambled around her desk.

When she reached the reception area, she saw him standing just inside the door with an exasperated-looking man wearing what appeared to be an expensive suit.

"What...what are you doing here?" she asked, glancing between them.

"I couldn't do it," Brandon said. "I couldn't leave without you."

Was she hearing him right? He seemed in earnest.... "But your...your operation!"

"It can wait."

"Not if he wants to ski next season, it can't," the man he'd brought with him cut in. "But he can still make it if he's on the next plane."

"When does it leave?" she asked.

"In three hours."

"I'll only go if you go with me," Brandon said. "Do I have any hope of talking you into that?"

"I—" Her mind whirled as she thought of her apartment, her business.

"Come here, honey," Brandon said, reaching for her.

He didn't have to ask twice. She walked right into his arms and pressed her body against his, so grateful to see him, to touch him, her chest ached at the prospect of letting go.

He'd come back. For her.

"I think what we feel deserves a chance," he explained, his voice low in her ear. "I don't want to walk away from it."

"I'd like to be there for the operation." She wanted nothing more than to watch over him, keep him safe. "But I have clients to take care of and rent to pay—"

The other man made a show of tapping his watch. "Maybe you could join him in a week or two."

"Olivia, meet Scott Jones, my agent," Brandon said. "You don't have to listen to anything he says. Personally I'm finding that quite liberating."

Now she understood why this other person was so upset. Brandon was risking his career by coming here. She grinned at Brandon's tongue-in-cheek comment but spoke to Scott. "Won't the operation be over by then?"

"You could make it for the recovery," Scott said. "That's the most important part, anyway."

Not to her. She wanted to be there to support Brandon through the whole thing. She wanted to go with him now.

She could refer her clients to another planner she knew in River City. That wasn't the tough part. The tough part was paying her rent without that income....

"He's right," Brandon said. "I'm being selfish. I've just missed you so much. If it's too hard, you can come later."

She considered the money in her savings account. She'd put that away to get her through difficult times, had promised herself she wouldn't touch it except in an emergency.

Was she willing to spend it on love?

Everyone she knew would probably tell her she was being foolish, reckless. If Brandon recovered, he'd return to his career. But when she was with Kyle, and even long before that, she'd been so responsible, methodical, cautious—and that hadn't saved her from heartbreak. If Brandon could risk his career for her, she supposed she could risk her career for him.

"I'll throw some clothes in a bag. The rest I can handle via the internet," she said and smiled happily as his arms tightened around her and he buried his face in her neck.

"I'll make you glad you did," he promised.

Epilogue

"SO WHAT HAPPENED?" LORIANNA LEANED forward, her hair now dry and her coffee long cold. "What was wrong with Brandon's leg? I mean, I've seen footage of the accident. I knew his injuries took him out of the sport. But why didn't his leg heal? What did the doctor find?"

Olivia tightened her ponytail, then turned her mug of tea in a slow circle. She was thinking about how lucky she was to have found Brandon.

Maybe letting go of her resentment over what Noelle had done wasn't completely outside the realm of possibility. Noelle had behaved badly and often behaved badly still, but she was so caught up in fulfilling her own needs that she seemed almost incapable of considering the needs of those around her.

She definitely didn't understand that the way she approached life would never bring her the satisfaction she craved. Look where she was. Not only had she lost Kyle, she'd tried to get together with several other men since, none of whom were interested in more than a quick fling. She was working as a day clerk at a gift shop, moonlighting as a waitress at Sexy Sadie's and living at home. She didn't even have any good friends. The type of people she associated with came and went.

Weren't the natural consequences of her actions punishment enough? Why did Olivia feel Noelle had to be remorseful in order to obtain forgiveness?

Maybe she was using Noelle's behavior as an excuse, Olivia realized. It was easier to move on without someone like that in her life. But they *were* sisters. And what kind of debt did she owe her parents? They weren't perfect, but they'd always done their best.

"Olivia? You still with me?" Lorianna prompted.

Olivia looked up. "Oh, sorry. You asked…"

"What was wrong with Brandon's leg."

"It was a bone infection," she said. "Dr. Shapiro wasn't sure how the doctors here missed that, considering it was so extensive. He had to scrape away the infected area and drain a couple of abscesses. But, thanks to his efforts, followed by some heavy antibiotic therapy, Brandon recovered completely. He has no pain now."

Lines appeared on her friend's forehead. "So it wasn't his injury that took him out of skiing?"

"Not really. He could've come back for one or two more seasons. He considered it."

"Why didn't he?"

A sense of warmth, of well-being, passed through her. "He wanted something different by then."

Lorianna's lips curved upward for probably the first time

since she'd arrived in Whiskey Creek. "He wanted *you*, a family."

Olivia's hand went to her stomach. "Yes."

"I bet Scott was upset to hear that news," Lorianna said with a laugh. "I don't know him well. Jeff had a different agent when he was skiing. But any sports agent who repped an athlete like Brandon wouldn't want him to quit too soon."

"Scott was definitely disappointed."

"But Brandon didn't change his mind."

"No."

Lorianna pushed her cup toward the center of the table. "How did you feel about his decision?"

"Torn. If he was going to give up skiing, I didn't want him to regret it, or blame me later. But I also didn't want him to take the same risks he'd been taking."

Lorianna bit her lip. "And? *Has* he missed it?"

Olivia went over the past three years in her mind, examining those days, as she often did, for any dissatisfaction on his part. "I'm sure he has. But he's never focused on that loss. He got involved in opening the store and giving ski lessons. He even started his own winter camps for kids, instead of just helping out with other people's, and he still skis for fun. He seems to be…content." And that made her content, as well.

After that, they both seemed to get lost in their thoughts, and the silence stretched out.

Several minutes later, Lorianna spoke again. "So that man who came to the door—your ex-boyfriend—he's also your brother-in-law?"

"Can you believe that?"

"I guess stranger things have happened. But it can't be comfortable to see him at family gatherings."

"It's getting easier. I believe he's glad I'm happy."

"Is he happy?"

"I think he'd like to find someone and settle down."

"He's a handsome man. I can't imagine that'll pose a problem—once he gets over you."

"I hope you're right. I'd like him to have what I have."

Lorianna pulled the top of her robe more tightly closed. "So what are you going to do?"

Olivia got up to set their cups in the sink. "About what?"

"Noelle. Isn't that the person you need to forgive? Because it sounds like you've forgiven Kyle."

"I'm not quite sure how to handle my sister," she admitted. "What would you do if you were me? Should I let the past go? I mean...*really* let it go?"

Lorianna toyed with her belt. "That's hard to say. She doesn't deserve it."

"Same thing Kyle said. But your husband probably doesn't deserve it, either," Olivia pointed out.

"At least *he* claims he's sorry," she responded.

"*Claims?* You don't believe it?"

She stared down at her hands. "Actually, I do. He was in tears when he told me what he'd done. I've never seen him cry like that."

Olivia leaned against the counter. "So...what does that mean?"

"It means, once I recover from the disappointment, I'll try to rebuild, give him another chance."

After what she'd been through herself, Olivia had a small inkling of what Lorianna must be feeling. "That won't be easy," she said as she rinsed the cups and put them in the dishwasher.

"No. But your story about Kyle made me realize that I don't want to throw away what we have over one mistake."

After wiping off the counter, Olivia went over and plugged in the Christmas-tree lights. She couldn't say if Lorianna was doing the right thing. Only time would tell whether Jeff was capable of appreciating her forgiveness for the gift it was. But as Olivia stood back and looked at all the twinkling lights, her heart lifted as if it had suddenly divested itself of a huge burden.

She was confident she'd arrived at her decision, too.

"You're *sure* we have to do this?" Brandon raised one eyebrow as they stood on the doorstep of her mother's house. Olivia was holding a casserole dish, while he was loaded down with the presents she'd purchased and wrapped.

"Not entirely," she replied. "But it's Christmas, right? I want to give a more meaningful gift than a new purse or... or a shirt."

That didn't seem to change his mind. "This is more of a sacrifice than I think you should be required to make."

"Anything that doesn't require a sacrifice isn't much of a gift. Remember that O. Henry story?"

"Sure. But when has Noelle ever sacrificed for anyone?"

"Don't confuse me," she said. "My decision can't be contingent on that."

He winked at her. "Okay. I won't argue. I'm just happy you're the kind of person you are."

"We're going to have a baby. We want to have good relations with both our families, don't we?"

"Personally? I like things the way they are, but you mean enough to me that I'm willing to do anything—even if it involves your sister."

Her mother opened the door before she could respond. "Olivia! Brandon! What are you two doing here?"

"We came over to surprise you," Olivia said.

Her mother smoothed the apron covering her black polyester slacks and red sweater. She wore Christmas-tree earrings that blinked, with a matching brooch. "I was just doing some holiday baking. Smells like you've been doing the same."

"I made some hot crab dip for your dinner tonight."

"That cheesy one?" she asked with apparent enthusiasm.

Olivia nodded.

"I love that!"

"I know." She smiled, but she'd already warmed the dip and the heat was beginning to seep through her hot-pad holders. "Are you going to let us in?"

"Of course. I just—" Nancy lowered her voice "—Noelle's home tonight."

For a moment, Olivia's customary reaction to the prospect of seeing her sister nearly got the better of her, but she quickly beat back those negative feelings. "That's okay. We thought maybe we could all have dinner together for a change."

Her mother's gaze shifted disbelievingly from her to Brandon and back again.

"It's true," he said. "But she gets all the credit. I tried to talk her out of it."

He was teasing, trying to lighten the mood, but they all understood that it was basically true.

"Has Kyle talked to you?" her mother asked.

"He came by, yes," Olivia replied.

"Then I wish I'd gone to him sooner."

Olivia wasn't sure she would've been ready before now. But there was no time to respond. Her father spoke up from where he sat on the couch, watching TV. "Well, are you going to let them in, Nancy? Or are you going to make them stand out in the cold all night?"

At that, her mother stepped out of the way, and Olivia hurried inside to put the hot casserole dish on the stove, where it couldn't burn the countertop. She'd originally planned to have a talk with her family, to finally sit them down and hash out the past. After that, she'd imagined embracing Noelle and telling her she no longer held anything against her. But the coziness of her parents' home, and the fact that Noelle, when she walked out from the bedroom area in back, acted pleasantly surprised but didn't question their presence, made Olivia change her mind. Why go into all of that again? Why cause fresh tears by dredging up those negative emotions?

"How're things at the shop?" her father asked Brandon.

"Sales are strong, considering that we haven't had a lot of snow this year," he replied, and sat down with Ham while Nancy drew her and Noelle into the kitchen.

"Come see the pies I made this morning," she told them, as excited as though it was already Christmas morning.

If Noelle had already seen what her mother had baked, she didn't say so. Like Olivia, she admired the pies, which were sitting off to one side so they wouldn't be in the way of other preparations.

"They look and smell wonderful," Olivia said.

"Maybe someday I'll learn how to cook." Noelle sounded somewhat wistful, which reminded Olivia of everything they'd been missing out on since they'd stopped having much to do with each other.

"We could set aside a few hours and have Mom teach us both," she suggested.

Nancy's smile couldn't have stretched any wider. "There's a real knack to it, but I could show you."

"I don't know when I'd be able to do that." Noelle sounded genuinely disappointed. "I have to work so many shifts during the next two weeks."

"You'll have Christmas off, won't you?" Olivia asked. The boutique would be closed—Olivia knew that much—but Sexy Sadie's stayed open year-round.

"No, but people should be in a good mood that night." She shrugged. "Maybe I'll get some decent tips."

Olivia studied her.

"What?" Noelle sounded slightly defensive, as if she was expecting a comment—but Olivia smiled.

"I like the way you just turned that into a positive."

Noelle pressed a hand to her chest. "You like something about *me?*"

Olivia remembered how cute Noelle had been as a young girl, how enthusiastic she'd been about every aspect of life. "I like a lot of things about you," she said. And then, even though this hug wasn't the one she'd planned in her mind, she pulled her sister close. When she let go, Noelle looked absolutely stunned. "What was *that* for?"

"We're sisters," Olivia said simply. "And it's Christmas."

Their mother blinked as if holding back tears, but then a buzzer went off and she rushed to the oven. While her attention was elsewhere, Noelle lowered her voice. "I'm sorry. I don't know why I did what I did to...to you and Kyle. I don't know why I do half the things I do."

Olivia patted her arm. "It's okay," she said and, somehow, she meant it.

"This is going to be quite a Christmas," her mother piped up, joining them again. "I don't remember a time I've felt so optimistic."

With a laugh, Olivia slipped an arm around her mother's shoulders. "Merry Christmas."

★ ★ ★ ★ ★

Welcome to Icicle Falls

....

SHEILA ROBERTS

Prologue

Love and BFFs

WHO DIDN'T LIKE A COOKIE EXCHANGE? WELL, other than a surly teenager.

Muriel Sterling-Wittman's little house was filled with friends and the aroma of hot chocolate. And every inch of space on her dining room table was covered with plates of cookies—cookies smothered in frosting, cookies oozing chocolate, cookies with gumdrops peeking out like colored gems. Scented candles added to the good smells, and the room buzzed with conversation as three generations of Icicle Falls residents swapped recipes and gossip.

In one corner Olivia Wallace was making a face over some cheeky remark her friend Dot Morrison had just made. Muriel's daughters were gathered around the punch bowl, which was full of eggnog punch, while Janice Lind, the grand old dame of Christmas baking, was holding court on Muriel's sofa with Muriel, her friend Pat Wilder and Pat's daughter Isabel keeping her company. Some of the younger girls were hovering over the table, sneaking cookies.

Normally Pat's fourteen-year-old granddaughter, Clara, would have been with them, but right now she sat in a chair with her back to the group, scowling like a miniature Scrooge in drag. This was a first. Pat had been bringing her granddaughter to Muriel's cookie exchanges ever since she was five. And she'd always been excited to be there, happy to play with the other little girls whose mothers had deemed them worthy of the privilege of attending. Instead, here she sat, the expression on her face as dark as her hair.

"Why don't you go hang out with the girls?" asked Pat.

"No, thanks." Clara shot a dagger glare over to where the other girls were gathered in a giggling clump. All except for one, who was sneaking anxious looks in Clara's direction.

Pat and Muriel exchanged glances.

"She and Aurora are having issues," Isabel, her mother, explained.

Muriel's daughters Cecily and Bailey had joined them now, leaving Samantha in charge of the punch bowl. Cecily helped Muriel's oldest daughter, Samantha, run Sweet Dreams Chocolates, the family's chocolate company, and Bailey owned a successful tea shop in town. All three of them were happily settled with the right man now and busy with work, and Cecily was expecting a baby in February. But they always gave the cookie exchange top priority.

"I need this recipe," Bailey announced, holding up a chocolate cookie filled with candied cherries. She smiled at the scowling Clara and said, "You look like you need chocolate."

Clara shrugged.

"What's wrong?" Bailey asked.

"Nothing," Clara muttered.

Now one of the other girls had drifted over, a pretty girl with strawberry-blond hair and freckles, Clara's best friend, Aurora.

Make that former best friend, judging by the way Clara turned her back. "Go away. I'm not talking to you."

Tears sprang to Aurora's eyes. "Please don't be mad, Clara. It's not *my* fault Garth likes me now."

"Yes, it is. You stole him. He liked me first."

"And so now you're not speaking to her," Bailey deduced.

"She stole him," Clara hissed, in case they'd missed that piece of vital information the first time.

"We've been down that road," Cecily said, and put an arm around her sister. "It was a dumb road. Especially considering how well things worked out."

"What do you mean?" Aurora asked, settling onto the couch next to Muriel.

"I mean Bailey and I both wanted the same man. But in the end, we each got the person we were meant to be with."

"Well, I was meant to be with Garth," Clara said, her scowl deepening."

Pat smiled. "Yes, I understand those feelings. You know, I thought I was meant to be with someone once and my best friend got him."

"Who was that?" asked Clara, forgetting that she was supposed to be sulking.

Bailey and Cecily exchanged smiles. They'd heard the story back when they were fighting over a man. It looked as though it was time for a new generation to learn the importance of love and loyalty.

Muriel had both of the younger girls' attention now. "What happened?" Aurora asked.

Dot and Olivia had drifted into the living room area now along with two other young girls. "Tell 'em," Dot said. "I always like a good story at Christmas, especially when it has a happy ending."

"All right," Muriel said. "It happened a long time ago, but sometimes it seems like only yesterday."

One

Summer, 1969

"WE NEED MORE CUTE BOYS IN THIS TOWN," Olivia Green complained as she and Muriel and Pat Pearson walked home from Icicle Falls High.

"We have more than we used to," Muriel said.

By the late fifties, most of the cute boys and their families were all moving away. So were a lot of the girls, including her best friend, Doreen Smith. Muriel and Doreen wrote regularly for years, determined to stay best friends via the post office. But it wasn't the same as having her in town.

The town hadn't been much then. Icicle Falls had been dying for years, thanks to the railroad leaving and drying up the lumber business. After that there wasn't much left—a ramshackle downtown with derelict buildings housing a general store, a bank and a post office. There was a run-down motel and a diner to cater to people going over the pass. Add to that a few houses, a church, a grade school and tiny high school, and that was about all there was.

When Muriel was eight, she'd eavesdropped on the conversation of various grown-ups gathered in her parents' living room.

"We've got a mountain setting as nice as anything you'd find in the Alps," her daddy had said. "We could turn this place into a Bavarian village, make it a real destination town. We've already got the mountains and the rivers to lure skiers and fishermen. Let's give 'em a reason to stay and spend their money."

"I don't know, Joe. It's a big gamble," Mr. Johnson had said.

"If we don't take this gamble it's a sure thing Icicle Falls will be nothing but a ghost town in another ten years. We've got more people moving away all the time," her daddy had pointed out.

Ghosts? Were there *ghosts* haunting the place?

She'd asked her mother about that later. Mother had kissed her and assured her there was no such thing as ghosts.

"What did Daddy mean, then?" she'd demanded.

"He meant that we need to find a way to make our town a place where people want to be."

"*I* want to be here," she'd said. She'd wanted her best friend there, too.

"So do I, darling," her mother had said. "Don't you worry. Your daddy's going to fix everything."

Daddy made chocolate. She had no doubt he'd be able to fix this problem, too. The one all the grown-ups were so concerned about.

And he had. In the summer of 1962, while her friend Doreen was enjoying the Seattle World's Fair, Muriel was helping with town cleanup, collecting old cans in a field with Pat Pearson and Olivia Green. That had been a bonding experience.

And while they bonded over bits of garbage, other townspeople bonded hauling away old tires and abandoned cars from empty lots. Architects and builders were put to work, and the ramshackle buildings began to get a face-lift, changing Center Street from a Wild West ghost town to a quaint Bavarian village.

Muriel's correspondence with Doreen finally dried up, but life in Icicle Falls moved on. The following year new faces began to show up in town. They came in a slow trickle at first, like the drip from icicles on their roof when the snow began to melt. These visitors sometimes brought along cute boys. Some of them even returned to stay, opening up shops. Like Dale Holdsworth, who opened Kringle Mart and imported snow globes and handblown ornaments from Germany to sell to people who came to check out the newly minted tourist village. And Andy Marks, who started a small wood-carving shop, and Gerhardt Geissel, who built Gerhardt's Gasthaus. The Mountain Inn got a face-lift and a new name—the Bavarian Inn.

By the time Muriel was in high school, the student body had nearly doubled in size. Now it was up to a whopping hundred and forty-eight students. Thirty-two of them, including Muriel and her friends, were seniors that year.

"We may have more boys than we used to," Olivia said, "but most of them are underclassmen. Who's there in our class to choose from?"

For Muriel? No one matched the man of her dreams, the man she hoped would someday come into her life. Waiting for a perfect man seemed silly to her friends, but she was a big believer in true love. And in dreams. Her grandmother had dreamed an entire company into being, so Muriel had no doubt she could find the man she'd envisioned—someone dashing and romantic, who would make her heart skip a beat.

"There's Arnie Amundsen," Muriel suggested. For Olivia, not her. Arnie was skinny and wore glasses but he was sweet. Olivia could do a lot worse.

"He's got a crush on you," Olivia said.

"Everybody's got a crush on Muriel," Pat added in mock disgust.

"That is a gross overstatement," Muriel said.

Pat complained about being tall. She hated her auburn hair and lamented on a regular basis that she wasn't blonde like Olivia or a brunette like Muriel. Still, she'd had her share of invitations to the senior prom, which had taken place the week before. Muriel had gone with Arnie. Just as friends, she'd reminded him.

She wished he'd asked Olivia. Olivia had ended up with Gerald Parker, who'd wanted her to go all the way. They'd come close but she'd chickened out at the last minute. Now she was regretting her decision because Gerald was ignoring her, making her last week of school miserable. He'd enlisted in the marines, though, and would soon be gone. Muriel was secretly relieved. Of course, she didn't want anything bad to happen to Gerald, but it was best to remove temptation from Olivia.

"There's Hank Carp," said Pat.

Muriel frowned. "He's a hood."

"But he's a cute hood," Olivia said.

That was all Olivia needed, to get tangled up with Hank.

"I'd take him," Olivia continued, "except he likes Stephie."

"She's fast," Muriel said.

"That's probably why he likes her," Olivia muttered.

"Anyway," Pat went on, "that man is going nowhere. You can do better."

"I don't think so," Olivia said. "Nobody wants a fat girl."

"You're not fat," Muriel insisted. "You're—"

"Curvy," Pat supplied. "And boys like curves."

"No," Olivia corrected her. "Boys like Muriel. I bet you'll be married by the time you're twenty."

Muriel shook her head. "Not if my father has anything to say about it." She sighed. "He's got my whole life planned."

"Yeah, well, it's tough having a family chocolate factory," Pat said. "Poor girl. You'll have to work there, get rich and eat all the chocolate you want." She and Olivia giggled.

"I don't mind working there, doing fun things like helping with recipes or answering phones. I just don't want to run the place. I want to get married and have a family."

"And be a famous writer," Olivia reminded her. "Did you hear back from *Seventeen* yet?"

The rejection letter for her article, "How to Have Fun in a Small Town," had arrived the day before. Muriel hadn't even wanted to tell her best friends. It was so humiliating to be a failure. She bit her lip.

"Oh, no," said Pat. "They didn't like your article?"

Muriel shook her head again.

"Well, they're stupid," Olivia said.

"Don't worry," Pat told her. "You'll sell something. Maybe you'll even write a bestseller like Jacqueline Susann."

Muriel wrinkled her nose. "I wouldn't want to write that kind of thing."

"I would," Pat said. "If I wanted to write, that is. I'd rather read."

"I'd rather make out," Olivia said with a grin. "You know, it's going to be really hard to find men to marry once we all graduate. It seems like half the boys are leaving for college." Her expression grew sad. "I sure hope God brings some new ones to town."

Two weeks after graduation, God did. And Olivia and Pat

dropped into the gift shop of Sweet Dreams Chocolate Company, where Muriel was on duty, to tell her about it.

"We were walking down the highway, and he stopped and asked us where there was a good place to eat," Pat said.

"He's gorgeous," breathed Olivia. "He's tall and he's got muscles, and he looks like Mick Jagger. Even his hair. Well, except his hair is blond."

Long hair. Muriel's father wouldn't approve. "He's a hippie, then?"

"No," Pat said. "He rides a motorcycle."

"And he wears a leather jacket," Olivia added. "We're going to meet him at Herman's Hamburgers."

And with that they were off, leaving Muriel to run the candy shop. This was unfair. And wrong. Summer vacation had barely started and Daddy had her in here working! Pat and Olivia didn't have to work.

"Pat and Olivia don't have a family business," her father pointed out when she complained to him a few minutes later.

"Well, I wish I didn't."

"Muriel, don't ever let me hear you say that again," he said sternly. "This is a wonderful business, and it all started from your grandmother's vision. That's something you, as a young woman, should be proud of."

"I am," she protested before he could, yet again, tell her the story of how Grandma Rose had literally dreamed up those first chocolate recipes that had become the foundation of Sweet Dreams. "But that doesn't mean I want to *work* here."

"This is your inheritance, and you have a responsibility to yourself and future generations to respect that."

Muriel showed her respect by rolling her eyes.

"You may not like this now..."

She didn't, especially making change. She hated making change. She couldn't count backward no matter how hard she tried. Heck, she could barely count forward. Anyway, she didn't want to be a career girl. She loved the idea of owning the company and enjoying an endless supply of chocolate, but she didn't want to run it. Unlike her mother, who was always at the office helping Daddy, she wanted to stay home and concentrate on raising a family. Oh, and get articles published in prestigious magazines like *Seventeen* and *Mademoiselle,* or maybe even *Woman's Day.*

"But," her father continued, "down the road you'll be glad I insisted you get involved. Women don't stay home anymore, you know. I want you to be able to do something with your life."

Yes, she wanted to do something with her life, and right now the something she wanted to do was have fun.

Her father chucked her under the chin. "Come on now. No pouting. Do you know how many of your friends would kill to work in a chocolate shop?"

At the moment? None of them. They were all at Herman's Hamburgers, the new hamburger joint, downing cheeseburgers, shakes and fries. With a handsome motorcycle-riding stranger....

Her father hurried out the door, off to have lunch with the mayor, and she leaned her elbows on the counter and moped. And then decided to comfort herself with a chocolate-covered caramel. And another. And another. And just one more. And...pretty soon she wasn't feeling so good. Hmm. Could a girl really get too much of a good thing?

She was still pondering that question when Mrs. Lind came in for a box of truffles.

"These are for my sister's birthday," Mrs. Lind said. "I hope I can stay out of them."

The way Muriel was feeling after her chocolate caramel binge she was sure she'd have no trouble staying out of the chocolate for, oh, say, the next twenty years. "This might help you...." She put a mint truffle in a small gift bag and slipped it across the counter.

Janice Lind's face lit up as though she'd just won the Publishers Clearing House sweepstakes. "Oh, you're such a dear. Thank you, Muriel."

"My pleasure," Muriel said. All right, this was the part of the business she loved, the people part. She had to admit, as she sampled a truffle herself, that it was great to have access to such wonderful chocolate treats.

Still, she spent the rest of her shift watching the clock, willing the time to pass quickly so she could go find everyone and maybe get a glimpse of the new arrival in town. He was probably swarmed with girls right now.

Olivia was right. There weren't enough cute boys in Icicle Falls. How was she going to fulfill her dream of living happily ever after with someone special when there was no one here she wanted to live happily ever after with?

The bell over the shop door jingled. Oh, my. What was this?

Two

IN WALKED PAT AND OLIVIA. OLIVIA WAS GIG-gling; Pat was sulking. Behind them came the newcomer.

He did, indeed, look like a blond Mick Jagger. Muriel's heart rate kicked up several beats. She wished she'd put on more lipstick.

"This is Stephen Sterling," Olivia said. "He wanted to meet you."

That would explain Pat's sulk. Obviously she hadn't been thrilled with the idea of introducing Stephen to Muriel. She'd probably had plans for this man that didn't include anyone else.

And Muriel couldn't blame her. Man, he was. Stephen Sterling wore an air of maturity the local boys had yet to acquire, and he looked both dangerous and intriguing in his leather jacket and jeans. His hair was long and shaggy, falling around his chin. Did he play in a rock band?

Muriel smiled and said hello.

"When I told him about you and your family's chocolate company he wanted to come see it," Olivia explained.

"Do you like chocolate?" Muriel asked.

"I like sweet things," he said, and the way he smiled at her sent a flush racing to her cheeks.

"What kind of chocolate do you prefer, dark or light?"

He shrugged. "Chocolate is chocolate."

That made Olivia giggle. "Boy, have you got a lot to learn."

Muriel would be happy to educate him.

She was just getting ready to sneak them some free chocolate—none for her, thank you—when her father came back in. "Hi, kids."

His greeting was amiable enough, but Muriel could see the disapproval in his eyes when he glanced at Stephen. Of course, the long hair. Her father believed that men should look like men. Well, this one looked manly enough to her.

"Muriel, give your friends each a chocolate," Daddy said.

"Wow, thanks, Mr. Patrick," Olivia said, and Pat, too, murmured her thanks.

"Thank you, sir," said Stephen, proving he had manners. Muriel hoped that would score him some daddy points.

Daddy nodded. "Then I'm afraid you'll have to go. Muriel has to get back to work."

Doing what? Serving imaginary customers?

With that parting shot, he went upstairs to the office, leaving his daughter fuming over his rudeness and the fact that her friends were going to skip off and take the good-looking newcomer with them.

Muriel gave them each two chocolates. Petty revenge, but it made her feel better. Slightly.

Stephen popped a truffle in his mouth and chewed. "This is good."

"Of course they are," Muriel said. "We make the best chocolate in Washington."

"Looks to me like you've got a lot of good things here," he said, and smiled at her.

Pat frowned and tugged on his arm. "Come on, Stephen, we should go."

Fine. Eat my candy, take the cute guy and leave. See if I ever give you free chocolate again.

"Yeah, we don't want you to get in trouble with your dad," Olivia said to Muriel.

"Stephen's decided to stick around for a couple of days," she added, "so we're having a bonfire down by the river tonight."

"I'll be there," Muriel said. If her father asked her where she was going, she'd say out with Arnie. Daddy liked Arnie.

"Bring Arnie," Pat suggested, and Muriel knew she wasn't concerned with helping Muriel find a cover for the night.

"I'll invite a bunch of people," Muriel said. "Oh, Pat, I'll be sure to see if Hank can come." Not that Pat and Hank were a couple. His was simply the first name that came to mind.

Pat narrowed her eyes, fully aware that Muriel was trying to pull the same stunt she'd just tried. "Don't do it for me."

"Invite everybody." Olivia was so clueless. "The more the merrier."

"Let's go," Pat said. "We're going to show him Lost Bride Trail," she threw over her shoulder as they left.

Muriel wanted to call after her, "You'll never see her," but she resisted the temptation.

Everyone knew the legend of the lost bride. Rebecca Cane had come to town as a mail-order bride, but her husband, Joshua Cane, had trouble keeping the beautiful woman to himself. She fell in love with his younger brother, Gideon. There were threats and public fights enough to have the whole town talking. And when Rebecca and Gideon both went missing, there was more talk, especially when Joshua turned into a bitter hermit. Speculation ran wild. Soon the court of public opinion convicted Joshua of murdering both his wife and his brother. And when someone saw Rebecca's ghost over by Icicle Falls, that proved it.

For a while, people were afraid to go near the falls. But then a spinster, who was up there picking huckleberries with her cousins, saw Rebecca's ghost the very day before she received a proposal of marriage. After that, it became a lucky thing to catch sight of the lost bride's ghost flitting behind the falls—a sure sign that the woman who saw Rebecca Cane would soon be getting married.

So now Pat was going ghost-hunting. Really, could she be any more obvious?

"She wants him, doesn't she?" Muriel asked Olivia as she lay across her bed later that afternoon, talking on her princess phone.

"Well, who wouldn't?" Olivia replied. "He's so cool. You know he was in Vietnam?"

"My gosh, how old is he?"

"He's twenty-two."

Another dream-man qualification met. The mysterious man of Muriel's dreams was older and wiser than her. "What does he do now?" What kind of job did he have that allowed him to ride around in the middle of the week on a motorcycle?

"He isn't working."

That would not go over well with Daddy.

"He says he has some money in savings. He picks up jobs when he needs them. He's already done a year of college."

Handsome, smart and older—oh, and he made her heart race. *Another* important qualification met.

"I've got to go," she said. She needed to wash her hair and redo her nails before dinner.

★ ★ ★

"What do you have planned for tonight?" her father asked her as they ate macaroni-and-cheese and fish sticks, one of her mother's standard work-night meals.

"Arnie and I are going out," she answered, glad she'd invited Arnie to join the fun. She never liked to lie to her parents.

"He's a sweet boy," her mother said.

He was sweet, but he wasn't the stuff dreams were made of. This Stephen, on the other hand...

"I hope you're not going to anything where that long-haired hippie will be," said Daddy.

Did he listen in on her phone conversations?

"I'm sure if she's with Arnie she'll be fine," Mother said calmly.

"You stay with Arnie," Daddy said, pointing a fork at Muriel.

It was at times like this that Muriel hated being an only child. There was no one else to take the spotlight off her.

"Is he coming here to pick you up?" Daddy persisted.

"No, I'm meeting him at the park."

Daddy frowned. "Well, see that he brings you home."

"Yes, Daddy," she murmured. If things went according to plan someone very different would be bringing her home.

She helped her mother with the dishes, then escaped the house, dressed for a party in bell-bottom jeans and a batik top, a sweater tied around her waist.

By the time she got to the river, a lot of the newly graduated seniors were already making themselves at home on blankets on the riverbank, some seated on fallen logs, some roasting hot dogs over a roaring fire, others drinking pop. A few, like Hank Carp, were drinking beer. The legal drinking age was twenty-one, but the older teens often scored contraband beer and met in fields or down by the river to indulge in illegal activity.

Muriel wasn't much of a drinker and she was worried this thing would get out of control, especially when she saw that Olivia's ten-year-old sister, Wendy, was present, along with Nils's twelve-year-old brother, Peter, and Hank's wild kid sister, Josie. Usually it was just the older kids who came to these parties. If everyone started drinking, who would look out for the younger ones?

Arnie stood by the fire next to Olivia and Hank, uncomfortable and out of place. He was visibly relieved by the sight of Muriel and hurried over to greet her. "Hi, Muriel. I wondered if your dad would let you come."

"He knew you'd be here so he said yes." That made Arnie smile. Oh, dear. "Olivia looks cute tonight, doesn't she?"

Arnie spared Olivia a glance. "Yeah, she looks okay. You look *great*, Muriel."

Why couldn't boys see what was right in front of their eyes? All Arnie had to do was ask, and Olivia would go out with him. Olivia was frustrated and desperate. At this point she'd probably go out with anyone.

Not Muriel, though. She was holding out for her perfect man. She smiled at Stephen, who was talking to Pat. He gave her an appreciative once-over, but stayed where he was. Had Pat hypnotized him?

Lenny Luebecker took his guitar out of its case. "Hey, Muriel, got a song for you," he called, then began singing Tommy Roe's "Dizzy," grinning hopefully at her. Muriel didn't want to give him any encouragement so she merely smiled. But Olivia drifted over to where he sat with Nils and began singing along. So did some of the other kids. Pat and Stephen remained at the edge of the party, talking, and Muriel found herself frowning. This party wasn't going to be as much fun as she'd thought.

Definitely not fun. She kept looking to where Stephen and Pat were camped out, hoping to catch his eye but not succeeding. She tried to channel Scarlett O'Hara, tossing her hair, throwing her head back and laughing uproariously at something Lenny said. "Hah, hah, hah, hah."

But all she succeeded in doing was losing her balance and falling backward off the log she was sitting on. Oh, great. This was the way to get a man's attention. Act like a fool and wind up looking like an upended turtle.

When Lenny and Arnie pulled her back up her face was flaming. She sneaked a look in Stephen's direction and saw that he was watching her now, an amused smile on his face.

Good grief. Here was an article she could write for *Seventeen,* now that she knew what not to do. *"How to Get His Attention," by Muriel Patrick, town fool.*

The evening wore on, with more revelers arriving. The children darted in and out of the trees, playing tag, while the teenagers drank. The singing got louder and the laughter more raucous. Some drifted to the dark edges of the fire and became kissing silhouettes. Hank and Stephie were going at it as if they meant it. A shotgun wedding in the making, Muriel thought, and then realized she was jealous. She wanted to be off in the shadows necking with Stephen.

Where *was* Stephen? He and Pat were nowhere to be seen. Well, maybe he wasn't the man for her after all. Maybe she'd imagined the similarity between him and that tall, blond vision she'd seen so often in her dreams.

A shriek cut through the noise, like an ugly obbligato, and a moment later Josie came running to the campfire. "Wendy fell in the river!"

"Oh, my God!" cried Olivia, jumping up immediately.

The current could be swift, and a kid trapped in the river at night was enough to mobilize everyone. They ran to the water's edge, Olivia calling her little sister's name all the way.

They'd barely spotted her, a small body bobbing down the angry river, when out of nowhere a tall male form splashed into the water. Stephen Sterling.

Muriel held her breath and watched as he plunged toward the little girl, fighting against the rushing water. It was a struggle worthy of Greek myth. The river didn't yield its catch easily and on the first try he missed. The second time he caught her but it looked as if he needed every ounce of strength to get them both back to shore.

"Somebody help him!" Olivia yelled.

Hank found a long branch and extended it to Stephen, who caught hold and used it to pull himself and the child back to the safety of the shallows.

Wendy was in tears now and so was Olivia.

Josie was crying, too, and Peter looked as if he wanted to.

Nils grabbed his brother's arm and said, "What the hell were you guys doing?"

"We were just playing tag," Peter protested. "She ran into the water to get away and..." He burst into tears.

"She went too far," Muriel finished for him as she draped her sweater around the dripping girl. "Oh, Wendy, what were you thinking? You know better!"

"I slipped," the child sobbed.

"Let's take her back to the fire," Pat said, taking charge. "Come on, honey. We'll get you warmed up in no time."

Pat and Olivia were busy calming Wendy down. Muriel picked up a blanket and went over to Stephen, who stood talking with Nils. "I thought maybe you could use this."

"Thanks," he said, and swung it around his shoulders.

Nils was smart enough to know when a woman wanted a

man to herself, and he moved away, giving Muriel the first chance she'd had all night to talk to the newcomer alone.

"What you did was so heroic."

He shook his head and stared into the flames. "Not really."

"But it was," she argued. "No one else went in."

"Someone would have. I just happened to be first."

"Isn't that what heroes do, go into danger first?"

"I've had enough of that, believe me."

"Some men are meant to be heroes, whether they want to or not."

His smile was mocking. "Are you looking for a hero, Muriel?"

Maybe she was. "Is there anything wrong with that?"

Now Arnie had joined them. "Olivia's going home. I'm thinking maybe we should, too."

As if he was her boyfriend. She could have kicked him. "I'm not ready to go yet."

"Okay. Do you want to say goodbye to Olivia?"

Of course she wanted to say goodbye to Olivia! Except now, just as she was staking her claim on Stephen, here came Pat, smiling at him as if they were already a couple.

Still, a girl didn't ignore her good friend for a man. Muriel walked over to Olivia, who was gathering her things and seemed on the verge of tears. "Are you okay?"

"My parents are going to kill me and I don't blame them. This is all my fault."

"You didn't push her in the river."

"I didn't watch her. I was too busy flirting with Nils."

There was no denying that. But from an early age children in Icicle Falls were taught to respect the river. "It was an accident, pure and simple," Muriel said. "The important thing is, she's all right."

"No thanks to me," Olivia said miserably. "Tag," she added in disgust.

"We've all played it," Muriel reminded her.

"Not by the river."

Muriel gave her a hug and assured her all would be well. Then, having done what she could to encourage her friend, she looked for Stephen. He was no longer standing by the fire. Neither was Pat. She caught sight of them, walking off toward the river walk, probably toward the Bavarian Inn, where he was staying. Maybe she was ready to go home after all.

The incident had sucked the energy out of the party, and people began to leave. Having made her point earlier, Muriel let Arnie walk her home.

She turned to go in the door when Arnie took her arm. "Muriel."

She knew by his tone of voice what was coming.

Sure enough. "You know how I feel about you."

She nodded. "I'm sorry, Arnie. I like you, but just…not that way."

He frowned. "It's that new guy, isn't it? I saw you staring at him."

"A girl can't help who she's attracted to." Now Arnie looked heartbroken and she felt awful.

But he wasn't the man of her dreams.

He heaved a sigh. "If you ever change your mind, you know I'll always be there for you."

"You're a good friend, Arnie," she whispered.

"Thanks," he said, but his tone of voice showed what he thought of that.

The path to true love was as twisted and tangled as Lost Bride Trail, Muriel told herself sadly as she slipped inside the house.

Three

WHEN THE CHURCH YOUTH GROUP MET ON
Sunday night, Muriel pulled Pat aside. "Where'd you
go with Stephen after the party?"

"We went for a walk. Not that it's any of your business."

"*I* was talking to him."

Pat shrugged. "And then you left."

"I was saying goodbye to Olivia. I was coming back."

"How was I supposed to know that?" Pat snapped. "Look,
Muriel, you can have any man in town. You don't need to
add this one to your collection."

"I'm not collecting men!"

"Yes, you are. You like having every boy in town crazy
over you. Well, this one isn't, and I want him."

"So do I," Muriel said. "And I can't just walk away and let
you have him, not when he might be the man I've dreamed
of all these years."

Pat rolled her eyes. "Oh, please. That stupid dream."

"It's not stupid!"

"It is, and it's selfish, too. And if you think I'm stepping aside because you say so, you can think again."

That had been the end of the conversation. Maybe even the end of their friendship. For the first time since anyone could remember, Pat and Muriel didn't sit next to each other at a church function.

"This is making it awkward for everyone," Olivia said when she came into the shop the following Friday.

"Tell that to Pat," Muriel said stiffly.

"You guys shouldn't be fighting over a boy."

"He's not a boy. He's a man, and he's—"

Olivia cut her off. "I know, the man you've dreamed about."

"We're meant to be together. I'm sure of it," Muriel said earnestly.

"But you're *not* together. He's seeing Pat. And it looks like he's going to keep on seeing her. You know he's renting a room at the Schoemakers'? And he's started working part-time over at Swede's garage. He's here to stay—and he's here to stay with Pat."

Muriel got busy straightening a display of gift boxes.

"Can't you be happy for her?" Olivia coaxed.

If Stephen wanted Pat instead of her... "I guess I can try," Muriel said. That was as much as she could promise.

Still, it was painful when she and Olivia went to Herman's Hamburgers that night and ran into Stephen and Pat there. Pat already had a booth staked out and he was waiting in line to order.

"Good. We can sit with them," Olivia said. "Here's your chance to show there's no hard feelings." She handed a five-dollar bill to Muriel. "Order me a cheeseburger and a brown cow, will you?" Then she went to join Pat.

"What to Do When Your Best Friend Gets the Man of Your Dreams," by Muriel Patrick, loser. Feeling awkward and self-conscious, Muriel stepped into line, two people behind Stephen.

He saw her and let the other people go ahead. "Out for a big night in Icicle Falls?" he teased.

"Something like that," she replied.

"How come you're not with Arnie?"

"Because I'm not. Should I be?"

"You two are a couple, right?"

She thought she'd made it clear they weren't. "Who told you that?"

"Pat."

Pat, her former good friend. "People say a lot of things in a small town. Not everything they say is true."

He cocked an eyebrow. "Yeah?"

"Arnie and I are friends. That's all we'll ever be."

"So, if someone else was to ask you out?"

"How to Play It Cool When He Shows Interest," by Muriel Patrick, whose life is looking up. She smiled. "I might say yes."

By the time they'd picked up their orders and joined Pat and Olivia at the table, Pat was seething. "I don't remember inviting you to this table," she said.

"Don't worry, we're not staying," Muriel said frostily. She nudged Olivia. "Let's go sit with Hildy and Nils." Olivia had been looking from one friend to the other in concern. Now she nodded and scooted out of the booth. "This isn't good," she said as she followed Muriel to the other side of the restaurant.

"No, it's not," Muriel agreed.

"We've all been friends since we were kids. This just isn't right."

Muriel sighed. "I guess there's nothing like love to ruin a friendship."

★ ★ ★

Stephen switched loyalties the next week, coming into the shop and asking Muriel to see *True Grit* at the new Falls Cinema. She said yes and then felt guilty. Pat had fallen hard for this man and here she was going out with him. Was Pat right? *Was* she a selfish man-collector?

They shared a popcorn, and he slid an arm around her, and there in the dark, with John Wayne busy fighting bad guys on the screen, her heart fought its own battle. She wanted this man, knew deep down that he was the one for her and that they'd wind up together. But she didn't want to lose her friend. How would that work with all of them here in Icicle Falls?

A new thought dawned. Did Stephen want to stay in Icicle Falls?

"Do you like it here?" she asked later as they had root beer floats at Herman's.

"Sure. It's a nice little town, a heck of a lot smaller than Seattle. Don't know if I'd want to live here all my life."

That made the ice cream in Muriel's stomach harden into a rock. "Where would you want to live?"

He shrugged. "Don't know yet. I've got a lot of country left to check out."

"You could look all over the world but you'd never find a place as nice as Icicle Falls."

"It's okay," he said. "Might be hard to find success in such a small place, though."

"What kind of success are you looking for?" Muriel had always felt that simply having a life filled with family and close friends qualified as success.

Friends. She thought of Pat and pushed away her glass.

"I don't know that, either," Stephen said. "I know I want to make something of myself, but I haven't figured out what." He frowned. "One thing I do know, I'm going to be successful. My old man wasn't much," he added. "He doesn't think I'll be much, either, but I will."

"I believe you," she said. "But you don't need a big city to do that. A man can make something of himself in a small town."

"People can be prejudiced in a small town."

"People can be prejudiced anywhere." She remembered how her father had looked at Stephen, the "long-haired hippie" when he came into the Sweet Dreams gift shop. Was Stephen remembering that, too?

He glanced around the restaurant. "Doesn't look like there's much to do here except run a shop."

"Or own an orchard," she put in. *Or a chocolate factory.*

"Nah. I'm not a farmer. I'll figure it out, though. One thing I *can* tell you, I want a woman who's willing to leave everything to be with me."

Muriel got the message. For Stephen she could do that. She nodded. "That's what love is—giving up what you care about the most for the person you want to be with."

He smiled at her as though she'd just passed some kind of test. Well, she'd said the right thing. But could she really leave her home?

Of course she could. *Home is more than a place,* she told herself, *it's wherever two people in love can be together.* It was probably too soon to talk about love, but she knew what she felt and she knew what she wanted. Stephen.

Now she had to find a way to convince her father that she wanted the right man. At some point she was going to have to bring Stephen home. But not yet.

So she kept insisting on meeting him places—Riverwalk Park, the pool, the movies. And June slipped by like a dream. The only part of the dream that wasn't perfect was the fact that every time she saw Pat, her friend turned her back and went the other way.

So what? Maybe she wouldn't be here much longer. Maybe she'd marry Stephen and move away. That thought cheered her up. Almost.

By July 3, the town of Icicle Falls was surrounded by campers, and people were taking rafts down the river, picnicking in mountain meadows and enjoying the town's amenities. The Fourth of July celebrations were underway, with food booths set up on Alpine Street and an arts-and-crafts show in the park. And Stephen and Muriel were getting out of town.

She met him by the gazebo and hopped on the back of his motorcycle to go for a drive. It always made her nervous climbing on the back of that big, noisy bike, and she'd hold on to Stephen for dear life every time they hit the open road. But she also got a secret thrill out of being seen by the other kids. The guys all wanted to be Stephen and the girls all wanted to have him. Too bad. He was hers.

She was just looking around, gloating, when she saw someone staring at her from the corner across the street. And that person didn't seem happy at all.

She gasped, but Stephen didn't hear her. He was gunning the bike. Then, before she could gather her thoughts, they were speeding off down the street. If she survived riding this big scary monster, it would be to come home to something even scarier—Daddy's wrath.

"How to Deal with an Angry Father," by Muriel Patrick. She'd have plenty of time to write that article because she was going to be on restriction for life.

Four

MURIEL HAD BARELY WALKED INTO HER HOUSE when the fireworks started. A day early.

She could smell her mother's meat loaf baking but she had no appetite. Her stomach had been churning for the past two hours.

Daddy was home and waiting for Muriel in the living room, Mother keeping him company. She looked concerned. He looked ready to explode.

"What were you doing with that long-haired motorcycle bum?" he demanded.

"He's not a bum," Muriel protested. "He's nice."

"I can tell by looking at him that there's nothing nice about the boy. He doesn't even have a job."

That showed how much her father knew. "Yes, he does. He's working part-time at the garage."

Daddy pointed a finger at her. "At his age he should have a full-time job."

"Now, Joe," Mama said in her most soothing voice. "He's young."

"He's old enough to ride a noisy motorcycle all over town. He's old enough to have a full-time job," Daddy said, his voice rising.

"Then maybe you should give him one," Muriel suggested boldly.

"I'll do that when hell freezes over. Now, I don't want you seeing him again."

"You can't tell me what to do, Daddy!"

"As long as you're living under my roof I can," her father roared, "and I expect you to listen."

He could expect all he wanted but it didn't mean she would. She turned and stormed out of the room and up the stairs to her bedroom.

"I'm not done with you, young lady!"

But she was done with him. She kept right on going. Upstairs she slammed her bedroom door, just so Daddy would know she meant business.

A few minutes later, a gentle tap at the door told her he'd sent a negotiator. "May I come in?" Mother asked.

As if she had a choice? She sat on her bed and watched sullenly as her mother slipped into the room. Mother joined her and laid a hand over hers. "Muriel, your father's only concerned about your happiness."

"No, he's not. If he was, he wouldn't make snap judgments. Stephen's fun and noble and… I love him." There, she'd said it. Her parents needed to be aware of this immutable fact.

Mother sighed. "You hardly know the boy."

"You hardly knew Daddy," Muriel argued. Her parents had met when their families were vacationing at the ocean and it had been love at first sight. They'd written letters back and forth for six months, had a total of three dates and then gotten engaged.

Her mother gave her a reluctant smile. "I'll talk to your father. Meanwhile, don't rush into anything."

Muriel understood what that translated to. Don't have sex; don't get pregnant. Well, she wasn't planning on running right out and sleeping with Stephen. But if he asked her to marry him, she'd do it tomorrow. Rather than upset her mother with that bit of information she simply nodded.

Her mother kissed the top of her head. "Now, let's go have dinner."

The last thing she wanted to do was sit across the table from her father. "I'm not hungry."

"Honey, come make up with your father."

Muriel shook her head. "I'm going to the street dance with Olivia."

It was a bold-faced lie and her mother knew it, but she pretended to be stupid and nodded. "Okay. Remember what I said, though. And give your father grace. He loves you dearly and doesn't want to see you hurt."

Muriel kept her eyes lowered and nodded. She couldn't look her mother in the face after lying to her. She couldn't let her father off the hook, either. He should have understood but he refused to.

When she got there, Center Street was alive and throbbing with holiday revelers consuming corn dogs and cotton candy. The Pink Poodle Skirts, a fifties and sixties cover group, were setting up over at the gazebo in the park and testing their equipment, and the sounds of electric guitar drifted on the air. She ran into Olivia right away, which made her feel better about the lie she'd told her parents.

And now, here came Stephen wearing jeans and a T-shirt, his hair pulled back in a ponytail.

Olivia sighed loudly. "He is so gorgeous."

"Yes, he is," Muriel agreed.

"You two are the perfect couple."

"Tell that to my father," Muriel said grumpily.

"He'll come around."

She'd said that about Pat, too. She'd been wrong. Pat wouldn't come back, not unless Muriel gave up Stephen. And she wasn't giving him up, not for her father and certainly not for Pat. This bad attitude of Pat's just showed how selfish she was. A true friend would have been happy to see her best friend since grade school find the man of her dreams.

"Hey there, you two," he greeted them. "You both look great tonight."

Olivia's cheeks turned pink. "You don't look so bad yourself."

"How about a corn dog?" he offered.

"Sure," Olivia said, falling into step with them.

At the corn dog stand they found Nils and Lenny, and Hildy and Sue Lind, and in a matter of moments Stephen had managed to separate Muriel and himself from the others, leaving Olivia in their care.

That was fine with Muriel. She wanted him all to herself. They wandered the street, hand in hand, and then later, as the light began to fade, made their way to the bandstand. The band had just started, their girl singer belting out "He's a Rebel." Stephen draped an arm around Muriel's shoulders as they stood there in the growing crowd, listening.

She smiled at him. "Are you a good dancer?"

"The best."

He proved it when the band played "Proud Mary" and everyone started dancing. Stephen had the moves. The band shifted down to a slower tempo, playing "Never My Love," and he took her in his arms and they swayed.

"Who knew I'd find treasure here in the mountains," he murmured in her ear and drew her closer.

Slow dancing with him was like dancing in a dream. She looked up at him and thought, *My life is perfect.* And later, as they walked by the river, she said as much.

"I think it's time I got to know your parents," he said after a very long and luscious kiss.

She bit her lip and stared out at the river, which was now a dark ribbon. She could hear the current rushing past.

"You do want me to meet your parents, don't you?"

"You've already met Daddy," she hedged.

"That wasn't much of a meeting."

How was she going to make this happen? She felt Stephen's assessing gaze on her and pulled her sweater tighter.

Next to her, he let out a frustrated sigh. "Your dad doesn't approve of me, does he?"

"I wouldn't say that exactly." Another lie.

"Muriel, I'm not dumb. Don't you think I've figured out why you always insist on meeting me places?"

"I just thought—"

"That I wouldn't notice how he looked at me that day in the candy shop?"

Muriel felt her cheeks heating. "My father will come around."

"Will he?"

"I know he will," she said firmly.

"And what if he doesn't?"

"I guess we'll cross that bridge when we come to it."

Even in the dark, it wasn't hard to see him stiffen. Then he pulled away. She'd failed some kind of test.

"Stephen, what?"

"Nothing. It's getting late. I'll walk you home."

She could envision her father waiting on the front porch, a welcoming scowl on his face. "I'll be fine on my own."

"Yeah, you probably will. I'll walk you to your street anyway," he said.

They left the park in an uncomfortable silence, and Muriel found herself at a loss, unsure of how to fill it.

Once they got to her street corner he stopped. "Goodbye, Muriel."

"I'll see you at the river tomorrow night for the fireworks," she said.

He nodded. Then he turned and walked away without so much as a goodbye kiss.

Muriel went the rest of the way down the street with a heavy heart. Everything had been going so well until the subject of her father came up. Daddy was ruining her life.

Just as she'd suspected, she got to the house to find him waiting for her on the front porch. He frowned as she walked up the porch steps. "You were with that boy, after I told you not to see him."

"Daddy, I'm not a little girl anymore. You can't tell me who to see," she snapped, and marched inside the house.

"Muriel!"

Ignoring the frustration in his voice, she kept moving. Once again, her bedroom door slammed, but this time nobody came to talk to her. Which was fine. She didn't *want* to talk to anyone. She fell on her bed and indulged in a good cry. This was all wrong. She'd never fought like this with her father before— but then her father had never been so mean-spirited before.

The next morning she entered the kitchen and found him at the red Formica table, nursing a cup of coffee. "You still mad at me?" he asked.

"Yes." She opened the refrigerator and pulled out a carton of eggs. "Do you want an egg?"

"Sure," he said, trying to sound amiable.

She fried him one and made toast, then put bread in the toaster for Mother, who was strictly a toast-and-coffee girl.

By the time Mother entered the kitchen, Muriel and her father were both seated at the table, eating in silence. "Well, we have a lovely day for a picnic, don't we?" she said.

"I'm not going." The last thing Muriel wanted was to spend the day pretending she wasn't mad at her father.

"Of course you are," Mother said in typical mother fashion. "We picnic with the Greens every year. Think how disappointed Olivia would be if you didn't show up."

"How about a truce for the day?" her father offered.

As if she was a child, pouting because she'd been denied a toy? "Daddy, you don't get it. This isn't some fad I'm going to get over. I'm in love. Stephen is the man I want to spend the rest of my life with."

Her father set aside his coffee cup with a frown. "Muriel."

"You haven't even given him a chance. What would have happened to you and Mother if Grandpa hadn't given *you* a chance? Did he like you at first? How well did he like you when he learned you wanted to marry Mother and move her over here?"

Her father held up a hand. "Okay, point taken. Now, can we enjoy our day?"

Muriel smiled at him. She'd battered down her father's defenses and was well on her way to securing her future independence—a fitting victory for the Fourth of July.

But she'd just exited the kitchen when she heard a snippet of conversation that left her lurking around the corner, eavesdropping.

"That was good of you," said Mother.

"Not really. I know Muriel thinks she and Galahad are going to be together, but the kid's a drifter. He won't stay beyond summer. There's no sense arguing over something that isn't going to happen."

"I'm not so sure," Mother said.

"I am," Daddy said.

Her father was wrong. Stephen was here to stay and Daddy would simply have to accept that.

The two families met for their traditional picnic lunch by the river. Little Wendy stayed far away from the water. Mrs. Green made her famous fried chicken and Mother had picked up potato salad and cold cuts from Schwartz's deli. The cooler was stocked with soda pop for the younger generation and beer for the dads. Mrs. Green's chocolate cake finished off the meal and shortly thereafter everyone packed up and went to watch the parade.

It was in full swing when Muriel caught sight of Stephen across the crowded street. Tonight they'd meet at the river where they'd partied only a few weeks ago and watch while the town's younger generation set the sky on fire shooting fireworks over the river. She could hardly wait to set off her own fireworks with Stephen when he kissed her. Her heart rate picked up, and she gave him a smile and a tiny wave. He nodded and waved back. Surely she was imagining that his answering smile failed to reach his eyes.

Darkness took its time coming, but at last the sun slipped behind the mountains. The whistle and boom of fireworks filled the night and the sky lit up with showers of colored sparks.

"It's beautiful, isn't it?" she said to Stephen as they sat together on a log by the campfire Nils had built for the gang. "Not bad for a small town," she teased.

"Not bad," he agreed, then fell silent as he chewed on his lower lip.

"What is it?"

"Let's take a walk." He stood and held out a hand to her.

Foreboding settled on her heavily. This wasn't a happy, romantic walk they were about to go on. She hesitated and he reached down, took her hand and gently towed her to her feet. Then he led her away from the fire.

Five

THEY WERE AWAY FROM THE OTHER PEOPLE.
They should have been about to kiss. Instead, Stephen
drove his hands into his pants pockets.

"What's wrong?" Muriel asked, not wanting to hear the
answer. *Something* was wrong. She'd known it all evening.
Heck, she'd known it since she saw him at the parade. Yes,
he'd smiled at her, but it hadn't been a lover's smile.

"I'm leaving town."

She blinked. Proof was mounting up but she refused to see
it. "For how long? When will you be back?"

"I won't. It's time to move on."

"Move on?" she repeated. "Why don't you want to stay?"

He looked beyond the park, beyond the town, to the highway. "This isn't working out."

"What's not working out?" she persisted. "Us?" He couldn't
mean them.

"Muriel, you know what I'm talking about. I saw the way your dad looked at me at the parade today."

So while she'd been smiling encouragement, her father had been sending a very different message. And to think she'd made breakfast for him.

"He doesn't approve of me. He's never going to."

"And so you're leaving? Just like that? You're not even going to stay and fight for me?"

"Look, it's been great. *You're* great. But I don't want to be tied down," Stephen said. "Life's too short."

"I wouldn't tie you down," she protested. "I'll go anywhere you want to go."

"Would you really, Muriel?"

"Of course!"

"Prove it. Get on my bike right now and ride out of town with me."

"N-now?" she stammered. Without even saying goodbye? That didn't make sense.

He shook his head. "That's what I thought."

"You thought wrong!"

He shook his head again. "No. I know you think you'd follow me anywhere. And maybe you would for a while, but you'd wind up wanting to come back here."

She ground her teeth in frustration. "I want to be with *you,* Stephen."

"This town is in your blood. It's your life, the center of your world. You own a chocolate company for crying out loud."

"I don't own it. My father owns it."

"You'll run it. It's your inheritance."

She didn't want an inheritance. She wanted Stephen.

"And a good one at that. You're lucky, Muriel. You have a place where you belong, family and friends who love you. Don't give that up on a whim."

"Do you think all you are to me is a whim? I'll be packed in half an hour."

He closed his eyes. Then he kissed her. It wasn't a kiss filled with promise. "Goodbye, Muriel," he said and turned and started walking.

She chased after him, catching his arm. "Stephen, don't do this. We belong together."

"Ah, Muriel, you're so naive. Everybody isn't equal in America. I'm just a guy from the wrong side of the tracks and that's all I'll ever be to your dad."

"That's not true," she insisted, even though she knew it was.

He gave a disbelieving grunt. "People judge you no matter what. Never mind that I put my ass on the line in 'Nam. You know what happened to me when I first came home? I was at the airport, still in my uniform, and some kid spat on me. I got rid of the uniform and grew my hair and people are still spitting on me. I'm gonna keep riding till I find someplace where they won't."

"No one's spitting on you here," Muriel said. He had such a big chip on his shoulder he couldn't see past it.

"I don't belong."

"Yes, you do. You belong with me!"

His only response was to remove her hand from his arm. "I'm done," he said, and walked away.

Stephen had been right, Muriel thought bitterly. He was no hero. And he wasn't the man of her dreams, either. That man wouldn't give up, wouldn't walk away. The dream was over. She stood for a moment, watching him, then buried her face in her hands and wept.

News spreads fast in a small town. By the sixth of July all her friends knew Stephen was gone. Her father had taken the car in to Swede's for servicing, so he knew, too. She was grateful he didn't say anything. Instead he gave her a hug and a kiss and told her he loved her before he left for the Sweet Dreams office.

How sad that it was her father's love that drove Stephen away. And how sad that the two most important men in her life had been such a huge disappointment to her. *"What to Do When the Men in Your Life Disappoint You."* She wished she knew.

Later that day, when she was working in the gift shop, Pat stepped inside.

"Did you come to buy chocolate?" Muriel greeted her stiffly.

Pat shrugged. "I'm looking for my friend. I think I've lost her, but I'm hoping..." She stopped and bit her lip. "Oh, Muriel, I'm sorry. I'm sorry he's gone and I'm sorry we fought."

That was all it took to bring Muriel around the counter for a hug and a good cry.

As they dried their tears, Pat said, "Fighting over Stephen was stupid."

Muriel nodded. "It was."

Pat stood there for a moment, running a hand along the counter. "You know, if you'd gotten engaged I'd have come to the wedding."

"Come to the wedding? You would've been a bridesmaid."

That made Pat cry all over again, which called for another hug. Finally she said, "Let's never fight over a man again. Promise?"

Muriel nodded. "Promise."

"Next time we'll flip a coin, okay?"

Muriel managed a smile. "Okay." Would there ever be a next time? She thought she knew the answer to that, and it was all she could do not to start crying all over again.

Summer dragged on, hot and heavy, and Muriel slogged through it listlessly. Her friends tried to cheer her up. Pat and Olivia assured her on a regular basis that someone else would come along. Arnie brought her bouquets of mountain meadow flowers. Lenny wrote her a song about better times ahead that thoroughly depressed her. And she consoled herself with so much chocolate that she gained seven pounds.

Her father took her out to dinner at Schwangau, the fancy new restaurant in town, and talked about things working out for the best. Meanwhile, she had her family and friends, and the company. He wanted her to work full-time in the office come September. She could start out as a receptionist.

"This is all going to be yours someday," he reminded her. She nodded.

"This company will take care of you and your family long after I'm gone," he continued.

Before she could have a family, she had to have a man. She wiped at her teary eyes with a corner of her napkin.

Her father reached across the table and laid a hand on her arm. "Honey, he wasn't good enough for you. If he was, he would have stayed."

"Maybe he would've stayed if he thought he was welcome."

"No," her father said adamantly. "If he'd really cared about you, he'd have stayed."

Deep down she knew he was right. Maybe Stephen had simply been looking for an excuse to leave.

She'd finally had all she could take of well-meaning friends and fatherly advice. She slipped away on a Sunday afternoon and went for a walk. The walk led her to Lost Bride Trail.

As she hiked she could hear the thunder of the falls. That poor, miserable bride. Her life hadn't turned out as she planned, but at least she'd had a chance to *be* a bride. Muriel never would.

"You have to stop this," she told herself.

All this wallowing in self-pity was becoming ridiculous. She was too young for her life to be over. She could still make something good of it. She'd learn more about her family's business, and maybe, down the road, she'd marry Arnie and he could help her run Sweet Dreams. They could have a family.

Little Arnies running everywhere.

Maybe she'd stay single and hope her father lived until he was ninety.

She was at the falls now. She stood in awe, watching the water plunge over the rocks. How many women had something as incredible as this practically in their backyards? And how many women had a chance to live in such a beautiful town with so many wonderful people? So she was alone. But she had family and friends to be alone with. And— What was that? She strained to see more clearly.

A woman in a long, white dress darted under the cataract.

Muriel blinked. All right, she was imagining things.

But no, there was the woman again. A shiver ran down Muriel's spine and she gasped. The lost bride! She dashed off the trail, moving toward the edge of Icicle Creek to get a closer look.

Muriel had never been the most athletic girl in town. She still wasn't. She tripped over a tree root and tumbled down the bank, oomphing her way right into the shallows of the creek. She staggered to her feet, muddy and wet, and stared up at the falls.

All she saw was water.

Wishful seeing, she told herself in disgust as she made her way back up the bank. There was no proposal in her future.

She was never walking Lost Bride Trail again. Ever.

Labor Day weekend. It was the last hurrah for the grade school and high school kids, and the starting flag for many of the older ones. Pat would soon be attending Cascade Junior College and Olivia was looking into culinary school. Lenny was going to nearby Washington State University and Nils had been accepted at the University of Washington, where he wanted to study to become a pharmacist. Before leaving, though, he'd proposed to Hildy and she'd promised to wait for him. Hank Carp had gotten Stephie pregnant and they were getting married the following weekend. Even Arnie was moving on, bound for the University of Washington, like Nils, where he was planning on majoring in business.

Muriel was staying put, working at Sweet Dreams. And she'd decided she was happy about that. Daddy had given her an assignment that she was truly enjoying—designing a logo for their growing company. And he'd promised to let her write the ad copy for their next catalog. It wouldn't be quite as exciting as writing for *Seventeen* or *Woman's Day,* but it would come close.

Yes, she'd decided she was perfectly happy with where she was in life. After all, how many women had their very own chocolate factory?

Still, as Friday wound down, she found herself looking out the office window at the Wenatchee River, thinking about her life and sighing. Something was missing.

Make that *someone.*

She shook her head. What was the point of revisiting that old dream? She needed to move on with her life. Maybe she'd take some evening classes at Cascade Junior College, try her hand at writing a novel. Or possibly submit some more magazine articles. *"How to Survive a Breakup," by Muriel Patrick, chocoholic.* Except moping probably didn't count as good advice.

She was just locking up the gift shop when she heard the roar of a motorcycle coming down the street. She turned and saw a lean man in jeans and a black leather jacket with blond hair. Short blond hair? Still, there was no mistaking who it was.

"Stephen!" She dropped her purse and ran to meet him, barely giving him time to stop and turn off his bike. "You're back," she said gleefully, stating the obvious. Then she grabbed his arms and kissed him, right there on the street for anyone passing by to see.

"I've missed you," he said.

"Is that why you're back?" This was too good to be true. Was he really here? She held on to his arms, sure he'd vanish if she let go.

"Yeah, it is. I need you in my life."

"I'll go away with you."

"No. You'd just be helping me run away from my own insecurities. Anyway, this is where you belong so this is where I need to be." He smiled. "It's where I want to be."

"Oh, Stephen!" she cried, and kissed him again.

"Get your purse, then hop on back," he said. "I'll take you home. It's time your dad and I had a talk."

If her father was surprised to find Stephen in the living room, sipping lemonade with Muriel and Mother when he came home from work, he didn't show it. "I see you're back."

"Yes, sir, I am. I came to talk to you."

"Come on, Muriel," Mother said, "let's go see about dinner."

She didn't want to see about dinner. She wanted to stay right here in the living room and supervise this all-important talk.

"We'll be fine," Stephen assured her, and Mother nudged her out of the room. Daddy made it final by shutting the pocket door in her face.

Happily, the phone rang. Her mother picked up the kitchen extension. "Oh, hello, Betty."

That was a gift. Mother would be talking to Mrs. Green for a good fifteen minutes. Muriel escaped and hurried down the hall, where she positioned herself by the pocket door. She pressed her ear to it.

"I see you cut your hair," Daddy was saying.

Muriel had to stifle a groan. This wasn't going well.

"It's easier to take care of when it's short."

"Is that what you're about, young man? Taking the easy way?"

"If it was, I wouldn't be here, sir. If it was, I'd have gone to Canada instead of 'Nam."

"You were in Vietnam?"

"Yes." The word came out curtly.

"Well," Daddy said slowly. "I had no idea. Did a tour in Korea myself. A man sees things."

"Yeah, he does."

"So, why are you back in town?"

"I think you can figure that out, Mr. Patrick."

Muriel smiled.

"You could've come to me the first time, you know," Daddy said sternly.

"I could have. But Muriel made it clear you didn't want to meet me."

All that sneaking off to meet him, it had seemed like such a smart idea. Now she realized it had been immature and foolish and had done nothing to help the cause.

"Did she?" Daddy said thoughtfully. "Well, she was right. You didn't look like the kind of man I want for my daughter. And I'm still not convinced you are. What are your plans for the future?"

"I'm not sure yet," Stephen admitted. "But one thing I do know—Muriel's the most important part of it."

It was all she could do not to open the door, fly into the room and throw herself into Stephen's arms.

"Look, I'm not a bum," Stephen said, "and I want to marry your daughter."

"She's too young," Daddy told him.

"I'll wait until she's old enough, then."

"And just what will you do while you're waiting, ride around on that motorcycle of yours?"

"I'll do whatever I need to do—dig ditches, drive a delivery truck."

"And that's how you plan to support my daughter?"

Muriel knew that tone of voice. She pressed a fist to her mouth.

"No. There are colleges nearby. I'll go back to school on the G.I. bill."

Now all Muriel could hear was silence. She pressed her ear harder against the door.

"Okay, son," Daddy said at last. "Show me you mean business and then we'll talk."

"No offense, sir, but I'm not waiting four years to date your daughter."

Good for you, Stephen. Good for us! Muriel smiled. She thought she heard her father chuckle.

"Tell you what," Daddy said. "You get a year of school under your belt. Go back to Swede's or get a job in the grocery store. If you can hold down a job for a year and I hear good things about you, then maybe I can find a place for you at Sweet Dreams."

Muriel could hardly believe her ears. It was like the king promising a peasant part of his kingdom.

"You've got a deal," Stephen said.

A moment later, her father called out, "You can come in now, Muriel. I know you're out there listening."

How had he known? Who cared? She entered the room smiling and linked her arms through Stephen's. "I told you that you were wrong about him, Daddy."

"Time will tell," said her father.

Six

COME CHRISTMAS THAT YEAR, MURIEL HAD AN engagement ring.

"It's beautiful," Pat said, when she'd stopped by to exchange gifts. "I'm so happy for you." She handed over Muriel's present. "I hope you'll like this."

Muriel opened the box to find a photo album inside. "Someplace to put the pictures of you and Stephen."

It was a perfect present, and Muriel thanked her and hugged her. Then she pulled a small box out from under the Christmas tree. "And here's yours."

Pat opened it and gasped in delight at the sight of the silver heart necklace. She picked it up and read what had been engraved on it. Best friends forever. "It's perfect," she said. "I love it!"

"That's us," Muriel said. "Let's never forget it, because friendship is the best gift a woman could ever get."

Epilogue

"STEPHEN WOUND UP GOING TO COLLEGE, AND after he graduated he went to work for my father," Muriel said to the girls gathered around her. "A few months later we were married. Sweet Dreams turned out to be a perfect fit for my husband. He fell in love with the business, and he and my father actually became good friends. Eventually, Daddy retired and Stephen took over running the company. I helped out in the early days, but then I got busy running our home. And writing.

"We had three wonderful daughters and a wonderful life together. So, as you can see, all ended well for us."

"You lived happily ever after," Aurora said dreamily.

"Because my grandma didn't steal your boyfriend," Clara added, and shot an angry look at her former BFF.

"No," Muriel said gently. "Because we both wound up with

the men we were supposed to be with. Jimmy Wilder came to town and your grandma found the man of her dreams, too. And one of the things that's made me so happy all these years is my friendship with her. I'd hate to have lost that because we quarreled over a man."

"Anyway, people can't help who they love," put in Bailey.

"If a guy's not into you he's not the right one for you," Cecily added.

"Besides, being mad at your friends is bad for your digestion," Dot said, and popped a mini quiche into her mouth.

Clara frowned, still not convinced that losing the boy of her dreams was a good thing.

Cecily sat next to her on the floor and put an arm around her. "I have a feeling that the perfect boyfriend for you is right around the corner."

Clara looked at Cecily as if she knew the secrets of the universe. "Who?"

"I can't tell you that," Cecily said. "But I can tell you he'll be worth the wait."

"So that means you can keep your girlfriend," Bailey added.

"Keep the girlfriend and lose the guy," Dot advised. "Men are a pain in the patootie."

That made the girls giggle and Dot's friends frown in disapproval.

Aurora stole a look at Clara, who was suddenly very busy picking lint off her sweater. "Want to get some punch?" she ventured.

Clara nodded and they made their way to the punch bowl with the other girls following suit.

"Crisis averted," Samantha said as she watched the two girls hug each other. "Good job, Mom."

Muriel smiled and shook her head. "I can't really take credit for that. The girls would have made up eventually."

"Yeah, but you saved us from having to endure teen girl drama," Dot said.

"And maybe you opened their eyes just a little," Pat said. "Friendship is one of God's greatest gifts."

"Right up there with family," Cecily said, and smiled at Bailey.

"And so is being together at Christmas," put in Olivia.

"Gack," said Dot in disgust. "Next, one of you is going to say, 'God bless us, everyone.'"

"God bless us, everyone," Samantha said, deadpan, making Dot frown and the other women laugh.

Dot shook her head. "Never mind all that sweet, syrupy stuff." She raised her cup of punch. "Let's stick to our traditional toast," she said to her friends. "Here's to us, none like us."

"Amen to that," said Pat, raising her cup. "And here's to Christmas and to being able to gather with family and friends."

"To love and BFFs," added Cecily, looking at the next generation, gathered around the punch bowl and giggling.

Muriel followed her daughter's gaze and smiled. Family, friendship, romance—love had a way of working things out no matter where trouble sprang up. Oh, yes, it was going to be another wonderful Christmas in Icicle Falls.

★ ★ ★ ★ ★

Starstruck

....

RaeAnne Thayne

Also available from HQN
The Cowboys of Cold Creek series
from *New York Times* bestselling author RaeAnne Thayne

STARSTRUCK
LIGHT THE STARS
DANCING IN THE MOONLIGHT
DALTON'S UNDOING
THE COWBOY'S CHRISTMAS MIRACLE
A COLD CREEK HOMECOMING
A COLD CREEK HOLIDAY
A COLD CREEK SECRET
A COLD CREEK BABY
CHRISTMAS IN COLD CREEK
A COLD CREEK REUNION
A COLD CREEK NOEL
A COLD CREEK CHRISTMAS SURPRISE
A COLD CREEK STORY
THE CHRISTMAS RANCH
THE HOLIDAY GIFT
THE RANCHER'S CHRISTMAS SONG

Prologue

As usual, the annual Christmas party at Carson and Jenna McRaven's house was crowded, crazy and her absolute favorite night of the year—next to Christmas Eve itself, of course.

Ruby Hartford sat with her three BFFs, Destry Bowman, Gabi Parsons and Ava Webster, in their favorite corner, looking through the big glass windows into the pool inside the McRavens' supercool house.

They had a big plate of delish snacks in front of them—cookies of every description, a few melt-in-your-mouth brownies and these little swirly appetizer things that looked as if they would be gross but were absolutely fantastic.

Her best friends, Christmas decorations and music all around them, and good stuff to eat. Best. Party. Ever. In all her thirteen years, she'd never been to a better one.

She glanced through the glass and spied the very cute Drew Wheeler standing at the pool's edge. He seemed to be talking to his little sister Jolie, but his attention was most definitely on her and her friends.

Ruby nudged Destry. "He's so checking you out. I told you. I think Drew has a thing for you."

"What happened to that kid?" Gabi said. "Last year he was this quiet kid in glasses who always had his nose in a book. This year he's suddenly, whoa."

It was definitely true. In the board shorts he was wearing, Ruby could see the muscles that had suddenly popped out overnight and he must have shot up a foot since the Christmas before. He wasn't as built as his brother Hayden, but Hayden was sixteen and in high school.

"He is cute, I'll admit," Destry said, peeking out the corner of her gaze at him and then quickly turning back to them. "Why would you think he's looking at me?"

"Just trust me. He is," Ruby assured her. Even though he was a year ahead of the rest of them in school, Ruby considered herself pretty good friends with Drew since their ranches were close to each other and they rode the bus together.

More than once, Drew had not-quite-casually asked about Destry, but she didn't want to betray their friendship by admitting that since she knew it would embarrass him.

Gabi, always the skeptic, gave a snort. "He doesn't even have his glasses on. He's not looking at anything. He probably doesn't even know we're here."

"Oh, he knows," Ruby insisted.

"Who is *he* and what does he know?"

At the curious adult voice, she turned around and saw her mom and dad had wandered over. They were holding hands, as usual, which always made her heart happy.

"Oh, nothing. I think Drew likes Destry, that's all."

"Ruby!" Destry exclaimed, her face turning almost the same red as the ornaments on the tree next to them.

"I just think you guys would be cute together. What's the harm in a little matchmaking? Tell them what a good track record I have at it!"

Her dad made a face but her mom only smiled softly. Ruby never called Ashley her stepmother. Even though her parents hadn't married until she was six, Ashley was the only mom she had ever known.

"Who else have you brought together?" Ava asked curiously.

Ruby grinned and pointed at her parents. Yeah. She rocked at matchmaking.

"Really?" Destry asked, eyes wide. "I always wondered how a Hollywood movie star met and married the best kindergarten teacher in Pine Gulch."

"It's a *great* story," Ruby assured her.

"I bet it's so romantic," Ava said, her voice barely a whisper. It weirded Ruby out, but Ava—who used to be so normal—could barely talk around Justin Hartford after watching several of his movies with her cousins when she went back to Chicago for a week over the summer.

"Oh, yeah." Her father grinned. "Romantic. I was a regular knight in shining armor."

"You were. Eventually." Her mom gave him the kind of secretive, goofy look they were always exchanging. "Of course, it took a while for me to see you that way after you thought I was some kind of celebrity stalker and threatened to have me arrested."

"Oh, you have to tell us the whole story now!" Destry exclaimed.

"Well, if you insist." Her mom handed Ruby's little brother Jess over to Ruby's dad and settled onto the sofa next to Des. "You see, it all started with a rascal of a kindergartener who wouldn't do her schoolwork...."

One

JUSTIN HARTFORD WAS A JERK.

Ashley Barnes leaned against the hood of her car glaring at the locked gates to the sprawling Blue Sage ranch and repeated the words like a mantra. Jerk. Jerk. *Jerk.*

He was a narcissistic egomaniac who thought the entire world had nothing better to do but impinge on his personal space. Of course he would have locked gates. He wasn't about to give mere mortals easy access to him.

Too darn bad. She had to talk to him *today.* If repeated phone calls, letters and emails weren't going to do the trick, she would just have to bust down these gates until the man agreed to talk to her.

She sighed. Well, okay, that probably wasn't the most brilliant idea she had ever come up with. As much as she adored her lime-green VW bug, she was afraid it didn't have the necessary gumption to break through a couple of eight-foot-high iron gates.

Failure was *not* an option, though. She and the jerk in question had been heading for this shoot-out for three weeks. Whether he knew it or not—or whether he even cared—she had given Justin Hartford an ultimatum in her mind. His time for avoiding her had just run out.

She eyed the gates, all eight menacing feet of them. She hadn't grown up on a horse ranch with four older brothers without learning a thing or two about hurdling fences, shinnying up trees and swinging out of barn lofts on old, fraying ropes. Climbing the man's gate wouldn't exactly be easy, but he wasn't giving her a lot to work with here.

She sighed, grateful at least that she was wearing jeans. She had to jump three times before she could reach the crossbar on the fence. From there, it was easy enough to hoist herself up. She perched along the top bar for just a moment—only long enough to catch a terrifying glimpse of a horse and rider heading toward her at a neck-or-nothing pace.

Rats. It was too far to jump unless she wanted to risk a broken ankle, so she had to slither down like one of her kindergarten children on the monkey bars. She hit the ground and turned around just as a gorgeous Arabian raced up in a swirling cloud of dust.

Ashley caught a quick glimpse of the horse's rider and her pulse rate kicked up a notch. Her mouth suddenly felt as dry as a Cold Creek tributary after a three-year drought. It was the jerk himself. She couldn't mistake those chiseled features and that strong jaw for anyone else.

She had a quick mental picture of him in *Last Chance,* when he had played a wounded outlaw with a tragic secret. She loved that movie. She loved *all* his movies.

Too bad they were all Hollywood make-believe.

Two

STORY:
Justin reined the horse in and tipped his hat back. Ashley took an instinctive step back at the menace on his features. Had she ever really been so young and so stupid to think she was hopelessly in love with him?

"You've got two choices here, lady," he growled. "You either climb back the way you came or we wait here until the sheriff shows up to arrest you for trespassing. Which one do you prefer?"

A chorus line of nerves started tap-dancing in her stomach, and she couldn't seem to think straight with those midnight-blue eyes boring into her.

"Go ahead and call the sheriff, Mr. Hartford. In fact," she added brightly, "I can do it for you if you'd like, since I've got him on speed dial on my cell phone. I have *all* my brothers on speed dial. Luke is number two, right after Mom and Dad. It's only fair, since he's the oldest and that seemed the easiest way to keep the numbers straight. I should probably put Evan at number two since I call him most often. He's the brother just older than me. We're only two years apart so we are probably the closest. Still, he's at number three. I don't call the twins very often since they live on the coast, so they're at five and six. But like I said, Luke is number two, so it would be easy to get him here fast if that's what you want to do—"

By the time she had the sense to realize she was rambling and could manage to clamp her teeth together to stem the gushing flow of stupidity, Justin Hartford's famously gorgeous eyes had started to cross.

This was all his own fault, she thought, crabby all over again. He didn't need to sit there on his horse and glower at her as if she was the treasonous spy in one of his movies.

"I'm sorry," she said stiffly. "You don't care about any of that. When I'm nervous I ramble."

"I hadn't noticed," he muttered, with such condescension she wanted to smack him. "Enlightening family history aside, you're still trespassing—an eight-foot-high locked iron gate is usually a big tip-off there."

She drew in a cleansing breath and let it out again. This wasn't going well. She needed to put aside her instinctive nervous reaction to her silly teenage heartthrob and focus on the crisis at hand—the reason she was there.

"It's your own fault. If you weren't such a…a darn *hermit* maybe I wouldn't have to resort to such drastic measures."

He blinked. "A hermit?"

"Yes! How am I supposed to talk to you if you hardly leave the Blue Sage?"

"I happen to like my privacy, Ms.…."

She drew herself up to her full five-foot-three inches tall

and glared at him with all the frustration that had been burning through her for three weeks. "Ashley Barnes. Ruby's kindergarten teacher. Whether you want to be bothered or not, it is imperative I talk to you about your daughter."

Three

JUSTIN LOOKED DOWN AT THE SOFT LITTLE blonde peach in the dusty-pink sweater who had just scaled his gate like some kind of Olympic gymnast. Ruby's kindergarten teacher. He winced, embarrassed he had mistaken her for an obsessed fan.

Though he had walked away from Hollywood six years ago and moved to eastern Idaho without a backward glance, away from the attention he had never wanted, sometimes it followed him. He wasn't obsessive about security. But what else was he supposed to think when he spied a woman climbing over his gate?

"Kind of drastic measures to take for a parent-teacher conference, don't you think?" he asked as he slid down from his horse.

Her hazel eyes narrowed at him and he had to admit, up

close she was seriously cute. Small and feminine, with short blond curls held back in a headband and dimples that appeared even when she was glaring at him.

She looked like a cream puff. Like a delicious, sugary, melt-in-your-mouth confection. He had sworn off sweets a long time ago, but that didn't make the sudden intense craving any easier to ignore.

"I wouldn't have *had* to resort to such drastic measures as climbing your stupid gate if you could be bothered just once to answer one of my *dozens* of pleas to set up a meeting."

She didn't let him answer—not that he had the first idea what she was talking about.

"I realize you're a very busy, very important man," she snapped, her hands fisted on her hips.

How did the curl of those luscious lips make the words sound like an epithet? he wondered.

"I'm sure you must have scores of people to see and all that," she went on. "But you're an actor—or you used to be, anyway. Couldn't you at least *pretend* you care about your child?"

He jerked his attention from her lips as her words filtered through. "Excuse me?"

"You probably pay more attention to that horse of yours than you do to your own daughter!"

Justin was usually pretty good at keeping his temper under wraps. But he wasn't about to let some sanctimonious school-teacher question how he raised his daughter. Ruby was the most important thing in his life. The only thing that mattered. Everything he did was for her and he didn't take kindly to anyone insinuating otherwise.

"You don't know anything about me or about my daughter if you can say that."

The cream puff didn't exactly deflate in the face of his anger, but she did back down a little.

"I'm sorry," she said stiffly. "But for three weeks I have been trying every method under the sun, except carrier pigeons, to get your attention, and you have ignored every single one of my attempts to contact you. If you were in my shoes, wouldn't you have the same impression, of an uninvolved parent who doesn't care a hill of beans about his daughter's education? I finally decided I would talk to you today, even if I had to climb your gate to do it."

Four

HE TIPPED HIS HAT BACK FARTHER, COMPLETELY baffled by the obvious concern in her voice. "I'm sure this is some kind of a mistake. I haven't heard anything about any problems Ruby might be having in school. Did you talk to her great-aunt about it?"

She moved forward, so close he could smell her, like vanilla and almonds. His mouth instantly watered but he pushed it aside.

"Several times," she answered, oblivious—he hoped—to his sudden hunger.

"Lydia has promised me that she and Ruby talked about it and Ruby promised her things would change. But nothing has."

The school term had been underway for a month now and he had been under the impression everything was fine. Pine

Gulch, Idaho, wasn't exactly overflowing with educational opportunities and the local public school was the only option for his five-year-old daughter. He could have hired tutors for Ruby when she reached school-age, but he wanted her to have the most normal life possible. To him, that meant school lunch and recess and spelling bees.

All the things he never had.

It was tough enough on a kid having a dad who had once been a celebrity. He hadn't wanted to make things harder on Ruby by showing up at her school all the time and reminding everyone of it, so he and his aunt had agreed she would be his go-between with the school.

Lydia served as his housekeeper, nanny and confidante. She had raised him, after all, and had been the logical person to turn to for help raising Ruby the day she had been dumped on him when she was only two months old.

He loved Lydia dearly, but she did have a bad habit of trying to solve all his problems for him.

"Lydia and Ruby never said a word about any trouble at school. In fact, all I hear from Ruby is how much she loves it. She talks about it all the time. About her friends and how much she's learning and how much she loves her teacher. I guess that would be you."

Miss Barnes had been the major topic of conversation since school started a month ago, he reflected. Ruby had jabbered endlessly about how pretty and nice and smart her teacher was, until he had begun to dislike the woman before he'd even met her.

Just now the nice, pretty teacher was staring at him as if he were the alien space creature from the single sci-fi picture he'd made.

"She said she loved her teacher? Are we talking about the same child here? Mr. Hartford, your daughter *hates* school!

And me! Or at least she manages to give a very convincing impression of a child who does."

"Hates it? You've got to be kidding! She doesn't talk about anything else!"

"The first week of the school year, things seemed fine. Ruby was making friends, she was enthusiastic about learning, she was attentive in class and participated in discussions. Then three weeks ago, everything changed."

"Three weeks ago?"

"Right. I've seen a dramatic turnaround. Ruby has gone from being a sweet little girl to one who seems absolutely miserable, from the moment she arrives at lunchtime to when she leaves at the end of the day. She is sullen and uncooperative. If I call on her in class, she clamps her lips together, and she turns every assignment over on her desk without even putting her name on it."

Five

HE STARED, HIS MIND CHURNING TO MAKE sense of this. "That's not like Ruby at all. This can't be right."

"Look, Mr. Hartford, I'm only trying to get to the bottom of the rapid change in Ruby's behavior. Have you noticed a similar change at home?"

"No. She's been the same as always—energetic, curious, a little on the mischievous side, maybe. But overall, she's a great kid."

Her prickly attitude seemed to soften a little at his words. "I'll admit, I'm stumped. Did anything happen about three weeks ago that might have contributed to her acting out?"

He racked his brain, trying to think back. They had made a quick weekend trip to L.A. to visit a friend who was having an engagement party to celebrate her second marriage. That was the only thing that came to mind. "I don't know. I can't think of anything specific."

"I must tell you, I'm wondering if perhaps Ruby is not quite ready for kindergarten. Some children take longer to mature than others, especially if there is some...upheaval in their lives."

She said the last part with such subtle contempt that he simmered. She didn't know anything about him—except maybe what she read in the tabloids.

"You're wrong, Miss Barnes. Ruby has been ready for kindergarten since she was three years old. She is smart and precocious and curious and loves learning. I can't imagine what's happened since she started in your classroom to change that."

Her gaze narrowed and he realized how his words could be misconstrued. "You can bet I intend to find out," he said quickly. "I'm sure once we sit down together we can figure out what's going on. Ruby and Lydia have gone to Jackson, shopping for the day, or I would go grab her right now and have this out. Any chance you can come back later?"

"I have plans tonight," she said stiffly, a hint of color in her cheeks. A hot date? he wondered, and was stunned at his disappointment.

"We can make an appointment to meet one day this week after school," she offered.

"I'm leaving Monday to go to Denver on a horse-buying trip until Friday. What about tomorrow night? We'll even throw in dinner for your trouble."

A host of emotions flashed through those expressive eyes—reluctance at the forefront among them, something that suddenly annoyed him. "I... Yes. I suppose that would be all right."

"Does seven sound okay?"

She nodded those soft curls. "Yes."

"This has got to be a big misunderstanding. Ruby is a great kid. You'll see. We'll get to the bottom of it."

"I hope so. Ruby's negative attitude is becoming disruptive to the entire afternoon class."

"I'll see you tomorrow night, then. Oh, and Miss Barnes," he said with a smile as he pushed the button to open the gate, "perhaps it would be better if you rang the buzzer when you arrive for dinner tomorrow. I wouldn't want you to fall from the top of the gate next time and miss the appetizer."

He laughed at the hot glare she sliced at him. As he watched her march back through the gates and climb into her fluorescent car, he was aware of the unwilling attraction settling low in his gut.

Six

H E WAS CHARMED BY HER, JUSTIN THOUGHT AS he watched Ruby's teacher drive away. He had to admire any woman passionate enough about her job to climb a fence, just to get her point across. Not to mention those delectable lips....

Nothing could come of it. He knew that. Miss Ashley Barnes had *commitment* written all over her cute little face and he had a terrible track record in that department.

He had decided after Ruby came into his life that he just had to close the door on anything long-term. He had been burned too many times. He picked the wrong kind of women to tangle with and then ended up paying for it.

Ruby's mother had been the final straw. Tamara Drake had been an aspiring actress he met at a party and dated a few times, unaware that underneath her fun, sexy act was a predatory woman who thought trapping him by becoming pregnant with his child would seal her celebrity status. Tamara's pregnancy and her increasingly strident demands on him had been Justin's wake-up call that his life was not traveling a course he wanted. He had fathered a child with a woman he barely knew and one he had come to despise, and the grim reality of it all forced him to take a good, hard look at himself.

He hadn't been very crazy about what he saw. He was just like Tamara, he had realized. He had become selfish, materialistic, shallow. He went after what he wanted at the moment without thought of the consequences, and he knew he couldn't continue on that road.

He started looking for a quiet western town to settle in, told Tamara he was leaving Hollywood and offered a financial settlement and annuity in return for her signing over parental rights to Ruby to him. Though she had been livid at him for walking away, she certainly hadn't wanted to be saddled with a baby. She agreed with alacrity and died a year later of a drug overdose.

It was an ugly story, one that still made him ashamed of the man he had been six years ago.

He had changed. Ruby had seen to that, but he still didn't trust his own judgment about women. Tamara had just been the last in a long line of mistakes, and with a child's fragile emotions to consider, he couldn't afford the high price anymore.

He avoided the spotlight now as much as he could, but to his jaded eye, it seemed as if every woman he met since Tamara was mostly interested in him for his ex-celebrity status, enthralled, for some crazy reason, to be seen with a man who had once been moderately famous.

It turned his stomach. He wanted them to see beyond the image that had appeared on far too much movie-related merchandise. To see the man whose favorite things now were mowing the lawn on a warm summer afternoon, playing outside in the sunshine with his daughter, training a good horse.

He didn't trust many women and he certainly didn't trust his own judgment. This way was better. Just him and Ruby and Lydia. They made a good team and there just wasn't room for any more players.

Not even cute-as-pie schoolteachers with dimples and hazel eyes and blond, starlit curls.

Seven

"*ALL A BIG MISUNDERSTANDING.* RIGHT. CAN YOU believe that man? Does he think I don't know what's going on in my own classroom?"

"The nerve!" Josie Roundy exclaimed.

"He should be horsewhipped," Marcy Weller agreed.

Her two best friends looked at each other and grinned, and Ashley fought the urge to bean them both with the wok she was setting up on the stove top.

She should be grateful they were there, she told herself. They had both agreed to her last-minute invitation so she wouldn't be consumed with guilt for lying to Jason Hartford.

She hadn't wanted to tell him the truth—that she had no plans other than lesson prep work—but she also hadn't been ready to turn around and drive back to the Blue Sage that night, not without a little more time to psych herself up to facing him again. As salve to her conscience, she had called Josie and Marcy over for an impromptu party watching movies and making Chinese food and venting about the man himself.

"You should have seen the way he looked at me, like I was some deranged fan come to steal his boxers or something. Good grief."

"Well, you did climb over his gate," Marcy pointed out from the sink, where she was washing vegetables. "You can't blame the man for being a little suspicious about you."

"If I were going to become a stalker, why would I pick a washed-up recluse of an actor?"

"Because he's a big hot bundle of yum?" Josie suggested.

Marcy made a face. "Yum factor aside, you know perfectly well he's not washed-up, Ash. He walked away at the top of his game. I bet right this minute he could still step into any role he wanted and find himself back on the A-list. He just doesn't want to be there."

She had to admit, Marcy was right about that. Justin had the intensity and range of a truly great actor. And the cameras had loved him.

"I still cry every time I watch him in *Warrior*," Josie said.

Ashley didn't want to admit that she did, too—and that she'd watched the DVD just the other night.

"How many times did we drive to Idaho Falls to see *Last Chance* when we were sixteen?" Marcy laughed. "At least a dozen. Remember how you used to have that picture of him in your locker with his shirt half ripped off and his sexy black Stetson and that hard look in his eyes?"

Josie snickered as she twisted another egg roll. "If there was ever an obsessed stalker fan back then, it would have been you, Ash. I seem to remember you writing *Mrs. Justin Hart-*

ford on everything from your algebra homework to the pizza napkins at Stoneys."

"Will you two just forget about that? For heaven's sake! It was more than a decade ago. Marcy's already given me a hard time about my stupid crush."

She loved her friends dearly. They had been friends since *they* were all in kindergarten and she found great comfort in that kind of continuity. She just sometimes wished they didn't know every single detail about her life.

"You're supposed to be sympathetic here. I was a silly teenager. What did I know about what to look for in a man? All I cared about ten years ago were dreamy eyes and six-pack abs."

"Two things Justin Hartford still has," Josie pointed out with a slightly overheated gleam in her own eyes. "He came into the hardware store last week for hex screws and I just about drooled all over his cowboy boots."

"Dreamy eyes are fine but not when they come as a package deal with a man willing to abdicate his responsibility to his child."

"That's unfair," Marcy spoke up as she drained the vegetables. "He invited you to come back and talk to Ruby about her behavior, didn't he? I wonder if you would be so mad at him right now if you hadn't had such a crush on him back in the day."

"Yeah," Josie warmed to the theory. "Maybe you built him up in your wild little fantasy world for so long that finding out the real man is just a struggling father with the same problems as the rest of us has left you heartbroken and disillusioned."

She had to admit, there might be some truth in what they said. She had this image in her head of him as the hard-driving, hard-living hero he played so well. It was a little hard to reconcile that with the father of her biggest behavior problem.

She sighed. She was *not* looking forward to dinner the next night. How did a girl dress to have dinner with her teenage crush?

Eight

BY THE NEXT EVENING, AS HE WAS PREPPING THE steaks for dinner, Justin still didn't have a clue what was going on with Ruby and school.

He had tried to talk to his daughter about it a dozen times, but she had been acting strangely ever since she found out Miss Barnes was coming to dinner. She was popping out of her skin with an odd kind of excitement and every time he tried to bring up school, she made some excuse to escape.

He hadn't pushed it, though he knew he should. He didn't really have a good handle on the extent of the problem, and he thought maybe it would be better if he waited until the teacher was there.

Lydia hadn't been much help, either. When he talked to her the night before, he found his aunt was firmly of the opinion that Ruby was only misbehaving as a coping mechanism to adjust to school. She wasn't used to being around other children all the time, everything was new and she had the added complication of being the daughter of the town's only celebrity, which automatically set her apart, Lydia thought.

She had talked to Ruby several times and the girl had promised she would do better. Lydia wanted to give her a little more time to adjust and she hadn't wanted to bother Justin with it, especially as they had agreed she would be the liaison with the school.

She had nothing but praise for the teacher, though. Justin had had just about enough of hearing about all of Ashley Barnes's wonderful qualities.

He sighed. He already had enough trouble with the females in his life. Why did he even think for a moment he needed to add more? Still, he hadn't been able to get the teacher out of his mind. He had dreamed of her last night and had awoken aroused and embarrassed and with an intense hunger for cream puffs.

He jerked his mind away from those unruly images. "Ruby, you need to set the table," he called. "Your teacher will be here any minute now."

"Coming, Daddy," she called from the other room and a moment later she flounced into the room. *Flounce* was exactly the word for it—she was wearing the ruffly girlie dress she and Lydia had bought the day before in Jackson.

She was all taffeta and lace, with mismatched ankle socks and her favorite sparkly sneakers.

He hid a smile. "Honey, you can't wear that. You'll ruin the pretty dress you and Aunt Lydia bought to wear to Sierra's mom's wedding next month."

"I want Miss Barnes to see it. She'll like the way it twirls. See, Daddy?" She spun in a circle, eyes wide with delight, and a lump rose in his throat. He loved this crazy, funny little thing so much it was a physical ache in his chest sometimes.

"You're having a hot dog, though, and you know how messy those can be. You wouldn't want to spill mustard on your dress, would you?"

Her brow furrowed as she considered and he pushed his advantage while he had it. "Set the table out on the deck and then go up and change into something else. After dinner maybe you can change into your new dress to show Miss Barnes."

He knew that before too much longer, he wouldn't be able to convince her of anything so easily, but for now his logic could still sway her.

"Okay." She ran to the cupboard for the plates then stopped and gave him a considering look. "You should wear your blue shirt, Daddy. The one that's soft and silky. Aunt Lydia said you turn all the ladies to mush when you wear it."

Before he could ask why she might want him to turn her kindergarten teacher to mush—a task he doubted he had the ability to perform, much as he and his libidinous dreams might like to—she rushed outside with an armload of plates and silverware.

She had just returned for glasses when the buzzer on the front gates rang. Ruby shrieked with excitement. "She's here! She's here! She's really here!"

Nine

RUBY RACED TO THE INTERCOM AND CONTROL console for the electronic gates. "Miss Barnes! Miss Barnes! Hi, Miss Barnes! I'm going to push the button and open the gate, okay? Okay?"

There was a slight pause then Ashley's voice filled the kitchen and even through the intercom he could hear the amusement in it. "Thank you very much, Ruby."

She pushed the button then jumped away from the console. "You let her in while I go change, Daddy. I'll be right back."

He started to call her back—since she was already in the dress, she might as well show it off now instead of later—but she was gone, heading up the stairs at a full-out run.

The doorbell rang and Justin was startled at the way his pulse kicked up against his will.

He walked out to the entryway and opened the door then

forgot to even say hello. She looked sweet and lovely and delicious enough to gobble up in one bite. He was so busy trying to convince himself he wasn't hungry that he almost missed the wary look in her eyes.

"Hi. I'm early. I'm sorry."

He was a little rusty as a host but he tried to do his best. "Not at all. Come in. Ruby's gone to change her clothes and I'm not sure where my aunt has vanished to. I'm sure she'll be along soon."

She held out something in a white box wrapped in string. "I brought dessert. I didn't know what you were serving so I didn't know what kind of wine would be appropriate. And, anyway, I thought Ruby might enjoy something sweet more."

"What is it?"

"Raspberry ribbon cheesecake. It's my mom's recipe."

"Ruby will love it. I'll just put it in the refrigerator. Why don't you come outside with me while I put the steaks on?"

"You're cooking?"

He had to smile at the utter disbelief in her voice. "I'm grilling. There's a world of difference between the two. Throwing a couple steaks on the grill doesn't exactly take much except a good spice rub recipe and a meat thermometer."

She still looked flabbergasted as he gestured her ahead of him into the kitchen. She walked past him and again the tantalizing scents of vanilla and almonds—with a hint of raspberry now—teased him.

He closed his eyes, stunned by the overwhelming urge to lean forward and bury his face in her curls and just inhale.

It had been far too long since he had been with a woman. Months. That must be the reason for this sudden fascination with this soft schoolteacher.

One of the downsides of being a responsible single father was the serious crimp it put in any casual encounters. It never seemed right to bring women home for the night with Ruby in the house and lately he had been taking her along on the few trips he took out of town.

He had entertained some vague idea about calling Lexie Walker when he went to Denver on the horse-buying trip next week to see if she might be interested in flying out to meet him, as she had done a few times before. Lexie was a producer he had known in L.A. She was sharp, beautiful and sexy as silk sheets.

Oddly, the idea suddenly didn't appeal to him at all. He didn't have to look far to figure out why.

Ten

"THIS IS LOVELY," ASHLEY EXCLAIMED WHEN they moved out onto the wide deck overlooking the western slope of the Tetons. With delight evident on her delicate features, she took in the twinkling lights in the trees shading the deck, the swimming pool with its waterfalls and spa, and the outdoor fireplace, where a merry blaze took out the slight chill of the September air.

Beyond the backyard, horses grazed near the whitewashed barn, and in the evening everything looked peaceful and still.

"We live out here when the weather is nice," he admitted. "And even sometimes when it's not. With the fireplace, we can enjoy it from March to early December sometimes, until the snow gets too deep on the deck."

"She must adore it out here! My word, look at that play set.

I think it's more elaborate than the playground equipment we have at school."

He smiled at her enthusiasm. "We'll have to have your class out for a party in the springtime when it's warm enough to swim again. Ruby would love it."

Her eyes glowed at the idea and she smiled, the first genuine, heartfelt smile she had ever given him.

He couldn't seem to look away from it, at the curve of her lips, at the way the left side lifted just a little higher than the right, at the dimples he suddenly hungered to taste.

The heated dreams of the night before suddenly rocketed through his brain and in his mind he was once more tangled in all that softness, touching his mouth to hers, tasting that sweetly curved mouth.

He heard a ragged-sounding breath and managed to drag his attention from her mouth—and from his own feverish imagination—to meet her gaze. Her pupils were wide, her color high, and thick, heady awareness suddenly bloomed between them.

He needed to kiss her. He didn't want to, he knew he shouldn't, but he had to know if she tasted as delicious as he had imagined. He couldn't seem to stop himself from leaning forward.

An instant before he reached her, he heard the bang of the screen door and jerked back just as Ruby raced out of the house.

"Here I am! I changed and everything. Hi, Miss Barnes!" She hugged her teacher's legs and Ashley looked dazed—whether from Ruby's affection or their almost-kiss, he couldn't guess.

"Do you want to come see my bedroom? It's pink and green and my bed is in a real playhouse!"

Ashley cast a furtive look at him, her color high. "I… Of course," she murmured, looking relieved at any excuse to escape.

"The steaks won't take long," he said, calling on all his long-neglected acting skills to keep any trace of embarrassment from his voice.

She nodded and walked out with Ruby's hand tucked in hers, leaving him alone in the starlight to wonder what the hell had just happened.

Eleven

JUSTIN HARTFORD HAD NEARLY KISSED HER. IF HIS daughter hadn't come bursting out onto the deck, Ashley had no doubt that with a half second more alone with him, she would have been in his arms.

She followed Ruby up a sweeping staircase constructed of hewn half logs, painfully aware of the way her knees trembled and her stomach still felt jittery and weak.

Justin Hartford. Almost. Kissed. Her.

He had wanted to, anyway. She had seen the sudden heat in those heartbreaking eyes of his, the slight parting of his lips, and hadn't been able to stop her body's instinctive sway toward him.

What a jerk, she thought, but the familiar imprecation held no heat whatsoever. She had wanted him to kiss her. Another minute or two and she probably would have *begged* him to.

They reached Ruby's bedroom and she could only stare. "Wow. This is your room?"

"Yep. It's cool, huh?"

"Very cool." It was a dream of a room for a little girl. Everything was pink and flowery and Ruby had told the truth— her bed was built into a massive playhouse built into the center of the large room. It was like a room inside of a room, with a door and windows and a gabled roof that touched the ceiling.

"Daddy and me built the playhouse. I helped hammer the nails and measure the wood and everything."

"Oh?" It was very hard to dislike a man who could create such a wonderland for his child.

"Yep. My daddy makes really good things. My aunt Liddy says he has always been good with his hands. She said when he was a kid, he was always making stuff from junk wood he found around. And he's strong, too. When we builded my bed, he carried all the wood in by himself."

Ruby frowned for a moment, her brow furrowed in concentration, then it cleared and she smiled. "Oh, and he makes up funny stories. My favorite is about the ugly hedgehog. Daddy does all kinds of voices when he tells stories and he always makes me laugh. You should hear him."

"Oh?" She tried to pretend disinterest, but in truth she was fascinated to hear about Justin's interactions with his daughter.

"Yeah, and he can swim superfast! You should see him. And he rides horses better than anybody else in the whole wide world. I have my own horse, but my favorite is when I ride with my daddy."

Why did Ruby suddenly remind her of a used car salesman trying to unload a junker? Ashley wondered uneasily. She really shouldn't be listening to all these things about Justin. It made him seem too real, entirely too likable.

Still, she forced herself to smile. "It sounds like you have a lot of fun with your dad."

"We're best buds. Me and Daddy and Aunt Liddy are a team. Daddy says so. I love him a ton."

She suddenly gave Ashley a funny sidelong look she couldn't quite interpret.

"Except I think maybe he's lonely."

Twelve

JUSTIN HARTFORD LONELY?

She couldn't even imagine it. Still, the conviction in the girl's voice set off warning bells. "Ruby, is that why you've been misbehaving in class? Because you think if you're naughty enough in school and don't do your work, you'll be sent home to the Blue Sage, where you can be with your father?"

Ruby's big blue eyes opened wide and she looked so genuinely startled at the suggestion that Ashley knew she must be completely off the mark.

The little girl giggled. "No! That's not why. You're silly."

Oh, she certainly was, especially if she thought a gorgeous, compelling man like Justin Hartford could ever be interested in a boring, naive schoolteacher like her.

"Will you tell me the reason?" she pressed. "I don't think you really hate school, even though you pretend you do."

"I don't hate it," she whispered. She looked down at the thick carpet of her room, digging the toe of her sneakers into the floral pattern.

Ashley paused, totally at sea to figure out what all this was about. "Is it me you don't like? Perhaps we could switch you to the other kindergarten teacher's class."

"Noooo!" Ruby looked horrified by the very idea. "I don't want another teacher. I *have* to be in your class. Please, Miss Barnes. Please don't make me go to another class!"

She was trying to process that impassioned plea when she heard footsteps in the hallway and a moment later, Justin stuck his head in.

He looked incongruous in the girlie room, dark and gorgeous and uber-masculine, and her heart gave a foolish little thump just at the sight of him.

Ruby jumped into his arms. "Hi, Daddy. I've been telling Miss Barnes about all the fun things we do and how you're such a good swimmer and a good horse rider. I bet she'd like to see you sometime."

He raised an eyebrow and Ashley refrained from commenting that she had seen his particular riding style when he had nearly mowed her over the day before.

"Oh, and Miss Barnes thinks the playhouse you made for me is cool," Ruby added.

He managed a smile. "Good to know. Uh, dinner is ready. I just checked on Lydia and she said she's feeling a little under the weather tonight so it's just the three of us, I guess. I hope you're hungry."

"I'm *starving!*" Ruby said with so much pathos in her voice, Ashley had to assume she had inherited more from her father than midnight-blue eyes and dark hair.

The little girl skipped ahead down the stairs, leaving the two of them alone.

She was intensely aware of Justin as they walked down the stairs. They didn't say anything, but the thick awareness flowed between them, leaving her jittery and unsettled as they walked out into the moonlit night.

Thirteen

DINNER WOULD LIVE ON FOREVER IN HER MEMory as one of the most surreal experiences of Ashley's life. She was having dinner with Justin Hartford—and not just any dinner, but one he prepared with his own hands. The fourteen-year-old girl who—she was ashamed to say—still sometimes popped up in her psyche wanted to swoon.

She found the whole experience disorienting. It was extraordinarily difficult to reconcile her different images of him—sexy, intense big-screen hero, then disinterested father—with the man who cut his daughter's hot dog and did really lousy impersonations.

Somehow they managed to put aside their discomfort over that awkward scene before dinner as they talked and laughed and listened to Ruby's apparently endless repertoire of bad knock-knock jokes.

She was charmed by both of them. This Ruby was a far different girl at home than she had been the past three weeks. Here was the girl she had met those first few days at school and Ashley wanted to know why she had disappeared.

And Justin. Every once in a while she would find him watching her with a baffled kind of heat in his eyes and her insides would flutter and sigh.

She was doing her best to ignore it, but she had never been so fiercely aware of a man.

Her heart was in serious danger here. She realized it sometime before they finished eating and he brought out her cheesecake. The man across the table was exactly the kind she dreamed of now, and that scared the heck out of her.

"I'm all done eating," Ruby said after she had all but licked her dessert plate clean. "Can I go change into my party dress to show Miss Barnes, Daddy? Can I?"

He looked reluctant but he nodded. "Go ahead. Hurry, though."

Without the buffer of Ruby and her chatter, Ashley's awareness of him became almost unbearable. She couldn't shake the disbelief that she was actually sitting on a starlit deck with Justin Hartford, a man she was finding increasingly attractive.

Without thinking, needing only to move suddenly, she stood up and started to clear away the dinner dishes.

"You don't have to do that," he said. "We usually don't make our guests clean up."

She felt her face heat. "Habit. Sorry. With five kids in my family, we all had to pitch in to help. I don't mind, though. Really, I don't. This way you don't have to clear them yourself later."

He rose and started helping her, and they worked in a silence that would have been companionable except for the vibes zinging between them like the kids on the zip line at the school playground.

"The sheriff is really your brother?" he asked after a moment.

She nodded. "He's always been good at telling people what to do. I guess that's because he's the oldest."

"I've met him a few times. He's a good man. Does that mean you grew up around here?"

She searched his rugged features for any clue that he might be patronizing her, but all she saw was genuine interest. "I've lived here all my life, except for the years I spent in college in Oregon. I suppose that must seem pretty provincial to someone like you."

"Not at all." He gave an almost bittersweet smile. "I envy you."

Fourteen

SHE BLINKED. "ME? I'M A BORING KINDERGARTEN teacher. I've never done anything exciting in my life."

Before tonight, anyway, she corrected to herself.

"Climbing over my gates doesn't count?"

She smiled. "Well, there was that. And the time I drove my dad's pickup over the mayor's mailbox."

His laugh did funny things to her insides. "I'm serious," he said. "It must be wonderful to have roots in a nice town like Pine Gulch. When I was looking at property to purchase, I knew the moment I stepped into town that this was what I wanted for Ruby."

"You didn't? Have roots, I mean?"

He was quiet for a long moment, leaning against the railing of the deck with the stars spilling across the sky behind him. "No. I grew up living out of suitcases and cheap hotels and sometimes even the backseat of my mom's old Pontiac. She was a wanderer who didn't like to stay in one place very long. When I was twelve, she dumped me off with Lydia in Chicago and never bothered to come back."

She heard the old pain in his voice and her heart ached with sympathy.

"I'm so sorry," she murmured, leaning against the railing beside him. "But I'm glad you had Lydia. I've taught children with no one at all to call their own."

"You're right. I was lucky, though I didn't think so at the time. Lydia tried. But by age twelve I had been basically on my own for a long time and didn't want much help from her. I equated caring with smothering. I took off when I was seventeen and headed for sunshine. L.A. I worked odd jobs for a while and ended up doing some stunt work as a favor to a friend and before I knew it, I was in movies."

She remembered the bones of his story from those early days when she used to scour *People* and *Us Weekly* looking for information about him, in the days before the internet would have put all those details at her fingertips. But, of course, she couldn't tell him that.

"What about you?" he asked. "What led you to teaching?"

"It's all I've ever wanted to do. I love children. I always have." She smiled. "I was the world's best babysitter because I could have done it all day for free just for the fun of it and everyone knew it. There is something so magical about early childhood, the innocence and the wonder and the sheer delight of it. I love watching them grow and start to test life. Setting them on a path to discover the world of possibilities waiting for them."

Her voice trailed off and she flushed. "I'm sorry. I'm rambling again."

"Not at all. I could listen to you all night."

Her gaze flashed to his and the heat in the midnight depths sent those nerves twirling through her insides again. She swallowed hard and had time only to wonder if this could possibly be real, when his mouth captured hers.

Fifteen

ASHLEY FROZE, THE BREATH CAUGHT IN HER throat and her pulse thundered in her ears.

Oh. Oh, my. His kiss was unbearably soft, almost tender, and she leaned into it, into him. Her hands rested on the hard muscles of his chest and she could feel the jump of his heartbeat beneath her fingertips. His arms slid around her, pulling her close, and she surrendered to the magic and wonder of his kiss.

She could definitely fall hard for this man.

His kiss suddenly deepened, his tongue licking at the corner of her mouth, and she lost any chance at coherent thought for several long, drugging moments.

"Okay, get ready!" she suddenly heard Ruby call from inside the house and the two of them sprang apart, both breathing hard, just as the girl burst through the door in all her finery.

★ ★ ★

What in the hell was he doing?

He invites the woman to dinner to talk about his daughter's problems in school then ends up dumping his life story on her before all but jumping her on his back deck.

The crazy thing was, he wanted to do it all over again. The kissing part, anyway. Justin could still taste her on his lips, that subtle, sweetly erotic taste of raspberry and cream and Ashley.

It was crazy. He knew it was impossible, but he ached to taste her again.

Focus, he chided himself and jerked his attention back to the conversation between Ruby and her teacher.

"See how twirly it is?" Ruby exclaimed, her arms wide as she did circles around the living room, where they had adjourned since there was more light to show off the sparkles.

Justin wasn't sure he was prepared for this primpy stage to start. Ruby was showing all the signs of someone who would be seriously girlie and he had no idea how to handle the rest of it. Just thinking about makeup and boyfriends and hair spray made him break into a cold sweat.

At least he had a few more years before he had to worry about that.

"You look just like a princess," Ashley assured Ruby. Her color was high, he saw, and she didn't look at him as she spoke.

Ruby preened, oblivious to the tension between them. "I'm going to wear it to a wedding. My friend Sierra's mom is getting married next month and we're going to Hawaii for it and I get to swim in the ocean and maybe see a dolphin."

She had been delirious with excitement about the whole thing, from the moment Natalie Brooks invited them along. Nat was his first leading lady and one of the few people he stayed in touch with in Hollywood.

"I don't get to be the flower girl because Sierra does," Ruby went on, "but I can wear my new dress and maybe have a lei, too."

Ashley gave a smile that looked forced and he would have given just about anything to know what was running through her head right about now. "How fun," she murmured. "You and your father will have to take lots of pictures so you can bring them back for the rest of the class to see."

"Okay. I will." She looked thrilled at the idea for just a moment before she frowned and her excitement slipped away. "Um, I'll have to see. I'll probably forget."

Right. Ruby remembered the names and birthdays and favorite colors of everyone she had ever met. This sudden reluctance was part of whatever game she had been playing at school. He sighed, knowing the time for socializing was over.

"Ruby, if you're done showing off your new dress, we need to talk about what's happening in school. You know that's why Miss Barnes is here."

Panic flared in her eyes suddenly, and she started edging for the stairs. "I better go change out of my dress before I get it all dirty."

"Come back here," he said, his voice stern. "We're going to sit down right now and discuss how you've been acting."

Sixteen

"DO I HAVE TO?" RUBY ASKED, LOOKING SUD-
denly miserable.

"Yeah, you do, shortcake."

"You'll be mad."

"Probably. But we still have to talk about it."

She perched on the edge of a leather ottoman, her hands tightly folded on her lap. He sighed, not sure where to start.

"I thought you loved school," he finally said. "You talk about it all the time. But Miss Barnes says you're not doing your work and you're not participating in class. What's going on?"

"I was just pretending I didn't like school," she said, her voice small. She lifted her gaze to give her teacher a look of earnest entreaty. "I really do, Miss Barnes. I promise. I love playtime and I love circle time and I love snack time. My favorite is story time. I love, love, *love* story time."

Ashley gazed at her, her lovely features baffled. "Why would you want to pretend you don't like it? It's wonderful to love learning!"

Ruby's chin wobbled. "It was Sierra's idea. She's my friend in California. She said if I was bad in class, my dad would have to come to school for a conference. And then he would fall in love with you and you would get married like Sierra's mom is getting married and then you could be my new mom."

Okay. This was just about the most horrifying moment of his life. A dead silence greeted Ruby's stunning declaration and Justin couldn't think what to do, what to say. He risked a look at Ashley and saw her features had leached of all color. Not a good sign.

He knew he had to step into the terrible silence. "Ruby..." he began, then faltered as he found himself at a loss for words. "People don't, uh, fall in love like that," he said after a moment. "You can't manipulate them into doing what you want just because you want it. Life doesn't work that way."

Sometimes it did, though. He had to be crazy, but he suddenly knew he was in serious danger of falling for this soft, sweet woman who loved children and smelled like a dream.

"But Miss Barnes already loves you, Daddy. You just have to fall in love with her."

"What?" Ashley exclaimed. To his somewhat thunderstruck fascination, all the color soaked back into her cheeks in a hot, relentless tide.

Ruby fidgeted, looking almost as miserable as Ashley. "I heard Miss Weller in the school office talking to you about Daddy a few days after school started. I had a stomachache and went to lie down in the sick-kid place, and I heard her ask if you had met Daddy yet and you said no and Miss Weller asked if you would mention at parent-teacher conference that you had his picture in your locker in school and that you used to write Mrs. Justin Hartford on things."

Seventeen

H E HEARD A SOFT SOUND OF DISTRESS COMING from somewhere in Ashley's vicinity, but he didn't dare look at her.

"So then I thought how nice you are," Ruby went on, "and how I wanted you to be my mom but I didn't know what to do. I told Sierra when we went to visit them and she thought I should be bad in school. It was really hard and I didn't want to. But I wanted you to be my mommy really bad, so I did it, anyway. I'm sorry."

After she finished, there was a long, terrible silence and all Justin could focus on was how much he would have preferred it if Ashley hadn't known who he was back then. He had a wild, sudden wish that she had met him only the day before.

He wanted her to know only the man he was today, not some image on a screen that had never been real. His chest ached suddenly and he had to fight the urge to rub his hand against it.

Finally, he managed to speak. "That was very wrong of you, Ruby. I'm disappointed that you would be so deceitful. You've wasted three weeks of the school year for nothing and now you're going to be behind all the others in your class."

"I'm sorry, Daddy."

"I don't think I'm the one you need to apologize to."

Her chin quivered but she rose and stood in front of Ashley, who looked close to tears herself. "I'm sorry, Miss Barnes. I do like you and I can be good. I promise."

Ashley cleared her throat, still not looking at him. "Does this mean you're going to do better from now on? No more of these...these crazy ideas?"

"I promise. You'll see. I'll be the best kid in the whole class! I'll do all my work on time and I'll raise my hand and everything."

"Good. I'm, uh, certainly glad to hear that." She rose abruptly. "I... Now that we've cleared that up, I should go."

"You don't have to," Justin said.

"Yes. I do."

He couldn't argue with the vehemence in her voice, and in truth he knew he would be relieved when she was gone. She still didn't look at him once as he and a now-dejected Ruby walked her to her impractical little car.

"Ruby, I'll see you Monday in school," she said, with what sounded like false brightness in her voice. "Thank you again for dinner."

She climbed into her car, started it and took off down the driveway. He hit the buzzer to open the gates just as she reached them, wondering if it could possibly be only a day since he had found her climbing over them.

As her taillights headed down Cold Creek Road, he held Ruby's hand and watched them disappear.

How insane. She only blew into his life the day before, but he knew as he watched her drive away that she had left footprints on his heart. He would miss her laughter and her softness and her sweet, infectious smile.

He had to let her go. He had no choice. Anything between them was impossible. Even before he found out she had once been a fan of his movies, he knew he could never do anything about this terrifying tenderness growing inside him.

That didn't make the regret any less bitter.

Eighteen

S HE WAS GOING TO DIE—JUST PULL HER BUG OVER somewhere along the banks of the Cold Creek, curl up in the front seat and wither away from absolute mortification.

But Miss Barnes already loves you, Daddy. You just have to fall in love with her.

Oh, this was the most awful moment of Ashley's life. It was bad enough that he should find out from his *daughter* about the crush she used to have on him. It was far worse that she had to be sitting three feet away from him when he did!

She forced herself to concentrate on the driving until she had reached the town limits and her own little white clapboard house. Once home, she pulled into her driveway and buried her face in her hands. She felt miserable. Completely wretched. All she could think about was the soft, seductive heat of their kiss and the way she wanted to lean into him and let him hold her forever.

Tears burned behind her eyes. She used to have a crush on a one-dimensional image on the screen, gorgeous and strong and heroic. But she was very much afraid she had lost her heart to the man behind that image. Even through her absolute horror as she had listened to Ruby's scheme, as the girl had talked about how much she wanted a mommy—how much she had wanted *Ashley* for a mommy—she had wanted it, too.

She still did. She ached with it, with the possibilities he had stirred up inside her by the tender heat of that kiss. She indulged in those possibilities—okay, those *im*possibilities—for only a moment then she dropped her hands and squared her shoulders.

It was over. She had shared one wonderful starlit night with him and with Ruby and that was all she would ever have. She just needed to put the whole humiliating experience behind her, forget about her teenage crush and the wonderful man she had found in real life, and figure out how to move on.

The weather turned cold and grim the next day as an icy rain blew down out of Montana to soak the mountains. It matched her mood perfectly, but did nothing to help lift her spirits.

As promised, Monday saw a dramatic turnaround in the Ruby Problem. The girl reverted to the sweet, sunny child she had been the first few days of school. No more belligerence or defiance. She handed in perfect assignments, she answered more questions than anyone else in class, she sat as still as a five-year-old could possibly manage during circle time.

The only black mark Ashley could have put in the Ruby column was that the girl apparently hadn't given up her ridiculous matchmaking. Every day at recess, she would hover around Ashley, filling her ears with stories about her father that only made Ashley fall deeper for him. She tried her best to discourage her, but Ruby wouldn't be deterred.

She could only wonder what kinds of stories about *her* Ruby was carrying back to Justin.

She had to admit, she was always glad to see the last of the girl when her great-aunt Lydia arrived to pick her up every afternoon in a sleek Range Rover.

On Friday, though, Ruby was the last child waiting at pickup and Lydia and her Range Rover were nowhere in sight. The cold, relentless rain dropped in sheets and even under the awning in front of the elementary school, it was miserable.

"Let's go inside and wait," she said to Ruby. "We can go back to the classroom and call your great-aunt to find out what's going on."

To her dismay, Ruby looked thrilled for a little more time in her company and Ashley sighed. She was growing to care far too much about the little girl, too. She set Ruby up with crayons and paper and looked through her files for Ruby's contact information so she could dial Lydia's cell number. She had just found the right paper and pulled it out when she heard a noise by the door and Ruby shrieked with delight.

"Daddy! Daddy!"

Nineteen

ASHLEY JERKED HER GAZE UP, JUST IN TIME TO see Justin standing in the doorway, looking strong and masculine and wonderful, before Ruby rushed to him and threw her arms around his waist.

"I missed you so much, Daddy. Did you buy a new horse on your trip?"

"A couple of them." He hugged his daughter, but his gaze rested on Ashley and she felt hot and cold at the same time.

"Are they pretty?" Ruby asked.

"Beautiful," he murmured, but his gaze never left her. A wild heat flared inside her and she couldn't seem to catch her breath. *Try,* she ordered herself harshly. The last thing she needed right now was to hyperventilate and pass out at his feet. Then he would *really* think she was an obsessed fan.

"I was really good for Miss Barnes all week," Ruby told him. "Wasn't I, Miss Barnes?"

She cleared her throat and tried to force her oxygen-starved brain to function again. "Uh, yes. You were wonderful."

"Oh!" Ruby said suddenly. "I forgot my leaf pictures. I left them in Mrs. Cook's classroom in art class so they could dry, but I need to take them home and show Aunt Liddy."

In a heartbeat, she rushed out the door, leaving the two of them alone.

Ashley couldn't look at Justin, but she was aware of him moving into the classroom and walking closer to her desk.

"How are you?" he asked.

She finally lifted her gaze at the quiet sincerity in his voice. "Still more embarrassed than I've ever been in my life," she admitted.

"You have no reason to be embarrassed. It was my daughter who tried to play matchmaker."

"Ruby would never have gotten the crazy idea in her head if I hadn't been talking about you with Marcy." She sighed, knowing she had to confront this or she would never be able to look him in the eye again. "Marcy has been my best friend since second grade. She knew all about my silly crush on you. Everyone knew. I'm afraid I was a little obsessed. I was fourteen and you were, well, you. You were heroic and passionate and...and gorgeous."

Her face flared with color and she knew she had to be beet-red, but she cleared her throat and plowed on. "Marcy thinks it's a hilarious twist of fate that I'm teaching your daughter, all these years later, and she's been teasing me about it since school started. That's what Ruby overheard, just two old friends remembering something that seems another lifetime ago."

He was quiet and she thought she saw something like pain flicker in his eyes.

"You know I'm not that man, right? I hated being a celebrity. I never wanted it. Everything just sort of fell into my lap. I was more surprised than anybody when I turned out to be moderately good at making movies, and for a while it was heady and addicting and I got sucked into the whole thing. But for my own survival, I had to get out when I did and I've never been sorry."

"I know. I don't see that heartthrob anymore when I look at you, Justin. Not after the other night."

He seemed to absorb that for a moment, then to her shock, he reached for her hand. "What do you see?" he asked, and the sudden intensity in his voice snatched away her breath again.

Twenty

ASHLEY'S HEART RACED AND SHE WAS CERTAIN Justin must be able to hear the blood pulsing loudly in her ears. "I see a man who loves his daughter. Someone trying to do his best by her. I see someone funny and sweet who cooks a mean steak and does a lousy John Wayne impression. And I see someone who made me forget my own name when he kissed me," she added in a whisper.

His fingers tightened on hers. "I've spent six days thinking about that kiss, Ashley. Thinking about you."

She blinked as his words soaked through her lingering discomfort. He had thought about it, too? About her, about the magic she thought she had only dreamed?

"Oh?" she managed.

"For years I've been telling myself I didn't need a woman

in my life, that Ruby and I were doing just fine on our own. Suddenly, I'm not so sure."

"You're...not?"

He shook his head and pulled her to her feet. "I don't know how it happened, and I certainly wasn't looking for it. But when you climbed the gates of my ranch, somehow you climbed through the walls I've built around my heart."

As his arms slid around her, a heady kind of joy flooded through her like that rain outside, only this was sweet and cleansing. He kissed her, his mouth strong and warm, and she sighed a welcome.

This was real, she realized with shock. Real and right and worlds better than anything she could have imagined as a silly, giddy teenager.

She lost herself in the kiss, yanking off his Stetson and burying her hands in his thick hair as she poured all the emotions of her heart into her response. When he pulled away, they were both breathing hard. Through the delicious haze, she sensed movement in the doorway and they both turned to find Ruby standing there.

Her leaf pictures were scattered at her feet, her clasped hands were pressed to her heart and her wide eyes glittered with a thousand stars.

"It worked," she breathed. "It really worked!"

Justin groaned. "I think we've created a monster."

Ashley smiled, happier than she ever dreamed she could be. "That's all right. I'm a kindergarten teacher. Taming monsters is part of the job description."

Epilogue

RUBY SIGHED WITH DELIGHT AS ASHLEY TALKED about how they had married the summer after Ruby graduated from her kindergarten class.

She had been so wrapped up in the familiar story that she hadn't noticed others had gathered, too, while her mom and dad were taking turns telling the story. Her little sister Caitlin and Cait's best friend, Addie Larrimore, and Addie's mom, Faith, who was her mom's best friend, were there along with Caroline Dalton and Emery Cavazos and a few of their kids.

She never got tired of hearing that story. She could only vaguely remember a time when Ashley wasn't in their lives—when it was just her and her dad and her great-aunt Lydia.

Mostly, she remembered her dad had been far too serious. He worked superhard on the ranch and didn't laugh much. Not as he did now, anyway.

They had made a pretty good team before, her and her father and great-aunt, but with Ashley in their lives and then the little ones, now they had a completely awesome family.

"You were right. That *is* a great story," Gabi exclaimed. "Jeez, Rue, I can't believe you told your dad that your teacher used to have his picture in her locker!"

"It was the most mortifying moment of my life," her mom said, "but in the end, all that embarrassment was worth it."

She smiled at Justin, who reached out and squeezed her hand and gave her one of those gooey looks they were always passing back and forth. Beside her, Ava let out an audible sigh.

Ruby wanted the very same kind of love story someday to share with her kids. A million years from now, of course.

"See?" she told Destry. "I told you I know what I'm talking about when it comes to romance."

"Maybe you can be a matchmaker for me in fifteen years or so—after I graduate from college and travel through Europe and barrel race in the PRCA rodeo finals."

"Sounds like a plan," Ashley said with a smile. "But here's a thought. Why don't we focus on the joy and magic of Christmas first? I heard a rumor that a special visitor might be on his way later."

"Is it Santa?" Caitlin asked, her eyes wide.

"Santa!" Jess clapped his hands, looking his completely adorable two-year-old self.

Ruby and her friends gave each other cynical looks. Even Ava, the youngest of them at twelve, didn't believe in Santa anymore, but it was still fun for the little kids so they didn't say anything to spoil it.

As the group broke up and the grown-ups and the little ones headed off in different directions, Ruby gazed at the tree beside her and her friends.

Yeah, she was excited about the new iPhone she was almost

positive would be in her stocking and really hoped she would get the tooled leather saddle for her horse, Rita, that she had pointed out to her dad. But when it came down to it, she already had everything she needed.

She might not believe in Santa anymore now that she was thirteen, but she *did* believe in dreams coming true.

She had wonderful friends who would do anything for her, a more-than-comfortable house, a dog and a horse of her very own, and a family she adored—a family that never would have happened if not for her.

★ ★ ★ ★ ★